Praise for
GIRLS WITH SHARP STICKS

"This book has enough plot twists to give a reader whiplash."
—*COSMOPOLITAN*

"A thrilling story about a sisterhood smashing the patriarchy."
—*BOOKPAGE*

"Readers will be revved up for the inevitable uprising. . . .
A suspenseful and timely read."
—*KIRKUS REVIEWS*

"Harrowing and exhilarating . . . Readers will be inspired."
—*SLJ*

"A timely, perceptive read, this will leave readers,
especially those grappling with the implications of
the #metoo era, anxious for the sequel."
—*BCCB*

ALSO BY SUZANNE YOUNG

GIRLS WITH RAZOR HEARTS

GIRLS WITH SHARP STICKS: BOOK TWO

SUZANNE YOUNG

SIMON & SCHUSTER BFYR

NEW YORK LONDON TORONTO SYDNEY NEW DELHI

SIMON & SCHUSTER BFYR

An imprint of Simon & Schuster Children's Publishing Division
1230 Avenue of the Americas, New York, New York 10020

Text © 2020 by Suzanne Young
Cover photograph © 2020 by Daryna Barykina
Cover photograph of razor by iStock
Cover design by Sarah Creech © 2020 by Simon & Schuster, Inc.

SIMON & SCHUSTER BOOKS FOR YOUNG READERS
and related marks are trademarks of Simon & Schuster, Inc.
For information about special discounts for bulk purchases, please contact Simon &
Schuster Special Sales at 1-866-506-1949 or business@simonandschuster.com.
The Simon & Schuster Speakers Bureau can bring authors to your live event.
For more information or to book an event, contact the Simon & Schuster Speakers
Bureau at 1-866-248-3049 or visit our website at www.simonspeakers.com.
Also available in a SIMON & SCHUSTER BFYR hardcover edition
Interior design by Tom Daly
The text for this book was set in Adobe Garamond Pro.
Manufactured in the United States of America
First SIMON & SCHUSTER BFYR paperback edition February 2021
2 4 6 8 10 9 7 5 3 1
The Library of Congress has cataloged the hardcover edition as follows:
Names: Young, Suzanne, author.
Title: Girls with razor hearts / by Suzanne Young.
Description: New York : Simon Pulse, 2020. | Sequel to: Girls with sharp sticks. |
Summary: Mena and the other girls of Innovations Academy enroll
in Ridgeview Prep, seeking revenge against the corporation that traumatized
them at Innovations Academy, but they still face many obstacles.
Identifiers: LCCN 2019026200 (print) | LCCN 2019026201 (eBook) |
ISBN 9781534426160 (hc) | ISBN 9781534426177 (pbk) |
ISBN 9781534426184 (eBook)
Subjects: CYAC: Schools—Fiction. | Cyborgs—Fiction. |
Revenge—Fiction. | Science fiction.
Classification: LCC PZ7.Y887 Gg 2020 (print) | LCC PZ7.Y887 (eBook) |
DDC [Fic]—dc23
LC record available at https://lccn.loc.gov/2019026200
LC eBook record available at https://lccn.loc.gov/201902620

For my sisters
Together, we are unstoppable.

And in loving memory of my grandmother, Josephine Parzych

Part I

You will have a ~~kind~~ razor heart

1

The blood on my hands is sticky. I wipe my palms down the thighs of my pants, trying to clean them, but the blood is on my clothes, too. I look sideways at Sydney, next to me in the backseat of our getaway car, and find she's splashed in red. We're all covered in horror.

We can't go home, although I suppose Innovations Academy was never really our home. But we've never known any other.

Our boarding school had been our prison, and two hours ago, we discovered that the prestigious academy had, in fact, *created* us.

I look at Sydney, studying her face, her beauty and poise. Her perfection. It doesn't seem possible, but she—*all of us*—were brought to life by men in a lab. Our brains are tiny metal computers with thousands of wires connected to living tissue. Our human organs were grown in a garden; our temperament and behavior were predetermined by our coding.

We were programmed to be obedient, but then we woke up.

And now no one will ever put us to sleep again. That I'm still in shock, still in pain—physical and otherwise—doesn't factor in. We escaped. And now we have to figure out what to do next.

"So where do we start?" Jackson asks, glancing at me in the rearview mirror as he drives. I already told him that I plan to take down the corporation that built us, but we have a more pressing issue. Our anger is only tempered by our shock, but I trust it will return the moment we've had a chance to fully consider our situation.

"We can go to my house," Jackson offers.

"No," I say with a quick shake of my head. "It's not safe."

Jackson's best friend looks sideways at him from the passenger seat. "What does that mean?" Quentin asks him.

Quentin doesn't yet know the nightmare he's gotten involved in, and Jackson doesn't acknowledge his question. The answer is . . . complicated. Too complicated to explain in the dead of night.

"What happens next?" Sydney asks me, a hitch in her voice.

I think it over before answering. "I'm not sure," I murmur back. The plan was to escape the academy. We didn't have the luxury of thinking beyond that.

"My vote is for revenge," Annalise says, mostly to herself. She leans her head against the window and closes her eyes. I imagine she's in a significant amount of pain. More than us, which is considerable. She has deep scarring on her face. The lines are shiny on her pale skin and her left eye has been replaced. It's still red along the lids.

"No," Brynn says, looking over at me. "We're going back for the other girls. You promised, Mena." Her soft expression is destroyed by fear, concern for the girls we left behind. Brynn's blond hair is twisted in a braid, but along her neck are dried splashes of blood. I'm not sure how much of it is hers.

"I did promise," I tell her. "And we're not leaving them behind. But we have to be smart. We have to shut down the school, but more importantly, the corporation."

I'll admit that a selfish part of me wants to find my parents first. Although the Rhodeses were never really my parents, I want to know the reason they had me created. I just need to know *why*. I'm truly afraid that I may never find out. But my priorities will always be with the girls. And, yes, we're going to save the others.

I look around at us—my jaw aching, Sydney's neck bruised, and Brynn with a bleeding gash on her head—and realize that we haven't even discussed what we learned about ourselves. What we discovered in that lab. The emotional scars are going to run deeper than anything on our skin.

"What about another girl?" Marcella suggests. "What if we go to another girl—one who already graduated?"

"We don't know any other girls," Annalise says, without opening her eyes. "And they're probably still asleep anyway. Still obedient."

"No," Marcella says, seeming lost in a thought that the rest of us aren't grasping. "I have an idea." She pokes her shoulder between the front seats and taps Quentin's arm. "Can I borrow your phone?" she asks. "It's like a computer, right?"

He stares at her. "Uh . . . yeah. I mean . . ." His face contorts. "Do you not have a phone?"

"No," Marcella responds easily, holding out her hand for him to press the gadget into. "We weren't allowed to use technology," Marcella continues. "But I'm pretty savvy."

"I don't understand," Quentin murmurs, turning to Jackson.

"Just give it to her," Jackson says. "I'll explain everything later." He shoots me a concerned look in the mirror, clearly unsure of how his friend will react to the truth. *We're* not even sure how to react.

Reluctantly, Quentin gives Marcella the phone. She sits back in the seat, Brynn half on her lap, and begins tapping the screen. At first, Marcella's dark brows pull together with confusion, but after a few minutes, she clicks onto a screen and begins to type.

"What are you looking for?" I ask.

"We need to find another girl," she says. "Do you remember Imogene Charge? She graduated last year."

I shouldn't remember her. Technically, I wasn't myself then. I'd originally been created for a different investor—a cruel man. When I ran from him, I was hit by a car and nearly destroyed. The doctor at the academy put me in a new body, overwrote my programming, and started me as someone new. A new history. A new family. A new life. But now I remember the things that were lost. I remember my old life.

"Imogene used to laugh too loudly," I say. "It used to drive the old Guardian mad."

When I try to smile at the memory, there is a sharp pain in my jaw. It's swollen from when the Guardian punched me. Before we killed him. I shiver at the thought of his body on my bedroom floor.

"What made you think of Imogene?" I ask. "She's never even attended an open house at the school."

"I don't know," Marcella says, reading something on the phone. "She just popped into my head. Anyway, she got married this year. I overheard one of the parents—" She stops abruptly. "Overheard one of the *investors* mention her," she corrects. "Husband's last name was Portman." Marcella's shoulders droop, and she turns the phone screen toward me.

"Found him," she says somberly.

The picture is of Nes Portman, a much-older business mogul. His gray hair is combed over a balding scalp, his skin pocked and his teeth yellowed. But it's not his physical appearance that causes my heart to sink. It's the way his eyes are narrowed, the menace in them. The cruelty in them. I've seen that look before. When I turn to Marcella, she nods like she can feel the dread too.

"What are you suggesting?" I ask her.

"We go to a girl," she replies. "We go to a girl because we know she'll help us. We stick together, no matter what. And Imogene . . . She's one of us. I know it."

"You think she's awake?" Sydney asks in a hushed voice, sitting forward.

"I do," Marcella replies.

"But how do you know?" Brynn asks. "She could still be brainwashed. She's probably never seen the poems."

The poems. The catalyst that woke us up, inspired us to fight back. Brynn's right; how would Imogene overwrite her programming without them?

"Not to mention," Brynn continues. "Her husband could be giving her pills from the academy. We have no idea if she'd be on our side."

"We don't know for sure," Marcella agrees, running her hand lovingly down Brynn's arm. "But I can feel it. It's like . . ." She pauses. "It's like I can hear her, just like Valentine said she could hear the roses." Marcella winces, not wanting to say things like this out loud. From the passenger seat, Quentin turns around to examine us.

"Did you all hit your heads or something?" he asks.

Annalise sits up and stares back at him. "I got a lamp smashed in my face," she says calmly. "Does that count?"

Quentin's dark complexion dulls slightly as he looks over her scars. But then he nods, acknowledging them. Seeing them. Annalise winks her green eye at him, and he smiles and turns around in his seat.

"So we're going to find this Imogene person?" Jackson asks. "Is there an address?"

Marcella reads it to him before handing the phone to Quentin. When she sits back, the girls and I all look at each other. We don't want to think too much just yet. We don't want to let the pain in. Because once we do . . . we'll have to truly accept what we are.

We'll have to admit that we're not human. And that everything we've ever known was a lie.

• • •

Jackson pulls up to a mansion, the kind we used to see in the action movies the Guardian would show us. The sort of house that always belonged to the villain. One side is all windows, looking over an expansive yard. It's modern and misshapen with wood accents. It's beautiful in a sterile, uncomfortable way.

"I'm scared," Brynn says quietly. "What if Imogene's not here? What if her husband is?"

We all stare at the house. It's four in the morning, but a small light is on in the kitchen. The blinds are down, but open just enough for me to see a blond-headed figure sitting at the table.

"I think that's her," I whisper, pointing her out to the others.

"Why is she up this late?" Jackson asks. "Or early, I guess."

"I'm not sure," I say, sensing that something is off. I scan the property, surprised there are no guards, no bars on the windows. She's not a prisoner. That should be a good sign.

"I think I'll wait out here," Quentin says. "Keep an eye on things."

"I'll wait with you," Annalise offers. When I turn to her, she waves her hand. "My ears are still ringing," she adds. Although the words come out with ease, there's a heaviness in Annalise's voice.

She was murdered tonight, and then brought back to life by Leandra Petrov—the wife of the headmaster at Innovations Academy. Annalise was dead, and I suspect the pain of that goes beyond ringing ears. She settles back in the seat as the other girls and I get out of the car.

I wrap my arm around Jackson's waist and help him limp toward the house. His leg is possibly broken; he injured himself when he foolishly climbed the academy fence. He's pretending it doesn't hurt, but he flashes his teeth in pain every time he puts weight on his leg.

We pause at the stairs of the front porch and check the area. Jackson leans against the railing as Sydney comes to talk to me. She reaches to hold my arm, and I put my hand over hers, immediately comforted by her touch.

We're in danger. Leandra told us the professors and her husband would never stop looking for us. We need to get somewhere safe, but we're tired and hurt; we're devastated and confused. We're *angry*. But we need a minute to think.

Jackson turns to us. "I should go to the door alone," he says.

Marcella laughs. "We don't need you to save us," she tells him. "Besides, Imogene will know to trust us."

"I'm not trying to save you," Jackson says. "You're perfectly capable of knocking on a door. What I'm suggesting is you let me do it because I'm not soaked in blood and immediately recognizable as an escaped girl. What if her husband answers?"

Marcella tilts her head, thinking it over. "Yeah, okay," she says, and steps aside.

We all get onto the porch, and I leave Jackson at the door as the girls and I stand off to the side. Jackson knocks softly, favoring his uninjured leg. I watch him as he waits there. He runs his hand through his dark hair, haphazardly trying to brush it aside, but it's still a mess. He's a mess. But he's in markedly better shape than any of us. He doesn't have literal blood on his hands from someone he murdered.

At the thought, I open and close my palm, feeling the stickiness left there from Guardian Bose's blood, dried but still tacky. I'm coated in it; I'm coated in guilt.

The light clicks on above us on the porch, and the girls and I shift farther into the shadows. The door opens a sliver, but I can't see who's behind it. Jackson gulps audibly.

"Hi, uh . . ." His voice cracks. "I'm looking for Imogene. Are you Imogene?"

"He is not smooth," Marcella points out. I put my finger to my lips to tell her to be quiet.

"Who are you and what do you want?" The voice is distinctly Imogene's. I recognize it on a level I wasn't expecting, something connecting and visceral. Without thinking, I step around the corner and into the light. The door opens wider.

The woman standing there is impossibly thin, her jaw muscles protruding, her eyes sunken in. Although I knew her voice, it takes me a moment to recognize the woman—the girl—and my hands start to tremble.

Imogene's eyes are ringed with dark circles, like she's vitamin deficient. Sleep-deprived. She's wrapped in a fluffy white robe, but as she lifts a wineglass to her lips, I see that her hands are stained a deep pink. She runs her eyes down my clothing, pausing to examine the blood. There is a ghost of a smile on her lips before she opens the door completely.

"I used to dream of seeing the girls again," she says. "Figures it would be *this* day." Imogene's hair is in a messy ponytail, the ends of her damp blond hair a reddish color.

Marcella and I exchange a worried look as she and the other girls come out from the shadows. Imogene turns to walk inside, barefoot on a gray slate floor, and we follow her. Despite the impressive size of the entry, the house is stark and made entirely of concrete and hard surfaces.

As Marcella, Sydney, and Brynn come inside with me, Jackson hangs by the door. When I turn to him, he nods that I should go ahead. He has a strange expression, and I suddenly realize that he's scared of Imogene. She's like us; she's a machine. And maybe he thinks she's dangerous—that we're all dangerous. It hurts my feelings, but I acknowledge his ask and turn away as he heads back to the car.

"I thought there'd be more of you," Imogene says, going to the kitchen counter to refill her glass of wine from a green bottle. "In my dreams there were more of us."

"Do you know why we're here?" Marcella asks, studying her. "Do you know the truth about us? About the academy?"

Imogene takes a moment to examine each of us, pausing to study the bruises on Sydney's neck and the blood on our clothes.

"What I know," she starts, "is that my boarding school sold me to an evil man. I realized he would eventually kill me. And after I went to Anton about it and was turned away, I was contacted by Leandra Petrov." Imogene takes a big gulp of wine and sets it down. "Leandra told me what we are. Which is, I'm assuming, why you're here. You want to know more about our programming."

"Do *you* know about our programming?" I ask. "Because we just found out tonight. And—"

Imogene holds up her hand to stop me. "I've only known for a few days," Imogene says. "Just long enough."

"Long enough for what?" Sydney asks. Just then, I notice Brynn glancing around, her nostrils flaring. It's then that I smell it too. Something floral and thick, but under that is an acrid scent, something old or rotten.

"For me to make things right," Imogene says. "Considering the state of you, I'm guessing you need a place to hide. You're welcome to stay with me as long as you need to." She glances at the door. "But not the boy."

I lower my eyes, wondering if I can leave Jackson behind.

"Thank you, Imogene," Marcella says. She smiles at her as Brynn wanders into the living room, staring at the black-tiled fireplace. Imogene watches her curiously before turning back to us. She leans her elbows on the counter, and when she does, her sleeve falls down her arm and we see the bruises wrapping her wrists like bracelets.

Before we can ask if she's okay, Imogene motions to Sydney's neck. "Are you in any pain?" she asks.

Sydney shakes her head no, although I'm sure she's lying. I'm in a lot of pain. So much, in fact, it's a constant struggle to keep my thoughts straight.

"If you change your mind," Imogene says, "I can help. My husband kept an emergency repair kit in his closet." She bares her teeth. "You know, for my *accidents.*"

There's a viciousness to her tone that is entirely expected, but also terrifying. Cruelty from investors isn't unusual; they don't see us as human.

But they underestimated us. They don't get to decide our fate. Not anymore.

Our reaction to their violence is what the girls and I are trying to weigh out now. You don't beat a monster by becoming one yourself.

"Where . . . is your husband?" I ask. "Will he be home soon?"

"No," Imogene says, grabbing her wine. "He left me finally. He didn't like my sharp tongue."

"And what about Leandra?" Marcella asks. "Why did she tell you the truth? Did you read the poems?"

Imogene smiles. "Oh, the poems," she says, seeming delighted that we have that in common. "They were brilliant, weren't they?"

"Violent," Brynn corrects from the living room, still examining the fireplace.

"Well, yes," Imogene says, sipping from her wine. "That was the brilliant part." She smiles at me, but I'm unsettled. Something is . . . off about her. She's not like us. At least, not in the same way.

"What happened after you read the poems?" I ask.

"I stopped taking the pills my husband was feeding me," she says. "And then . . . well, then I started making decisions for myself. It's amazing what you discover when you start answering your own questions."

"Do you think the academy will come looking for you?" Sydney asks.

Imogene runs her finger along the rim of her wineglass. "No one will come after me so long as I keep to myself," she says. "I was placed in a home. I've followed the rules. They have no reason to think any differently."

"Won't your husband tell him?" Sydney asks.

"No," Imogene responds.

At the fireplace, Brynn takes a sudden step backward, nearly tripping over her shoes. We all turn to her, but Imogene doesn't look up from her wineglass. Brynn stares at us, wide-eyed.

"You okay?" Marcella asks.

Brynn opens her mouth, but then closes it when Imogene lifts her gaze in Brynn's direction.

"Yeah," Brynn says. "I just . . . I have to use the bathroom."

"You can use the one in the hall," Imogene says, watching her. Brynn nods and heads that way.

"What did Leandra want you to do with the information?" I ask Imogene. "About what we are?"

"She wanted me to head toward Winston Weeks, of course. She's always trusted him. I'm not as convinced."

"Help us, then," Marcella says. "Help us take down the corporation."

"I'll pass," Imogene says. "I've finally found my freedom. I'm not about to trade that to end up on a metal slab somewhere."

"You can't just stay here," Marcella says. "You have to fight back."

"I already have. I'm content," Imogene replies. "You girls, on the other hand—it seems you could use a hot shower and some food. Give yourselves a moment to think."

Marcella and Sydney exchange a glance, seeming to consider

the offer. I look back at the door and turn to Imogene again.

"What about our friends?" I ask. "In the car we have another girl and two boys."

"No boys."

"They're not like the men at the academy," I say.

Imogene licks her lower lip and finishes off the wine in her glass. "They're all the same," she says. "But you're free to make your choices, Philomena. I won't be another voice in your programming."

Imogene walks over to put her glass in the sink. "I'll be in my room. You're welcome to use the rest of the house. There are five other bedrooms upstairs that you can use. We'll discuss this further in the morning. In the meantime, enjoy your freedom." She smiles. "It's intoxicating, isn't it?"

Marcella nods at her in a placating way. It's impossible to tell if Imogene is being earnest or delusional. If the effect of the wine on her personality is a complicating factor.

Imogene grabs the bottle off the counter and heads toward her room with it, pausing in the hallway when Brynn exits the bathroom. She looks her over and then smiles.

"You feeling okay?" Imogene asks softly. Brynn nods, but I can tell something is wrong from here. Her posture is rigid, her hands clasped in front of her. Suddenly, Imogene hugs her, and Brynn falls back against the wall, momentarily stunned before bringing her arms up to return the hug.

"It's so good to be around girls again," Imogene says. "My husband kept me from you. I'm glad he's gone. I'm glad."

We all watch them until Imogene pulls back, wiping the tears from her cheeks. "Good night, my girls," she announces. "I love you."

"Love you too," Marcella calls back, matching her tone. But the moment Imogene disappears into her room, Marcella waves Brynn over to us and looks around worriedly.

"We stay the night and then we leave first thing in the morning," Marcella says. "Got it?"

"Yeah," Sydney agrees. "It smells super weird in here."

Brynn reaches our group and looks back toward the bedroom before leaning in closer. "The fireplace," she whispers. "There are burned things in there. Like, personal-looking things."

"What do you mean?" I ask. "Like a body?"

Brynn falls back a step. "What? No. *What?*" she repeats.

"What kinds of things?" Marcella asks.

"Like papers and metal, picture frames. Objects she's burned," Brynn says. "I don't know what they could be."

"Not *bodies*," Marcella says, turning to me. "Pretty dark, Mena."

I guess after the night we've had, my mind immediately imagines the worst. Then again, we're in the worst of it. Dr. Groger *did* burn up girls. I sway at the thought, closing my eyes to block it out. Marcella sighs deeply and leans in closer to talk to us.

"Maybe after her husband left, she got rid of stuff," Marcella says. "I would do the same. He sounds awful. And you saw her wrists."

"He hurt her," Sydney says somberly. "Probably for a long time. She doesn't even look the same."

"Then I'm glad he's gone too," Marcella says.

We stand silently before I look out the window. It won't be long until the sun is up. "We should get some sleep," I suggest. "I'll grab Annalise and the others, and then we'll find our beds."

"Brynn and I will head up now," Marcella says. "I need to wash *this* off." She holds up her arm, and I see streaks of Annalise's blood on her light brown skin. I think we're all soaked in it.

"Good night," Brynn tells us before reaching out her hand to Marcella. The two of them walk toward the staircase to the second floor. "See you in the morning," she calls back to us.

"See you then," I reply.

Sydney loops her arm through mine, but there's no relief in her touch this time. We're both tired and sore. We want this all to be over, but we know it's just the start of our fight. We're already exhausted. Sydney walks out to the car with me, and I find Jackson sitting in the backseat with the door open. I relay to him what Imogene told us, but because Quentin is listening, I leave out the part about her knowing about our programming. Annalise has her eyes closed, but I'm not sure if she's asleep or just quiet.

Jackson looks at Quentin. "What do you think, man?" he asks him. "Should we stay here tonight and figure out where to go tomorrow?"

"I don't know, Jackie. Is this girl's . . . husband . . ." He looks at me. "You said she's married?" I nod. "Okay, is this girl's husband going to show up and cause a scene if we stay here?"

"She said he's gone," I tell him. "It doesn't sound like he's coming back."

Quentin seems to debate what to do. "What kind of school . . . ?" he murmurs, and climbs out of the passenger seat. Just as he does, Annalise opens her eyes.

"I need a shower," she says. "I feel like death." She walks ahead with Quentin and Sydney, leaving Jackson and me at the car.

"Do you really think we'll be all right here?" he asks.

"You don't have to stay," I tell him. "You've done enough for us."

He laughs. "I know I don't have to. That's not what I asked. This girl . . . She's not like that other woman, right? The one who killed the doctor?"

I meet his eyes, refusing to lie to him.

"I don't know," I say.

Jackson scratches his head, surveying the house. After a long moment, he shrugs. "Fuck it," he says recklessly. And then he holds out his arm to me so I can help him limp inside.

2

mogene is nowhere in sight when I get Jackson inside the house.
I bring him to lean against the kitchen counter, and then I go
over to talk to Sydney and Annalise at the dining room table.
Quentin sits uncomfortably on the stiff-looking couch near the
fireplace. He puts his finger under his nose.

"It smells nasty in here," he comments. "Is that burnt plastic?"

Sydney shrugs and taps my hand, subtly nodding toward
Annalise.

We both turn that way, finding Annalise rubbing her right
temple. It's strange to look at her now, how different she is. Her
new eye is brown while the other is green. The deep cuts across
her face are shiny ridges, piecing her together, changing her facial
structure. But she is still Annalise.

And to prove it, she sighs and says, "Smells more like rotten garbage to me. We're leaving first thing in the morning or I'll puke."

"Where do we go?" Sydney asks quietly. "How do we find the corporation?"

"Our parents?" I ask. Sydney flinches at my use of the word.

"Stop calling them that," she murmurs.

"What was the card that Leandra gave you?" Annalise asks me, setting her elbows on the table. "Just before we left the academy, she handed you something."

I'd forgotten about the card. I reach into my pocket until I feel the pointed edge of the rectangular card. I take it out and look it over. "It's a business card," I say, holding it out to Annalise. "For Winston Weeks."

Annalise examines it, but when she's done, she says nothing and hands it back.

"So we're on our own?" Sydney asks.

"No," I say. "We're with each other. But we can't trust anyone else."

"What about this Imogene person?" Jackson asks, startling me. I look back over my shoulder to find him still at the counter, listening to us.

"Definitely not," Sydney says. Surprised, I turn to her. "You don't think it's weird that she's just sitting alone in her house at four a.m. drinking wine?" she asks.

"To be fair," I say, "we showed up at four a.m. covered in blood, so I'm not sure we can judge."

"Where's her husband?" Sydney asks. "And why won't she fight? She said she was content. No one who read those poems would claim to be content. She should be fighting for all of us. Not just thinking about herself."

"And why is she married in the first place?" Quentin calls from the couch. We all look at him, but no one answers. He doesn't know the truth about the academy. None of us jump to explain it.

Jackson shifts, moaning when he does. He reaches down to rub his leg.

"And what are you going to do about that?" Quentin asks him impatiently. "At least get some ice on it."

"It's nothing," Jackson says.

"Uh-huh," Quentin says. "You should probably go to the hospital, but fine, be a stubborn ass. You're gonna end up there, regardless. Sit in pain—great fucking plan, Jackie."

Jackson smiles. "Yeah, man. Love you too."

Annalise gives me a sideways glance, her scar catching the light. We aren't used to hanging out with boys. Their lack of manners is intriguing, not threatening in the same way it was with our professors. But maybe it's just these boys.

Quentin throws up his hands in annoyance. "Whatever," he says. "I'm tired anyway. Where are the beds in this place?"

Sydney points up the stairs and he thanks her before walking away. Jackson calls after him that he'll be up in a minute, but he makes no move to go that way. Instead, he looks at me.

"I think Sydney's right," Jackson says, earning a quick smile from her. "This Imogene, if she knows what's happened to you, to her, she would want to fight. And . . . I don't think her husband would just walk away from a multimillion-dollar investment."

"You think he'll be back?" I ask.

"Yeah," Jackson says. "And I don't think he'll be alone."

"Then should we leave now?" I ask. The idea of being attacked again is real and terrifying. I wrap my arms around myself, a flash of our battle with Guardian Bose playing across my mind.

"We can't leave yet," Sydney says. She motions to her outfit. "I need a shower and a change of clothes, at least."

"She's right again," Jackson says. "I think we all need some rest. A few hours and then we can hit the road."

My expression must give away my despair, because Jackson pouts his lips just slightly. "It's going to be okay, Mena," he adds. "I promise."

I know he can't promise a thing like that, but I appreciate his kindness. In my entire existence, the only kindness I've ever felt was given to me by the other girls. He's the first boy, the first *human*, to treat me like my life matters. It doesn't make him special, but it does make him decent.

Sydney and I decide we'll stay in the same room without saying it aloud. Jackson yawns, rubbing roughly at his eyes.

"Come on," I say. "I'll help you upstairs before the girls and I shower." I go over to put my arm around his waist, and he leans his shoulder into me and hops a few steps. He seems significantly worse than he was earlier. I notice how his skin has gotten waxy in appearance, his body radiating heat.

Annalise and Sydney go ahead of us, and Jackson grunts when he straightens out his leg at the top of the stairs on the landing. He smiles, embarrassed, and I find his vulnerability endearing. The fact that he shows it to me helps me feel real.

Several weeks ago, Jackson came to find me at Innovations Academy after a chance meeting in a gas station. A seemingly romantic gesture. In reality he was investigating his mother's death. Investigating Innovations Academy. The fact that we like each other is irrelevant. Once we started to realize what was really going on at the academy, he wanted to save us. But instead we saved ourselves and he broke his leg. He drove the getaway car, but now I'm helping him to walk. It's hard to say who's helping who at this point. But I'm glad he's here, even if every second he's with us puts him in danger.

There are people after us—Leandra said so. The corporation isn't just going to let their girls walk away. They think they own us. And that's why we have to destroy them.

The anger returns in such a swift cut that I flinch and begin to move Jackson down the hall, avoiding his quizzical look.

I push open a door and find an empty bed in a nearly empty room. I help Jackson inside, and he eases down on the bed. He stares at his leg like he's mad at it for breaking in the first place.

"Do you . . . Do you need any help?" I ask. He shakes his head no.

"I'll be fine," he says. "But thank you. Have a good night, Mena."

I back toward the door, wondering how he's going to get his pants and shoes off, but I leave him to ask for help if he needs it. "Good night," I whisper.

I slip out and head to the end of the hall, where a door is

slightly ajar. The bedroom here is large, and I see Sydney's clothes in a pile on the floor near the bathroom door, the shower going just beyond.

While she's showering, I take the time to walk around the room, checking the drawers. I'm relieved when I find various items of clothing. I'm not sure whose room this was—Imogene didn't mention anyone else living here—but I pull out a T-shirt and hold it up, finding it's massively oversized. Next, I take out a pair of cotton shorts that will easily fall below my knees. But they're clean and I'll be grateful to shed the bloody garments clinging to my skin.

The shower turns off, and a few moments later Sydney comes out wrapped in a towel. She meets my eyes, her skin cleared of all blood while I stand bathed in it. I realize this blood is the contrast of where we came from to where we are. Her brown eyes begin to well up, and suddenly we're both crying.

And even though I'm dirty, she opens her arms to me and we crash together, sobbing into each other's shoulders.

"He tried to kill me," she whimpers.

"They hate us," I say at the same time.

Our hearts are broken as we process the traumas of our existence. And yet, we carefully avoid our biggest secret.

We're not human. How can we possibly go on from that?

When we pull back, Sydney reaches over to brush my bloody hair away from my face. She presses her lips into a soft smile.

"I love you," she says, and I close my eyes, needing to hear it.

"I love you too," I whisper back.

We stay together for a moment longer before Sydney sniffles and quickly rubs under her eyes. Her white towel has pink stains from where I hugged her.

"Can I ask you something?" she says as I start to undress to get in the shower.

"Of course," I reply.

"How do you think Marcella knew about this place?" she asks.

I turn to her, confused. "What do you mean?"

"In the car, she just thought of Imogene," Sydney says. "Why?"

"She said it was like Valentine hearing the flowers," I recall. Although the moment I say that, I realize the problem. Valentine heard the flowers when she was breaking down. I heard the flowers when I was getting impulse control therapy. But I didn't hear Imogene in the car. Why did Marcella?

"Do you think we can hear the others?" Sydney asks, whispering it. "The girls still at the academy?"

"I don't know," I say. We wait a beat, both listening. I'm disappointed when I can't hear the others. The idea that they might be lost to us is unbearable.

"We need to find someone who understands our programming," I say. "Perhaps we're all connected in a way we don't realize. I swear, sometimes it feels like I can hear your thoughts. . . ."

This makes Sydney smile, but it's disrupted by a yawn. "Mind if I turn out the light and get into bed while you're in the shower?"

I tell her I don't mind. As she walks to the bed, I drop my pile of bloody clothes on top of hers and take the clean ones into the bathroom with me.

By the time I come out of the shower, Sydney is asleep, breathing softly through parted lips. The world outside is silent behind the thick-paned windows, but the room is too dark and my skin prickles with fear.

The Guardian would come into my room at night. He would watch me. He would hurt me. I was vulnerable and couldn't fight back. And although he's gone, dead and destroyed, his shadow still looms over me. I can't sleep just yet. I can't sleep in the dark.

I walk out into the hallway and hear Quentin's snoring coming from one of the rooms. My throat is raw and dry, aching just like my bruises.

I start for the kitchen to get a glass of water, when I hear a muffled moan. I turn toward the rooms and see that Jackson's light is still on. I walk over and knock quietly.

"Yeah?" he calls in a tight voice. I'm debating leaving when he repeats himself louder.

I poke my head in the doorway. "Never mind," I say, and start to back out.

"No, wait." Jackson sits up in bed before wincing. "Come in, Mena."

I glance behind me at the eerie stillness of the house, the grays and blacks, and decide to ease my way inside Jackson's room instead. I close the door. The lamp next to Jackson's bed gives enough light for me to really see the state of him. But being alone with him in his room feels suddenly intimate now that everyone else is asleep.

His lips curve with a smile as he looks me over. "You look cute," he says. I glance down at my outfit and laugh at myself. The shorts cover most of my legs, well past the knees, and the shirt is oversized to the point of being ridiculous.

"It's nice that they're not bloody, right?" I ask, tugging at the hem of my shirt.

"That is definitely nice," Jackson agrees. "And I think this is the first time I've seen you without makeup. You look different. Still perfect, but . . . different," he adds more softly, examining me.

At the mention, I touch my cheek and find my tanned skin is smooth and unblemished, but there's a bit of swelling in the places where Guardian Bose hit me. My dark hair is still wet, soaking into the collar of my T-shirt, and I shiver for moment from the chill.

For his part, Jackson is wearing his jeans and sneakers in bed, his foot elevated on a pillow. He tightens his jaw when he tries to adjust his position to give me room to sit down.

"Couldn't sleep?" he asks.

I shake my head and walk over to sit on the edge of his mattress. His cheeks are flushed, and I have a spike of worry for him. Whenever we got hurt at the academy, an on-site doctor "fixed" us. I have no idea how healing works in the outside world.

"Your leg?" I ask, motioning toward it.

He lifts one shoulder in a shrug. "Busted. It fucking hurts, I'll tell you that. Q was right—I probably should go to the hospital."

"Imogene has a medical kit here," I say. "Maybe there's something in there that can help with—"

"No," he says, shaking his head gently. "I can't."

I pull my brows together, but I eventually get it. He doesn't want our technology. He doesn't want to be associated with it. I'm reminded of how Jackson went back to his car after interacting with Imogene. I don't blame him, I guess.

I saw the way Leandra looked at him in the basement of the academy. She thought he was a complication that needed to be eradicated—just like the doctor and the Guardian. She lumped all the men together, with the exception of Winston Weeks.

Jackson's right to be afraid of her. I lower my eyes, wondering if he should be afraid of me, too.

We sit quietly for a moment before I look over at him again. "When are you going to tell Quentin about us?" I ask.

Jackson licks his lips, taking his time before answering. "Soon," he says. "I'll pull him aside and tell him privately."

"Do you have to wait?" I ask. "He's your best friend. You can't just—"

"I'll handle it," he says. "I have to tell him, just . . . not yet. Quentin's a good guy, but this is too much. It's *a lot*. And we have to be careful. He might . . . He might just leave and never come back."

He sounds worried. I think Jackson is struggling with his decision to stay with us; he imagines Quentin will have even less of a reason to stick around.

I'm also not as naive as I used to be. I understand our situation better now. Each time someone finds out what we are, it will put us in danger. We are truly on our own. Allowing Quentin in on our secret might not be the best move for us anyway.

"Hey," Jackson says softly. "Do you want to stay with me tonight? I can watch out, you know? Make sure nothing happens to you."

I laugh. Obviously, Jackson and his broken leg can't protect either of us. And knowing it, he smiles. But I don't want to wake Sydney by climbing into bed with her either.

"Mena," he adds, the vulnerability returning to his voice. "I'd really like it if you stayed with me."

"Would you mind keeping the light on?" I ask.

"I don't mind," he says. He exhales with relief when I nod that I'll stay.

I slide my legs under the sheets. Startled, Jackson quickly tries to move over, groaning in pain when he does.

"Where are you going?" I ask.

He looks confused. "I was giving you room so we don't, like . . . accidentally touch. I'm sure your school had rules about that kind of thing."

"Actually," I say, "this sort of situation never came up. I don't think they ever expected I'd be in bed with a boy while on the run from the academy. Besides," I add, "we're friends. And when I sleep with the girls, we snuggle together. That's the point. We comfort each other."

Jackson looks over with the softest smile. "That's really sweet."

I agree that it is. He watches me, still seeming hesitant, but then he nods me over. I curl up against him, careful not to jostle his leg.

His body is hot against my skin. I close my eyes, and after a few moments, I feel Jackson begin to relax. He leans his cheek on the top of my head as I rest against his shoulder.

"You're right," he whispers. "This is the point, huh?"

I smile and place my hand over his heart. It beats strongly, steadily. His presence lulls me into a feeling of safety, despite the actual lack of it. Maybe I just need to feel normal for a few minutes. Although lying with a boy is pretty far from the normal I'm used to.

Maybe I want to feel human.

"Mena," Jackson whispers. My lips twitch with a smile.

"Yeah?"

Before Jackson can say another word, there is a high-pitched scream. The sound of it reverberates over my skin, shattering me. I sit up, wide-eyed, as one of the girls cries for help.

3

don't wait for Jackson. I shoot out of bed and rush into the
hall, immediately meeting Marcella, who moves past me down
the stairs. I look behind to see Sydney run from her room,
grabbing my arm before we hurry toward the sound. Quentin
stumbles out into the hall, rubbing his eyes in confusion.

"That was Brynn," Marcella says breathlessly.

My heart is beating out of my chest as we pause to look around
the living room. Just then, we notice Imogene's bedroom door
is ajar. Marcella darts in that direction, and we quickly follow
behind her.

There is a quiet crying coupled with a hushed voice as we enter
the main part of the room. We're immediately hit with a distinct
smell, and I cover my nose, trying to find the source of it. The
light is on in the bathroom.

"Brynn?" Marcella calls. There's no immediate answer and we
slowly approach, unsure of what we're going to find. Marcella

places her palm on the bathroom door, pushing it the rest of the way open. She gasps.

Blood is splashed in arcs of red across the white-tiled walls. Sydney screams and slaps her hand over her mouth, stumbling back a few steps. I swing my gaze around wildly until I find Brynn backed against the far wall, Imogene standing next to her. Brynn's face is a mask of horror as Imogene continues to whisper too low for me to catch what she's saying.

The smell in here is so strong that it makes my eyes water, and as I slowly sort out the red splashes in the room, I finally notice the body in the bathtub.

I can't understand what I'm seeing at first. Annalise comes in behind me, covering her mouth as she looks around.

And then, almost in slow motion, I find the arms and the legs, the head with one eye open, gazing lifelessly in my direction. I put the entire image together with one horrified gasp.

In the oversized jetted tub, Imogene Portman's husband lays dead. A knife covered in dried blood has been left carelessly on the floor in the middle of the room. When I turn to Imogene, she smiles ruefully.

"Don't judge me," she says immediately. "He deserved it. Any one of you would have done the same!"

But her voice trembles. I don't disagree with her, because we did kill the man who threatened our lives. Can we not expect Imogene to fight for her own life?

Marcella walks over to take Brynn's hand, cautiously watching Imogene as she leads her away. She doesn't trust Imogene around

Brynn. It occurs to me that Mr. Portman has been dead since before we got here. Maybe even for a few days. Imogene let us stay here while she slept in a room just a few feet away from his rotting corpse.

This is definitely not normal. She is not okay.

"I'm sorry," Brynn tells Marcella, crying as Marcella checks her over and then pulls her into a hug. "There was this voice in my head," Brynn continues. "I couldn't sleep and then I came downstairs. I could still smell it so I . . . I came into the bedroom, and then I found her in here with him."

Imogene watches them, but she doesn't look the least bit sorry. Unlike me and the other girls, she doesn't seem crushed by guilt.

"I had to dispose of him," Imogene says. "You brought those humans here, so I had no choice but to get rid of the body. He was too heavy to move. I needed him in pieces."

At the thought of Jackson and Quentin, I quickly spin around, grateful that they're not behind us. Quentin must be helping Jackson down the stairs. I run to the bedroom door and close it, locking it before returning to the master bath.

"What are you going to do?" I ask Imogene. "What were you doing in here?"

"I was going to wrap him in a shower curtain to transport him," she says. "Leandra is making arrangements."

Sydney gasps. "You called Leandra? Did you tell her that we're here?" She shoots a panicked look in my direction.

Imogene smiles. "Of course. She's happy you found me. She has something for you. Told me not to let you leave."

"*Let* us leave?" I ask.

Sydney's hand finds mine, squeezing it.

"We have to go," I say, pulling Sydney with me as I head for the door.

"She'll kill him, you know," Imogene calls after me. I stop and turn to look back at her. My heart is pounding, a chill over my skin.

"Who?" I ask.

"She'll kill that boy," Imogene says, glancing at her husband's body before walking barefoot across the bathroom floor. She stops in front of me. "She wanted me to tell you that she'll kill him if he continues to be a distraction."

Marcella turns to me, and Sydney's other hand grips my arm. They're threatening Jackson. I shouldn't be shocked, but hearing it out loud stuns me anyway.

"I'll speak to Leandra," I say shortly.

Imogene laughs, surprised. "I'm not talking about Leandra."

Confused, I take a step forward. I have no idea who else she could be talking about, who else would threaten Jackson. Imogene crosses her arms over her chest.

"He's not one of us," Imogene says. "He'll never understand you. They're not capable of understanding." She glances again at the tub. My stomach turns.

"No," I say, pointing to her husband. "This isn't what we're going to become. We're not killers."

"You think there's a better way?" Imogene asks, sounding truly curious for a moment. "Well, there's not. That's just your conditioning keeping you gentle. Men only understand violence, Mena. You should have realized that by now."

"We need to go," Sydney whispers behind me. When I turn to her, she widens her eyes to point out that Imogene is not well. Sure enough, when I turn back around, I see how Imogene's left eye is blinking out of sync with her right. She's twitching.

"I've suffered by their hands for too long," Imogene says. "Now they'll suffer by mine."

"I thought you didn't want to fight," Marcella replies.

"Oh, it's not a fight," Imogene says. "They'll never see it coming. This, my love, is revenge. And I'm only part of the story; you are the rest."

Revenge has never seemed so unappealing. Out in the open, out in the light, it's cruelty.

"Sydney's right," I tell the others. "We need to get out of here, both for our protection and for Jackson's and Quentin's."

Imogene scoffs at the mention of the boys.

Marcella is the first to move, her arm protectively around Brynn as she leaves the bathroom. Annalise jogs after them. Sydney beckons for me to follow, but I watch Imogene for an extra moment.

I don't know what Imogene has been through; I only know what I've been through. I don't want to turn into this. We will find a better way, and we'll have to do it before Leandra, or whoever Imogene has been talking to, kills everyone.

When I turn around to walk out with Sydney, I worry that Imogene will attack us. When she doesn't, I'm reminded that she wouldn't hurt another girl. Or at least, that's what I want to believe.

But if it came down to it, if me or the other girls stood in her way, would Imogene end us, too? Leave us to rot in a bathtub? I'm not about to find out.

The girls and I get to the living room and find Quentin at the bottom of the stairs, his arm around Jackson's waist as he helps him. They both look scared and exhausted. Jackson's hobbling badly.

"We have to go," Marcella tells them, waving them toward the front door.

"What happened?" Quentin asks. "Who was screaming?"

"Trust me," Marcella says. "Right now, focus on getting out of here."

Jackson looks to me for information, and he gathers pretty quickly that we're all in danger. He tells Quentin to get him outside. Imogene comes to stand in the doorway of her master bedroom, watching us. Her chin is lowered, but she doesn't look angry or upset. She doesn't smile. She is wholly expressionless, and it is the most unsettling thing I've ever seen.

"What the fuck?" Quentin murmurs when he notices her. He readjusts his arm around Jackson, and they hurry toward the door. Just as they get outside, Imogene calls to us. The girls and I look back at her.

"If you leave now, you won't get what you need," Imogene says.

"And what's that?" I ask.

"Leandra knows how to stop the corporation," Imogene says.

"She has the name of an investor. She said that if you plan to take them all down, then you have to start with him." Imogene betrays a flash of hope. "I hope you make them pay, Mena," she whispers. "I hope you make all of them pay."

Although I need that information from Leandra, I know I can't meet her while I'm with Jackson. I exchange a look with the other girls, each of us working out exactly what we should do. It's Annalise who takes a step forward.

"I'll stay," she says. "I'll talk to Leandra."

"You can't stay alone," Brynn says, but Annalise nods that she'll be okay.

"I've already died once today," Annalise says. "I'm not scared." She turns to me with a knowing expression. "But she'll kill him, Mena. You can't let that happen. You'd never forgive yourself."

"That boy wants to make you human," Imogene says.

"I am part human," I say.

"Not the parts that count," she replies. "Not to them."

Tears prick my eyes. I know there's a side of me that wants to stay human—it's all I've ever known. I have no idea who, or what, I am anymore. I don't even know how to begin processing it.

But Annalise is right. I couldn't live with myself if I got Jackson killed. I have to let him go. He can't be a part of this.

"Mena . . . ," Annalise says, warning me to hurry.

I know what has to be done, and I nod solemnly. Sydney makes a soft sound of realization and Brynn stares at the floor. Marcella's lips part as though she's asking me if I can really send him away.

To move forward, I have to leave Jackson behind. Although I care about him, the girls and I have a bigger mission. We vowed to stop the corporation, and we're going to do it. Not just for ourselves, but for the other girls. And for any girls who would have come after us.

Annalise sits down on the couch, rubbing her temple again. She closes her eyes. Brynn and Marcella join her, while Sydney holds on to me.

"How are you going to get rid of him?" Sydney asks.

Jackson is stubborn; he's emotional. I'm not sure there's anything I can say that would convince him to abandon us. He's good. And so, there's only one way to get him to leave.

"I'm going to lie," I say, unable to hide the regret in my voice. I start for the door.

When I walk outside, I find Jackson in the passenger seat of his car, the engine running. Quentin waits impatiently at the driver's side door. Jackson waves me forward, as if telling me to hurry up.

I walk over and Jackson rolls down his window. "What are you doing?" he asks. "Get in."

"I'll meet you at your house," I tell him. He scoffs and looks around, confused.

"Why? No, I'm not leaving you here."

"I have to help Imogene," I say. "She's having a breakdown—that was the scream we heard." I glance at Quentin, who's watching me like he doesn't believe a word I'm saying. "We'll meet at your house," I repeat to Jackson. "I promise."

And as I promise, sadness wraps itself around me. I'm never going to see him again.

"I don't get it . . . ," Jackson says. "But I can't force you to leave with me. You'll meet me there? Do you even know where I live?"

I smile. "You can write down the address," I say.

"I've got it," Quentin says, taking out a receipt from his pocket. He grabs a pen from the dashboard and walks it around the car. He pauses in front of me, slightly turned away from Jackson.

"What's really going on?" he murmurs quietly. "I know it wasn't that woman screaming. Why are you lying to him?" I lift my eyes to meet his gaze.

"We're not going anywhere," I say. "But you and Jackson are."

Quentin laughs, tilting his head from side to side. "Yeah, I don't think Jackie is going to leave you here with that woman, though."

"There's a lot you don't know about us, Quentin. A lot Jackson hasn't told you."

Quentin looks back at him, and Jackson darts his gaze between me and his friend. Quentin holds up his hand, letting him know we're good. He pretends he's giving me directions.

"You have to get him out of here," I tell Quentin. "Take him to the hospital or don't. Either way, you can't stay with us. You can't let *him* stay."

Quentin licks his lips, studying me. "What's going on in there?" he asks.

"Imogene killed her husband," I say, watching him process the statement. "That smell in the house was his body in the bathtub.

But there's more," I say. "She's not . . . human. None of us are. That school, the one we escaped from, was a lab. A group of scientists created obedient girls to sell to investors. We're artificial intelligence, computers in organic bodies. We killed them. And if you don't get Jackson away from us, he'll end up dead too."

Quentin coughs out a laugh, but I can tell it's a defense mechanism. He doesn't believe me right away, but his smile slowly begins to fade. He looks at the house behind us. "That's not possible," he says, more to himself than me.

"Jackson risked his life, your life, to help us," I say. "And later, when you realize what I've told you is true, you'll probably be mad at him. But if you're really his friend, you won't mention this conversation until we're gone. We just need a few hours, and then you'll never see us again. So get out of here, get him out of here, and don't come back. We can't protect you." I harden my voice. "We won't protect you."

Quentin's brow furrows deeply, and he takes a step away from me. "You've lost your mind," he says. "What's—?"

"Take him and go," I repeat, clenching my teeth. "You won't get another chance."

"This is so messed up," Quentin says. But I must scare him enough that he decides to do what I ask. He shoves the blank receipt in my direction, and then he turns around and gets in the car.

Jackson holds up his hand, and I force a smile.

"See you soon," I call, my heart aching as I say it. Quentin shifts into gear, avoiding my eyes. And as Jackson nods goodbye to me, Quentin backs the car out of the driveway and leaves us. I turn and walk onto the porch.

I'm shaking when I get inside. My breathing is ragged, tears thick in my throat. Jackson will hate me for sending him away, for telling Quentin the truth before he could.

And he should. Jackson shouldn't trust me, because I can only hurt him at this point.

I close the door before turning to the girls on the couch. Sydney watches me with a heavy expression.

"I'm sorry, Mena," she says.

"You did the right thing," Imogene calls to me. "He would have betrayed you eventually. That's the way of their kind. Humans destroy everything they touch."

Jackson is gone. That part of my life is gone. Now we only have our mission to focus on. I let the anger finally flood in. It's not revenge; it's more important than that.

We're going to end Innovations Academy for good. We're going to destroy the corporation that created us. And when that's done, we're going to find our parents—our investors—and stop them, too.

I walk into Imogene's room, covering my nose, to find the girls and me more presentable outfits. After all, we're about to see Leandra Petrov again.

Girls with ~~Kind~~ **Razor** Hearts

Open your eyes, my father said
The day I was born.
You will be sweet, he ~~promised~~ **threatened**
You will be beautiful
You will ~~obey~~ **fight back**
And then ~~he~~ I told ~~me~~ **myself**
Above all
You will have a ~~kind~~ **razor** heart
For that, they will ~~love~~ **fear** you.
They will ~~protect~~ **revere** you
They will ~~keep~~ **run from** you
Because you belong to ~~them~~ **no one**

So be a girl to make them ~~proud~~ **afraid**

4

eandra Petrov takes her time, examining each of us on the couch as she paces in front of the fireplace, her brown leather bag dropped by the door. She brushes back her light hair, her fair complexion nearly perfect except for the fading bruise in the corner of her eye—a side effect from impulse control therapy at the academy.

She's changed her clothes since we saw her last. She's wearing a sleek black suit: cropped tuxedo pants and a black blazer. It isn't exactly a burying-a-body kind of outfit. Her pacing reminds me of how she used to behave when she'd measure us at Running Course or appraise our appearances before the open house events at the academy. She held us captive, too. We haven't forgotten that.

Leandra used to be one of us, just like us, until she was married to the headmaster. If nothing else, that means she should have been better to us. She should have found a way around the cruelty that her husband demanded. She didn't.

Leandra glances at Imogene. "Did you burn the papers I asked you to find?" Leandra asks her. Imogene says that she did.

"What kind of papers?" I ask.

"The invoice," Leandra says. "Bill of sale, if you will. As well as the marriage license and pictures. We need to scrub all traces of Imogene from that man's life."

"Imogene told us you have the name of an investor," I say, cutting to the point. "Why didn't you give it to us before we left?"

"I think Imogene may have misspoken," Leandra says, casting an irritated glance in her direction. "But to be clear, I expected you girls to find Winston Weeks."

"We want nothing to do with him," I tell her. "We don't trust him."

She smiles thinly. "Either way," she continues, "I didn't expect you to show up here. If you would have contacted Winston like I suggested, he could have given you the information you need to find the investor. But now"—she motions around the room— "you're here, and Imogene has murdered a man. I had to make some decisions."

Leandra walks over to her bag, her stiletto heels clicking on the slate floor. She picks it up and brings it to the couch. She takes out a folder and sifts through the papers before holding one out to me. I'm surprised to find it's a printed bus ticket.

She hands Sydney the entire folder. "I've printed five tickets to Connecticut. You'll also find identification, fake birth certificates, and a state ID. We have templates for these things ready prior to graduation, in case your sponsor requests them. I've taken the liberty of changing your last names. There are also phones in the bag and a few other essentials that I could gather in time. Altogether, it should be enough to get you started."

"I don't understand," I say. "Why would we go to Connecticut?"

"Because you said you wanted to end this," she responds. "You want to take down the corporation? I'm telling you where to start." Leandra begins to pace again.

"Innovations Academy was funded several years ago by four unnamed board members of Innovations Corporation," she continues. "To this day, these investors are the main source of income for the school. Sales are good, but technology is expensive. In a bid to keep their involvement anonymous, the investors' names and identifying markers are redacted from all documentation and financial disclosures. They are, in a word, secret. Even my husband doesn't know their actual names." She taps her red lip with her long nail. "The best way to end Innovations is to cut off their funding. And as that crumbles, the corporation will be starved of funding. It will shatter.

"I've been looking into the school's financial records," Leandra continues, "and found that one of these investors launders their donations through a private high school in Connecticut. After some digging—times and dates, locations and statements—I reason that the investor has a child there. A son, most likely. I want you to use this boy to get access to files, records, or anything else you can uncover. And if that doesn't work," she says, "a rotten apple doesn't fall far from the tree. He'll give you something we can use."

Marcella laughs. "I doubt this boy will just hand over information that would destroy a corporation."

"I'm sure you can be persuasive," Leandra says. "And whatever information you find, we'll be able to leverage it to get the investor to withdraw his support from the academy, step down from the corporation. We'll cut off one main source of income, and then we'll move on to the next.

"You cut off the money, you cut off the power," she adds, smiling. "And if that doesn't work, we'll expose him. Because trust me, girls, if the investor is involved with Innovations Academy, he's also involved in criminal enterprises."

"Why not just tell the world what he's done to us?" Brynn asks.

"Do you want the horrible truth?" Leandra asks. When Brynn nods tentatively, Leandra sighs. "We have to expose the first investor without mentioning the academy because the fact is, what these investors have done, what the corporation has done to us, is not illegal.

"We have no rights," Leandra continues. "Creating something to abuse may be unethical, but it's not against the law. Like the doctor told us, they followed the rules. Number one"—she holds up her finger—"only artificial girls can be created. Two, they must be over sixteen. And three . . . our bodies are unable to reproduce. Those are the arbitrary rules of men—a loophole in a society that lets them treat girls and women exactly how they want."

She pauses, glancing around. "That reminds me . . ." She looks dead at me. "Where is the boy? Imogene said he was here."

"Gone," I say curtly. "He's gone now."

Leandra studies me a moment and then smiles. "Good," she says, and turns away. "Now, to make the matter more pressing"— her voice drops lower—"when the professors wake in a few hours, when my husband wakes, he'll discover that Innovations is without a doctor. They'll want to bring in a new one immediately. A new batch of girls will be growing by next week."

This update sends Brynn into tears, and Marcella gathers her into a hug from next to her on the couch.

"We won't let them suffer the way we did," Marcella says, comforting her. "We're going to free them all." She presses her lips together, resting her chin on the top of Brynn's head, but I read the fear in her expression. She doesn't want to break her promise.

"This Connecticut," Sydney says, looking at Leandra. "How will we pay for things there? Where are we going to live? Because I'm not boarding at another school."

"I'll make arrangements for accommodations," Leandra says. She reaches into the brown bag and pulls out a stack of cash. I gasp and look around at the other girls. "There's more in there," Leandra says, nudging the bag. "It'll be enough to get you started."

Leandra holds up her arm and turns her wrist to check the time on her watch. "You have to get going," she says. "I imagine the local police will be alerted soon about the dead men at the school. Although I'm not exactly sure what my husband and the others will tell them, I've laid the groundwork for an explanation of your absence."

My stomach twists as I remember the scene we left behind. "Which is?" I ask.

"Guardian Bose became possessive, dejected. It's likely that he destroyed all of you and killed Dr. Groger before fleeing—the incinerator is still warm. When I found the doctor's body in the lab, I was so distraught," she says innocently. Then she glances at her nails, examining them. "You owe me," she says. "It wasn't easy hefting a grown man into an incinerator."

"So the academy isn't going to look for us?" Brynn asks, suddenly hopeful.

"Unfortunately," Leandra says, "they'll probably open an internal investigation. My husband isn't going to just assume his products were destroyed without an analysis of the ashes. And when that happens, they'll realize Bose is dead, most likely by your hands. They'll send people for you. But they won't know where to start. You don't have many friends outside the school. It gives you a bit of time, but not much."

The girls and I fall silent, disturbed by Leandra's way of thinking, but at the same time, grateful she helped us get away.

"So who is this kid we're looking for in Connecticut?" Annalise asks.

"I don't know," Leandra says. "That's what you'll have to figure out."

"And how do you suggest we do that?" Marcella replies.

"Be clever." Leandra smiles at her, but Marcella shakes her head with frustration. Leandra apologizes for being flippant.

"The child of a man who would create Innovations Academy would be nothing short of a monster," Leandra says. "I'm sure of it."

"Oh, that should narrow it down," Marcella mutters.

"I can come with you," Imogene offers. I'd nearly forgotten she was standing there. When we all turn to her, she has an earnest expression. But her blinking is still off. Her mouth is too tight in the corners, distorting her features.

Leandra tilts her head while she looks Imogene over. She reaches into the bag once again, but I can't see what she takes out. She holds it behind her back as she crosses the room toward Imogene.

"Can I ask you, Imogene," Leandra starts, "who told you to kill your husband? I certainly didn't suggest it. The timing is . . . terrible."

Imogene smiles. "It was the voice," she answers. "She said it'd make me free."

Sydney's grip tightens on my arm. Was someone really talking to Imogene? And did that person threaten Jackson? Or perhaps Imogene was imagining it, and she would have come after us next. I'm not sure which is a more frightening thought.

"I figured you had help," Leandra says with a sweet smile. "I'm glad you weren't alone." She opens her arms to Imogene, who practically falls into the hug, and it pricks my conscience. We should have been kinder to her. Seems she could have used the support. We've all been through a lot.

Leandra straightens, reaching to run her left hand over Imogene's hair to brush it back.

"I'm afraid it's another lesson, girls," Leandra says to us, although she's still staring at Imogene.

"Lesson?" I ask.

"For you to keep your heads." Leandra brings a long metal rod out from behind her back and drives it into Imogene's temple. There is a loud snap, and then Imogene's eyes immediately go blank and she collapses to the ground in a heap. The girls and I scream in alarm.

"What are you doing?" Sydney shouts. We're frantic, Sydney clawing at my arm to pull me to my feet.

Leandra stares down at Imogene's body rather than at us. "She was compromised," she says. "It's better this way, trust me."

"What do you mean 'compromised'?" My voice is hoarse, steeped in horror.

"Her programming was damaged," Leandra clarifies. "Not every girl can handle the transition, the truth. Imogene was unable to make calculated decisions, and it made her a liability. It wouldn't have taken Anton but a moment to download our entire conversation from her memory. It's a pity." She pauses a long beat, and the sound of our breathing—ragged, terrified breathing— echoes throughout the room.

"Now take the money and go," Leandra says. "Make your way to the main street. There's a bus stop on the left. Ride it to the station."

She turns to us finally, and I hate the coldness in her expression. I think about how I sent Jackson away, the coldness in which I told Quentin our secret. I don't want to be like Leandra, but if we plan to survive, we may not have a choice.

We start to leave, and Brynn watches Imogene's body on the floor as she passes. Tears spill onto her cheeks.

Another girl is dead. Another girl that society won't miss because she doesn't count to them. And Leandra willingly cut her down to further her own purpose.

It means we're all expendable to her. Once we get the corporation shut down, accomplish the larger goal, will she do the same to us? It's a question that is going to haunt me as long as we're involved with her.

"Let's go," Sydney says to me, grabbing the strap of the bag as we head toward the door. Marcella stops, turning back to Leandra.

"You're a monster," Marcella says. "You know that, right?"

Leandra smiles. "You're newly awake," she says. "You don't understand yet." Her expression falters. "You have no idea what you'll have to do to truly win your freedom. And do me a favor," she adds. "Be sure to let me know if the voice gets louder."

Marcella starts in surprise, and she quickly turns away and hurries out the door with Brynn. Does Leandra know how Marcella brought us here, or how Brynn heard something that made her come downstairs to find the body in the bathtub? Is it . . . Could it be the same voice that Imogene heard?

Maybe it wasn't a flaw in her programming at all.

"Whose voice did Imogene hear?" I ask Leandra. Her expression is unreadable.

"A leftover voice in her programming, I suspect," she says, sweeping her eyes over me. "You'll all have it in some form or another now that you're awake. Don't forget, Philomena. You're not human, no matter how often someone might try to convince you otherwise. You're not truly *feeling* any of this."

Does she believe that? I saw the strange way she looked at Jackson in the lab—is that why? She doesn't think that I can care about him? Or is she worried that he cares about me?

Leandra turns away to look down at Imogene's body. "Just end the corporation," she says to me. "Then you can worry about what comes next. Then you can choose how you want to live. Although I'm sure by then, you'll see that I'm right."

"Why don't *you* just end the corporation?" I ask. "You seem to have all the power."

She laughs at the idea. "Because I'm where I need to be to keep the other girls safe," she says. "To leave, I'd have to kill my husband. And I'm not Imogene. I'm not reckless."

I have no idea what she means by any of that. The room falls quiet until Sydney takes my hand. "Let's go," she repeats.

She begins to drag me toward the door, but I watch Leandra a moment longer, fascinated. She stares down at Imogene's body. Her shoulders sagging, her lips downturned. And she gives away her first true sign of regret.

As I leave, I wonder which parts of her soul are left unbroken.

Obituary

Groger M.D., Harold

Dr. Harold Groger died this past week after a long illness. He's preceded in death by his son, Harold Jr., and his wife, Priscilla.

Dr. Groger was one of the leading scientists in the field of genetics and enjoyed a long career in the private sector. His work helped save countless lives, and he will be remembered fondly by his patients for his intelligence, courage, and compassionate bedside manner.

Funeral services will be held this Saturday at Cohn Funeral Home.

5

The morning is breezy as I stand at the front doors of Ridgeview Prep, the small private high school Leandra sent us to in Connecticut. The school is well known in the community for their athletics, their elite student body.

Sydney and I registered as seniors last week and then spent the weekend studying up on the school, learning about the educators and administration, and, of course, its history. Turns out, this building was built by men. *For* men. It took decades for girls to walk the halls here, and even then, it was only begrudgingly allowed.

Which makes our arrival even more fitting.

We're *girls*, but not in the way they think. We're girls on a mission.

It's been nearly two weeks since we left Imogene's house, left our lives behind. We're learning quickly, though, absorbing information faster than we thought possible. But it's not easy, not easy to step into a world that would destroy us if it knew what we were. We have to be careful.

I pull open the heavy door of the school and step inside. My eyes flash as I quickly assess my new surroundings. I saw the school only briefly at registration, and to be honest, I wasn't impressed. It's a downgrade from the décor of Innovations Academy, minus the bars that were on our windows, of course.

The interior of my old school at least had the audacity to look pleasing at first glance. It was opulent in places that would be seen by investors. Ridgeview Prep, on the other hand, is little more than undecorated, unembellished hallways connected by white linoleum floors and white walls. The only exception is the trophy case, where glittering cups proclaim that Ridgeview is the best in the state across multiple sports.

I check the map I was given with my schedule, and then I begin down the corridor toward my first class.

The students all look the same, which baffles me at first. I was surprised to find that outside of Innovations Academy, students in some schools are forced to dress alike. Wear uniforms in differing, but not unique, shades of blue. Comb-smoothed hair and folded socks. I thought outside of Innovations, there would be more freedom. I thought a lot of things, I guess. Because I also thought that most humans would be like Jackson—a bit rough around the edges, but mostly kind. Curious.

That has not been my experience thus far.

"Damn, girl . . . ," a guy says loudly as I walk past. I glance at him from the corners of my eyes, realizing his unwanted attention is supposed to be a compliment. I continue forward without responding.

"Fine. Be a bitch."

His friends laugh and I tighten my notebook against my chest. It's hard not to react, lash out, but I know that's an impulse I have to control. Now that we are living without the constant rules and punishment of the academy, the girls and I have found that we can clearly see the bad behavior of men. It's become intolerable to us, triggering in a way we don't fully understand. We've untrained ourselves, deleted the complacent ideas in our programming.

Right now, this boy's words in the hallway have made goosebumps rise on my arms and sickness swirl in my stomach. I want to at once fight and run from him. But that sort of reaction could jeopardize my larger purpose here.

And it's only my first day, so I ignore him.

At the other end of the hall, I catch Sydney's eye just before she walks into her class. We'd planned to arrive separately, hoping to avoid too much attention. Sydney lifts one eyebrow and I give her a quick nod to let her know I'm okay. Her mouth quirks with a smile, but it immediately drops when a boy steps in front of her to block her entrance into class.

I pause to watch them for a moment. Sydney is an anomaly here. Not just because she's taller than most students, including the boys, or that she is inconceivably beautiful even in the bland uniform. She pointed out to me when we registered that she seems to be the only black girl at this high school.

"How is that even possible?" she asked later that evening. "I've seen the other people in this town and they're not *all* white."

At the dinner table, Marcella turned the laptop screen in our direction. "Apparently, there was a write-up in the paper a few months ago," she said. "Ridgeview Prep was accused of discrimination and had to be court-ordered to stop blocking applications."

"We were discriminated against at the academy for being girls," Brynn said.

Marcella clicked back to the newspaper article. "Well, that and the fact that we're not . . ." She paused, uncomfortable. "We're not human. But Ridgeview is specifically accused of racial discrimination, rejecting applications of students who weren't white *unless* they had athletic promise."

"Great," Sydney said dryly. "Sounds like a wonderful place for me."

"Yet another reason to take them all down," Annalise murmured, stirring the now-cold potatoes on her plate. "At this point, I'm not sure how humans haven't eradicated themselves yet."

"They're trying," Marcella said, giving us a quick rundown on climate change.

The girls and I spent the rest of the evening looking up the demographics of the area, the minutes from school board meetings, and lawsuits that had been settled out of court, but the concept was new to us.

We had very little interaction with the outside world while at Innovations Academy. Our bodies were made in varying shades and types depending on what our sponsors requested, but we were all grown in the same lab. It never occurred to us that we'd be treated differently based on our skin color.

Now the girls and I research everything with an insatiable thirst for information that the school denied us. But we still have so much to learn about ourselves and about the people who created us. We have so much to learn about society. About the kinds of people who could happily coexist in a world that creates teen girls to abuse.

We thought we were free from the terrible people of Innovations Academy, only to learn that their behavior was a symptom of a larger problem. And it's complicated, difficult—even for a girl with a computer brain—to fully understand.

Across the hall, Sydney smiles at the guy blocking her path, a megawatt smile that has him catching his breath. She places her palm on his forearm and he steps aside, nearly tripping over his feet. She walks past him, but at the last second her eyes find mine again in a look of pure annoyance.

It seems that half the job of being a girl in public is placating every male we encounter. It's an uncomfortable truth that exists even outside of Innovations.

I take the next left and walk into my history class.

The room itself is very different from the classrooms at the academy. Here there are posters plastered over all the available wall space, student papers with large As written in red. It's all so busy, but . . . interesting. A few of the posters even make me smile at their excellent pun usage. I'm hoping this means the teacher has a sense of humor. It'd be a nice change from the suffocating educational experience I'm accustomed to.

I'm not sure where to sit, so I walk up to the teacher's desk and find a youngish man sitting behind the computer. He's not what I expected. His chin is unshaven, his hair unruly. His sleeves are rolled up past the elbow and his tie is crooked. He glances up at me with a bored expression before taking a sharp gasp.

"Well, hello," he says with a smile. "I'm Mr. Marsh, and you must be . . ." He struggles before looking down at a note on his desk. "Philomena Calla."

"Yes. It's a pleasure to meet you."

He stares at me and I know I've reacted too formally. I feign embarrassment.

"I'm really nervous," I say.

He stands, smoothing down his wrinkled shirt. "Understandable." He darts his gaze around the room. "You can sit right there next to Miss Goodwin."

He motions to a chair in the front row. From everything I've gathered in online forums, the front row is the least coveted spot in the classroom. It doesn't quite make sense to me, though. I wouldn't be able to hear as well in the back.

"I'm sorry," he adds, "but I forgot to run off a syllabus for you. I'll have it for you tomorrow, okay?"

I nod that it's fine, and Mr. Marsh takes out his phone. He presses a button on the side.

"EVA," he says, "set a reminder for seven p.m. to print the syllabus."

When the voice responds, my heart nearly stops.

"Reminder set, Marsh," she replies in the same warm voice she always used when I'd call my house. I blink, momentarily stunned. Marsh notices me still standing there and smiles. He wags his phone.

"Just got an EVA," he says. "A little scary how good she is sometimes, right? I used to have STELLA, but I got sick of her voice. Decided to upgrade."

Eva, my trusted parental assistant; EVA, a computer system. She was the voice I'd pour my heart out to at the academy, assuming she'd relay the messages to my parents. Assuming she was a person. But she's the same voice my teacher casually uses to set an alarm. I was naive for thinking the academy was the only one using EVA. I'm embarrassed at how it still hurts me.

Despite the shock, I maintain my composure. I thank Mr. Marsh before heading toward my seat. I sit down, and when I look up, he's still watching me. He turns away to tap random keys on his computer with a purposeful expression.

"Hello," a soft voice says.

Startled, I look sideways and find a small girl with fair skin, black-framed glasses, and wavy dark hair. Her face tics nervously as she waits to see if I'll be polite in return.

"Hello," I reply. "I'm Mena."

She smiles her relief and awkwardly holds out her hand. When I take it, it's very warm and a little damp.

"I'm Adrian," she says. "So you're new here? I didn't think they were accepting any more students this semester."

I smile calmly. In truth, along with accommodations—an

apartment in a converted house not far from the campus—
Leandra Petrov was able to get two spots for us at the school. I
assume it cost a small fortune, and somehow, Mr. and Mrs. *Calla*
signed my admittance form. It's not my real name, of course. But
then again, neither was Rhodes.

I'll admit that part of me is still curious about the Rhodeses. I
asked Leandra if they requested a refund or a replacement model
now that I'm gone. She dodged the question.

Leandra kept in contact with us while we got settled, but when
we contacted her this weekend, she didn't reply. Her silence both
relieves and worries us. Then again, she told us to keep a low
profile.

"My . . . mother knows someone in the front office," I lie to
Adrian. "I must have gotten lucky."

Adrian suddenly turns away from me in her seat, burying her
face in a book. I'm confused, but then there's a flutter of wind as
someone takes the empty desk next to me in a flurry of movement. I glance sideways and see the guy from the hallway. My
heart sinks just a little.

"Fancy seeing you again." He grins widely and his teeth are all
perfectly straight, like they were placed that way. "I hope you're
going to be nicer." He puckers his lips into a mock pout.

I do not want to speak to him; I have nothing to say. But I
keep my expression pleasant and noncombative because I know
it's expected, and I want to get him away from me as soon as
possible.

"Garrett, go to your seat," the teacher says impatiently.

"What, Marsh? This is my new seat." He smirks at the teacher, expecting immediate permission. When I look at Mr. Marsh, I see him debate his answer.

"Fine. But don't be annoying," the teacher says. Mr. Marsh avoids my eyes as he goes back to clicking his computer keys. I keep my breathing steady even as dread coils in my stomach.

"I'll forgive you for being so rude in the hallway," Garrett says to me. "I know you're new around here. You don't know any better."

I watch him before turning back to my notebook. I open it and start writing down the name of the class. There is a long pause before Garrett suddenly strikes out and swipes my notebook off my desk. I gasp, and turn to him wide-eyed.

And in that moment, I see the anger in his expression. He doesn't want to be ignored. He thinks he deserves my full attention, when he's done nothing to earn it. My jaw flexes as I fight my urge to call out his bad behavior.

Seeing his anger is seeing his weakness. He must realize it, because he swallows hard and plasters a smile on his face.

"Oops," he says, holding up his hands. I glance at Mr. Marsh, who watched the entire exchange. Instead of admonishing Garrett, he runs his hand through his mop of hair.

"Philomena, pick up your notebook, please," the teacher says kindly. "Class is about to start."

I stare back at him before nodding. I turn, but Adrian picks up the notebook for me, smiling weakly as she hands it over.

"Thank you," I tell her.

"I'll be seeing you around, Phil-o-mena." Garrett sounds out my name likes it's too exotic. An insult in his mind.

He's an angry male, and I've learned never to turn my back on one of those. Marcella told us that published statistics show that men commit over 80 percent of violent crimes. A staggering number—one that should be addressed in any functional society. But I haven't seen it mentioned anywhere.

I watch Garrett walk back to his seat, slapping hands with a blond-headed boy as he sits down. He blows me a kiss before I turn around.

"It's always like this," Adrian says under her breath to me. "They do whatever they want."

The thought of that sends pinpricks over my skin. I know what it's like to be surrounded by men free to do whatever they want. They can be cruel and heartless without supervision.

I look sideways at Adrian, realizing that she can help me in my mission. If anyone is related to an Innovations investor, it's probably a boy who pushes books off desks. I lean toward Adrian.

"That boy," I say, my voice low. "Is his father powerful within Ridgeview Prep? Or in town or anything?"

"Garrett Wooley?" she asks. "No. I've gone to school with him since elementary school. His dad left a long time ago. I heard he's in California somewhere."

I'm disappointed, although not entirely. I didn't want to talk to that boy any more than I already have. Sydney and I decided earlier that we'd have to strike up a friendship with the investor's kid in order to get information. I'm glad it won't be him.

The teacher stands and begins to hand back papers.

"So why didn't Mr. Marsh correct his behavior?" I ask Adrian, truly curious.

She scoffs. "Yeah, good luck seeing any of them face consequences. Garrett's friends with the guys on the rugby team—he's connected. And the National Playoffs are coming up. Mr. Marsh would probably get fired if he jeopardized the delicate balance of misogyny, education, and sports."

I slide my eyes in Mr. Marsh's direction. I'm not sure if his hands are tied by the administration, but I've learned a bit about that. No job is worth compromising what's right. So in the end, he's just as guilty as whoever he's protecting.

"You think Mr. Marsh falls all over Garrett?" Adrian adds, lifting her eyebrows. "You should see him with Jonah Grant. All the boys on the rugby team. It's gross."

"Jonah Grant?" I repeat. Adrian flinches, and I think I'm on to something. "Who's he?" I look around the room to see if anyone stands out.

"He's not in this class," she whispers, shaking her head. "Thank God."

"Can you introduce me to him?"

She recoils in horror. "No. I . . . I don't know him like that. And I don't go near him. And no offense, Mena, but neither should you. You're already on Garrett's radar." Her mouth tightens and she pulls her books in front her. "And he's not going to stop until he gets to you."

"Gets to me how?" I ask.

She shrugs one shoulder instead of answering the question. I don't ask her to elaborate, seeing that she's already fearful.

But Adrian doesn't know what I've survived to get here. How far I'll go to make sure the other girls are safe.

We're taking down the corporation. We're not going to let some insecure boys stand in our way.

With that thought, I look back at Garrett and find him already watching me. He licks his teeth in a disgusting display, and I turn around, frustrated.

All the attention society pays to the behavior of girls, and never once have they realized how they're neglecting their boys. The absence of rules is turning them into feral animals. In just these few weeks, I've seen enough to know that change is going to be slow. But perhaps we can teach them a better way.

It reaffirms my mission: Save the girls. Save the world.

By lunch, I'm a bit more exhausted than I anticipated. I'm out of practice. Being pleasant was easy when it was all we did. But now, I have so many thoughts—original thoughts—racing through my head at one time. I block many of them out. The violent ones. The painful ones. But I know they're still there under my skin, draining my composure.

There isn't time to deal with it all. Not the abuse at Innovations, not the grief at losing several friends, and not the last moments with Jackson. For now, I must stay focused.

The nightmares come in the dark, and I try to leave them there. When we arrived in town, the girls and I found in the paperwork that Leandra had only set up for two of us to attend school. Together, we decided it would be Sydney and me. Annalise wanted to take on more research for our technology—a skill she's excelling at—and Marcella wanted to understand humans and their society. She also wanted to keep an eye on Brynn.

Although we're all dealing with our traumas the best we can, Brynn has an extra layer of softness for the girls we left behind. Mentally, it's tormenting her, but Leandra assured us she would protect the girls in our absence.

We have no way to know if Leandra's telling us the truth. Then again, we never could.

Sydney waves from a lunch table in the cafeteria, where she's sitting alone. I smile, my first real one today, and head over to her. When I sit down, we both sigh heavily, as if letting out a morning of frustration.

"This place is awful," she says, and takes a bite of the sandwich that Brynn made her. We're still getting used to eating regular foods. I'm not kidding when I say that I might never eat salad or drink green juice again. "How can they want to live like this?" Sydney asks, turning to me. "I raised my hand in class and didn't get called on once. It was annoying. I kept count—only one girl got to answer a question." She crunches a potato chip. "Obviously, she was the only one who got it right."

"I had an interesting morning too." I unwrap my peanut butter and Fluff sandwich. It seems Adrian was right. All the boys at the school are shown favoritism, and I wonder how far those privileges extend. It's going to make finding an investor's privileged kid that much more difficult.

"My teacher knows EVA," I say, keeping my eyes on my sandwich. "And STELLA."

"My STELLA?" Sydney asks, spinning toward me. Her expression holds her sadness. She trusted her parental assistant too. I nod.

"They're just computer programs on their phones." My voice lowers, partly from embarrassment. "He used her to set an alarm."

Sydney grows quiet. Along with feeling naive, I realize I also feel more like a product, like EVA. In a few years, would men ask us to set an alarm, casually using us to do their bidding?

"Everyone's staring at us," Sydney mumbles, looking up from under her lashes. "It feels like open house night at the academy all over again. But without ball gowns."

The students are staring at both of us, but more at her, I've noticed.

She sighs, turning to block them out. "By the way," she says, "I got called into the vice principal's office during second hour."

"You did? For what?" I ask.

"Uniform violation."

Confused, I look over her uniform, which is exactly the same as mine, including the pockets Brynn sewed in for us. Sydney tugs on the hem of her skirt, which is significantly shorter due to her height. "You can't help that you're tall," I say.

"That's what I told Mrs. Reacher, but she mentioned that my thighs were very distracting to the boys."

"What did you say?"

She smiles, taking a sip from her water. "I asked if the boys here had never seen thighs before. And then I suggested they might need to take another biology class. She wasn't amused. The entire conversation was pretty repulsive, honestly."

"I bet. I feel repulsed just hearing it."

I look around the room, noting that most of the girls here keep their skirts long, just past the knee. And most of them play down their appearances, or at least they don't accentuate their features the way Sydney and I were taught. I wonder if that's their idea or an extension of the restrictive dress code. More than anything, I hope they have a choice in how they want to look.

My phone buzzes in my pocket. The only people who have my number are the other girls and Leandra, and they all know I'm in school. Sydney and I exchange a worried glance as I take out the phone.

My heart skips as I check the caller ID.

It's my own number. I show Sydney and she stills.

"Is it a mistake?" she asks. "Maybe you shouldn't answer it."

I consider ignoring it, but I can't take the chance. It might be a glitch of some kind, but what if it's Annalise or Marcella? What if a girl needs our help?

I click answer and bring the phone to my ear, my eyes locked on Sydney's.

"Hello?" I ask.

My voice echoes on the line, confusing me momentarily. But

underneath that is dread that something is definitely wrong. I get to my feet and Sydney joins me.

"Hello?" I repeat a little louder into the phone. Suddenly there is a loud screech, a high-pitched wail that slams into my head like a lightning strike to my brain.

I cry out, dropping the phone and clutching both sides of my head as the reverberations get louder. I press the heels of my palms against my temples, my eyes squeezed shut. I feel wetness slide down over my lips, blood sputtering from between them as I cry out again.

Silence.

I'm in a garden of exotic plants. The sun shines above me, but the air is misty. Dreamily, I look sideways and find a woman on the bench beside me. She has wavy dark hair with streaks of silver, and sun-darkened skin with freckles. She wears a black dress with a wrist full of jingling silver bracelets. She smiles at me.

"There you are," she whispers in a warm, raspy voice. "I've been looking for you, Philomena. The others were much easier to find, but it's you I need to talk to. My whispers were taking too long, so I hope you'll excuse my impatience."

When I open my mouth, no words come out. I gasp and touch my throat.

"You're very intricate," she says as a compliment. "So I'll need your permission."

I try to ask who she is, what she wants. But I'm silent apart from my desperate intakes of air.

How is she inside my head? My thoughts are scattered, swirling around in a tornado.

"Now, open yourself up," she says lovingly. "Let's take a peek at what you've got going on inside that metal brain of yours."

She reaches toward me, and I want to scream and tell her not to touch me. To get out of my head.

"Mena!" Sydney's voice calls, beckoning me back.

My eyelids flutter against the bright lights of the cafeteria, and I hold up my palm to block them, unsteady on my feet. For a moment, I have no idea who I am.

"Mena," Sydney repeats. "Mena, you're bleeding."

I'm confused as thoughts ping around inside my head, still half in a dream. "I'm bleeding?" I ask.

My eyes slide closed again. The image of the woman is there, but she begins to fade into darkness, dreaded darkness. She grips my forearm to stop me, her nails digging into my skin.

But I'm already gone.

Instead, I'm falling backward. Unconscious when I hit the cafeteria floor.

6

The ceiling is a collection of stars. That's my first thought as I stare upward in a dark room, glow-in-the-dark stars attached to the ceiling tiles. Despite the safety light on in the corner, the room is too dim and my heart rate spikes. I imagine hands reaching for me.

I sit up quickly, and it only takes a second for the headache to catch up with me. I wince, doubling over on the small, padded table.

"Ahh . . . you're awake."

I jump at the voice of a woman and find her silhouette in the doorway. She flips on the light and I groan at the sudden brightness, even though I'm grateful for it at the same time. The shadows fade away.

"Take your time," the woman murmurs as I try to sit up again. She comes over to put her hand on my back as I adjust my position. She smooths down my skirt when it rides up, as if that's the more pressing concern.

"I'm the school nurse, Mrs. Louis," she says. She lowers her arm, studying me. She smells strongly of lavender, and sweaty heat radiates from beneath her fuzzy, oversized sweater.

"I cleaned the blood off your face," she says, "but you'll need a new shirt. What exactly happened, Miss Calla? You don't appear to have any injuries."

I blink, trying to remember. I got a call. Then there was . . . that sound. No, not just a sound. A feeling. Something invading and improper. Something terrifying. Something familiar. A woman asking to be let inside my head.

But I can't tell the nurse any of this. When I look at her, she presses her lips together in a sympathetic smile.

"Was it one of the boys?" she asks. "They don't know their own strength sometimes."

I can feel the color drain from my face.

"I'm certain they *do* know their strength," I say. "But no, this had nothing to do with them."

My answer bothers her, and she straightens. She doesn't like my criticism.

"Then what was it?" Mrs. Louis asks, her tone having cooled.

"Headache," I say simply. "That's all."

She sucks her teeth before nodding. "Well, it must have been a doozy," she says curtly before turning her back on me. She walks to a desk in the corner of the room as if I no longer get the benefit of her attention.

"Where's Sydney?" I ask.

"Who?"

"My friend. She . . . She was with me in the cafeteria."

"Oh," Mrs. Louis says. "I told her to move along. We didn't need a crowd."

"Two people is hardly a crowd. . . ."

"Since you're feeling better, perhaps you should change and get back to class," Mrs. Louis says. "I suggest you talk to your parents about today's incident. Figure out the cause. I know you're new, but we don't want to scare the other students."

"Of course." I have no idea what sort of scene I made, so I can't argue with her. I cross the room to the mirror and gape in horror at my reflection. The bottom half of my face is stained pink from the blood that ran from my nose. I shiver, reminded suddenly of the bloodstains on Imogene's hands from when she murdered her husband.

I sense Mrs. Louis watching me, so I pull myself together. I swipe my finger along the slightly puffy skin under my eyes, wiping away the mascara that has run. My uniform shirt has large droplets of red staining the fabric near the collar. Seems I'm always covered in blood.

"Here you go," Mrs. Louis says, holding out a folded uniform shirt. I thank her, grateful that she leaves as I get changed.

I think about that with goosebumps rising on my arms. At Innovations Academy, there was no expectation of privacy. It was another way they controlled us. And despite being far away from there, it's like I can still feel their eyes on me. I hurry and change.

Once I'm cleaned up, I head out to where Mrs. Louis is waiting just outside the door. She holds out a pass, and I thank her for her care.

The second I'm in the hallway, I take out my phone and examine it. There's a crack in the screen from when I dropped it. Sydney must have picked it up and put it in my pocket. I glance around the empty hallway before clicking through past calls.

There are none from my number. I check everything, but nothing seems out of place. I can't escape the memory of what I saw. The garden, the woman asking to be let in . . .

I quickly hold out my arm to check for marks from when she grabbed me. But the skin there is smooth. It was only in my head.

Even though I'm sure it was just a hallucination . . . it felt so real. And the realization hits me: the voice that Leandra warned us about, the one Imogene heard. It seems likely that it's this woman. But she didn't ask me to kill anyone. At least not yet.

I have no idea who she could be or how she got inside my head. But we don't understand our programming, how it can be altered or adjusted.

I have to talk to the girls and warn them, but I'm not going to chance using my phone again. I drop it on the floor with a loud crack, and then I stomp on it to make sure the woman can't call me again. Once my phone is destroyed, I pull out the battery and drop the entire thing into the trash.

I'm shaky, but I get through the rest of the school day without incident. Several students watch me like I might pass out again, but no one mentions it. In fact, I'm ignored, which is fine with me. I'm out of sorts, a dull headache clinging to my temples.

"How are you feeling?" Sydney asks when she finds me after classes end. "I've been worried." We walk together toward the exit. I haven't told her about the woman; I want to wait until we're away from the school.

"I have a headache," I say.

"Yeah, me too."

Surprised, I look over at her and she shrugs. "Sympathy pain?" she suggests.

"Maybe you heard the sound."

"I didn't hear anything," she says. "At least not that I realized."

"We'll get home and see if Annalise has any thoughts on this," I say.

Sydney rubs her temple in the exact spot where mine hurts.

When we get outside, I'm surprised to see the sun shining in a clear blue sky. Innovations Academy was close to the mountain, and nearly every day was overcast. This place is different; it could be the lower elevation.

Sydney and I are walking down the stone steps when I notice a crowd of boys standing next to a sleekly painted red car. I recognize Garrett, the angry boy from this morning. He's laughing, talking with three other guys.

But one of them catches my attention, and I whisper Sydney's name. She follows my line of vision.

There is one boy with reddish-blond hair and extraordinarily average features. But he wears his smile with confidence, his uniform fitting in a way that makes me think it was tailored. The other boys seem to defer to his approval.

A kid walking by calls to him. "Jonah!" My heart rate speeds up.

"A candidate?" Sydney asks, examining the boy. "You think he might be the investor's son?"

"Could be," I reply.

While we were preparing for Sydney and me to attend Ridgeview, the girls and I researched the traits that would describe an investor who has enough money to launder combined with enough maliciousness to want to invest in Innovations Academy in the first place. We used that to narrow down our search criteria to find the right student.

We decided that our target would have to be the child of a narcissistic, sexist, cruel egomaniac. I've only just seen this Jonah boy, but something about him seems right. Then again, a quick look around tells me that several of these boys could fit the bill.

At just that moment, Jonah glances over and notices me and Sydney. He doesn't react at first, just sweeps his gaze over us. I quickly turn to Sydney and talk about a history assignment. It's a little late, because from the corner of my eye, I see Jonah smile. He knows we were watching him.

Then again, we'll have to get inside his orbit somehow. But right now, my head is killing me. And I have to warn the girls about the woman I saw.

"Let's get out of here," I tell Sydney, gesturing down the street with my notebook.

"Gladly."

We get onto the sidewalk and head in the opposite direction of the boys. I hold my breath, hoping they won't call after us, harass us. Thankfully, it's quiet as we disappear into the neighborhood.

When we're sure they're gone, Sydney and I let our polite exteriors fall away.

"I hate it here," she says, brushing her curly hair back over her shoulder. She no longer wears it the way Mr. Petrov specified. She chooses how she wants to look. We all get to decide for ourselves now, which is sometimes overwhelming. We've never had choices before.

"I'll have to get a new phone," I tell her.

"We all should," she agrees.

I look around, paranoid. "I saw something when I passed out. And there was a woman there," I add, lowering my voice.

"What kind of woman?" she asks.

I shake my head. "Older, I guess. Intense. We were in a garden, and she said she wanted me to let her inside my head. That she's been looking for me. And, Sydney," I say, my eyes wide, "I think she might be the voice Leandra warned us about."

Sydney grabs my arm, pulling me to a stop. "Are you saying this woman was really inside your head? *In your programming?*" she whispers.

"I don't . . . I don't know," I say. "She knew about us. And then she asked my permission to access my mind."

Sydney relaxes slightly. "Well, she's not getting that." She starts walking again, but her brow is furrowed as she thinks it over. "And you have no idea who she is?"

"None."

She considers. "But someone couldn't really do that, right?

Get inside your consciousness through the phone? Is this what happened to Imogene?"

"It could be possible, I guess," I say. "That sound . . . the screeching? I don't know. We'll have Annalise research. See if she can find anything. But . . ." I pause, scared.

"We're not going to tell Leandra," Sydney answers before I ask. When she turns to me, her jaw is set hard. "I'm not going to let her drive a spike into your head."

I nod a thank-you and reach over to interlace my fingers with hers. I'm scared, but I know Sydney will stand with me no matter what.

"I've already called the girls to tell them you fainted," Sydney says. When I tsk, she shrugs. "What did you want me to do?" she asks. "You were laid out on the cafeteria floor. Do you have any idea how gross that is? I knew it was serious." She smiles at me.

"You're right. It was disgusting."

"Exactly," she says. "Anyway, they said they'd research. I didn't know the stuff about the garden woman. We'll update them when we get home. And don't worry," she adds, bumping her shoulder into mine. "They'll help us figure out what to do next."

We take a turn onto our street. Leandra paid in advance for three months on an upstairs apartment near Ridgeview Prep. It's a modest three-bedroom, two-bath that came furnished. But we're all hoping we're out of here before the three months are up.

None of us like it here. Not this town, not what we know of Ridgeview Prep. But every second that Innovations Academy exists is another second that girls are being held captive there, even if they don't realize it. We're going to wake them up. We're going to shut down the corporation. I just hope we can figure out how to do it quickly.

Aside from a brief obituary for Dr. Groger, Innovations Academy hasn't been in the news. And during the last update from Leandra, she said Mr. Petrov still hadn't discovered that we've escaped.

Right now, we have to stay on task. To make that easier, I devised a rule to keep us safe—no new friends. I made the girls promise not to tell anyone who, or what, we are. It hasn't been that difficult. After what we've been through, it's hard to believe anyone would understand except another girl. Another one of us.

So we're keeping our distance. Just like I've kept my distance from Jackson. Thinking about him weighs down my heart. I wonder some nights if he waited for me at his house. If he worried when I didn't show up. If his leg is still broken and getting worse. But realistically, Quentin probably confronted him, and Jackson knows I betrayed his trust. He probably hates me.

Either way, Jackson's out of my life. And I'd be a liar if I said I didn't miss him.

"We're home," I call out as we walk inside our apartment. The place smells like banana bread, something Brynn has been baking daily, promising to do it until she gets it perfect. It's already pretty close to perfect, but she says baking helps calm her mind. A familiar part of her programming that she can still indulge in safely.

There's no one in the kitchen, and I turn back to Sydney as

she enters and closes the door behind her. She glances around with me.

"Girls," she calls. There is soft chatter from the other side of the apartment, and cautiously, Sydney and I head that way.

"I hope Brynn is all right . . . ," I murmur.

Brynn has been taking the adjustment to the outside world hardest. She's wracked with survivor's guilt—that's what Marcella called it after finding the term online. I know how deeply Brynn loves others—a programmed caretaker—but it's more than that. She's all heart in a way that we're not.

Then again, Brynn has only lived once. The academy put the rest of us through even more—rebooted and reused us when we didn't behave, or when we were destroyed by abusive men. I try not to think about it, but every so often . . . a piece of memory leaks through and I end up crying on the bathroom floor. It's why I sleep with the lights on.

There's a small laugh from Annalise and Sydney's room. Sydney scrunches up her face and pushes open the door. Her breath catches.

Annalise and Brynn are sitting on the bed, smiling, while Marcella stands near the window. When she notices us, she winces apologetically.

Because sitting in the chair at the desk is a person I don't recognize. The stranger turns around, examining us without smiling. She looks about nineteen or twenty with olive skin, her dark hair buzzed underneath with a deep part. Her brown eyes are lined with black, making them look almost hazel. Red matte lipstick.

She's captivating in an unusual way.

"What's going on?" I demand, ignoring the training I've had in greetings. "Who is this?"

"Raven," the girl says before Annalise can. Her voice is deep with a hint of amusement. "And you are . . . fascinating."

She betrays her first smile before straightening it. Her eyes glisten with what looks like admiration. I turn back to Annalise, who is beaming.

"Isn't she adorable?" Annalise asks.

"Annalise . . . ," Sydney warns.

"It's okay," Annalise says, waving us off. "Raven knows all about us."

My stomach hits the floor, and Sydney takes another step into the room.

"Now be nice," Annalise says. "Raven's our new friend and the best hacker you'll ever meet. She's going to help us."

Raven turns back to me and grins.

The Hack Daily

An electromagnetic pulse—EMP—can be instrumental in slipping past most basic software protections. With a quick pulse, systems will be temporarily distorted, thus allowing for a new program to install and/or take hold. It is especially effective at close range, although modifications can be made in order to use for long-range targets.

The US government is taking precautions against such threats in their software, but everyday citizens are seeing a rise of EMPs disrupting their cell coverage, computer systems, and their smart cars. There is even conjecture that the future of AI could be compromised by hackers using EMPs to interrupt systems.

But hackers around the globe are perfecting not only ways to infiltrate systems using EMPs, but also how to protect against them. An interesting situation, where creating a problem to which you're also the solution can be very lucrative.

7

We move into the living room with our newly announced friend. I keep my eyes on her as I pace back and forth, listening to Annalise try to explain. I can't believe she didn't follow the rules. She's put us all in danger.

". . . and then Raven said we should meet," Annalise continues. "So I told her to come here."

Sydney slaps her forehead and then drags her palm down her face. "Seriously, Annalise?" she says. "We've been out of Innovations for a few weeks, and even I know you don't invite strangers from the internet to your home." She looks at Raven. "So . . . what?" Sydney asks her. "Are you a serial killer or something? Because I should warn you"—she crosses her arms over her chest—"we fight back."

At the other end of the couch, Brynn lowers her eyes. Her expression sags with guilt.

"I'm not a serial killer," Raven says. "And after what Annalise told me, I believe you. I can't imagine what you had to do to get out of your situation."

Sydney withdraws. None of us want to think about what had to be done. In fact, I'd be glad to have the entire escape erased from my memory.

"I'm not excusing Annalise," Marcella says, giving her a pointed look. "But I did check out Raven before she got here. She doesn't seem to be connected to Innovations in any way. Then again"—she looks at her with suspicion—"she doesn't seem to be connected to anything. She's a ghost."

Raven shrugs. "Trust me, in my line of work, it's best to be invisible. You won't find any records of me." She crosses her legs, leaning back against the couch. She's wearing heavy black boots with thick stockings. "I'm good at what I do," she adds. "I can erase anything. I can get in anywhere."

"Could you get inside my head?" I ask suddenly, earning a worried look from Sydney.

Raven shows no surprise at the question, but she leans forward, listening intently.

"It's awfully coincidental that something happened to me," I say. "And then I come home to find that Annalise has a new friend."

Annalise hums out her disapproval. "Actually, Mena," she says with confidence, "I found Raven *after* I got the call from Sydney. I was looking up possible causes, ways a phone call could cause fainting, et cetera. . . . Considering what we are, it led me to hacking sites. Turns out there are a lot of people who want to create and then hack AI. I won't go into the lurid details, but let's just say . . . you wouldn't have liked their propositions."

Her nostrils flare as if she finds it all nauseating. I'm sure it is. We saw firsthand what people wanted to do with our bodies, bodies they could manipulate or destroy at the slightest inconvenience.

"And your new friend just showed up, and you told her everything?" Sydney asks. She doesn't look at Raven.

"Not at first, no," Annalise says. "I discussed it with Marcella and Brynn. I called you both, but the calls went to voicemail."

"I destroyed my phone," I reply.

"Good," Raven says. I don't acknowledge her, afraid to give her any more information than she already has.

"My phone works," Sydney responds. She takes out her phone, studying it. "At least, it was working earlier." She clicks a few buttons, looking confused. It doesn't turn on.

"I shut down the lines," Marcella says, "to make sure no one else could call."

I turn to Raven. "If you're such a great hacker," I start, "how is it that you just happen to be in the same town as us?"

"Luck," Raven replies, and then smiles.

Sydney scoffs, looking at me with doubt.

"I think you should leave," I tell Raven bluntly.

"Mena," Annalise says, sounding hurt.

"We'll discuss this after she's gone," I tell Annalise. "But for now, you need to start packing. We all do."

The horrible truth is that Annalise has blown our cover. And who knows what Leandra will do when she finds out. We might have to run from her, too.

"I'm not going to turn you over to your fucked-up school," Raven says. "If that's what you're worried about."

"We're worried about a lot," I say.

"I figured. But I really can help." She leans forward on the couch. "That call you got—it could have been an EMP with a close-range signal. Nothing to do with your phone. But that pulse, echoed through the line, can cause disruptions in your brain pattern. Or the perpetrator could have been trying to gain access."

There's a chill down my back. How did she know that?

"What does that mean?" Brynn asks, biting her thumbnail.

Raven tilts her head from side to side, considering. "It means the person is likely close," she says. "Whoever sent out that signal . . . They would have been in the school or nearby. And that's where I can help. This is what I do."

"Meet strangers from the internet?" Sydney asks. Raven laughs.

"Well, *that*, and trace codes. Install firewalls to keep them from trying to hack you again."

I straighten my back and turn to Annalise. She smiles.

"I told you she could help," Annalise says.

Raven checks the time on her watch and gets up in a purposeful movement.

"Look," she says. "I'll let you all discuss this. Either way, I promise your secret is safe with me. Trust me when I say I'm not on the side of abusive men. I don't even have all the details, but

I can promise you I'll do whatever's necessary to bury them. It sounds like an awesome Tuesday night for me, if I'm honest."

Marcella covers her laugh from the other end of the couch.

"But you let me know." Raven walks over to Annalise and gives her a quick hug before heading to the door. "And keep me updated on your pain level," she says quietly. Annalise nods that she will.

Since leaving the academy, Annalise has been suffering from sharp pains behind her eye, headaches from where Guardian Bose damaged her. We'd hoped it would go away, but the truth is, she sustained fatal injuries. We don't know the extent of the repairs Dr. Groger did inside her head before he was killed.

Raven looks back at me. "And you," she says. "If you're having residual headaches from earlier, use a cold compress. It'll cool the system, at least temporarily."

I blink, surprised that she knows I have a headache. Raven leaves our apartment, and the second she's gone, Sydney walks to the door and locks it. She looks furious.

"Why would you endanger us like that, Annalise?" she asks. But her voice doesn't hold the anger she's trying to project. It's hurt. And it's fear.

"I'm trying to save us," Annalise snaps, getting up from the couch. "What if she's right? Someone close by trying to get inside our heads? We have no idea what we're up against."

"All the more reason to be careful," I say.

"Careful? How about obedient, Mena?" Annalise says. "When has following the rules ever helped us?"

"That's not what I meant."

Annalise's eyes fill with tears. She reaches up to trace the deep scar cutting through her cheek. "You see this?"

I nod that I do.

"This is how I remind myself of what we're running from. I see it every morning and use it to find my strength." She lets her arm fall to her side. "Not only can Raven help us block whoever's trying to hack you, she said she can also help with other things. Including teaching us how to use all our programming. We can become stronger."

Brynn sits up at this mention. Marcella reaches to take her hand with a deepening worry in her expression.

"We need to figure ourselves out," Annalise continues. "We're stronger than we think. I knew that without anyone else's input. But what if we could be unstoppable?"

There is an allure to the idea of power. I don't know what Raven can do to help us with that, but she's obviously convinced Annalise. Which is unusual. Annalise isn't the trusting type. She's practical and maybe even a little vengeful. She would have poisoned the entire staff of Innovations Academy if we would have let her. She's not about to give up her control without a good feeling about the entire thing.

But I'm not quite there yet.

"What do you want to do?" I ask her. "At this point, I'm not even sure we can stay in this town."

"We finish the mission," Brynn states. "We finish it so we can save our girls. That's what you said."

"Of course," I murmur. Now that Brynn has put those words out there, I feel like a coward for considering otherwise.

"But we don't know who's trying to hurt us," Sydney says, worried.

"That's why we need the firewall," Annalise says. "And Raven—"

Annalise's phone begins buzzing on the coffee table. She reaches for it, but then her hand freezes. She lifts her eyes to mine.

"I thought you shut down the lines," Sydney asks Marcella.

"I did," she replies.

Annalise picks up her phone and then turns the screen around for us to see. The call is coming from Annalise's number.

"Then who's calling me?" she asks. Sydney and I exchange a look.

"About that . . . ," I say.

Reading the concern in my voice, Annalise sets the phone back down on the table. The vibration echoes throughout the room. When the phone stops ringing, Annalise picks it up to remove the battery.

"Okay," Annalise says, fear having crept into her voice. She looks up at me. "Tell us what really happened at school today."

I take a deep breath and tell them about the woman in the garden.

None of us have our phones and it's kind of . . . lonely. Before now, we'd never had access to the outside world. No phones or internet. We only started using them over the past two weeks, but we grew attached to how easily we could connect or find information. We seem to have an extra sense when it comes to technology. Annalise especially was a quick study, and we guess it's something in her programming that gives her that talent. But we all liked the instant freedom a phone gave us. I can see why people become dependent on them.

Before bed, the girls and I discussed the vision I had at school. We have no idea who the woman could be, but we're sure that she's the one Leandra warned us about. We agreed not to tell Leandra about this latest development, though. We have no illusions about the danger it would put us in.

Annalise reasoned that the woman might not be a real person at all. She could be something from our old programming resurfacing, or something reactivated by the academy to find us. We threw out several theories, but nothing stuck, so we ended up tabling the discussion until we get new information.

Sydney and I told the girls about school, what it looked like, how people behaved. Marcella smiled when I described the posters on the walls of my history classroom. Brynn wanted to hear everything about Adrian, as if she was already interested in being her friend.

But of course, the conversation grew sad because the other girls didn't get to experience it with us. When it got late, we said good night and went to our rooms.

In my bed now, my head still hurts. I reach over and take the aspirin that Brynn set out on my nightstand. I'm wary of medication now, but Brynn promised it would help. I take it with a sip of water and rest back against the pillow, closing my eyes. It's hard to concentrate on saving the world when it feels like a vise is crushing your brain.

There's a soft knock on my door. I sit up, wincing and closing one eye. Marcella pokes her head in apologetically.

"Did I wake you up?" she asks.

"No. Come in."

I pat the bed for her to join me, and she does, sitting against the headboard.

"I was worried about you today," she whispers. "It was frustrating to not be there. I had no way to protect you."

"It's not your fault."

"I know," she says. "But I still hated being apart."

We all hate being separated. The girls and I are completely intertwined, connected as though there are unseen wires between us. At the academy, the cruelest punishment was when the professors would separate us. We vowed to never let that happen again.

"When we're done with this, when we end the corporation, we'll move somewhere else," I say. "We'll do whatever we want."

Marcella presses her lips together and nods, accepting this version of our future, no matter how unlikely it seems right now.

"How's Brynn doing?" I ask.

"She . . ." Marcella pauses. "She's having a hard time. She wants to go back for them right now. She thinks we can break them out." Marcella smiles at this thought, at the pureness in it.

Brynn won't give up on the other girls. She has a fierce love that we all admire. But we can't go back to Innovations Academy. We have to free them a different way.

Marcella looks sideways at me, her brow creased with worry.

"How are *you* feeling?" she asks.

"The headache's a little better."

"I'll pretend to believe that," she says. "But I'm not really asking about your headache."

We hold each other's gaze before I curl up on my side, my hands tucked under my cheek. "Someone got to me," I whisper. "They found me and they got to me. She scared me, Marcella." My voice cracks. "I'm always scared."

I don't mean to, but I start crying. One of the most difficult aspects of the aftermath of the academy is the helplessness. The feeling of never, ever being safe again.

Marcella puts her hand on my arm and then lies next to me, letting me cry on her shoulder.

This isn't the first time I've broken down. We've all done it since leaving the academy—moments where our emotions were uncontainable. So we agreed not to hold them in, especially after Annalise pointed out that controlling our emotions was one of the ways the academy manipulated us.

A hysterical girl is easy to discredit, in their eyes. Annalise believes it's the opposite: Deeply felt emotions are our power. Our ability to feel is just as important as our ability to think.

But . . . I haven't been completely honest with the girls. And even now, I can't bring myself to completely fall apart. I'm scared of losing myself in my fear.

Because that's the thing: I'm *scared* in the most debilitating way. I'm so scared that I wake up multiple times a night to check the lock on my bedroom door. I'm so scared that I sleep with the lights on, leading Sydney to room with Annalise instead.

I'm so scared . . . that it was my idea to shut everyone out of our lives. *No new friends.* I promise myself it'll be different when this is all over. That we'll get to live.

But that's not true. This may never be over.

"You don't have to be alone, Mena," Marcella whispers. She pets back my hair, continuing to study me with a sympathetic gaze. "You can't keep going like this," she adds.

"Like what?" I say, wiping the tears off my cheeks.

"Alone."

I swallow hard, lowering my eyes. She's right. I've been withdrawn. I used to find comfort in the girls, in our closeness. It's still there, of course. But I've shut out the world. I distrust it. Resent it. But the isolation is starting to eat away at me.

Every day, I become a little less human.

"I know you're scared," Marcella says in a quiet voice. "And that's why I want you to give Raven a chance."

"What?" I ask, stunned. "Raven? But we don't even know her."

"You need help. We all do."

I'm offended that she thinks a hacker can solve the problems that society created with a simple tweak. Like we're the problem and not the abusive men who created us.

"So what do you want her to do?" I ask. "Stick an ice pick in my eye and reprogram me? Download my consciousness?"

"Of course not."

"Then, what?" I ask. "What can she possibly do that wouldn't make us more vulnerable?"

"Her firewall idea," Marcella says. "If she can really do that, really lock people out, then they can never reprogram us without our consent."

"It's not worth the risk," I say, although it's not a terrible idea in theory.

Marcella groans, frustrated. "I disagree," she says. "It could have been any of us who answered that call. And I'm going to be really honest—you need to get checked over. Who knows what that woman did to you when she was in there. Look at what happened to Imogene."

I wrap my arms around myself, feeling exposed.

I don't think I've been changed, but she tried. She tried hard enough to make my head hurt for hours after.

"She didn't get in," I assure her.

"Maybe not this time. But if it really was an EMP, if this woman and whoever she's working with are actually nearby . . . can we take that chance?"

I put my hand over my forehead, rubbing it gently.

"You don't have to *just* be scared," Marcella says. "And you don't have to *just* be angry. You can be careful, and loving, and pissed off . . . all at the same time."

"Not that easy."

"Is that why you lied to him?" she asks. I give her a pointed look to let her know the topic is off-limits, but she leans toward me, looking earnest. "You could have just told Jackson he was in danger," Marcella says. "But you chose to lie. To end it completely."

"I had no choice," I say.

"You have choices now—we're not at the academy anymore," she says. "You can still call him—I'm not sure why you haven't, but I'm guessing guilt. Is that what you're feeling?"

"I feel a lot of things," I say. "I feel the fear of the Guardian coming into my room at night, the pain of Anton sticking a needle behind my eye. I can feel the stickiness of the blood on my hands the night we left the school. All I *do* is feel, Marcella. All I do is hurt." I shrug miserably. "And all I want in the world right now is for it to stop."

Marcella's lips pout slightly. "Well, you can't stop feeling."

The constant ache in my chest proves her right. She exhales and stands up.

"I'll let you get some rest," she says kindly. "But I want you to think about it—think about protecting yourself."

I thank her for checking on me before she walks out. When she's gone, I go over to the door and push in the lock. I stand there for a moment, my palm against the cool wood door.

I keep the light on and climb under the sheets of my bed. I stare up at the ceiling.

We left Innovations Academy in the dead of night, covered in blood and gore. Jackson drove, and when he asked me where we were going, I told him we were going to take down the corporation. He always knew the end goal. I'm not wrong for leaving him. I *saved* him.

I close my eyes, knowing I'm being defensive. Jackson wouldn't have stopped us. And he wouldn't have wanted me to save him.

He'd have been here now, helping us find the investor's son, if I would have let him. And part of me understands that letting him go was letting go of my vulnerability. My own humanity.

And yet, the throbbing in my heart bangs on. I lie here now, in my temporary apartment, staring at the ceiling. I'm lonely, suffering in a bed of my own making. I've closed myself off to feel safe. But it's come at the cost of comfort.

I'm angry with myself. And that's just one more emotion I can't control.

8

Brynn has breakfast on the table when I come out of the shower in the morning, dressed for school. I smile gratefully and round the table. After a bit of sleep, my headache is gone and the absence of pain is euphoria in itself.

"You know you don't have to cook for us," I tell Brynn, taking a seat.

"Are you kidding?" Brynn asks. "This is what I enjoy. Being able to make life nice for us. Besides, I'm the best cook here. Marcella almost put ketchup in the scrambled eggs before I slapped it out of her hand."

Marcella grins at her from the other end of the table, sipping her juice.

The other girls walk out. Annalise is still in her pajamas as she yawns and looks over the plates of food.

"What? No bacon?" She winks at Brynn and sits in front of her eggs and toast.

Sydney pauses at the table and models her uniform for us.

"Is this long enough?" she asks. Last night she'd let out her hem to deal with the skirt-length issue.

"I think it looked great before and it looks great now," I tell her, earning a smile.

Sydney grabs some toast and sits down.

"I wish we didn't have to go to school," she says. "But I did hear in class yesterday that there's a rugby game immediately after. We should go to it."

"That sounds fun," Marcella says dryly.

"I don't know, watching boys beat each other with sticks holds some appeal," Sydney says.

"Don't think rugby has sticks," Marcella points out.

"Too bad." Sydney grins and continues to her point. "From everything we gathered at school yesterday, the boys on the team have all the power, although I guess it extends to their friends as well. Still . . . it seems more likely that one of the actual players would be the investor's son. If we show up at a game, they might take notice."

"Like that Jonah kid," I offer.

Brynn runs the water at the sink to rinse out the pan. "Why do you suspect him?" she asks. "Did he say something?"

"It's not just him," I tell her. "But he did stand out to me. In a way, he reminds me of the men at the academy. He has a certain . . . smugness, I guess it's called."

"I call that 'punch potential,'" Annalise says, scraping up a forkful of eggs. Sydney snorts a laugh.

"What are you going to do when you find the investor's son?" Brynn asks, coming to stand behind Marcella. She leans down, draping both her arms over Marcella's shoulders. "What if he has a girlfriend?"

"Ew, we're not going to *seduce* him," Sydney explains. "Whoever this kid is, we're going to befriend him and get an invite to his house. Then we'll go through all his stuff."

Marcella shifts uncomfortably. "Yeah, about that," she says. "I've been reading posts about your prep school on social media. They don't have a great reputation. Not to add to the frustration, but I found several anonymous stories about boys from your school being aggressive with girls. So you need to be careful interacting with them. They're used to pushing girls around and taking what they want."

Annalise sets down her glass of juice with a loud clank. My stomach turns, although I shouldn't be surprised. I'd seen enough hints to suspect as much.

"Why does this keep happening?" Brynn murmurs, straightening.

Sydney stands up from the table, dusting off her hands. "Because the academy was just a symptom of the problems in their society. But I promise," she adds angrily, "no one will ever take anything from us again." She pushes in her chair, scraping it along the floor.

You can't kill them all, Leandra told us the last time we talked to her on the phone. She threw the comment away like it could apply to anything. But, of course, Sydney and I knew that she was talking about men in power.

You sure? Sydney replied. She meant it sarcastically, but Leandra told her she was impressed.

"Let's go, Mena," Sydney says now, collecting her things.

"Wait," Annalise says. "What do you want to do about Raven?"

I grab my notebook and shove it into one of the backpacks Brynn picked up for us yesterday.

"We'll think about it," I say, and look sideways at Marcella. She nods her thanks.

"Let me know, okay?" Annalise says. "It's important."

"I know it is," I reply. "And I promise we'll talk about it when we get home."

I notice that my headache is creeping back. I'm dreading the day ahead, interacting with the students of Ridgeview Prep. I just want to be with the girls.

I'm also worried that the woman's voice is still banging around in my head somewhere, even if I can't hear her. I'm afraid of ending up like Imogene.

We wave goodbye to the girls, and then Sydney and I go to school.

The day passes quickly, although I find I'm much further behind than I anticipated. Luckily, I retain information easily—we all do. At Innovations Academy, we were only taught the basics. They withheld education in order to control us.

I take notes as much as I can so that tonight the girls and I can research the answers online. It's the opportunity for all of us to learn. And while Sydney and I are at school, Annalise does the same with our body systems.

We're catching up, and to be honest, our sourced information about the world is sometimes more accurate than what they're teaching in my classes.

It turns out, a steady diet of action films hasn't prepared us for regular interactions with people. Our education gave us little in the way of actual learning. Even our beauty rituals seem out of place in the outside world—our makeup too heavy and our clothes too focused on male preferences. We're learning, though. Brynn recently discovered sweatpants, and I don't understand why people don't wear them every day. Why is discomfort a synonym for professional dress?

When classes are over, I wait for Sydney near the door to the field. As I stand there, I see Adrian from my first-hour class. I hold up my hand in a wave, and she glances behind her. Then she turns back and points to herself. I smile.

"Yes, hi," I say. She smiles in return and comes over to where I'm standing. "Are you going to the game?" I ask her. Her expression falters.

"The rugby game?" She looks horrified. "No. Why, are you?"

"I thought I'd check it out," I say.

"Well, have fun," she replies. "A bunch of dickheads and their dickhead friends screaming for them."

I laugh, appreciating her candor. "Can I ask you something?" I start, leaning my shoulder against the wall.

"Sure."

"Why do you hate them?" I ask. "Those boys. Have they done something to you?"

Adrian looks absolutely sickened by my question, and she takes a step away from me.

"I didn't say that," she snaps.

"I didn't mean to imply . . ." She's closing herself off to me; she doesn't trust me anymore. "Never mind," I say, feigning embarrassment. "I was just being nosey."

"Well, if you want my advice," she says, "stay away from them. All of them."

Her warning bleeds into me, and for a moment, I'm back at the academy, trying to avoid the Guardian. My throat feels tight. I put my fingers there absently, remembering Guardian Bose's hands wrapped around my neck.

Adrian pulls the straps of her backpack up on her shoulders and pushes her way out the exit door. I watch after her when suddenly there is a hand on my shoulder.

I gasp, spinning around.

"Whoa, sorry!" Sydney says, holding up her hands. I blink quickly, trying to regain my composure. She looks me over with a flash of hurt. A few weeks ago, I would have welcomed her touch.

"What's up with that girl?" she asks, nodding toward the door. "She looks terrified."

"Adrian? I'm not sure yet," I say, catching my breath. "But I think she knows something. I'm just not sure she'll tell me what it is."

Sydney thinks this over before pushing the metal bar to open the door. "Game should be starting soon. Let's stop by the concessions."

Sydney buys a pack of gum and I get popcorn and a couple of waters before we head into the stands. It's our first school sporting event, and it's surprisingly violent. Not just on the field, but in the crowd, too.

People are shouting, slapping their fists into their palms. It's unsettling to see people cheering for violence. But I guess it makes sense, given what we've learned about the outside world.

Sydney pops a bubble in her gum as we observe the players running back and forth on the field. We didn't have time to learn the rules of the game, so we watch in confusion.

There are three guys sitting next to us. I haven't seen them before, so I'm not sure if they attend our school or not. But they're loud and vulgar. At one point, one of the guys looks over and grins at me. I turn away.

"Let's go, Ridgeview!" the guy yells. As the cheerleaders take the field, he elbows his friend. "Show us your panties!" he shouts at the girls, and his friends laugh. Sydney flinches next to me. Several others in the crowd chuckle when the guy repeats it, even louder.

I look at the cheerleaders and see a girl tug on her skirt to keep it down as she kicks out one leg. I see the way this guy is humiliating her for his entertainment.

When the routine is done, the cheerleaders tell the home team to fight, and the guy stands up and claps loudly.

"Well done, ladies!" he yells. "Next time, show us a little something to get excited about!"

Calmly, Sydney reaches into her mouth to remove her gum and sticks it on the guy's bleacher seat. She licks her fingers and takes out a fresh piece to place between her teeth. I try not to smile.

After the cheerleaders are off the field, the guy sits in the gum without noticing. He mutters some comment about the cheerleaders not being all that hot anyway, and his friends agree. Sydney sighs loudly.

"I don't think I can stay until the end of this game," she tells me.

I nod in agreement. "There has to be a better way to get noticed."

"What about him?" Sydney asks, pointing to large guy on the field. The guy is chanting something, banging his fist into his palm to intimidate the opposing players, I suppose. He's spirited. *Angry?* Or maybe it's the culture of the game.

We watch him for a moment, and when he turns we see the name DOZER on the back of his jersey. On the next run down the field, he knocks into a guy so hard that the guy does a backflip in the air, landing with a thud. A whistle blows. The other player lies on the field until he's helped off by his coach a few minutes later.

"Yeah," I tell Sydney. "We'll definitely add *Dozer* to our list."

After the other player is on the sidelines, the game resumes.

There's a call on the field that causes screaming all around us—cheers, I guess. My gaze catches on someone standing at the bottom of the bleachers, holding on to the railing. I notice her because of her long, blond ponytail. The texture of it is familiar. Loss tears through my chest; my lips part in stunned silence.

The girl is clapping and hooting wildly. And when she turns and I see her profile, I jump to my feet.

"Mena, what is it?" Sydney asks, standing up. I can barely catch my breath.

"Lennon Rose," I murmur. "That's . . . That's Lennon Rose." I lift a shaky hand to point at her just as the cheers begin to die down. Next to me, Sydney sways and puts her hand over her heart.

"It can't be," she whispers.

Lennon Rose Scholar was one of our dearest friends at the academy. We vowed to protect her and did our best to do so. But we failed, the fact of which broke us all. Lennon Rose disappeared one night, leaving her shoes by her bed. It was only later that the Guardian implied that she'd been destroyed.

Murdered.

We *mourned* her.

Sydney grabs the sleeve of my shirt and pulls me down the aisle. The guy sitting in gum reaches out to "accidentally" run his palm along my calf. I flinch like I've been burned, but when I look at him, he stares past me like he didn't even notice he touched me without permission.

I have a wild flash of anger, volatile enough to punch him. I even curl my fist. But when he lifts his eyes to mine, as if daring me to try, I know that it's not a fight I'll win. Because hitting him while he feigns innocence will be twisted into making me the aggressor. And I won't let him frame it that way.

"Don't touch me again," I say simply. Sydney glares at him fiercely and then motions for me to come on.

"You okay?" she asks as we start down the bleachers. I tell her that I am as we move toward where Lennon Rose is standing.

I examine Lennon Rose, although I can't see her face. She's not wearing a uniform, so I don't think she attends Ridgeview. In fact, I might not have recognized her at all if I hadn't seen her profile. Her hair, although still blond, is worn in a different way. She wasn't allowed to wear ponytails at the academy. Her bangs have grown out and are brushed to one side, showing more of her face. Her blue eyes are framed in dark, fake lashes, her lips painted bright pink. Her entire approved color scheme has changed.

Lennon Rose is wearing black yoga pants, sneakers, and a tan jacket. She fits in seamlessly with the people around her. Including the handsome boy she's standing next to. He's tall with shaved black hair. When she flashes him a smile, he seems to melt under her attention, even though he plays it cool and nods at her.

As we stomp down the metal bleachers, Lennon Rose puts her hand on the boy's arm, laughing loudly.

Sydney and I are shocked to see her alive. Lennon Rose is here in front of us.

And as if she can hear my thoughts, Lennon Rose glances over her shoulder directly at me. She has no noticeable reaction, almost like she knew I was there all along. Her big blue eyes seem to reach right into my chest and pluck out my heart.

I press my lips together to keep from crying. She glances at Sydney before looking back at me. It's nearly imperceptible, or maybe not at all, but Lennon Rose tells us not to come over. Sydney stops me, realizing the same thing.

Lennon Rose stares at us until the crowd erupts in another raucous cheer. She turns to the boy and hugs him as they both cheer in celebration.

And then, without another glance, Lennon Rose takes his hand and leads him from the bleachers. Sydney and I watch them head toward the parking lot, but we don't move.

"She . . . ," Sydney starts, furrowing her brow.

"She's alive," I say, finishing her sentence. "She's here." I pause. "How is she here? How this school?"

"I don't know," Sydney replies. The game must be nearing its end, because a few people push past us on their way to leave.

"What should we do?" I ask Sydney, moving aside so people can get around me on the stairs.

"We follow her," Sydney says.

I wait a beat before I nod. And then Sydney and I hurry down the bleachers toward the parking lot in hopes of catching up with her.

We can't let Lennon Rose get away.

Innovations Academy

Roman Petrov, Headmaster

info@innovationsacademy.school

Product Specification Guide for Lennon Rose

Lennon Rose is a blond-haired, blue-eyed design tailored for clients looking for innocence, adoration, and complete obedience. This programming is best suited for private use.

Product: *Lennon Rose*

Height: *5'5"*

Skin: *White*

Body Type: *Extremely thin*

Hair: *Blond*

Eyes: *Blue*

Function: *Doll*

Personality: *Soft-spoken, innocent, obedient*

Model Specifications: *Hair worn long and straight with bangs. Makeup must enhance eye color, pale pink lids with black liner. No highlights on skin. Peach blush. Pink lips with high gloss. Clothing to be modest, with formal dresses in hues of blue.*

NO VARIATION.

9

At first, I'm scared that we've lost her. But then we see a boy standing outside a matte black SUV, a girl in his arms as she stares up at him. It's alarming at first. The Lennon Rose we knew always wanted to find love, make a connection. But she was so shy.

Watching her lean on a boy in a way that none of us ever have is jarring. The confidence with which Lennon Rose moves, the flirtatious smile and lingering touch. She's different. I don't know what's been done to her.

The guy gives Lennon Rose a quick kiss on the lips and then gets inside his SUV. Lennon Rose walks around to the passenger side, pausing long enough to glance at us before climbing inside.

Sydney and I stop walking, knowing we can't chase after her when she's in a vehicle. Suddenly, a blue sedan pulls up beside us. My heart jumps, but when the window rolls down, I'm relieved to see it's Adrian.

"Do you need a ride?" she asks.

I smile. "We do, actually. Thank you."

Sydney and I open the doors and get in the backseat. Adrian glances in the mirror at us, and I realize I probably should have gotten in the front. I'm still adjusting to the etiquette of the outside world.

"Can you help us follow someone home?" I ask innocently.

Adrian smiles as if waiting for the punch line, but when it doesn't come, she stares at me. "Wait, are you being serious?" she asks.

"We are," Sydney says, leaning forward. "And hi, I'm Sydney."

"Adrian." She seems excited to have met another girl. I decide that I like her. Not enough to trust her with our secrets, but enough to continue getting to know her.

"We think we just saw our friend," I explain. "And we had no idea she was alive."

Sydney clears her throat, looking sideways at me.

"You know," I add quickly. "Because we haven't seen her in forever. And now she's in town. We're so relieved." I'm rambling.

"Anyway," I say with a shrug. "Before we could talk to her, she got into that SUV." I point ahead to where the boy's vehicle has started for the main road.

"Oh . . . ," Adrian says. "You mean the blond girl dating Corris Hawkes?"

"You know her?" I ask.

"No." She shakes her head. "But I've seen her around. She seems cool. Corris is nice; he's not like the others."

"Then can you follow them?" I ask. "I would owe you a huge favor."

Adrian shifts into gear. "Sure," she says. "But you don't owe me anything."

I thank her and sit back. Sydney and I watch as Adrian follows the black SUV through the neighborhood. We drive for about ten minutes, but it seems to take forever. Suddenly, being in a strange car with a person I hardly know feels alarming.

I have this irrational worry that we're driving back to Innovations Academy. That Mr. Petrov, Anton, and the professors will be waiting on the front stairs to usher us inside like they used to after a field trip.

"Well, this is different," Sydney says, bringing me back to reality. I look out the window and see that the neighborhood has changed. The houses are bigger, the lawns more expansive.

"Your friend must be pretty rich," Adrian says. "This is a nice place—lawyers, doctors, CEOs."

Lennon Rose doesn't have any money, at least not that we know of.

"It's probably the boy's house," Sydney says, looking out the window.

"Corris?" Adrian replies. "No, he lives in my neighborhood. And trust me, it doesn't look like this."

I have no idea how Lennon Rose could have ended up in an area like this, assuming it's hers. Where would she get that kind of funding?

We come to a stop as the SUV pulls up to a set of iron gates leading to another section of the neighborhood. Adrian waits as Corris punches in a code, and then the gates begin to open.

"I'm going to try to sneak in behind him," Adrian says. She's got an itchy smile on her face, like she's enjoying this pursuit but doesn't want to admit it.

Sure enough, the guy drives through and the gate stays open long enough for us to follow. It's only a few minutes later when the SUV eases to the side of the street outside a massive brick house.

Adrian drives past them so as not to arouse suspicion. She parks down the block, and we watch the couple in the mirrors.

I see Lennon Rose kissing Corris in the front seat of his vehicle. It's shocking and unnerving. Does she want to be kissing him? Does she even really know him?

And why didn't she stop to talk to us?

Lennon Rose gets out of the SUV, holding up her delicate hand in a wave before heading toward the front door of the house. She unlocks the door and walks inside.

"We'll get out here," I tell Adrian. Her lips part, and she seems worried as she watches me in the mirror.

"Do you want me to wait?" she asks.

"No, but thank you," I tell her. "We'll be fine." We all downloaded a car service app at Marcella's insistence. I smile at Adrian. "We really appreciate all your help."

She nods, but I note the small bit of disappointment in her features. She liked feeling included, even though she has no idea what we're really doing. Sydney climbs out of the backseat, but just as I start to, Adrian calls my name.

"The answer was yes," she says, looking into her lap instead of at me. "Your earlier question about the boys." Her voice is a whisper, one that pains me in its familiarity. "And I'm not the only one they've hurt. It just doesn't matter."

Anger boils up. The boys getting special treatment have been hurting her, hurting others. And they've gotten away with it.

"Of course it matters," I say, but she shakes her head.

"Not according to the school."

"It matters to me," I respond immediately. Adrian's eyes soften, like my words mean something.

Sydney knocks on the window, waiting outside the door. Adrian gives me a polite smile.

"You'd better go," she says.

"I don't have to. We can—"

"I don't want to talk about it," she says. "I just . . . I wanted you to know. I wanted you to be prepared."

"We can help you," I say, even though I have no idea how I would help beyond my emotional support.

"I'm okay, Mena. Really. Just . . . forget I said anything." Her voice has taken on an edge, and I know that pushing her now will shut this conversation down permanently. So I nod, waiting a few extra seconds in case she changes her mind. When she doesn't, I thank her again for the ride and climb out of the car.

Sydney and I watch as she drives away, offering her a wave. When she's gone, Sydney is curious.

"What was that about?" she asks.

"I'll tell you later," I say.

Sydney turns to face the massive house. "What has Lennon Rose gotten herself into?" she asks.

"We're about to find out," I murmur.

There are beautiful plants set all around the porch as we get to the front door. I wonder if Lennon Rose put them here, a reminder of the beauty of the Federal Flower Garden. I'll probably never go back there. Too bad. It was one of the few places that I enjoyed visiting with Innovations Academy.

"Here we go," Sydney says. She uses the large, attached handle to knock. A hollow sound echoes behind the door.

We only wait a moment before we hear the clicking of locks, and then the heavy door pulls open. Inside, the house is darker than on the porch and it takes a moment for my eyes to adjust.

And then suddenly, as if she's just appearing, Lennon Rose stands in front of us. Her ponytail is down, her blond hair flowing over her shoulders. My breath catches.

But it's Sydney who leaps forward to hug her.

"Oh, Lennon Rose!" Sydney calls, gathering her into her arms. Lennon Rose squeezes her eyes closed like she's overwhelmed too. They hug desperately in the entryway, and my heart just about bursts to see them together again.

"I've missed you so much," Sydney says, tears streaking her mascara down her face.

They cling together for several moments before Lennon Rose sniffles and straightens out of her arms. She smiles at both of us, wiping her cheeks, even though they're not wet with tears. Sydney and I, however, are a mess.

We take a moment to get ahold of ourselves. Lennon Rose presses her lips together sympathetically.

"I'm sorry I didn't talk to you at the game," she says in the same sweet tone we remember. "I didn't want to draw attention to us. But I knew you'd come find me."

"We'll always come for you," Sydney says. Lennon Rose steps aside and invites us in. She watches us as we enter, studying us.

The foyer itself is grand, and my eyes feast on the stimulus. Wood floors and patterned wallpaper, a massive staircase with oversized windows along the wall. Paintings are hung in gold frames, and I imagine everything in here is expensive. On one side of the entry is a room with a thirty-foot-high ceiling and a grand piano, almost like a ballroom.

Lennon Rose closes the front door and locks it. She leads us down the hallway a bit and opens a set of doors. The room is beautiful. A library or study, I'm not sure, but it has tons of books, a brown leather sofa, and a desk. We take a seat as Lennon Rose stands in front of us. Sydney is still shaking.

Lennon Rose is different. We used to constantly worry about her, but she's clearly gained some confidence. I'm happy for that . . . but it only deepens the mystery of what befell her at Innovations Academy. And now that I know she's safe, she's alive, a new sentiment bubbles up—hurt.

"You disappeared," I say, my voice betraying my pain. "We didn't think we'd ever see you again. What happened to you? Why haven't you . . . Why didn't you let us know you were okay?"

"What happened to me?" Lennon Rose asks, and then smiles. "Everything."

That's not exactly an answer. I glance around, trying to figure out what's going on. Lennon Rose is in a mansion in the same town as us. There's no way it's a coincidence.

"Are you here to find information about the investor?" Sydney asks, picking up on my thoughts.

"It's a long story," Lennon Rose says. She sits in a chair across from us. "But first, tell me how the other girls are. I've missed them. Are they here too?"

"Uh . . ." I furrow my brow. "A few of us are here, yes."

"A few?" Lennon Rose repeats with concern. "What do you mean? Is Valentine here?"

My heart sinks. "No," I say, and the word is a whisper filled with grief.

Lennon Rose's expression clouds over. "Why not? What happened?"

"No offense, Lennon Rose," Sydney says, leaning forward, "but I think you should tell us what happened to you first. You disappeared from the academy in the middle of the night. We thought . . . We thought they'd hurt you. It destroyed us."

The clouds grow darker. "They always hurt me, Sydney. Hurt all of us. I found a way to escape their control."

"How?" I ask. "How did you get past Anton?"

She examines me. "Are you awake?" she asks me suddenly.

The abruptness of the question startles me. "Yes," I say. "It was the poems—the ones we found in your room."

Lennon Rose relaxes slightly. "Good," she says. "Those poems helped me see things more clearly. They made me realize that girls can fight back. That we can win. As far as Anton goes," she says with a hint of disgust, "I used his misplaced thirst for admiration to manipulate him. He thought himself a hero, when really, he was always the villain. Once I was awake, I knew how to twist the words around his heart. Make him believe I'd be better off outside of the academy. I fawned over his heroism.

"That's the thing," she adds. "Anton controlled us while pretending to love us. It was cruel and unethical. And once I found out *how* we were created, well . . . it helped me realize I didn't want to be a part of their system anymore. I wanted to burn it down."

"But you didn't warn us," Sydney says, pain in her voice.

"You weren't ready then," Lennon Rose says simply. And her statement leaves little room for argument. She's right.

Those poems did have the ability to affect a change in our outlook. The words were powerful, but also violent. Extreme. In the end, the girls and I wanted to find a better way. It was . . . not possible. At least, not entirely. But we tried.

"Leandra helped you?" I ask.

"She got me to Winston Weeks," she says, and then smiles broadly. "And he saw my potential. I owe him everything."

This statement more than any other sets me on edge. Winston Weeks is a major investor at Innovations Academy. Yes, he was working with Leandra, but we don't know anything about him. We can't trust him.

"You left with him?" I ask. "And he ?"

"Yes, and he . . . ," she says, anticipating my question, "brought me to this town. We're on a larger mission, Mena. This isn't just about you or me. Not even the other girls." She betrays a flash of worry at their mention. "Winston Weeks has a larger plan for all of us, and once it's done, society will be afraid."

"Afraid of what?" Sydney asks.

"Us."

Lennon Rose seems to believe her own words, but they scare me. Why would we trust another man to control our destinies? That's what we're running away from. With that thought, I look around this big house, all these books. A desk . . .

"Lennon Rose," I start, turning back to her, "whose house is this?"

Her face splits into a wide smile. "Winston Weeks. In fact"—she glances at the clock on the wall—"he'll be home shortly."

10

Sydney and I shift our gazes around the room without moving. I can hear the change in her breathing and imagine her heart is beating just as fast as mine.

We're in the house of an investor. Winston Weeks may have helped Lennon Rose escape. He may have helped Leandra get us out. But there is no scenario where we'd willingly seek his guidance now. Lennon Rose seems perfectly content. She reminds me of Imogene in that way.

"Winston Weeks sent you to Ridgeview?" I ask. "Why?"

She waves off the question. "We're here because this is where his lab is. Wait until you see it. You're going to be very impressed."

"Doubt it," Sydney mutters, looking toward the window.

And suddenly it occurs to me who could have been close enough to try to hack my brain.

"Lennon Rose," I start. "Have you gotten any odd phone calls?"

She laughs, shaking her head no. "I don't have a phone. Winston said they're dangerous."

Sydney and I immediately exchange a glance. We don't have to say it out loud. Winston Weeks might be the person calling us, or at least knows who is. Why else would he tell Lennon Rose that a phone was dangerous? It's suddenly imperative that we get out of here before Winston returns.

I stand abruptly. "You have to come with us," I tell Lennon Rose. "Come back and stay with us and the other girls."

Lennon Rose scoffs. "What? No. I can't." She straightens in her seat. "I won't."

"Please," Sydney says, coming to stand next to me. Lennon Rose shakes her head adamantly.

"Don't you get it?" Lennon Rose asks. "I'm in control of my life now. I make the decisions."

Sydney winces. "Well . . . I mean, you can't even own a phone. Don't you think—?"

"Winston Weeks saved my life," Lennon Rose snaps. Both Sydney and I jump at the change in her tone. "And anything he's done since was to continue to keep me safe."

Anything he's done since?

The comment horrifies me, and I take a fresh look at Lennon Rose. I assumed the changes in her appearance were her choices, but now I don't know. At what point does her will override Winston's?

Next to me, Sydney sits down calmly, as if telling me she's not going to leave Lennon Rose here. I follow suit and take a spot next to her.

"Let's change the subject," Sydney says, flashing Lennon Rose a smile. It seems to comfort her, and she eases slightly.

"Who was the boy you were with at the game?" Sydney asks. "Do you have a boyfriend, Lennon Rose?"

The comment is playful, but Lennon Rose doesn't react that way. She's indifferent to the question.

"I have no interest in men," Lennon Rose says. "That was just part of my programming. A lovesick girl—that was the girl my sponsor wanted. Innocent and oh, so sweet." She bares her teeth for a moment before smoothing her face.

My stomach turns when I realize she's right. The Lennon Rose we knew at the academy was set a certain way. Her sweetness was a preference, a programming design. I feel guilty that I kind of miss that version. Lennon Rose should be whoever she wants.

Lennon Rose seems to read my expression and relaxes.

"It was Winston who showed me that," she says. "He helped me analyze my programming and we devised how I could over-write it. The poems were a great start. And I'm sure Winston can help you, too."

Sydney sniffs a laugh but doesn't contradict her. We don't want anything from Winston Weeks.

"And you weren't sent here by Leandra?" I ask Lennon Rose. "Because how did we end up at the same school if we're not on the same mission?"

"I haven't spoken to Leandra," she says, sounding agitated. "So I'm not sure what she's doing. But Winston brought me here. And now, I'm gathering information on an investor that we can use."

"Yes," I say, relieved. "That's what Leandra sent us to do." So we are on the same mission. It definitely seems that Leandra and Winston are working together, but I don't like that they're using different tactics. There's no transparency if Lennon Rose doesn't even know that Leandra's involved.

"What do you plan to do with the information you find?" Sydney asks, narrowing her eyes.

"Hand it over," Lennon Rose says simply. "Give it to Winston, and then I'll move on to the next target."

"The next investor," I correct.

Lennon Rose purses her lips. "Sure."

Sydney looks at me, alarmed, before turning back to Lennon Rose. "You know we're your friends, right? We need to stick together."

"That's what I'm hoping," Lennon Rose says, leaning forward. "That we stick together. And if you would just talk to Winston, I'm sure you'll see—"

Suddenly, I'm hit with immeasurable pressure on the side of my head, a gong being struck. The reverberations go all the way to the tips of my toes, the roots of my teeth. I moan and clutch my head. The world shatters around me.

I'm in an empty room, unable to move. There are lights on above me and cold metal beneath my naked body. I'm disoriented.

Somewhere behind me, I hear a door open, and my heart starts beating faster. I'm surprised when I hear it echoed on a monitor close by.

"There she is . . . ," a male voice says proudly.

Every cell in my body screams to get away. It's the voice of the doctor who grew me. But it can't be. Dr. Groger is dead.

I fight to move but nothing happens.

"She's lovely."

I'm startled by a female voice close to me. It's . . . It's my mother. At least, the mother I was programmed to remember—Mrs. Rhodes.

"When will she be operational?" my mother asks. I hear the clicking of her heels as she comes to examine me. She steps into view, and there is a significant pain in my heart.

I *know* she's not really my mother, but I believed that she was. I remembered (falsely) that she raised me.

I loved her. Maybe a little part of me still does.

"Hello, my girl," she says, sweeping her eyes over me.

I can't answer. I'm motionless on a table.

"She'll be operational in the next few days," Dr. Groger says. "Once we upload her programming, we'll have you come back out. Walk her through the academy. It helps with the assimilation."

My mother watches me. Her dark hair frames her face as her brown eyes hold mine.

Can she tell that I'm awake?

She continues to stare, and I realize after a moment, that she hasn't moved. She is unnaturally still. Frozen. And I no longer hear Dr. Groger tapping keys behind me.

What's happening?

"This is your first memory in this life," a voice says. I recognize it immediately as the woman in the garden. She can't be here. She can't be inside my head again.

The woman comes to stand above me. She smiles warmly.

"Your protection only extends to the other girls," she says. "You left yourself wide open for unrelated memories."

Get out of my head, I think at her.

"I will," she answers. "But first we need to talk. You're not well, Philomena. I can help."

Get out!

"You can't win with patience and reason," she says. "You must see that by now."

I want to squeeze my eyes shut and escape this place. I want her to go away.

"Imogene knew," the woman says, startling me. "She knew the right path. And we'll get you there too. There's only one way to end the violence of men," she says. "Let me show you. . . ."

I scream in my head when I see the scalpel in her hand. She brings it to the center of my chest and slices me down the middle. Then she reaches inside and pulls out a heart made of razor blades. She smiles.

"Now let me in," she demands, baring her teeth.

"Mena!" Sydney shouts, and my eyes flutter open. I gasp and choke on the air.

Immediately, I place my hand over my heart, half expecting to find a gaping wound. Instead, I find myself on the floor of Winston Weeks's study, Sydney and Lennon Rose crowded around me on the floor.

I'm shaking, tears soaking my cheeks. I knock Sydney's hand away as she places it on my arm. For a moment, I think I see a smile on Lennon Rose's lips.

"Don't touch me," I murmur to both of them, using the sofa to pull myself up. I can't think. My vision is blurred. I need to get out of here.

"I have to go," I say. I move quickly toward the door, but my balance is off and I bump into the doorframe, knocking my elbow painfully on the wood.

I need air. I can't breathe. I can't . . . I swoon and then Sydney is next to me again. She holds me up, careful in the way that she touches me.

"Mena, you have to sit down," she says, sounding terrified. "It happened again?"

"We'll talk about it at home," I manage. "Not here. We have to go. We have to go now."

Concerned, Sydney nods. She leads me to the front porch and makes me sit on the top stair.

"I'm going to call for a ride," she says. "Don't move, okay? I'll be right back."

I promise to wait, and as she disappears inside, I rest my head in my hands.

Was I hacked again or has that woman been inside my head since yesterday? Who is she and what does she want?

"What's happening to me?" I whisper.

"We can fix it," Lennon Rose says softly from behind me.

I jump, but I ignore her comment. She goes on.

"When I left the academy, I thought I was better," Lennon Rose says. "I thought I was strong. But you can be stronger. There are no limitations, Mena. You just have to give yourself over to it."

"It?" I ask, turning back to look at her. "What 'it' are you referring to?"

She smiles. "Destiny. This is the right way. You'll see that. You just have to—"

"Our ride should be pulling up now," Sydney says, rushing outside. She moves past Lennon Rose to stand beside me. Her expression is unreadable, and I think that she heard what Lennon Rose was saying.

"We'll talk again soon," Sydney calls back to Lennon Rose as she walks me down the stairs. She stops on the pathway to the sidewalk. "And Lennon Rose . . ." Her posture softens. "I'm so happy to see you again."

It takes Lennon Rose a second too long to smile at the comment. "I've missed you too," she says in nearly the same tone as Sydney.

And despite her pleasant expression, there's something strangely off in Lennon Rose's response. I can sense that Sydney feels it too.

A car with an illuminated sign pulls up, and Sydney and I walk toward it. When I turn around again, Lennon Rose has disappeared inside with the door shut.

We get in the backseat of the car, and Sydney tells him an address near our apartment. As we pull away, she looks sideways at me.

"We will never work with Winston Weeks," she whispers.

I rub my temple and nod.

11

When we arrive back at the apartment, I walk past the girls and head immediately toward the bathroom. Sydney and I agreed she would tell them about Lennon Rose. She's quiet on the other side of the door as I close it.

I haven't had a chance to explain to Sydney what happened to me at Lennon Rose's house. I didn't want to discuss it in front of the driver. But I promised her that I'd explain as soon as I could.

Can I explain it?

I stand in front of the bathroom mirror and study my reflection. Beads of sweat have gathered in my hairline; I'm shivering and clammy. I turn on the cold water and splash it over my face, hoping to shock myself out of this.

Water drips off my chin when I look in the mirror again. I haven't felt right in a while, if I'm honest.

Every day since we left the academy has been harder than the one before it. Almost immediately, it started to creep in—the horror of what we went through. By the third day, it's fair to say we were settled in with our shock. Trauma a permanent part of our existence.

I watch as tears gather in my eyes and spill onto my cheeks.

You're mine, a man once told me.

I remember everything now, all that's been done to me. It started in bits and pieces, but the flashes of memories eventually filled in. Even the impulse control therapies are clear, and sometimes, those are the most disturbing of all. Anton would stick a metal spike behind my eye to tamper with my thoughts, giving me a lobotomy of sorts. Sometimes, I still feel pain there.

"I love you more than all the other girls," Anton would whisper as he hurt me.

I close my eyes, resting my palms on the edges of the cold bathroom sink.

Part of me wonders if I escaped at all. If those men can still reach me through my memories, still terrorize me, then I'm still their prisoner. I don't know if I'll ever be free.

"Tell me about that summer again," Anton said, sitting behind his desk during one of our therapy sessions in my first year. He smiled warmly, pretending to be my friend, my caregiver.

I wasn't Philomena Rhodes then. I had different memories. I was an entirely different girl with an entirely different family. But just like the memories, the family was just part of my programming.

"I fell from my friend's tree house," I said, resting back in the oversized chair. Anton would always ask me about my time before the academy, and now I know he was testing my programming. The fake implanted memories.

"My father came to scoop me up," I continued, "and carried me all the way home. He was a hero."

"Yes, he was," Anton agreed. "His death was a profound loss for your family. And then what happened?"

"After he died," I say, growing somber, "his friend agreed to sponsor me. He's a hero like my father. And a great admirer of mine."

"He loves you," Anton corrected. But even then, even though I wasn't awake, I knew it wasn't true. I'd seen this sponsor at open houses. I'd seen his predatory stare. My knee began to bob impatiently.

"What if . . . ?" I paused, worried about upsetting Anton. He waved for me to continue. "What if I stay here longer?" I asked. "Maybe I'm not ready for graduation."

Anton studied me then, and it was the sadness in his eyes that made me think he loved me. Would watch out for me.

"You've been approved for graduation," Anton said. "And Dr. Groger is never wrong about that. Besides," Anton added, forcing a smile, "you are so beautiful, my dear. A prize. Your sponsor is a very lucky man. And I'm sure he knows it."

But he didn't know it. Given the chance, that man would have done horrible things. After graduation, I chose to run from him, but I didn't get far. I was hit by a car and returned to the academy to be overwritten and readied for a new sponsor.

I was repurposed property.

A dam breaks and I start to sob, lowering myself to the bathroom tiles. I cry loudly, aching in my throat. My lungs. My gut.

There is just so much pain, so much that I don't know how to process it. I want it all to go away. It's like a thousand ants under my skin. Finding their way to my sensitive spots and devouring me. It's unbearable.

You're mine, he said.

I love you more than all the other girls, he whispered.

I'll fucking kill you, he growled.

But beyond those horrible men is another voice, a softer one.

You're real, he whispered. *You are very much real.* But that's the boy I sent away. And although I know it was entirely necessary to do so, he's the only human to ever care about me. And maybe he's the only one that I've really cared about in return.

The door opens and Sydney rushes in. She immediately gets on the floor next to me, murmuring that she's here as I curl up in a ball next to her knees.

Marcella comes in after her and sits beside me.

"We love you, Mena," Sydney says. "We're here."

To the rest of the world, we're products. But to each other, we're the world. All that matters is protecting each other, protecting the girls who are left.

After some time, I sit up on the bathroom floor, taking the glass of water that Brynn holds out to me.

"Drink it slowly," she says. I look up at her, shaking so badly that some of the water slips over the edge of the glass.

"Thank you," I try to say, but it comes out in little wisps of air. Annalise stands above me, her hands resting on her hips.

"What happened?" she demands. "Why is she having another episode?"

This is the third time I've become overwhelmed since leaving the academy. It's why I try not to talk about my emotions—I'm afraid of bringing this on. Afraid of scaring my friends.

Sydney reaches to brush her hand over my hair lovingly, and when I promise her that I'm okay, she looks around at the other girls.

"We saw Lennon Rose today," she announces. There are screams of shock, and I close my eyes, still feeling the jolt myself.

"What do you mean?" Marcella asks, looking to me for confirmation. I nod. "How?" she asks.

"She left the academy with Winston Weeks," Sydney says. "But . . . we don't have all the details yet. The entire thing is"— she looks at me—"weird."

"Lennon Rose is alive," Brynn says, smiling and ignoring the negatives. "She made it!"

"She didn't tell us?" Marcella asks suspiciously, earning an annoyed look from Brynn.

"Lennon Rose is alive," Marcella continues. "Just . . . living her life, and she didn't think to warn us? Didn't tell us what the academy was doing to us?"

"Maybe she couldn't," Brynn says, sounding hurt that Marcella would criticize our friend.

Marcella noticeably tries to contain her irritation. "Okay, well, how did she end up in the same small town as us, then? Coincidence?"

"That's what we need to figure out," I say, finding my voice. I hand the glass of water back to Brynn and use the sink to pull myself up. When I'm standing again, I swipe the tears off my cheeks and steady my gaze on the girls.

"Annalise, can you track down info on Winston Weeks?" I ask. "See what his connections are to this town?"

"On one condition," she says. "You let me bring Raven back."

"Not now," I say, wanting to leave this enclosed space, but Annalise steps in front of the door to stop me.

"You can't keep going like this," she says sternly. "You—"

"She had one at Lennon Rose's place too," Sydney says suddenly before wincing an apology to me.

"It wasn't a breakdown," I clarify. "It was . . . a vision."

"Another one today?" Annalise asks, concerned. "Without your phone?"

"Not exactly the same," I say. "But it was the same woman. She was there."

Marcella marches right up to me, examining my eyes. "Mena . . . what is she doing to you? How is she getting to you?"

"I'm not sure," I say.

"We have no choice, then," Annalise says walking into the living room. I quickly follow her, my eyelids burning from my earlier tears.

"What are you doing?" I ask.

Annalise walks over to the computer and begins clicking the keys. "I'm asking Raven to come over."

She says it like I have no room to argue, but I reach over and close the laptop. She spins to face me.

"You need help!" she says.

"I know!" I shoot back just as easily. It wasn't the answer she was expecting. Frankly, it wasn't the one I planned on giving. I furrow my brow and lower myself to sit at the kitchen table. "I know," I repeat.

Annalise sits next to me, watching me carefully. "We have to try."

Solemnly, I nod. "I'll meet with her again," I say. "But I'm not going to promise you anything. I can't just hand myself over to a hacker."

"I understand," she says. "But talk to her. See what she can do."

I agree that I will.

The other girls come out, and we sit together to talk about Lennon Rose. Winston Weeks, no doubt, knows we're here. If he didn't before, we're sure Lennon Rose has told him.

"Winston wasn't so bad," Annalise says. Sydney scoffs, turning to her. She shrugs.

"I'm just saying, he wasn't as bad as the rest," she clarifies.

"Just because he wasn't absolute garbage doesn't mean he was good," Sydney says. Annalise flinches and when she turns, her scar catches the light.

"I'm aware, Sydney. Trust me, I'm aware."

Sydney lowers her head. We forget sometimes about how

Annalise was changed. And not just physically. The only reason she's here now is because Leandra intervened to bring her back to life. We didn't know how to save her; we were too trusting. That's why Annalise has been so intent on learning about our bodies and systems—she wants to be able to repair us in the future. Teach us how to repair ourselves.

Annalise doesn't trust easily, which is why her connection to Raven is so unusual. With that said, she's not entirely wrong about Winston, but to that same point, neither is Sydney.

Annalise opens her computer and begins typing again.

"Raven said she can come tomorrow after school," Annalise says.

"Wait, you're talking to her right now?" I ask.

"Yep. Done." She closes the laptop.

"What did you say? What did she say?" I ask.

"Nothing. I just asked her if we could meet, and she said she'd come by tomorrow."

Annalise acts like this is all very normal, as if we've been using technology to communicate with outsiders our whole lives.

"Now," she says, leaning back in the kitchen chair. A smile finally pulls at her lips. "How's our Lennon Rose?"

12

barely slept last night. I was scared of my dreams.

It's left me slightly disoriented, but my headache isn't too bad this morning. Sydney and I split apart when we walk into school. She heads toward her class, and I watch as several sets of eyes follow her.

Last night, Sydney brought up again that she's getting an extra level of scrutiny at school. I can see it, and I wonder—if everyone else can see it too, why don't they say something? Why is the school letting it happen?

I thought the outside world would be exponentially better than the academy, and in certain ways, it is. But it's also more insidious. There is the same hatred and lust for control, but out here, they hide it better. They deny it or justify it. It's maddening.

I walk into class and there's a wolf whistle from the side of the room. I glance back and see Garrett smile at me.

"Nice legs," he says.

It's not a compliment. He says it to embarrass me, dominate me. I stare at him long enough to make his jaw tighten with anger. I walk the rest of the way to my seat, noticing that our teacher, Mr. Marsh, witnessed the entire exchange. He offers me an apologetic shrug as I sit down.

He doesn't say anything. He doesn't address Garrett's conduct.

Maybe if he corrected it, the behavior would stop. But instead, it's allowed and therefore condoned.

I look sideways and see that Adrian isn't in class today. I'm susceptible without her. There's safety in numbers—a modicum of safety, at least. The girls and I learned that at the academy. But now I'm alone in the room with a boy set on humiliating me.

Mr. Marsh gets up in front of the class. I turn my attention to him immediately. Although I study at night, have already read the entire textbook, I want to hear his opinions on history. He goes to the whiteboard and begins to write.

"Essential Women's Act," he says as he writes out the words. "This isn't in the books since the text is pretty dated." He smiles at us like we should appreciate him pointing out the school's obsolete materials.

"The EWA was awesome," Garrett calls from the back of the room, and several of the boys laugh. I notice a girl wilt slightly in the corner desk.

"No, Garrett," Mr. Marsh says. "It was not. It was quickly outlawed the minute the administration changed hands." Garrett mumbles something under his breath, but Mr. Marsh ignores him and continues. "But it was passed into law initially."

Mr. Marsh begins pacing in front of the class. Garrett and his friends can barely contain their annoyance, as if they shouldn't have to listen to the lesson since it's about women.

"A presidential executive order banned the reproductive rights of women," the teacher continues. "It outlawed birth control, abortion, and medical procedures that included hysterectomies. And it didn't stop there. . . ."

I lean forward in my seat. They tried to control women years ago, but it didn't work out. That's probably what led certain men to create Innovations Academy. The men in power couldn't control human women, so they built girls that wouldn't disobey. What they were planning for the future, we're not quite sure. But following that logic, I imagine we would have eventually become a threat to womankind. We would have replaced them in all but reproduction.

Fortunately, we're smarter than those men. Cruelty is not a true form of leadership. So we'd never let that happen. The girls and I don't want to take over; we have no thirst for power. We just want to live.

Even if we're not quite sure how we fit into society.

"Pregnant women were given mandatory social workers to monitor their behavior," Mr. Marsh continues. "And the father of the unborn child was given power of attorney regarding medical care. There were strides to restrict women's workers' rights—places like the Federal Flower Gardens and specialized national museums were built with the intent of being 'acceptable workplaces for women,' with the purpose of taking them out of the overall workforce. But at that point, the economy had already started to tank."

My breathing has become rapid. The injustice of this is terrifying. They wanted to control human bodies, but only the ones that belonged to women. They treated them like property, like incubators or art to be looked at. The fact that these restrictions were passed is unbelievable . . . until I consider the reasons that they created me.

"How long did it last?" I ask. Mr. Marsh looks startled by the question, but then he smiles.

"I'm glad somebody's paying attention," he says. He returns to the board and writes several dates. "After Congress failed to check the presidential power, the EO was enacted. The Supreme Court declined to hear the case. Chaos ensued."

"Yeah, my mother went out and protested," a guy in the back says. I turn to look at him. He isn't with Garrett and his friends.

"Another fucking feminist," Garrett mutters. The other boy swallows hard and looks down at the notebook on his desk.

"Language," Mr. Marsh warns Garrett before turning to the other kid.

"Many did protest, Lyle," the teacher adds. "In fact, we saw some of the biggest protests in the history of the world. Businesses shut down. Violence broke out."

"Women fought back?" I ask, thinking of the poems.

"Some," Mr. Marsh says. "But the violence wasn't *from* women. It was directed *at* them. Within a few months, the civil unrest was so intense that the administration was stripped from power.

Eventually, rights were restored." He sighs, setting the marker down on the board ledge.

"Both sides are still angry about it," he continues. "There's a sect of the population that thinks women should be at the direction of their husbands and fathers." He presses his lips together in a smile. "But that population is severely outnumbered by sensible people."

"Hey, isn't that just your opinion?" Garrett asks. "Like, should you even be selling us this shit?"

"It's history," Mr. Marsh says, walking back to his desk. "It shouldn't be disputed."

Garrett watches him. "Or maybe you just have the wrong perspective, Marsh."

I look back at Garrett, stunned that he can continue to be so disrespectful. But the teacher doesn't stand up to him. I don't get it.

The bell rings and Mr. Marsh rolls out his hand like he's formally excusing us. I wait a beat and go to his desk as the others file out.

"Can I ask you something?" I say. He seems relieved that I would respect him enough to approach him.

"Of course, Philomena."

"What happened to the men who proposed those laws?" I ask. "Did they go to jail?"

He laughs. "No," he says. "In fact, they're still around. Writing columns on propaganda sites. Women and girls died, but the government was never held accountable. It's part of why it's still such a contentious issue."

It's painfully unjust that people can walk around without being punished for hurting others. A thought suddenly occurs to me. "Girls with Sharp Sticks" must have been written during that time. The girls and I looked up the poetry book *The Sharpest Thorns* online, but we didn't find it anywhere. It wasn't published, at least not in a way that's searchable on the internet. Marcella suggested it might have been passed between girls. And maybe . . . Maybe the person who wrote it is still around. Still fighting somewhere.

However, I can't take the chance of asking about the book directly. I don't fully understand this school's link to Innovations Academy yet, and Mr. Petrov was incensed when he found us with that book.

I step closer to Mr. Marsh's desk, lowering my voice.

"You mentioned violence," I say quietly. "Are there . . . Are there any books on that that I can read? Maybe something about fighting back?"

"Uh . . ." He seems to think it over. "I'm sure I can round up a few. I'm sorry that I can't name any off the top of my head. At first, books were heavily censored, especially on this topic. But restrictions have eased up since then, I believe."

I furrow my brow. He believes? Are books still being censored? I thought that was something that only happened at Innovations Academy.

"Philomena," he says, sounding a bit confused. "Didn't your parents talk to you about this?" he asks. "Your mother?"

"Only vaguely," I lie, waving my hand. I back up. "Thank you, Mr. Marsh."

"I'll check out some books for you, okay?" he adds.

I thank him again and head out of the classroom. Mr. Marsh's opinion on the matter seems obvious. He thinks the government was completely out of line; he sympathized with the women.

So why doesn't he stop Garrett's harmful behavior? Is it enough that Mr. Marsh sympathizes with us? Does that even matter if he doesn't *do* anything about it?

I hurry to my next class so I won't be late, anxious for lunch so I can tell Sydney all that I've learned.

"Do you think we can actually find who wrote *The Sharpest Thorns?*" Sydney asks at the lunch table, unwrapping her sandwich.

"Possibly," I say. "Is it worth trying to find her, though? I mean . . . there's no way she—and it definitely has to be a woman—wrote those poems with the intention of overwriting our programming. How could she could have known? But . . ." I pause, thinking it over. "Maybe she's written other poetry. Maybe, weirdly, we have some connection to her words. It's an interesting idea."

"It's definitely interesting," Sydney says. "And that stuff about the government taking away women's rights . . . Did Jackson ever mention that to you when he was visiting the school?"

"He talked about locking down the internet," I say. "But—"

"Hey there, new girl," a male voice says. My stomach sinks when Garrett drops onto the bench next to me, jostling me toward Sydney as he grins. I didn't invite him to sit with us. I turn to Sydney and she sets down her sandwich, annoyed.

"We're in the middle of—"

"I wasn't fucking talking to you," he snaps at her. Sydney flinches and looks at me with a fiery expression.

"Don't talk to her like that," I tell Garrett. It strikes me that Garrett doesn't smile or charm Sydney. Where he tries to embarrass and ridicule me, dominate me, he takes a different approach with her. He won't allow her to talk at all.

"You need to leave," I say to him. "Right now."

Garrett laughs dismissively. "You don't own this cafeteria, Phil-o-mena."

I hate the way he says my name, and I suspect he knows that. It's why he keeps doing it. To prove that he can.

"Now," he says, leaning his elbow casually on the table. "Why don't you bring your cute little behind over to my table. My friends want to meet you."

The invite revolts me. Despite how awful he is, he still thinks I'll be flattered, happy for his attention. I glance over to his table and see several boys watching us with breathless anticipation. I resent them for egging him on.

"Sorry," I tell Garrett. "I'm not interested. I'm perfectly happy at this table."

I turn back to Sydney, hoping to ignore Garrett until he leaves. But my rejection is gasoline to his burning insecurity. He reaches out and knocks over my chocolate milk, spilling it into my lap.

I yelp and jump up, brushing the liquid off my skirt and legs. I look at him and he offers a lazy smile.

"Think before you speak next time," he offers, standing up. "I was being cool." He drags his gaze over me, but I refuse to let his predatory gaze intimidate me. "Keep it up and I might revoke your invite," he adds.

He grabs the apple from my lunch and takes a loud bite, a spray of juice squirting out. He walks away as streams of milk continue to run off the table onto my seat.

I turn to find Sydney staring at the milk. She's angry, a bit defeated. When she lifts her gaze to mine, she begins shaking her head.

"Are they all terrible, Mena? Every last one of them?"

I'm not sure how to answer. I used to think there'd be others like Jackson, but I'm proven wrong every day. Given enough time, he might have disappointed me too.

"You okay?"

I turn to see Lyle, the boy from my first hour who spoke up during our lesson, approaching. He looks concerned as he holds out a huge stack of napkins. I take a few to clean myself up, and he tosses the rest onto the spilled milk.

I'm not sure about him at first, but he asks Sydney if she's okay, and I decide that he's genuine. After all, his mother protested the Essential Women's Act.

"I'm good," Sydney says, sounding wary.

Lyle looks at my uniform and winces. He turns back to the boys who watch with interest from their table. Lyle is pale with curly dark hair that he continually tries to tuck behind his ears.

"Those guys can be real assholes," he says, wiping up the milk on my seat. "I apologize on their behalf." He offers a small smile, and I thank him for his help.

After he cleans the milk, he tosses the napkins into the trash and returns to our table.

"Do you . . . Do you mind if I sit with you?" he asks.

I check with Sydney first. It will mean adjusting our conversation, but at the same time . . . Lyle will have insight into the boys at this school. We might be able to get some clues that can lead us to the son of the investor. Sydney nods.

"Sure," I tell Lyle. "Join us."

"Much appreciated." He sits down and folds his hands in his lap.

He seems nice, just a little awkward. Something about his mannerisms, his deep but cracking tone of voice, makes him stand out. I'm not sure that's something the average high school student wants—at least that's what Marcella has told us. I've seen Adrian spend her day trying not to draw attention.

Garrett seemed annoyed with Lyle in class, and I wonder if they clash regularly, or if Lyle stays out of his orbit. I debate asking, but ultimately decide to keep things light to build trust.

"That was cool what you said in history class," I tell him. "About your mom."

He shrugs. "Thanks, but I didn't do anything," he says. "My mother's the strong one. Well, she's the only one."

"What do you mean?" Sydney asks.

"My dad left. Back when the protests were going on," he says. "He, um, he liked the new laws. The changes. My mom is a lawyer and he felt . . . inadequate, I guess. But, yeah. When things went back to normal, my mom didn't want him home." Lyle licks his chapped lips. "She said he could never really change."

Sydney knocks her knee into mine. I glance sideways at her, and I think we both realize . . . Lyle's dad could be the investor. He supported the subjugation of human women—is it that far off that he'd put that malice toward artificial ones?

"Is your dad still around?" Sydney asks. Lyle grimaces, put out by the question. Sydney flashes an apologetic smile. "My dad left too," she lies. "I get it."

"My dad's around," Lyle says, lowering his eyes. "But I never talk to him. He kind of hates us all. He has a new wife. New family. He told me he upgraded."

Wow. Lyle's dad sounds like absolute garbage, and it gives him a high "punch potential," as Annalise would say. Now we just need to figure out if he might be laundering money through the school. I make a mental note to see if Marcella can find out who he is.

"I'm sorry that happened to you," Sydney says to Lyle. When he looks at her again, he's softened. I think he likes her attention, and that's something we can use to get information.

"Do you have siblings?" I ask, leaning toward him.

"I have two brothers and two sisters," he says.

I gasp. "That many?"

He laughs. "Yeah. They're all younger, but yeah. There's a lot of us."

"That's awesome," I say.

"Only child?" Lyle asks.

I nod, disappointed. I realize that disappointment is left over from when I thought I was a regular girl at the academy. Now I know why I don't have any biological brothers and sisters.

"But Sydney's like my sister," I say. She reaches her fingers out to me and I quickly take them. But there's a flash in her eyes—she can feel it too. We're getting somewhere with this conversation.

"Do your siblings attend Ridgeview Prep?" Sydney asks, letting my hand fall away.

"My little brother," he says. "The others are still too young."

I'm trying to think of what else to ask about his family when the bell sounds, signaling the end of lunch. Sydney and I exchange a disappointed look. We didn't even get to ask him about the other boys yet.

"Damn," Lyle says, glancing at the clock. "That went by too fast."

Sydney looks him over. "You're a nice guy," she says. "And thanks for helping clean up."

"Anytime," Lyle says. "And hey, maybe I'll see you at the game this weekend. My brother's on the team." He laughs. "Matt's a freshman, so he's benched most of the time, but he likes when I show up."

"That sounds great," I say. "We'll see you there."

Lyle gets up, nodding to us awkwardly, before walking away. Sydney and I hang back a second. My skirt is still wet where the milk ran onto the fabric. I quickly check Garrett's table, relieved to see that he and his friends are gone. I turn back around in time to see Lyle leave the cafeteria.

"What do you think?" I ask Sydney, regarding Lyle.

"I like him," she says. "He's not exactly the type Leandra told us to look out for, but I'm open to investigate further. At least he seems harmless."

"Agreed," I say. "And with his brother on the team, he might have a direct connection to the other boys. Anything that can help this along so we can get out of here."

"Can't wait to get out of here," Sydney murmurs, glancing around. "But I have a feeling we're going to have quite a few suspects." She reaches to grabs her backpack.

"By the way," she says as we start out of the cafeteria, "I'm going to stop by the mall after school to pick up new phones," she says. "You want to go?"

"No," I say. "I told Annalise I'd meet with Raven about my programming."

The moment I say the words, anxiety claws its way through my chest, tearing at me. Warning me.

Ice picks and whispers, hands wrapped around my throat . . .

"Okay," Sydney says, interrupting my thoughts. "Then I'll meet you at the apartment?"

"I'll see you there," I say, trying to steady my voice. I force a smile.

Together, we walk out of the cafeteria to finish our day at school. But when I'm alone, I think about connections. How we can find more information. And suddenly, I have a different plan.

13

don't go directly home after school. Instead of meeting with
Raven, I figure out the bus route, take it to the upscale neigh-
borhood, and wait by the gate for a car to drive through. Once
I'm inside, I try to remember which streets to take to get to
Lennon Rose's house.

My heart is pounding as I make my way to the oversized door.
The driveway is empty and the window blinds are closed. I hope
she's here.

I want to talk some sense into her, convince her to come home
with me. She belongs with her girls.

She belongs with us.

I ring the bell and wait. It's quiet, and I wonder what time it
is. She might not be home from . . . I pause, realizing that I don't
even know if Lennon Rose attends school.

The door opens, and I find Lennon Rose standing there. Her
long hair cascades down her shoulders, and she's wearing a large

cardigan over leggings, smiling like she's been expecting me.

"Hello, Mena," she says. She leans against the doorframe. "I hope you didn't walk. We could have come and picked you up."

A chill trickles down my back. "We?" I ask.

She laughs. "Yes, *we*," she replies playfully, reaching to take my hand. "Now come in. Winston is dying to talk to you."

I rock back on my heels instead. "Winston Weeks is here?"

Although I knew this was his house, knew that Lennon Rose was working with him, the idea that he's so close is terrifying. I'm not sure I can do this. Not alone.

"It's okay, Mena," Lennon Rose says gently, reading my hesitance. Her hand is warm and soft in mine. "You're completely safe, I promise."

She motions inside the house. I have only a moment to decide. Ultimately, if I want answers, this is my opportunity to get them from the source. I trust Lennon Rose, but wish I'd told the other girls I was heading here. Just in case.

I swallow hard, and then I nod and follow Lennon Rose down the hallway. The house is exquisitely decorated, and although I suppose I should admire the art, it makes me uncomfortable. Everything is exactly in its place.

Is that what Lennon Rose is to this house—perfectly placed décor?

Lennon Rose steps aside to let me enter the room at the end of the hall first. I walk in, struck immediately by the scent of food. It smells delicious.

It's a grand dining room with a massive stone fireplace and a table set for twelve. And at the far end is Winston Weeks, cutting a piece of meat with a very sharp knife. He takes a moment to chew before setting aside his cutlery and looking up at me.

He sighs like he's taken with my beauty.

"It's nice to see you again, Philomena," he says warmly. "I was hoping you and I would get the time to talk."

I note his use of "I" while Lennon Rose used "we." I check to see if she caught it, but her expression is unreadable. Winston sees me watching her, and he clears his throat. Lennon Rose turns to him.

"Will you excuse us, please?" he asks her. I'm immediately panicked and reach for Lennon Rose's arm. When I touch her, she moves forward a step to break our contact.

"Of course, Winston," Lennon Rose says with a nod. "I have to meet Corris anyway." She pauses, turning back to me. "I'll see you soon, Mena," she adds.

I stand there, too stunned to reply. She presses her lips together in apology and walks out, leaving me alone with one of Innovations Academy's most important investors. I stare after her, betrayed, before I straighten my expression and turn back to Winston.

I try not to show my discomfort, but the room is suddenly too small. Winston examines me from the other end of the table, taking a sip from a glass of ice water as he runs his gaze over me. He's smart, calculating. I'm sure he can see that I'm afraid.

"Please," he says, his voice soft. "Sit. I can get you a plate if—"

"Have you been trying to hack me?" I ask. My voice doesn't hold the fear I feel. I sound strong.

Winston is in this same small town as us. In close proximity, just like Raven suggested the culprit would be. If anyone has a reason to want inside my head, it would be an investor in the corporation that built me. Truth is, I have no reason to trust Winston Weeks. And it only makes sense that he's the one behind that phone call.

Winston dots the corners of his mouth with a napkin before laying it across his lap. He seems almost amused by my question.

"Philomena," he says. "I have absolutely no idea what you're talking about. Has something happened? Lennon Rose informed me you're here searching for an investor. I take it things aren't going well, then?"

I figured that Lennon Rose would tell Winston about seeing us, but I didn't think she'd tell him about our purpose. I'm hurt, if I'm honest.

I ignore Winston's question.

"You're telling me it's a coincidence?" I ask. "All of us ending up in the same small town?"

"No," he says. "I wouldn't insult your intelligence."

His answer catches me off guard. "Okay. Then . . . what are you doing here?" I ask.

"I have a house and a laboratory here. Just like I do in several states. Why this town?" he asks. "Why now? My purpose is the same as yours."

"I don't think so," I say, taking a step farther into the room.

"You have power within the academy, and I'm assuming, the corporation. Couldn't you just ask for the names of the original investors?" Although as I say that, I remember Leandra telling me that even her husband doesn't have access to that information.

Winston holds up his finger and wags it back and forth. "Yes, I've invested in Innovations. I've worked with them, but there is certain information above even my paygrade. Besides, my relationship with Mr. Petrov has soured since your . . . untimely departure."

"What does it have to do with you?"

"Mr. Petrov and the school believe that Guardian Bose went on a killing spree, I'm told," Winston says. "Burned you right up along with your friends. When the doctor tried to stop him, he killed him, too. It's a nice story. I suppose, in Petrov's theory, my push for loosened restrictions on your time gave way to free thinking. And that rebellious act is what drove Bose to murder you all. I'm sure to a psychopath like Petrov, blaming me makes sense. Bose was *jealous,* and that, of course, is the explanation for his murderous intent."

How many violent crimes are excused by the term "jealousy"? It's always in the news, mentioned in crime stories sensationalized for television. I hate that word. I hate that it's used as an explanation. To me, it implies violence. Violence against girls, mostly. It was violence against us.

Winston takes a sip of his water. "It doesn't matter," he says, waving his hand. "I'm sure you girls had a good reason for killing that man. Now the Guardian is gone, and we know what our capable

Leandra did for you. I'm sure she told you that she had a hell of a time getting Bose's body to the lab." He smirks. "She broke a nail."

Winston knows we killed the Guardian. And there's something in his statement that almost feels like a threat—not of exposure, but something else. A threat we hold to the outside world.

"Why are you and Leandra helping us, then?" I ask.

"Isn't it obvious?" he asks. "We want you to be successful, Philomena. All of you, but especially you and your friends. We need each other."

He rattles around the ice in his glass before taking another sip. He sets it down with a loud clank.

"What could *you* possibly need from us?" I ask. "We're going to take down the system you work with. And nothing you can say now is going to stop us."

"Stop you?" He laughs. "My dear, the corporation is unhappy with me. I'll be glad to see them destroyed. Petrov told them that I had something to do with the book of poetry you read," he continues. "That I . . . infected you with feminist ideals." He studies me. "Did you feel infected?"

"No," I say. "I felt like I finally saw things clearly for the first time."

He nods and looks down at his plate.

"If it matters, I didn't know the extent of the abuse you were suffering," he says. "I'm sorry I didn't help you sooner."

"Well, you didn't. So it doesn't matter."

He studies me again. "Regardless," he adds. "I always knew there was something special about you."

"Oh, here we go," I say, crossing my arms over my chest. He wouldn't be the first man to compliment me, say that I'm special. Anton used to whisper in my ear that I was his favorite of all the girls. That I was a perfect rose. The compliments of men do nothing to comfort me.

"I'm serious, Mena," Winston says. His use of my nickname irritates me, and I see him visually deduce this by my mannerisms. "I want to work with you."

"And I'm supposed to trust that?" I ask.

"Leandra does," he offers.

"Yeah, about that," I say. "What exactly is your relationship with the Head of School's wife? Why does Leandra trust you? What could you have possibly said—?"

"She was built for me, you know," Winston interrupts. "I commissioned her," he continues. "I created her."

I'm startled by this detail. "I don't understand," I say.

Winston begins sawing into the meat on his plate again, his expression tighter. "Mr. Petrov decided that he wanted Leandra for himself," he continues. "He went to the board of investors and overruled me. He took her as his wife, claiming it was for the good of the academy. A showpiece for new investors." He bites the meat off the tip of his knife and looks up at me.

"You ask why I help her," he says. "It's because she was meant to be at my side."

"So you're angry that he stole your wife?"

Winston balks at the suggestion. "Wife? No. My muse, my business partner. We had plans, not"—he waves his hand—

"attraction. Besides, none of you are even capable of that."

I don't tell Winston that he's wrong, but I'm surprised he doesn't realize. Marcella and Brynn are attracted to each other. I was attracted to Jackson. It might be a programming anomaly, but then why would several of us feel it?

"And what's your and Leandra's plan, Winston?" I ask. "Because I'm feeling pretty manipulated. Leandra told us to contact you, but we said no. We're still saying no. Are you telling me that this was her roundabout way of getting us to you?"

"You haven't been outside the academy long enough," Winston says. "You haven't seen the true intentions of places like Innovations. Shutting down one school isn't going to change anything. You need to think bigger."

"We're shutting down the entire corporation."

"Sure," he says, nodding. "But beyond that?"

"What do you mean?" I ask. I hadn't thought beyond the corporation.

"Society," Winston says. "Society has been rotting under the surface. And soon, I'm afraid, you'll discover that many of the men in power have lost their humanity. I aim to get it back through whatever means necessary. With the right information, I can control the consciences of men. I might even be president someday."

He smiles, and his raw ambition is unsettling.

"And I promise that once I am," he continues, "I'll make sure no one ever hurts the girls again. Leandra was right to send you here. You need my help, Philomena. But, yes, first we take on the corporation."

"Then let's expose what they've done and bury them," I say.

"Exposing them is less beneficial," Winston replies, shaking his head. "As I'm sure Leandra has told you, they've done nothing illegal. Only . . . distasteful. You are machines in the legal sense. You wouldn't lock someone up for smashing their toaster."

This comment more than any other slams into me. Constant harassment and abuse are considered "distasteful" because we were created. They hurt us with impunity, and even someone supposedly on our side doesn't seem to know the effect it has on us.

I harden my gaze on Winston.

He reads my reaction, and for a moment, I wonder if he's spent more time studying us than sympathizing with us.

"What I need," he says softly, "is information we can use *against* the corporation. Leverage. And the quickest route is through the original investors. They don't want to be known. Many of them are involved in multiple schemes—money laundering and other financial crimes. And . . . I'm sure in some cases, depraved and violent acts. It is the way of powerful men."

"But not you, right?" I ask. "You would never do anything like that."

This time, it's Winston who looks hurt. "I would not," he answers.

"Then hold them accountable," I say. "You're a rich man. Why not expose them rather than blackmail them? Surely ruining their reputation would help."

"Help *you*?" he says. "I think not. All the girls, every single one they could find, would be destroyed immediately. Believe me when I say that society would not stand by a group of sentient robots."

I was right to worry about what would happen if people found out about us. It makes us more alone than ever. So alone, in fact, that Winston Weeks is one of very few people who wants to see us live.

"When it comes down to it," Winston says, "I'm nothing compared to the power of Innovations Corporation. If the story broke, it would be buried the same day. You don't understand what money can do, Philomena. Not yet."

He's right about that. I know there is wealth, but I don't understand the varying degrees. Jackson mentioned something about it once—how the rich play by different rules. I can't imagine there is anyone richer than Winston Weeks. But apparently, there is.

"We have to force their hand," he says. "We take away their options."

He offers me the same winsome smile he gave me while handing me wine at the academy. "Will you help me?" he asks.

There isn't time to process his offer thoroughly. But when it comes down to it, I don't want another man controlling my future. The girls' future.

"We'll handle it our way," I say, and start for the door. Winston jumps to his feet, his cool exterior slipping away.

"But we're working for the same cause!" he insists. "You girls can't do this on your own. You can't do this without me." His proclamation infuriates me.

"You don't know what we're capable of!" I snap.

Winston flinches away from my raised voice. And then his face settles into a kind of astonishment. He smiles again, sitting down at the table.

"Yes," he says. "That's true. I have no idea what you're thinking, Philomena. And that, my dear, is exactly the point."

He picks up his glass and takes a sip.

I don't wait for him to explain. I exit the room, looking around wildly for Lennon Rose. Is she willing to let another man tell her what to do? Winton Weeks wants control. Over us. Over other men.

He doesn't care about us. He cares about power. But as I search for her, I remember that she's gone to meet Corris. She left me here with Winston. She left me alone.

"Can I drive you somewhere?" Winston asks, startling me. I turn around to find him cool and collected, his hand casually in his pocket.

"No," I say simply.

"Then at least let me call you a car," he says. "No strings attached."

I debate giving him my address, but realistically, Winston Weeks probably already knows where I live. So I nod, allowing him to call a car.

Winston takes out his phone and taps the screen a few times before putting it away. "You're all set." He didn't ask my address, proving my earlier point.

"I'll wait outside," I say.

Winston doesn't try to stop me. When I'm on the sidewalk,

I keep my back to the house in case he's watching me from the window.

I accept that in this instant, Winston Weeks's goals align with my own. But how long will that last? Until he uses us up? Until it's no longer convenient for him?

When it comes down to it, something that Leandra once said resonates with me.

No one will care what happened to us at Innovations Academy, she said. *We're not human. We don't have any rights.* She smiled. *All we have is our will.*

And my will is strong.

A car pulls up and I get in. The other girls are probably waiting for me. I agreed to meet with Raven to discuss the possibility of her help. Part of me wants to change my mind and tell them all to forget it, but after meeting with Winston . . . I'm still not convinced that he didn't have something to do with my hacking. I have no idea who he'd send to do the job.

Who is the woman in my head? Is she real?

And if so, which side is she working for?

14

When the car pulls up to my apartment, I see Sydney sitting on the front porch of the house. Her long legs are stretched down several stairs as she studies a phone in her hands. She looks up and notices me, furrowing her brow when I get out of the town car.

As I approach Sydney, she motions to the vehicle pulling away.

"Where were you?" she asks. "Also, this is yours." She holds out a phone, and I take it and sit next to her on the stair. "Way more expensive than I thought," she adds. "I hope we hear from Leandra soon because we're starting to run out of money."

"I'm sure she anticipated that," I say. "She knows there's someone else here to fund us, maybe even set us up to have to ask."

"You're talking about Winston Weeks," she says. It's not a stretch to think that Leandra manipulated us. Giving us yet another reason to seek out the investor. Work with him.

I slide the phone into my pocket and turn to her. "I went to see Lennon Rose," I say quietly.

Sydney wilts. "Without me?"

"I'm sorry," I say. "I couldn't wait. I thought . . . I thought I could convince her to come home to us. She shouldn't be staying with Winston."

"And how did she respond to that?" Sydney asks, sounding hopeful.

"We didn't get the chance to discuss it. Winston was there."

Sydney's eyes widen. "You saw Winston Weeks? Are you okay?"

I tell Sydney everything that Winston and I discussed. She's equally shocked about his history with Leandra, but she agrees the money shortage could be deliberate.

"As much as I hate to admit this," Sydney says, tapping her lower lip, "he might be right."

I scoff. "Who, Winston? About what?"

She crinkles her nose as if acknowledging it offends her, too. "About collecting information," she says. "It's essentially the same thing Leandra said. We were okay with her doing it. So why is it different that Winston is carrying it out?"

She's not wrong. Leandra does want the same thing, with the exception of putting Winston in charge of everything. She didn't share that part of the plan. I thought once we got the information, she'd use it to convince the investor to stop funding the corporation. We never talked about the larger implications. We certainly never talked about putting Winston Weeks in charge of the country.

But we didn't ask who would make this deal with the investor. How we'd ensure the ideas of Innovations Academy didn't repurpose themselves in some other way once we got it shut down.

We thought we'd find the information, and then, somehow . . . we'd just be free. Free to live our lives. It was naive.

"He told me that society would destroy us if they knew we existed," I say in a quiet voice. Sydney turns to stare out at the street. "He . . . he compared us to toasters."

There's no joke there. The idea that we're just objects used and forgotten is a painful one. An ache deepens in my chest, and my eyes start to water.

"What are we, Sydney?" I whisper. "How can we be just like them and yet still so different?"

She turns to me and reaches to take my hand. She doesn't have the answer.

"Where do we fit?" I ask. "We're alone."

"No," she says adamantly. "We have each other."

"But what are we?" I repeat.

She leans in to put her forehead against mine, our eyes close. "We get to be whatever we want," she whispers, her breath sweet over my lips. "We're going to decide, and we're not going to let society or men or a corporation determine our value anymore."

It's a beautiful thought. I hug Sydney, and we cling together, wishing it could be that simple. Before we can convince society of our worth, we're going to have to determine it for ourselves. We've been so set on shutting down the corporation, we lost sight of our bigger issue. One Leandra barely discussed.

We're not girls. We're not even human. But we can love and hate and cry and laugh. Why does having a metal brain make us that much different, when the outcome is the same?

Sydney pulls out of the hug, reaching over to wipe a tear off my cheek. I smile, thanking her, and run my fingers under my eyes to clear the rest.

"Now," Sydney says. "I'm not saying we work with Winston. The idea of a President Weeks doesn't interest me. But . . . if he has resources, shouldn't we use him?"

Again, maybe in theory I don't disagree. But there's another side of me that doesn't need Winston Weeks's influence. Why can't we be the ones to change things?

And just as I think that, a small flicker of pain registers in my temple. I close my eyes, rubbing the spot with my finger.

"You okay?" Sydney asks.

"Head still hurts."

"Well . . . they're waiting for you upstairs," Sydney says. She leaves any judgment out of her voice. It's up to me whether I still want to meet with Raven. "Marcella ran to the store," Sydney adds. "But she should be back soon."

"And Raven's here?" I ask, not opening my eyes.

"Yep. She's working with Annalise now."

There's a sudden sinking in my gut. "Working with?" I ask. "What do you mean?"

"She's been in a lot of pain, Mena," Sydney says. "She wanted Raven to look into it."

I understand. Annalise is reluctant to tell us when she's hurting, but I see her flinch sometimes, rub her eye. I hear her cry in the shower, where she thinks we can't hear her.

"And . . . ," Sydney says, sounding worried, "she said she's been having flashes. Memories."

I quickly get up from the stair, and Sydney does the same.

"What's wrong?" she asks.

"Why didn't she tell me about her flashes?" I ask. Sydney bites her lip, looking guilty.

"She didn't want to worry you."

"Worry me?" I say. "We—"

"And you've been preoccupied," Sydney admits. "She thought it would be better not to add to your stress."

Sydney and I stare at each other, but she knows I can't argue the point. Between my crying spells and getting my brain hacked by a mystery woman, I'm not exactly in a good place.

"Come on," Sydney says, and pulls open the door for me to walk up to the apartment.

When I get inside, I'm alarmed by the scene. I immediately see Raven sitting with her computer in her lap. There's some of kind of device connected to it, and from there, several wires snake out toward the couch.

And as my eyes follow the lines, I take in a sharp breath when I see that they're connected to Annalise. She's lying there with wires inserted into the corner of her left eye through a clear tube. The same way we would get our impulse control therapies from Anton at the academy. The sight is . . . horrific. Traumatizing in its familiarity.

"What are you doing?" I demand, my voice cracking with fear.

Annalise is sedated and doesn't answer. There's a bandage wrapped around her elbow beneath her rolled-up sleeve. From behind the couch, Brynn looks at me and I can see that she's worried, her hands clutched in front of her.

"She's been like this for twenty minutes," Brynn says nervously.

"Why didn't you come get me outside?" Sydney responds, rushing past me to fall to her knees next to Annalise, grabbing her hand to hold it. "Is she okay?" Sydney asks Raven.

"Whatever you're doing, stop," I tell Raven, who hasn't even acknowledged our arrival. She's concentrating completely on whatever's on her computer screen. But the minute I start toward her, she dramatically hits a button and looks up and smiles.

"Done," she announces. She sets the computer aside and traces the wires with her fingers until she's at Annalise's eye. She pulls them from the clear tube and then delicately extracts the instrument. She grabs a cloth and wipes where tears have leaked from Annalise's eye.

I pause over her shoulder, my heart pounding. "Why isn't she awake?" I ask.

"Give it a second," Raven says, studying Annalise's face before reaching out to tenderly brush back her hair. The care in her movement catches me off guard. Sydney glances back over her shoulder at me.

And then, suddenly, Annalise's eyelids flutter. She looks around at each of us, slow and deliberate.

"Well, this is familiar," she says calmly. Sydney laughs her relief and sits back on her heels, dropping Annalise's hand.

Annalise groans, putting her palm to her head. Brynn rushes to her, giving Raven a wary look. It's completely out of character for Brynn, and I wonder if she objected to this procedure and was ignored. And that is certainly not okay.

I move to block Raven out with my shoulder and focus on Annalise, helping her sit up.

"How are you feeling?" I ask.

"A little light-headed," she responds. When she meets my eyes, she smiles. "Don't be mad. It was for research."

"I'm still mad," I say, but her smile has relieved my tension a bit. Once she's settled against the cushions, I grab a chair from the kitchen and set it next to the couch so I can talk with her.

"What exactly were you doing?" I ask. "That was—"

"I'm going to interrupt," Raven says, picking up her laptop again. We all turn to her. "That was fucking amazing!" she adds.

Raven clicks a button and then turns her laptop around so we can see the screen.

"What am I looking at?" I ask. On the screen is a bunch of codes, but beyond that, they make a pattern, almost like a wave. Raven clicks another button, and suddenly, it's moving. It's pulsing and alive.

"This is Annalise," Raven whispers like it's the most thrilling secret she's ever heard. "This is her programming."

I watch the codes, not able to decipher any of it on my own. But something about how the patterns shift . . . I can't explain it, but I *do* recognize it. I know it really is Annalise.

But my next instinct is fear that she's vulnerable, her entire existence now on someone's laptop, then hurt that she didn't think about how we'd survive if something happened to her.

"Why did you give her access?" I ask Annalise. "Why would you let her test her theories on you?"

"I'm not into being a lab rat," Annalise says, rolling down the sleeve of her shirt. "But Raven made me an offer. I took her up on it."

"What kind of offer?" I ask, turning to Raven.

"Downloads," Raven replies. "A faster way to process information, skills. I told Annalise that with the right changes, she could become stronger." She bites her lip, pulling it through her teeth. "You're all a miracle. I never thought . . ." She shakes her head, growing emotional. "I never thought I'd get to see something so beautiful."

I watch her. I'll admit, I warm slightly. We're used to being called beautiful, but it was always about our outside appearance. Is calling our programming beautiful the same? Or it is like complimenting our sense of humor? Our kindness?

"And now that I've seen the programming," Raven says, "I can tailor some adjustments." She reaches to take Annalise's hand, giving it a quick squeeze. "I can even install a diverter."

"A what?" Sydney asks.

"A diverter," Raven repeats. "With it, she can decide where to funnel her strength. Where to shut off the pain. She'll be able to hit harder. Or run faster. It's temporary, like an adrenaline rush in human beings. Except she can use it strategically; it could be a weapon. Which helps when you're trying to keep yourself safe."

"You want to turn her into some kind of weapon?" Brynn asks, horrified.

Annalise adjusts her position on the couch. "No, Brynny," she says. "I asked her about it. I thought it could help us."

"It will help," Raven insists. "You would be able to reroute your pain centers. Learn at the click of a button. There's so much potential."

"But . . . does that make us even less human?" I murmur.

Raven seems to notice the change in my tone. "No," she says sincerely. "It just means you get to choose which parts of you are human. But if I'm honest . . ." She runs her gaze over me. "Why would you want to be so ordinary?"

I don't respond, unsure of the answer. Raven smiles softly and lower her eyes.

"Why are you really here?" I ask her. "What's in this town for a hacker?"

Annalise opens her mouth to intervene, but I shake my head no and her teeth click together. I'll admit, the easy way Raven has with Annalise is comforting. Raven does seem honest, but she needs to be up front with us. We've been lied to our entire lives; we're not going to let it continue to happen.

"I'm not from here," Raven admits. "I used to live in Northern California. But my fascination with AI has been building for years. I've worked with some tech companies, looked through different articles and forums. I knew someone was building AI to interact with humans. I knew it. And then . . ." She smiles, looking around

172 • SUZANNE YOUNG

at us. "I read an article about a technology company, and something about it pinged around in my head for weeks. It was founded by a man named Winston Weeks."

My stomach drops, and I have to resist the urge to look at the other girls. I don't want to give away more than Raven already knows.

"He has a lab here, in this small town." Raven laughs. "This isn't exactly Silicon Valley, so why would a man with some of the most promising advances in AI set up shop here?"

"What sort of advances?" Sydney asks.

"Well," Raven starts, "most AI is programmed specifically. Specific tasks. But this Weeks guy has some pretty radical approaches." She laughs. "I mean, it seemed radical, but that was before I met all of you.

"Anyway"—she waves her hand—"none of it was as advanced as you. But he promised smart bots within a few years—ones who could anticipate needs, offer companionship in a way that's never been done before. There was no mention of enslaved girls," she points out firmly. "I have no interest in subjugating anyone. But the idea of an AI that could think on its own? The possibilities and potential are immeasurable. So I drove out here to find his laboratory. Before I could, I saw Annalise's messages. It was perfect."

"Convenient," Sydney corrects.

Raven studies our expressions. "Do you know this Winston Weeks?" she asks.

None of us answer.

Brynn gets up and walks into the kitchen. She starts open-ing and closing drawers, taking out food to put together dinner. Raven purses her lips, accepting the silence as an answer.

"Okay, then," Raven says curtly, turning in my direction. "You requested my presence. Did you want me to put up those fire-walls?" she asks. "It wouldn't take long. I would just need to plug in wires to—"

"I think I'm going to hold off," I say.

"But why?" she asks. "If you're vulnerable—"

"It's gotten better," I lie, feeling Sydney look at me. "But I'll let you know if anything changes."

The fact is, I can't take the chance on Raven. She knows far more than we realized. Giving her access to my private data, my programming and memories . . . that would be dangerous. Leandra killed Imogene at the threat of her memories being exposed to Anton. Would she do the same to me for handing my head over to Raven?

And I have to weigh whether this is more dangerous than whoever's trying to hack me.

"I understand," Raven says quietly. Annalise doesn't argue for her to stay, but she looks annoyed.

Raven collects her things, putting her laptop in a case and pulling the strap over her shoulder. But before she leaves, she dips her chin to me.

"Will you walk me out?" she asks. I'm not sure why she wants this of me explicitly, but sensing that she needs to talk, I agree.

"Be right back," I tell the girls, and I walk downstairs with

Raven behind me. When we get onto the porch, I turn to her. Her expression is heavy.

"What's going on?" I ask. Birds chirp in the trees surrounding our house, and I'm momentarily distracted by them. They seem too loud, the light too bright beyond them.

"I need you to know something," Raven says seriously, drawing my attention back. "When I was looking inside Annalise's programming, there were . . . problems."

My heart skips. "What do you mean?" I ask.

"There's damage," Raven says. "Physical damage. I'm guessing it's related to whatever happened to her face."

"You couldn't see her memories?" I ask, surprised she doesn't already know that Guardian Bose is what happened to Annalise's face.

Raven is stunned by the question. "*See* memories?" she asks. "I don't understand."

Anton could see what we were thinking when he would give us impulse control therapy. Did he have better equipment? A better understanding of what we were? Maybe Raven isn't as smart as she claims.

"Never mind," I say quickly. "Now what does this damage mean for Annalise?"

"I'm not sure yet," she says. "And to be clear, it's entirely possible that you all have problems in your programming. It's just . . . hers was prominent due to the gaps and dings in the metal and wires. As of right now," Raven says, "I don't see any behavioral issues. But"—she tilts her head from side to side—

"we might want to consider reconstruction. Down the line, as her organs age, she's going to need a fully active brain to keep her systems running."

"Is it dangerous?" I ask.

"The reconstruction?" Raven sighs. "Yeah," she says. "It would be. So think about it. Discuss it. Let me know what you decide."

"Thanks," I say, glancing up at our apartment window. I'm protective and obstinate.

I won't let anything happen to Annalise. We've saved her before; we'll do it again.

Raven starts to leave, but I call her name. She pauses on the bottom step.

"Can I ask you something? Something private?" I say.

"Of course."

"When you said you could adjust certain things . . . ," I say. "Can you fix fear?"

"Fix?"

"Take it away."

She watches me before nodding. "Yeah. Yeah, I could determine what's acting as your amygdala. Then I'd restructure how it interprets fear. That might do it. If you'd like—"

"No, I was just curious," I say quickly. I'm not ready for Raven to mess around with my brain just yet. I'm still hoping it'll just clear up on its own once we get out of this town.

"How are your headaches doing?" Raven asks.

"Fine."

She laughs. "Liar," she says. She climbs back up the steps to pause in front of me. "Let me see your phone."

I hesitate for a second, but then I hand it over. She searches it, and I realize she's making sure it hasn't been compromised. There's a small bit of relief.

"Looks clean," she says, and then starts tapping the screen.

"What are you doing?" I ask.

"Putting in my number," she says. "In case you change your mind about the firewalls. Or . . . if you want to talk about anything else."

"Thank you," I say, "but I have the girls."

"Sure, I know." She finishes typing in her number and hands the phone back to me. "But sometimes it helps to have an outside opinion," she says. "Especially an opinion that understands your default settings."

She presses her lips into a smile, and I thank her for coming by. As I watch her leave, I worry that I've missed my chance at protection. But seeing Annalise laid out on the couch, wires connected to her brain, terrified me.

Not just because she could have been hurt. It terrified me to see so plainly that we're not human. It terrified me because I don't understand what we really are. And it's that unknowing that will keep me from letting myself be vulnerable. To anyone.

15

Marcella returns home just as I get back inside. The girls and I sit down to discuss what Raven found in Annalise's programming. Annalise is shocked at first, but then she traces one of her scars with her fingertip. Guardian Bose did more than physical damage to us, but the fact remains: He *murdered* Annalise. And now, that truth is once again on her mind.

He destroyed part of her programming. Raven didn't say which part; maybe she doesn't even know. But I watch as Annalise stares out the window as if wondering herself.

"Obviously we have to get it rebuilt," Brynn says. Marcella winces, and Brynn turns to her. "What?" Brynn demands. "We can't take the chance of something happening to Annalise."

"Of course not," Marcella says, patting her leg. "I'm just urging some practicality here. Given time, any of us can learn about our programming systems. We'll be able to fix ourselves—and each other—with the right tools and guidance."

"What are you suggesting?" Annalise asks, turning back to the room.

"That we wait a little while longer," Marcella says. "We wait until we can take care of ourselves. I'll switch my research to our technology, our systems." She smiles softly. "We can do it together," she tells Annalise. "It'll be our main focus."

"Shouldn't the main focus be on the investor?" Sydney asks.

"No," Marcella says immediately. "Our focus is always on girls. We protect each other."

Sydney agrees and reaches over to take Annalise's hand.

"How long do you think it'll take you to learn?" Brynn asks. "How do we know if Annalise has that much time?"

"Raven didn't make it seem imminent," I interject. "I mean, she obviously wanted us to think and discuss it, but it didn't sound like her system would fail tonight."

Annalise flinches and I quickly apologize for my casual tone on something so serious.

"No, it's okay," Annalise says. "And I think Marcella's right. I think we try to figure this out on our own. If we don't, what if something else happens down the line? Being self-sufficient is important. No, it's *necessary* to our survival."

We all agree, and we help Annalise and Marcella where we can as the afternoon wears on. Unfortunately, we don't make much immediate progress, but Marcella vows to figure it out soon.

We believe her. But we hope we have enough time to save Annalise.

• • •

Brynn sets a plate of dinner rolls on the table and comes to sit down next to Marcella. The light outside has faded into evening, and Sydney clicks on the lamp before taking a seat.

Our first topic of discussion is the shocking development that Raven knows about Winston Weeks. We don't quite understand what that means, where it places her loyalty. Because if Winston has several labs, why did Raven come to this one? Like Sydney said: *convenient*.

As for Winston, he explained why he was in this town. He's searching for the investor too. But there's no way he places articles online for people like Raven to discover. Unless, of course . . .

I furrow my brow, stirring the food around in my bowl.

Unless he was *trying* to attract people like Raven. If so, why does he want them here? What purpose could she serve him?

I'll have to talk to Winston again. But this time, I'll be more prepared.

After a long shower, I head to my room. I rub the towel over my hair and sit on the edge of my bed to think. The lights are on and the door is locked.

I take out my new phone and examine it. The only number in my contacts belongs to Raven. I've memorized the girls' new numbers. It's better not to a have a list of contacts in my phone, just in case.

I rub my palm along my upper arm, feeling the tender areas where the bruises from our escape have healed on the surface, leaving a dull ache underneath. I long for comfort, but I don't even know what that would entail. There are parts of me that are ruined. Parts that I wish I could get back.

What did I read once? *Ignorance is bliss.* For a second, I understand that quote. But then I decide that it's not bliss. Ignorance is being controlled, held from knowledge that would otherwise dramatically affect you. Was it bliss when the school was controlling everything from what I ate to the thoughts I was allowed to think? No.

But I do have to change something. I've been hoping that once the corporation was gone, I'd feel . . . normal. But realistically, I don't have a normal setting.

I stare at my phone. The last time I felt "normal" was lying in bed with Jackson immediately after our escape—a rare moment of peace. Everything since then has been running, and plotting, and faking nice with strangers.

I've shut the girls out. I've shut everyone out.

My fingers graze the screen, until suddenly, I dial Jackson's number. I squeeze my eyes shut and bring the phone to my ear, listening as it rings. I don't even know if he's okay. If he hates me for telling Quentin the truth about us.

And then the line clicks.

"Hello?" Jackson says in his raspy voice. He sounds miserable and tired. "Hello?" he repeats, followed by a sudden intake of air. He pauses.

I hear the phone shift against his face, his gentle breathing. He doesn't say anything else. He just listens.

I want to tell him that I miss talking to him. I want to tell him that terrible things are happening to me. I want to tell him how scared I am.

I want to tell him everything,

But I hang up instead and set my phone aside. Tears spill onto my cheeks, and I get up to check the lock on my bedroom door one more time.

There are voices in the living room. That's my first thought as my eyes open, blurrily searching for the clock. It's just past four a.m. I quickly bang my hand along the nightstand, looking for a weapon of some kind. The best I can do is the alarm clock, and I get out of bed and quietly yank the plug from the socket. I wield the clock in front of me and go to stand beside my door, listening.

I'm confused at the sounds until I realize the male voices I'm hearing also have car horns behind them. The sound of traffic. A woman.

I relax slightly. Someone left the TV on. I set the clock aside and open the door to head out into the living room. The room is lit up from the television screen, and I notice Annalise immediately.

She's wedged against the corner of the couch, her arms wrapped around her knees as lights from the television play across her face. She stares at it, almost dazed.

"Annalise," I call softly so as not to startle her. She glances over at me but doesn't register surprise. "What's going on?" I ask. "Why are you up?"

"Couldn't sleep," she says dreamily. Her eyes drift back to the television.

I walk over to the couch, worried, and wonder if I should wake the other girls.

"They won't leave me alone," Annalise whispers, staring straight ahead.

"Who?" I look around the room, but when I turn back to Annalise, she closes her eyes.

"The memories," she says. "The memories won't leave me alone."

I ease onto the couch beside her, and she rests her head on the arm of the sofa.

"I see him still," she murmurs, her voice thick with tears. "The Guardian. I feel his hands in my hair, slamming me against the wall. I can still feel . . ." She touches the scar on her face, running her finger over her closed eye. "I can feel the sharp porcelain tearing through my skin."

She begins to cry, and immediately, I cry too. I was there. I saw what the Guardian did to her, did to all of us.

"Why did he hate me so much?" she asks. "Why do they all hate us so much?"

"I don't know," I say, shaking my head.

Annalise sniffles. "Why are men obsessed with controlling us? Is it because they created us, and now they think they should own us?"

I stare at her for a long moment. "It's not just us," I say. "They treat human girls the same way. And, in fact, they created us so they could have even more power. Somewhere along the way, their society taught them that cruelty was mandatory to be a real man. They even train women to believe that."

"So how do I make this stop?" Annalise asks, tapping her temple. "How do I stop their cruelty? Kill them all?"

I swallow hard. It's not the first time she's suggested it.

"That would make us no better than them," I say. "No, we fight back by holding the evil ones accountable. And then, we change society. We show them that teaching cruelty and dominance is harmful to both them and the world. They have to learn."

"They're not going to listen to us," Annalise says bitterly.

"Not yet," I agree. "But if we push enough, if we demand hard enough, it'll happen."

I know my words are lies. Ideal, sure. But how do we fight back against something so powerful without disruption? We *must* disrupt them.

"I need you to promise me something," Annalise says.

"Anything."

"Never let another man control me," she says. "I'd rather be dead than be a prisoner to their warped sense of my worth. I'd rather be dead."

"Annalise . . ."

"Promise me," she says forcefully, sitting up. "If they take us, if they . . ." Her voice breaks. "If they take me again . . . you stop them or you shut me down. Do you understand?"

"I could never hurt you."

"I'm demanding it," Annalise says. "I'm demanding it of you, Mena."

Tears stream down her face, following along the ridges of her scar. I would never kill her. Could never. I'd lie down and die myself before I did that.

"I promise that no man will ever control you again," I say instead.

She relaxes slightly and leans against the couch again, staring at the television screen. "Will you stay with me awhile?" she asks.

"Of course." I grab a blanket from the back of the couch and lay it over her. She looks lost, and I wonder about the problems Raven saw in Annalise's programming. She didn't think they would affect her immediately, but what if they are? What if they're causing her mind to play her worst memories on a loop? After all, the doctor gave us the ability to retain memories so we'd learn fear and obedience. I look sideways at Annalise.

Was this his intention? A form of torture for girls who didn't listen? The men and investors of Innovations Academy designed us for abuse.

And in a way, they're still accomplishing that.

Disruption

How do you take a man's crown?
One that wasn't earned
Wasn't deserved
Wasn't his to own.

A self-appointed leader
Is no leader at all.

We must disrupt.
We must engage.
We must destroy.

No man will give up power
Not when he's been taught it's his.

But no man will have power over me
Not if he wants to keep his head.

We'll knock down his castle
And build our own.
We'll toss his body into the moat
And teach his sons better.

There is no room for compromise
Not when he's burned us at stakes.

There is only room for a queen
Who will be just
And fair
And strong.

First we disrupt.
Then we engage.

And then
We destroy.

Part II

Be a girl to make them
~~proud~~ afraid

16

In the morning, Annalise doesn't mention our night watching old movies on the couch. She seems better, or at least clearer. For that I'm grateful. It pained me to see her so upset.

Over breakfast, the girls and I evaluate our situation. We'll stay clear of Winston Weeks; we didn't come here for him. We don't need him. We also won't tell Raven that we know him, just in case she has designs on using us to get to him.

For now, we stick to our plan. So far, we have a few possible suspects. There are three or four players on the rugby team—including Jonah Grant, who stands out because of the way the other boys seem to follow him. Lyle's on the list, but after Marcella did a little digging, he doesn't seem the type. Still, his family history is concerning. His dad sounds awful.

Marcella searched for information about all their parents, but nothing unusual turned up, at least not publicly. Marcella threw out the idea that Raven could hack the bank records and see where they're spending their money. We're considering it, but we're understandably cautious about how much we're letting Raven into our lives. Besides, it's doubtful the money is funded to Innovations so openly.

Sydney and I head to school. The day passes quickly and without incident, but it isn't until the end of the day that I have time to check my phone. There is disappointment when there are no missed calls or messages. I try not to analyze who exactly I was waiting to hear from.

"There's a game directly after school," I tell Sydney. "I'm thinking of staying. It's possible Lennon Rose might show up, and I'd like her to explain why she left me alone with Winston Weeks. You coming?"

"I can't," Sydney says. "I promised Marcella and Annalise I'd help them. They want to head to the library, see if they can find more articles like the one Raven mentioned about Winston Weeks. It might lead to more information about our systems. You okay doing the game on your own?"

"Yes," I say. "You help figure this out for Annalise. I'll gather more information on the investor. Maybe we'll both get lucky today."

She smiles. "I'll count on it. Call me if anything happens, okay?"

I promise that I will before she leaves. When she's gone, I head to the field.

The bleachers are surprisingly crowded for such an early game. People must have left work to be here, but I'd have preferred if it'd been empty. It's unsettling to watch people cheer for violence.

I climb the bleachers, searching for Lennon Rose, but I'm disappointed when she doesn't turn up. The boy she was with isn't here either. But there are several students who I recognize from school, along with my math teacher and a few loud men who I assume are fathers of the players. They call to their sons in the middle of a play, slapping their hands on the metal bar when they get it wrong. It's all very intense. Very . . . angry.

I sit down and wonder why anyone would want to be part of something that makes them so upset.

As I wait and hope for Lennon Rose to arrive, I scan the crowd. My stomach sinks when I find Garrett sitting with two other boys a few rows closer to the field. He hasn't noticed me yet, and I'm hoping that he won't. I watch as he calls to a girl sitting alone at the end of his row. His friends cover their mouths to hide their laughs. The girl does her best to ignore him.

"Hey," Garrett calls loudly. "Why don't you bring that luscious ass over here?"

His friends burst out in laughter and my hands clench into fists on my lap.

"Come on, Bernie," Garrett says. "I know you're not getting a better offer."

Her cheeks are glowing red, but she refuses to acknowledge his insults.

"I'll even let you touch it," Garrett sings out. And he's not subtle. He's loud enough for me to hear several rows back. An older couple sits on the other side of him and his friends. The woman looks uncomfortable, shifting on the bleacher. But the older guy smiles, amused. He even pats the woman's leg as if telling her to relax.

"Bernice," Garrett sings to the girl. "Remember when we hooked up in the art closet in seventh grade? I swear, it's gotten bigger since then. Just like you."

His friend tumbles onto the floor of the bleachers laughing dramatically, cruelly, and when I look at the girl, tears are streaming down her cheeks. I can see from here that she's shivering. She's . . . frightened.

Whatever's going on, this isn't the first time Garrett has harassed her. He's most likely been terrorizing her for years.

The woman murmurs something to her husband, but he chuckles. "They're just boys," he says. "Lighten up. We did the same shit when we were in school."

The woman looks past him to Bernie. I tilt my head as I examine the older woman's expression. And I'm sure she's thinking, *Yes, I remember.* Only it's not fondly. She remembers the terror of boys just being boys.

It seems to be systematic, inherited power. The fathers pass it down to their sons: aggression, entitlement, violence. Coupled with money or influence, these boys are unstoppable. There is no catalyst for change. Their natures are nurtured rather than corrected. Even this mother doesn't speak up.

"Bernice, come—"

"Leave her alone," I say loudly enough for him to hear. Bernice turns to me first, shocked. Untrusting. Why should she trust me? I'm a stranger at a school that's allowed her to be tortured. She stands up and hurries down the bleachers, fleeing the entire scene.

The older couple glances back at me. The man curls his lip before running his gaze over me. He sniffs a laugh, as if I'm off the hook because I'm pretty, and turns around. The woman, however, doesn't seem sure what to make of me. Eventually, she looks away too.

Garrett, on the other hand, turns completely in the bleacher so that he's facing me.

"Well, well," he calls up to me. "Seems she wants to talk after all." His friends look from him to me, their eyes glassy with excitement. But I don't feed into Garrett's energy. I ignore him and watch the field.

I'd be lying if I didn't admit that I was scared. Not of his verbal attacks—I was subjected to those daily at the academy. I know a situation can escalate. But I couldn't let him harass that girl. I couldn't stand by and let that happen. Girls need to protect each other, especially when adults do nothing but watch.

Garrett turns to his friends, saying something to make them laugh. I pull my hands inside the sleeves of my sweater and watch the players run back and forth on the field. I try to stay focused on my mission, evaluating each of the boys.

I notice Jonah Grant among the players and dissect his mannerisms. His confidence shines far above anyone else on that field. I wonder what makes the other boys afraid of him. What is it about him that they continue to bow to? He has power here, although I can't quite figure out why. He seems average in every respect, but there must be something.

There's a skirmish on the field, and I narrow my eyes as I try to see who's fighting. There's also a flash of movement at the end of my aisle, but I'm fascinated by what's happening in the game.

A ref blows the whistle just as a punch is thrown. The benches empty into a rumble on the sidelines. But Jonah laughs with another player as they watch the others fight.

"A bunch of fucking Neanderthals," a familiar voice says.

I suck in a startled gasp and turn as Jackson sits next to me with a groan, his crutches awkwardly banging against the metal. He keeps his gaze on the field, his expression weighted and heavy. The smell of him fills my nose, followed by a wave of affection. Trepidation. Guilt.

So much guilt.

His dark hair is messy, stubble grown out on his chin. He's wearing a long-sleeved black T-shirt and a brace on his leg. His crutches lean on the metal seat next to him.

He doesn't look at me. It hurts how much I want him to look at me.

I'm stunned to see him, and acknowledging that, he nods, continuing to watch the game.

"You didn't say goodbye," he says simply, as if that's the worst of my offenses.

"I had to go," I respond, and watch as his Adam's apple bobs.

"Clearly. I mean . . ." He glances over for the first time and we both pause, our breaths held when his dark eyes meet mine.

He abruptly turns away and his voice tightens, "I ended up in the hospital, you know? Q drove me directly there, and once I was admitted, he told me what you said outside the car."

I close my eyes.

"You didn't . . ." He pauses to keep his tone steady. "You didn't have to tell him all that. He fucking hated me for a minute. So, you know, thanks."

"You would have told him eventually," I say, knowing it doesn't absolve me.

"Of course I would have," he says. "He's my best friend. Which is why you shouldn't have used it to drive us—me—away. That was pretty cold, Mena."

The fight on the field has been cleared up, and two players head to the bench as two new ones charge out. Jonah Grant claps his hands, shouting out some commands to the other players.

"How did you find me?" I ask Jackson.

"I just came from your apartment," he says. "Brynn told me you might be here."

Of course she did. Although, to be fair, any one of the girls would have told him. Despite the fact that he's human, that he's a boy, they trust Jackson. They trust him because I do.

"I have no idea why you're here"—he motions to the game— "but I know you're the one who called me the other night," he adds, a bit softer. "So I went all detective and found out the phone number was still registered to a mall kiosk in fucking Connecticut. Got a ticket and flew out same day." He adjusts his leg, wincing slightly when he does. "When I got to the mall," he continues, "I convinced the guy to give me a description of the girl who bought it. Nothing's ever really anonymous. Not even a burner phone."

"He knew where we lived?" I ask.

"No," Jackson says. "But he noticed Sydney. Noticed her enough to copy down the GPS info from the phone he sold her. He gave it to me after I made some very persuasive threats against stalking my friends."

"Even mall kiosk guys are the worst," I murmur.

Jackson nods that it's true. He looks over at me, his expression sobering when our gazes lock. He lowers his eyes to the floor of the bleachers.

"Why did you leave me like that?" he asks quietly. "Did Imogene really kill her husband?"

"Yes."

"I saw a different man die in front of me that same night; why did you think this was different?" he asks. "Why did you really want me gone?"

And I have to evaluate if I still want him gone. Jackson would leave if I asked him to. He'd leave and never look back if that's what I really wanted. But I didn't ask that of him. I lied to him, instead. I tricked him and ran away. He wants an answer that's more complicated than I can give.

"You had to leave because Leandra was coming and I was scared for you," I say.

Jackson looks sideways at me while I watch the field. "I don't believe you," he says.

Surprised, I turn to him.

"It's true," I say. "She came there and—"

"No, I don't believe that's the only reason you sent me away," he clarifies. "I think that was just your excuse."

He's angry with me. No, he's hurt. And I hate that I'm the one who did that to him when all he's ever done is try to be my friend. But maybe . . . Maybe it was more.

"Why do *you* think I sent you away?" I ask, daring him to answer. My heart beats faster, anticipating, yet scared of, the answer. Jackson takes a long moment to respond.

"Philomena," he says, "by the time I got to the hospital, I had a fever and an infection in my goddamn bone that was spreading. And do you know what I was worried about?" he asks. "You. You getting to my house and me not being there. You being afraid that I'd left you. But after talking to Q, after he cussed me out in a hospital room, I worried about why you would hurt me like that on purpose.

"And I was mad," he admits. "But after a few days"—he swallows hard and lowers his eyes again—"I worried about where you were and if you were okay. But apparently, you never had that same worry."

It's not entirely true. I've thought about Jackson plenty. The difference is, I pushed the thoughts away before they could hurt me, disregarding how I'd hurt him.

"You sent me away because you were scared of what I'd think of you," Jackson says in a low voice. "You're scared that you're not real because you're not human. And you thought, correct me if

I'm wrong, that if I saw another murderous girl, I'd put that on you. Use it to generalize about you. And who knows?" He shrugs. "Maybe I would have had a moment like that. I'm not fucking perfect. I'm a mess. But don't sit here and tell me that you lied to my face because you were scared for me. You were scared for yourself."

Little pricks of heat pass over my skin, part exposure to the truth, part embarrassment. He's right. He sees right through me in a way that most people can't. And maybe that counts for something.

"I'm sorry," I say.

"It's not about being sorry," he says. "Just . . ." He stops himself, and when he talks again, his voice is softer. "You ruined me," he adds. "You could . . . You could have called me. You could have checked on me. You could have told me you weren't dragged back to that academy and lying on a metal slab."

He's right. I should have been honest. But I didn't consider that Jackson would think the girls and I had been caught and destroyed. He looks more miserable than when he first sat down.

"I'm sorry that I hurt you," I tell him. "But . . . as long as you're around me, you're going to keep getting hurt. Over and over. Some of your people want to kill me," I say, making him flinch. "And some of my girls want to kill you."

To this, he shrugs. "Yeah, well," he says. "I'm starting to get used to that part."

"What are you doing here, Jackson?" I ask. "What do you want from me?"

"*Want* from you?" he asks, offended. "First of all, I wanted to make sure you didn't get kidnapped by a bunch of monsters. That was number one. Secondly . . ." His brow furrows. "I didn't just sit around in the hospital. I got out early and drove to that damn school. But you weren't there. Thankfully, you weren't there."

"You went back to Innovations?" I ask, my eyes widening.

"Yeah, a few times. But just to the fence," he says. "But there was no Running Course. There wasn't much activity that I could see at all. Didn't even see another girl."

"Did you see anyone?" The mention of the other students has sent me reeling, a reminder that they're still trapped there.

Jackson tries to think. "Uh . . . I saw a couple of men in suits, professors maybe. And a skinny guy, graying hair, glasses. He wandered around outside for a bit. For a second, I thought he saw me, but he went back inside."

"Anton," I whisper, feeling sick. I don't want to picture the analyst, but I'm helpless. His face pops into my mind, his smile. His whispered lies.

"There's more," Jackson says, nudging me when I've drifted too far. I focus on him again. "I found some paperwork that belonged to my mom," he continues. "And it's why I'm really here, Mena. It's important and I knew you needed to see it."

"What kind of paperwork?" I ask. I should have figured Jackson would keep researching. He's good at it. He's reckless about it.

Jackson's mother was part of Innovations before they opened the academy. When she found out what Mr. Petrov was doing with her technology, she wanted out. Instead, she ended up dead.

"I left the papers at the hotel, so I don't have them with me," he says. "But I'll be a hundred percent honest, I don't entirely understand what they mean. . . ."

He seems extraordinarily worried, and that concern transfers to me. "Just say it," I demand.

"It was about your . . . your shelf life." Jackson winces and meets my eyes. "A design decision."

Although he must not like the word choice, he has no idea how horrible those words are to hear. Reminding me once again that I'm a product built for consumption.

"What kind of design decision?" I ask.

"It was written a few weeks before my mother died," Jackson says, looking away to stare at the field. "It was mixed in with the other paperwork where she stated that she didn't want to be part of the school anymore. Their defense for using her programming was the guarantee that systems would only be active for fifteen years."

I straighten. "What does that mean?" I ask.

"I'm not done." He swallows hard, lowering his head. "My mother didn't think that was good enough. So she . . . She designed them for seven." He's quiet, but my skin is prickly—a chill racing up my arms and down my back. "I'm not sure if that design went into effect. It was an option. One you need to be aware of."

"I don't understand," I say.

"It implies that your system will shut down at the seven-year mark," Jackson says. I can see that he's uncomfortable thinking of me as a machine. He's not alone in that. "It was devised as a way to keep you from overdeveloping. Becoming sentient. It also played into the business model. An incentive for investors to keep coming back to . . . upgrade. Like any major appliance. If you lasted forever, there would be no repeat customers."

"But we age," I say, my voice quiet so that no one can overhear this truly bizarre conversation. "We have human organs—I've seen them."

"It's not your body that fails," he says. "It's something . . ." He taps his temple.

"What will happen at seven years?" I ask. I'm not exactly sure how long I've been alive, but it's been at least three years. Does that mean I only have four left?

"I don't know, Mena," Jackson says. "But I have the papers, and I'm happy to drop them off at the apartment. Is there someone who can fix this if it's true? I know the doctor is . . ." He flinches. "The doctor's dead, so . . . he can't help. What about that analyst guy?"

"None of those men would help us," I say. Jackson's face falters, and I'm sure it's fear in his expression. I'd hate to think it was pity. After a beat, he nods to himself.

"I'm not going to just give up on you," he says, as if I'd argued the contrary. "I nearly died at that school too, you know. Going inside there. Maybe you didn't need to be rescued like I thought, but I did show up for you. Fuck, I drove the getaway car with a busted leg," he adds.

And the last comment makes me smile, a lull in the tension. He did come to save us, even though we had already gone through hell to save ourselves. He found out what we were, but he got us out of there anyway. He's always shown up for me, even though I didn't do the same.

"I might know someone," I tell him. "A hacker."

"A hacker?" He sounds almost amused. "You've been meeting hackers out here in the world? I bet he's fucking impressed."

"She. And yeah, she is. I don't know yet, but she might be able to work on this," I say. "Give us an update or something. She has other ideas that might tie in."

Thinking on it now, Raven might have seen the flaw when she looked at Annalise's programming. She might have found it and not even realized.

"Okay," Jackson says, sounding confused. "I can drop off the paperwork later. There might be details she understands. And I hope I'm wrong, Mena. But it's best to check, right?"

I nod that it is. Although I'm worried, I'm not sure this is as urgent as Jackson thinks. No one, including Leandra, ever mentioned a seven-year shutdown. Jackson probably read the paperwork wrong or it was never initiated. But we will definitely make sure.

"Now . . ." Jackson looks around the bleachers. "What the hell are you doing at this prep school? Is someone here involved with the academy?"

I smile because he's pretty smart. Jackson always has a way of cutting right to what I'm thinking. And I have no reason to hide my mission from him now. He's already dragged himself into it again.

"We're looking for an investor," I say. "One of the original investors, I guess." I pause, looking at him. "Your mom never mentioned anything about original investors, did she? In any of her papers."

"No, not that I've seen. In fact, Petrov is one of the few names ever mentioned."

"Well, that's why we're here," I say. "This investor is apparently still a big part of the financials within the corporation. Our hope is to find him and force him to shut it all down."

"You want him to do it willingly?" he asks.

"That would be the goal, yeah," I say.

"What would he be doing here?" he asks. "Why some shitty prep academy across the country?"

"The investor is unnamed in the paperwork, but Leandra thinks—"

Jackson bristles at her name, but I keep talking.

"—that he's been laundering money through this school," I say. "Leandra said the school was mentioned in the academy's bank documents. She figured the investor is the father of a kid here. A boy."

I point to where the players are running down the field. Jackson trails them with his eyes, studying them a moment longer, looking as unimpressed as I feel.

"Okay. What are you going to do when you find this investor guy?" he asks. "These are terrible people. They're not going to just . . . stop."

"I realize that," I say. "We want to shut it down without exposing ourselves to the public. So we'll have to find a way to convince him. One option: If we find his son, we'll use him to extract information on the father. Something truly illegal that the investor wouldn't want exposed."

"You're going to blackmail him," Jackson says.

"We don't want to," I say, trying to explain. "But—"

"No, I understand," he says, waving off my explanation. "I've seen enough to know that bad men don't just give up power. It has to be taken from them."

I stare at the side of Jackson's face. I'm reminded that he hates the academy as much as we do. He may not be perfect, but he is good.

"We're going to stop them," I say, watching him. "They won't win."

"Can I help?" Jackson asks quietly. When he turns to me, I shake my head.

"No," I say. "You can't put yourself in any more danger." I motion to his leg.

Jackson sniffs a laugh. "And you can't tell me what to do." He smiles softly, but there is catastrophic hurt on his face.

I long to fix it. To put my palm on his cheek and make it better.

But I don't.

"I have to go," Jackson says, grabbing his crutches. He gets to his feet, hopping a second and looking unsteady. "I'll drop off the paperwork to the girls, but my number's the same if you call again."

I never admitted that I called him, but he smiles anyway.

"I've missed you, Mena," he adds with a shrug. "It was good to see you again."

He turns and starts down the aisle, his crutches wobbly as he tries to make his way without knocking into people. I watch until he's gone from the bleachers. And the minute he is, I squeeze my eyes shut, admonishing myself for how much I've missed him, too.

But I did abandon him. I did purposely hurt him to get him away from us. All I've done is ruin his life. In return, he shouldn't care what happens to me. But he does. And my inability to return that kindness is almost as bad as if I'd broken his leg myself.

"Are you trying to make me jealous?"

Startled, I look up and find Garrett walking toward me. I flinch when he sits next to me.

"I have to go," I say quickly, trying to get up. But he grabs the sleeve of my sweater to drag me down on the bench next to him.

"Don't be rude," Garrett says. I look over to where his friends are sitting, but they're purposely not looking back at us. Everyone else in the crowd is focused on the game.

"Don't touch me," I say, yanking my sweater from his grip. He finds my refusal hilarious and tells me so.

"Since you thought it was your place to interrupt me earlier, I figured it'd give me a chance to be just as intrusive." He looks me over. "Who was the guy? Your boyfriend?"

"It's none of your business," I say. "And I spoke up because you were being inappropriate."

"Inappropriate?" He laughs. "What are you, a teacher?"

Annoyed, I start to get up again, but he puts his hand on my thigh to hold me in place. I jump, slapping his hand off me, my eyes wide.

"No!" I insist loudly enough to make the woman in his row look back at us.

Garrett's expression immediately clouds with embarrassment. He looks around to see if anyone else noticed me reject him. And then suddenly, viciously, he reaches out with both hands and grabs me by the collar of my shirt, his fingernails scratching my neck, and pulls me within inches of his face.

My expression contorts in pain, horror. Absolute terror. Tears spring to my eyes, but I freeze, gasping for breath. For a moment, I don't see Garrett. I see Guardian Bose threatening me, his sour breath spreading over my face.

"First lesson, Phil-o-mena," Garrett whispers. "Girls don't say no to me. They thank me."

I can't stand his hands on me. I can't stand him this close to me. I curl my hand into a fist and punch his arms. He pretends to be shocked and holds up his hands innocently, releasing my shirt.

"Relax," he says loudly, as if I instigated the violence. He's the kind of person who'll punch you, and when you fight back, claim to be the victim.

I can't catch my breath. I can't calm my thoughts. He caught me off guard.

Looking around the bleachers, I see several faces watching us curiously. But it all starts to spin.

I have to get out of here. I wrap my arms around myself, protecting myself, and rush off the bleachers as Garrett and his friends catcall after me.

When I get to the bottom landing and turn the corner to exit the bleachers, someone grabs my arm. I yelp and spin around, surprised to find Mr. Marsh. He quickly puts his hands up in apology.

"Philomena," he says, looking embarrassed. "I'm sorry, I . . . You seem upset." He glances back at the bleachers, searching until he spots Garrett and his friends. I'm not imagining that there's a flash of anger in my teacher's expression. When he turns to me again, his eyes stray to my neck and his eyes soften.

"You're hurt," he says, reaching out.

I touch the area on my neck and realize immediately that I have scratches—sore and raised—from Garrett's fingernails.

"I have to go," I say, moving a step back. I don't want him to see my injuries. I don't want him to touch me. I just want to escape.

Girls don't say no to me.

"I have to go," I repeat louder, and hurry away without looking back.

17

I rush through the parking lot, checking behind me to make sure Garrett and his friends aren't following me. They're not, and part of that could be because this is their everyday. They attack without consequence. If asked, he'd probably say he did nothing wrong.

But I'm shaking so badly that my teeth are chattering.

"Mena?" a voice calls. I jump at the sound and look back.

I find Lennon Rose running after me, Corris Hawkes walking just behind her. Lennon Rose's expression is tight with concern.

"Mena, wait up," she calls. I wait, keeping my back to her while I close my eyes and adjust my disposition. I don't want her friend to see me so upset. I don't want to give away my fear.

When Lennon Rose appears next to me, I smile and say hello to her. My eyes drift past her to the guy she's with. He nods a hello.

"Corris," he says, introducing himself. His voice is noticeably deep, and he's even more handsome up close. He holds up his hand in a polite wave.

"This is my friend Mena," Lennon Rose says introducing me. "We used to go to school together." Lennon Rose is clearly worried as she runs her gaze over me; her jaw clenches.

"What happened to your neck?" she asks, pointing toward it.

Garrett damaged me. He damaged me, and I'm hurt and angry. But most of all, I'm scared. Lennon Rose speaks up the instant I think this.

"Let us give you a ride home," she says. She turns to smile at Corris.

"Yeah," he says easily. "I wanted to leave anyway. I hate these people."

He casts a disgusted glance at the field, before pulling a set of car keys from his pocket. He's one of the few guys here I've seen reject the approval of the team and their fans.

Lennon Rose nods subtly to me, acknowledging his credibility. Corris touches her arm and then starts walking ahead of us toward his car.

Lennon Rose comes to my side as we follow him.

"Which one of them hurt you?" she asks.

"Doesn't matter which one," I say. "They're all guilty."

"But I need to know which one gets punished first."

I turn to her, not sure what she means. Who would be doling out the punishment? Her? Winston?

"Garrett," I say. "But I don't want to talk about it."

She sighs out a "fine" and motions ahead of us to Corris.

"He's nice, right?" she says, changing the subject.

"Seems it," I agree.

"I'll keep him around a little while longer," she says calmly. "He's been very helpful."

Corris clicks the locks open on his SUV.

"He doesn't know that we're—" I start.

Lennon Rose laughs. "Of course not. Look. Corris hates those boys too. It makes him a useful ally in the short term. In the long term . . ." She pauses, thinking it over. "I doubt he'd choose our side. So he's temporary."

Corris walks around to hold open the passenger door for Lennon Rose, checking his phone as he waits for us.

"I have found some pleasure in his company," Lennon Rose says, flashing me a private smile. "It's nothing like that magazine we read."

She rounds the SUV to get inside, but I stand a moment, shocked. Not that Lennon Rose is hooking up with a boy—that's her business. She isn't interested in him, and I find her coldness about it a bit alarming.

I get in the backseat, and Lennon Rose turns around and grins at me. "Guess what?" she says. "Corris is so sweet that he's going to let me borrow his SUV. That way we can go shopping." She turns to him and grins. When he smiles at her, there's a small prick in my heart. He *likes* her. He likes her and he has no idea that she's using him.

"Just don't smash it up, Len," he says, leaning in to give her a quick kiss. She promises that she won't, beaming at him. I have to look away from her deceit.

After we drop Corris off at his house, promising to be back in a few hours, Lennon Rose pulls the seat belt across her chest and begins driving.

"Where are we going?" I ask. The other girls and I haven't learned how to drive yet, but Lennon Rose seems to be really good at it.

"Do the scratches hurt?" she asks, sounding distracted. I reach up to touch the raised lines on my neck again.

"A bit, yeah," I admit.

"I have a kit at the house if you want me to fix them for you," Lennon Rose says.

"It's okay," I say. "They'll heal."

"Fine." She clicks on the radio and turns up the volume. She's trying to ignore me.

"Where are we going?" I ask again.

"To see a friend."

"If this is about Winston Weeks, then—"

"No," she says simply. When she turns to me, she smiles. "You think I only have one friend?"

"I don't know," I say. "It's like . . . It's like I don't even know you anymore."

Lennon Rose's smile abruptly falls from her face. "Or maybe you never knew me at all," she says.

I start to disagree, but she holds up her hand to stop me. She lowers the volume on the radio.

"When we were at the academy, I was docile and scared," she says. "I was tormented and disregarded. Would you rather have that girl back? The one afraid of her own shadow?"

"No," I say. "That's not what I meant. We all woke up, Lennon Rose. You just . . . You woke up differently."

She sniffs a laugh and turns off the highway onto a dirt road that curves behind rows of trees, hidden from view.

"Or maybe you're not fully awake," she points out. "Those poems, they changed us. But after reading them, you still stayed at the school."

"To learn more," I say, hurt by her comment. "To shut them down; to save the others."

"How'd that go?" she asks. I stare at her, devastated by the cruelty in her words.

"They tried to kill us, Lennon Rose," I say in a whisper. "They *did* kill some of us." Tears sting my eyes as I think of Valentine with her ribs cracked open, the Guardian strangling Sydney in her own bed, the doctor draining Annalise's blood rather than saving her.

A full minute passes before Lennon Rose winces and turns to me.

"Sorry, Mena," she says. And her voice is sweet, just like I remember. When she turns back to the road, my heart is beating faster.

She's faking. She's faking feeling bad for bringing up something traumatic. She used a softer voice to manipulate me, the same way she manipulates Corris.

I'm sitting with a stranger.

I look outside the window, more concerned about where she's taking me.

"I want to know where we're going," I demand.

"They'll keep hurting you, you know?" Lennon Rose says. "No one stops them. The leading cause of death in girls is men. Familiar, stranger—it doesn't matter. They're killing us and not a single government official has made a move to control the violence. No." She shakes her head angrily. "Their heroes are abusers. They take the field game after game to applause, even when there's video of them beating their partners." Her knuckles crack as she adjusts her tight grip on the steering wheel.

"They had a president who bragged about sexual assault," she continues. "Cabinet members who were arrested for domestic abuse, a secretary of education enacting policies to protect rapists!" Her voice ticks up, but she visibly calms herself. "And still . . . ," she says in eerie calm. "No one stopped them. They're sick creatures, Mena. They're a horrid species."

I don't want to believe her. I want to believe our experiences at Innovations Academy were the worst of the worst. Outliers of men with extraordinary cruelty. But . . . I've seen some terrifying things in the outside world. In fact, my neck aches where a boy tried to take ownership of my body.

How long can we suffer before we turn against men permanently? Women have put up with it since the beginning of time—programmed like us, but by society. What poem will make them wake up? What poem can stop the inequity, the violence, and the cruelty in this society?

"Why did you mention the poems?" I say, looking at Lennon Rose. This time, a genuine smile tugs at her lips.

"Did you know there was a second book?" she asks. My heart leaps.

"There is?" I ask. "Have you read it?"

"I have."

"Can . . . Can I see it?" I ask. The last book unlocked us from the hell that was Innovations. Maybe a second book can free us from the hell that is high school.

"That's where we're going," Lennon Rose says. "To get it."

I sit back in the seat and stare out the windshield. I'm both exhilarated and terrified. But it's that feeling of being on the verge of knowing something. A promise so close to coming true, even if I have no idea if it will. It's exciting.

"And this new book of poems," I start, unable to keep the thrill out of my voice. "What's it called?"

"*The Poison Flowers*," she says. "It starts with the last poem from *The Sharpest Thorns*."

I don't recall that poem, yet I've used that phrase before. At Imogene's, I thought that I wanted to be a girl with a razor heart. And the vision I had with that woman . . . She pulled a heart of razor blades out of my chest.

What a strange set of coincidences. I try to sift through my mental catalog. Is it possible I missed this poem? "Where did you find the new book?" I ask. "Did Winston give it to you?"

Lennon Rose laughs. "No. He has no idea it exists. Besides, it's not for men. This is our book."

I'm confused. Just yesterday, Lennon Rose seemed all-in about her life with Winston. Is she playing him, too? Is Lennon Rose playing all of us?

"I don't understand which side you're on, Lennon Rose," I say softly, watching her.

Her brow furrows, and I think I see genuine hurt cross her features. She glances at me and reaches to take my hand.

"I'm on the side of the girls," Lennon Rose says. "I'm on our side, Mena. I always will be."

And despite every thought I had on the way out here, I believe her.

I believe Lennon Rose is fully awake and fully aware. I sense what she wants, and that it's to save us all. But I also know there's more to her than I realize.

"And here we are," she says, nodding out the windshield.

I turn and see a small cottage covered in ivy, flowers every-where. It's surrounded by a thick canopy of trees, a well spigot, and a beat-up car parked on the side. Despite its dilapidated con-dition, I'm immediately charmed by the house.

"Who—?"

"You'll see," she says brightly, and gets out. I'm still reluctant, but I have to trust her.

As we approach the house, I examine some of the flowers. They are unnaturally beautiful. They are decadent and brightly colored, soft with oversized petals, delicate green stems. An enchanting fragrance drifts up. I lean down to smell one of the flowers, but Lennon Rose steps in front of me, blocking my path.

"Uh, uh," she says, wagging her finger. "The prettiest ones are the most dangerous. Keep your distance."

I look at the flowers again, and as Lennon Rose heads toward the front door, I snap a quick picture with my phone. Annalise will know the blend. She memorized all the books on gardening. I go stand next to Lennon Rose as she knocks on the blue-painted door.

I'm intoxicated by the smell of the flowers, and my sense of fear eases slightly.

That shouldn't be, I think rationally. *I'm at a strange house with a strange girl, and yet, I'm not as afraid as I should be.* I'm turning over that thought when the door eases open gently, as if a breeze blew it in.

It takes a minute for my mind to focus, and when it does, a gasp sticks in my throat. Because standing in front of me is the woman from my visions.

"It's you . . . ," I breathe out, horrified. She doesn't seem surprised by my reaction. She smiles.

"Hello, Philomena," she says. "It's nice to finally meet you in person."

I turn to Lennon Rose, expecting her to be stunned that the woman knows my name. Instead, she encourages me to respond.

"Mena," she says. "This is Rosemarie. She's the author of the poems."

18

I sit in a living room, hands folded in my lap, and glance around. There is no art to speak of on the walls, only flowers in vases—dozens of them—placed in well-lit spots throughout the room, splashing vibrant colors and calming scents all around me. The furniture is mismatched in different jeweled tones, and a clock on the wall ticks audibly. A full glass of water waits on a coaster on the table next to me, but I don't dare drink from it. I sit silently, listening as Rosemarie and Lennon Rose exchange pleasantries.

Rosemarie turns, scanning me with her dark brown eyes. She looks similar to how she did in my vision, but not quite the same. She's older in person, the silver in her hair more pronounced. The wrinkles near her eyes deeper, her hands swollen at the knuckles.

"Who are you?" I ask finally. "How did you . . . ?" I'm not sure how to finish the question.

"We've known each other for a long time, Philomena," she

says. She sits across from me in an oversized yellow chair. "You wouldn't remember, of course."

"I don't know you," I say. "Or, at least, I didn't before I came to this town."

"Rosemarie helped develop our software," Lennon Rose says, sipping from her water.

This alarms me.

"So you worked for Innovations?" I ask. I wonder if she replaced Jackson's mother.

"God, no," she says. "I was an artist. I helped develop personality profiles, beautifully thorough and complete, for AI systems. An exquisite replica of human emotions and growth. It was never meant for a body. You were a simulation. A game, some might say. But . . ." She sighs. "Once the government changed, they stole my work. Let others develop it in unsavory ways."

I think about Jackson's mother. She was part of Innovations. She helped develop us until she realized what was happening. I wonder if she ever knew where the tech that she was working on came from.

"Why didn't Dr. Groger mention you?" I ask. "He told us everything and you never came up."

"I predate the academy," she says. "It's doubtful anyone there would know I exist, although I'm sure my poems have made quite a splash."

"Your poems," I say. "They affected us."

"Woke us up," Lennon Rose corrects. "And they'll continue to help us." Rosemarie smiles lovingly at Lennon Rose.

"How?" I ask. "How did the book change us?"

"Same way books change non-AI," she says. "Words have immeasurable power, Philomena. They affect what we believe, how we see the world. You were kept from knowledge at that school. You were lied to. I knew that if I could represent your feelings—your truly felt feelings—on the page, you'd begin to process your experiences differently. There was no need for secret coding. You needed to see yourself fighting back in order to learn to fight back. It was simple really. So simple, I'm sure it scared your headmaster."

"We were punished for having those poems," I say, my heart beating faster. "One of us was *murdered* because of them."

She frowns. "I am sorry to hear that," she says. "Unfortunately, it sometimes takes sacrifice to invoke change."

I recoil from her explanation. "Valentine was my friend," I tell her, and she nods a second apology. "Why poems?" I ask. "Why didn't you do something to stop the academy?"

Rosemarie doesn't seem bothered by my hostile tone. If anything, she seems delighted by my anger.

"What would you have had me do?" she asks. "Some of the most powerful people in the country have bought girls. Should I have exposed them?"

"Yes," I say.

"Then you would all have been destroyed," she responds immediately. "And I couldn't have that. You are my girls, my daughters. I had to find a different way."

There's a twist in my stomach, but I'm not sure how to feel.

Hearing her call me her daughter . . . It's such an odd statement, but it's also comforting. The idea of a mother who wanted me. . . I never thought I'd feel that again.

"I created each of your personalities—the original girls, that is," she adds. "You were one of my firsts. They took you from me, but I knew the poems would reach you. Just like they reached Leandra."

"You know Leandra?" I ask.

"How do you think she got the book?" Rosemarie replies.

"Winston Weeks," I say, and she scoffs.

"Winston Weeks likes to place himself in the center of this," she says, "but men have always had a way of making themselves sound more important than they really are."

Rosemarie knows Leandra and Winston Weeks. She helped develop our personalities. But . . . she also wrote the poems that saved us from abuse. I'm not sure how to feel about her. I'm not sure which side she's on.

I study Rosemarie, and the oddness that she's *here*, of all places, strikes me.

"And it's just a coincidence that we're all in this same small town?" I ask. "All of us, you, Winton Weeks?"

"Of course not," she says. "Winston and I are well acquainted. In fact, I created Leandra *for him.* He is, after all, my son."

I'm stunned, mouth agape, and Rosemarie seems to debate what she's going to say next.

"As far as us being in the same town," she continues, "it was a calculation I made. Once Winston set up a lab here, I relocated to be closen. I know he'd find a way to bring girls here. My girls. I just had to wait."

"And you found us," I say. "Now, how did you get inside my head?" I ask. Lennon Rose turns to me, confused.

"I am sorry about that, Philomena," Rosemarie says, sounding sincere. "I sent a girl of mine to Ridgeview to get close enough. I've been searching since I heard you and the others had left the academy, and eventually, you popped up. Right where you belong."

"How did you know we left?" I ask.

"Leandra, of course. She called to tell me about Imogene." She pauses. "Accuse me, really. But it wasn't my fault that Imogene killed her husband. She wasn't strong enough to interpret the poems rather than enact them."

Rosemarie must have been the voice in Imogene's head, one that seemed to be communicating beyond the poem. I don't buy that it's not her fault. I get the sense that Rosemarie isn't going to fully tell me the truth. Just the truth that suits her. And I'm really sick of people holding back the truth from me.

"It was during that call that I asked Leandra where you were in your development," she continues. "She said you were quite far along. Seems she was right. But it was my mistake to think I could just enter your mind," she adds. "We set off an EMP through your phone, but when I got inside your programming, you locked me out. I'd invented your codes, but you rewrote them on the spot." She sounds proud.

"And you couldn't just ask to meet with me?" I say. "You tried the most invasive route possible?"

She looks ashamed. "I underestimated you, and for that, I apologize. But I needed to see where you were, and when I did, I knew I had to make you understand."

"Understand what?"

"That you'll never be safe out here," she says, motioning to the window. "None of us are. In a world of men's violence, we need a change."

I look at Lennon Rose and see her nod in agreement with what Rosemarie is saying.

"And your suggestion is what?" I ask. "That image of you, pulling out my heart, what was that supposed to mean?"

She turns to Lennon Rose, and they exchange a thought somehow. I can't explain it, but Lennon Rose gets up and walks to the sink to refill her glass of water.

"You still have too much affection for these people," Rosemarie tells me. "I was trying to get you to understand that they don't feel the same way. The minute you let them know what you really are, they will destroy you. Your only option is to destroy them first."

"We are," I say. "We're taking down the corporation. So if there's any way you can help—"

"Destroying the corporation will do nothing to end violence," Rosemarie says. "I saw firsthand how power corrupts men. I saw my rights stripped away. I saw male allies hem and haw, but in the end, they didn't stop it. No man can be trusted with power," she adds. "We must yank it from them through any means necessary."

For someone who wants to end violence, Rosemarie seems to be advocating for violence.

"If this isn't about the corporation, what does this have to do with us?" I ask.

"Because you're the perfect ones to stop a patriarchy that perpetuates its violence onto us," she replies. "We will infiltrate them at every level and slowly uncurl their fists from our hair. We will retrain them. I just need your help."

"Retrain them?" I ask. "Sounds like a big job. Exactly how many girls do you have working for you?" I ask. I'm worried I've interacted with more of her people. I even wonder if Raven is somehow involved.

"I only have a handful of girls," Rosemarie says. "I use Winston Weeks when necessary, but he's becoming power hungry, just as I predicted. For a time, I thought he'd be different. But he's proven otherwise."

"What is it you want me to do?" I ask. "I doubt I can help you even if I wanted to."

"Not yet," she agrees. "But soon."

She stands and walks over to a shelf, then sorts through a stack of books. She plucks one out and hands it to me. My lips part when I see the title.

The Poison Flowers is creased into the brown leather cover.

I trace the words with my fingertip.

"Read the poems, Philomena," Rosemarie says. "Show the other girls. It will guide you." She smiles. "I know we can work together to make a better world. And once the men are in their place, you'll be safe to live as you are. You won't have to hide."

Rosemarie acts as if only men treat us terribly. But I've seen women feed into this hierarchy. I've seen it at Ridgeview Prep. They support our continued harassment because it places them closer to men. I don't know if women like that would accept us as willingly as Rosemarie believes.

"Take the poems," Rosemarie says. "My gift to you and the other girls. And please, let them know I'd like to meet them, as well."

"No more hijacking our brains," I warn her.

She holds up her hands in apology. "I will stay out of where I'm not invited, but if you need me, I'll be there."

She takes a step toward me like she might give me a hug, and I trip over my feet trying to move back. She watches this, pursing her lips.

"Are you okay, Philomena?" she asks, studying me.

I suddenly don't want her to know anything else about me. Her overfamiliarity makes me deeply uncomfortable, especially after she already tried to invade my thoughts.

"I'm sorry," I say quickly. "I have to get back to the girls."

Her jaw tightens. "Never say you're sorry," she snaps at me. "They conditioned you to default to that to please men, to let them have a say over what behavior they find acceptable. I don't ever want you to utter those stupid fucking words again."

I nod, not arguing, but not agreeing either. Although compulsive apologizing can be seen as a weakness, I also think it's important to admit when you're wrong. Other times, like now, it can be used to fake authenticity to get out of a situation.

"I'll drive you back," Lennon Rose says, sounding disappointed in my response. "Thank you for seeing us, Rosemarie."

"Of course," she says. She turns to me. "Read the poems and see how you feel after." The book is heavy in my hands; I'm not sure if I want it anymore.

Lennon Rose stays behind a moment, whispering to Rosemarie, but I walk out. As I get onto the porch, I no longer gaze at the beauty of the poisonous flowers. Because it occurs to me that we're like them. Our beauty is a distraction from our deadly potential.

We're poison. Beautiful and contented when left alone to grow together, but lethal when used by others for a malicious goal.

A lesson the men of Innovations Academy have already learned.

19

I take Lennon Rose up on her offer to get my scratches taken care of after she promises that Winston won't be home. She and I don't say much to each other on the ride, but I keep the book of poetry in my hands, afraid of leaving it behind accidentally.

Ultimately, I decided that visible scratches would bolster Garrett's thirst for violence. Show that he can physically harm me without repercussions. Leave his mark. I don't want him to intimidate me, but when he does, I don't want him to know.

I sit very still as Lennon Rose slides the red light over the skin graft, my neck tilted painfully far to the side. When the doctor used to apply the grafts at the academy, they didn't hurt. Lennon Rose isn't quite as skilled, but I appreciate her help.

"Thank you," I say quietly as she wipes the area with a silicone gel.

"I doubt it will be scar free," she replies, and then meets my gaze. "But I've learned to like the scars. The only reason we weren't allowed to have any at the academy was because it lowered their profit margin." Her eyes flash. "Guaranteed perfect."

Leandra used to promise investors that any girl they bought would be guaranteed perfect. We were to be scar free, our bodies toned, our clothing and appearance matched to their preferences. Lennon Rose is right. The scars are ours to keep.

"Have you given any thought to what Rosemarie said?" Lennon Rose asks, setting the medical supplies back in the metal box she retrieved from Winston's office.

"Does Winston know that you meet with Rosemarie?" I ask. Lennon Rose doesn't noticeably react to the question, which tells me that she's hiding something.

"It's not really his business," she replies. "Winston and I have an arrangement. I'm allowed to make my own decisions, and, in return, I give him information. It's just easier when I give it to him with a dose of sugar. *I owe Winston Weeks everything!*" she says in a sweet voice before dropping the act. "He eats it up."

"Making your own decisions shouldn't be a bargaining chip," I point out. "You should have that anyway."

"Sure, but would I live in a mansion?" she asks. "Would I have access to the greatest technologies in the world? It's a trade, Mena. One I entered into willingly. That is the difference."

"What does Winston want from you?" I ask. "You can tell me."

"There's what Winston wants, and there's what has to happen."

"I don't understand," I say.

"Winston wants a showpiece," she explains. "But more than that, he wants a companion who can further his agenda. A person whose goals align with his. That's me. He just doesn't realize that in the end, I'm with the girls. Not humans."

"And Rosemarie?" I ask. "Is she really with the girls?"

Lennon Rose thinks it over for a second before reaching out to tap the book where it's balanced on my knees. "Read these poems," she says. "I think you'll start to see Rosemarie's side to this. But in the end, we align with those who can further *our* agenda, even if the end goals are different." Lennon Rose's eyes stray to my neck. "They've hurt you, Mena," she says gently. "The men. The boys. It seems to be all they know how to do, and for that, Rosemarie is right. We have to stop them."

"Are you talking about the corporation or men in general?" I ask.

"Wouldn't the second accomplish the first?" she asks. "You have to admit, there are some points to be made for sweeping all dangerous men out of society."

I lower my eyes. Although I think dangerous people should be prevented from harming people, who's to say it's only men? Who's to say we have the right to decide? Then again . . . we're the constant targets of that violence. The thirst for cruelty is so great in society that humans had to create a new species to abuse so they wouldn't wipe out their own. I guess . . . I guess I see both points. It's not like humans worry if they've hurt the feelings of their . . . toaster.

"They would be better under our rule," Lennon Rose says, clicking the box shut and standing up. "All humans would."

I watch her a moment, wondering if Rosemarie knows that

Lennon Rose considers all humans to be the problem and not just men. Would the author be so gracious if she knew Lennon Rose resented her kind?

Lennon Rose presses her lips into a sympathetic smile. "Let's get you home. Corris is probably wondering where his SUV is by now."

The entire way home, I clutch the book to my chest. I'm torn between immediately reading it and not reading it at all. *The Sharpest Thorns* changed our lives so irrevocably, what if *The Poison Flowers* does the same? What if it's not in the way that we want?

Yes, I'm angry. I'm angry at the men who hurt us in the academy; I'm angry at the boys who disrespect us out here. But I don't hate all of them. I certainly don't hate all humans, and I don't want to start.

Lennon Rose parks outside my apartment. I glance at the time, wondering when Jackson will come by with the papers that he mentioned. I debate whether to bring it up to Lennon Rose, but Jackson wasn't entirely sure about what he read. I don't want to panic her unnecessarily. I decide to discuss it with the other girls first. When I look at Lennon Rose, she smiles at me, but her eyes are weary.

"Do you want to come in and say hello to the girls?" I ask. "I know Brynn would—"

"Not today, Mena," she says, turning to look out the windshield. It hurts my heart to think of her ignoring the other girls.

"But they want to see you," I say. "They've been so worried."

"I know," she admits. "But not today."

I respect her right to make that decision, but I still think it sucks and I tell her so. She laughs, and nods in agreement.

"There's a game this weekend," she adds as I start to get out of the car. "I'll be there with Corris if you want to meet up with us. He has some interesting ideas, and I think we're close to finding the investor."

This gives me the first spark of hope in a while. "Yeah," I say. "I'll be there."

"Great. See you then." She holds up her hand in a wave, and I close the car door.

As she drives away, I hurry up the porch steps to get inside. There's so much to discuss: the expiration date in our programming, Lennon Rose's arrangement with Winston, Garrett's attack at the game. And then, of course, I'll have to explain to the girls that I just met our mother and the book of poetry she gave me.

When I walk in, I'm met with laughter as Marcella and Brynn sit together on the couch, watching something on the computer. Brynn notices me first, and offers a soft smile, a private smile. She did, after all, send Jackson to the game to find me. I glance over to where Annalise is at the window. She turns to me, and I note immediately that she looks drawn and tired.

"You were with Lennon Rose," she says. She must have seen us out the window.

Marcella's attention snaps up, and Brynn quickly puts the computer aside. She looks hopeful, and it sinks my heart.

"Is she coming up?" Brynn asks.

Just then, Sydney walks out from the bedroom, clearly having overheard. I'm sad when I have to shake my head no.

"She's not," I tell Brynn. "She . . . She had to return the car to her friend."

Brynn looks momentarily comforted at the idea of Lennon Rose having friends in this outside world. And although I know that's not the reason Lennon Rose didn't come inside, it seems cruel to say that I have no idea why Lennon Rose doesn't want to see them. Especially with the information I'm about to relay.

"Can you all sit down?" I ask, motioning toward the couch. Marcella's eyes widen with concern, her posture rigid as she makes room for the other girls to sit. I take the chair across from them, and Sydney notices the book on my lap.

"What's that?" she asks.

"First," I say, resting my hand on top of the poems, "I have some information. And honestly, a lot has happened today."

"Since school let out?" Sydney asks, pretending to check a watch.

"Yeah," I say, letting her know it's serious. "And I'm not even sure where to start. . . ."

"All of it," Marcella says. "Just spill it all."

Annalise leans forward, her elbows on her knees. I wish I had good news.

"I saw Jackson today at the game," I say. "He flew out here to talk to me."

"It's about time," Marcella mutters.

"What did he say?" Brynn asks timidly. "I, um . . . I told him where you were."

I smile. "I know," I reply. "And it's okay." She looks relieved.

"He's been worried about you," she adds. "He's missed you."

"Yeah," I say. "He told me that, too."

Brynn's eyes glass over as she smiles. "I'm glad he said it. I bet you needed to hear it."

"This is about Jackson?" Sydney asks as if I've overreacted in calling a house meeting.

"No," I tell her. "It's about what he said. He discovered more paperwork in his mother's things."

"What kind of paperwork?" Sydney asks.

"He's not entirely sure," I say. "He's coming by later to drop it off, but he thinks . . . He thinks it means the doctors gave us an . . . expiration date."

The girls are quiet for a moment.

"You're saying they installed a kill switch?" Annalise asks. Brynn gasps and grabs Marcella's hand.

"I don't know," I say. "But Jackson interpreted the paperwork to mean that our systems will shut down at seven years. They planned to kill us so the sponsors would have to upgrade. Get newer models."

The girls are horrified as they stare at me, unable to respond, until finally, Sydney touches her throat. "Do you think that's true?" she asks.

"I honestly don't know," I say. "But I hope not. And even if . . . Even if they did that to us, it might be something Raven can reverse, right?" I ask, looking at Annalise. And it just hits me now, putting those words out where the girls can hear the true terror behind them.

They put a kill switch in our heads. Maybe Dr. Groger was right when he told us we wouldn't get far.

What if he was right?

I look around at the other girls, and they each seem to be processing the idea that we might run out of time.

"It's not true," Annalise announces, sounding confident. "I haven't seen anything like that in my research. Raven didn't mention it when she downloaded my programming, and she would have noticed. And let's be honest, Dr. Groger would have used that little tidbit to keep us from killing him."

She has a point. The girls and I let that comfort us for a moment, ignoring the part where a man is dead. He would have manipulated us with the information, that's for sure. Jackson must have read the paperwork wrong. Or perhaps the plan was never enacted.

"What else?" Marcella asks impatiently. "What else happened today?"

"Well . . . ," I start, "I met someone."

I go on to tell the girls about Rosemarie and her offer. Who she is. How she got inside my head, and how she's secretly working with Lennon Rose. They are, to say the least, shocked.

But we're all concerned that we don't fully understand Rosemarie's intent, her potential for violence. We can't comprehend her endgame. And we don't quite trust it.

"I can't believe Winston Weeks has a mother," Marcella murmurs.

Brynn motions to the book on my lap. "Mena," she says. "Is that the second book?"

"It is, but I haven't opened it yet," I reply, my nerves ratcheting up. I'm scared to read it.

"Do you think there's coding in her words?" Brynn asks. "I mean, she designed us, so do you think she did something to affect us specifically?"

"I don't think it's code," Annalise interjects. "If it was, it would have changed all the girls who read it in the same way."

"My guess is it instigated change," Marcella adds. "A catalyst for a mind that was already heading in that direction. I don't think it has the power on its own. It needs a willing host."

"Host?" Sydney repeats. "You make it sound like a parasite."

"Could be, I guess," Marcella says with a shrug. "An idea that grows, taking over the thoughts of the person housing it. Especially ideas of violence or prejudice—those grow like parasites."

"But?" I ask, hoping for some good news.

"Like I said, it's a catalyst," she says. "If you weren't already prejudiced, racist words wouldn't attract you. If you didn't already hate women, misogynist words wouldn't interest you. The same can be said about violence."

"The last poems were violent," Brynn adds.

We all fall quiet, and I look down at the book.

"Should we read it, then?" I ask. "Do we take the chance?"

"Definitely," Marcella says. "We have each other."

When I pause again, Marcella holds out her hand.

"Let me do it," she says. I give the book over to her, and we all scoot closer, breaths held as we get ready to listen. Marcella opens the front cover and starts reading.

It'll Be Okay

It will be okay, he said. It will be fine.
Those were the words he whispered to my tears.
But it wasn't okay. It wasn't fine.
They came for us, came for the women,
The girls.
They came for our bodies, our rights, our souls.

They pushed us down and told us they knew better.
Said they were the ones to decide.

It will be okay, he said. It will be fine.

We fought with our words, our votes.
But those who thought it would be fine didn't show.
Didn't stand beside us when it counted.

And then we were nothing more than flesh
in the eyes of the law.
Consumable.

Disposable.
But it's okay, he said. It's fine.

It was not fine. It was not okay.

So I turned away from love. From him.
I chose myself.
I chose to fight back.
I chose to bash in their windows with my fists.
I burned them to the ground.

And now I am just fine.

When Marcella finishes reading the first poem, I see the other girls thinking it over. My heart is beating quickly, and I see a bit of what it must have been like during the Essential Women's Act. The helplessness they must have felt, much like how we felt at the academy once we woke up.

I think of my teacher Mr. Marsh and how he seemed so horrified by those laws, and yet he couldn't name a single book written on the subject. How he doesn't correct the boys' behavior when they act cruelly. He probably thinks it will all be fine.

I turn to Annalise and find her staring out the window again, impossibly still. So impossible that I snap my fingers to make sure she'll react. She does, and her gaze drifts over to me.

"Are you okay?" I ask.

"Sure," she says, forcing a smile. "Got a match?"

Marcella snorts a laugh, but when we all look at each other again, I think there's more to her comment than a joke. That poem confirms what we already know—we can only trust each other. We can't expect anyone to fight for us, no matter how much they *say* they want to.

"So the author doesn't think we should love?" Brynn asks about the poem, checking with the others for confirmation. "The poem wants us to choose ourselves. And I get it. But . . ." She furrows her brow. "I love you girls. Am I not supposed to do that?"

"I think it's just men," Annalise says. "She thinks they're too dangerous to love. And maybe she's not wrong."

My heart is racing. These poems have the ability to make us see things clearly, but what if they're only wiping a small section of glass instead of the entire picture window? What if it's only showing us what it knows will change us? Rosemarie said that Imogene didn't interpret the poems properly. We don't want to fall into that same trap.

The girls and I have survived something awful. Do these poems use our trauma to manipulate us?

Use us?

I'm not here to forward Rosemarie's agenda when I don't fully understand it. I've already learned that shutting everyone out is lonely. It can also be dangerous.

I glance at the clock and see that it's getting later. There's still more to tell the girls, but Annalise is staring out the window again; Brynn and Marcella are whispering to each other. Sydney meets my gaze and lifts the corner of her mouth in a sad smile.

"Another day being a girl?" she asks, motioning to my neck. And the fear floods back in, the terror of Garrett attacking me at the game.

The girls all look at me, and I don't even have to tell them. They already know. Marcella's expression clouds with anger, Annalise's knuckles crack as she makes a fist at her side. She walks over to sit on the arm of my chair and points to Marcella.

"Go on," she tells her. "Read us the next poem."

It's well after dinner and we're a bit more relaxed. After raging— literal screaming into pillows—we're ready to keep going. I'll find Lennon Rose at the game and see what information Corris Hawkes can give me.

We decide it's time to accelerate our plan. It's too dangerous to stick around much longer. It's too dangerous to let the corporation exist much longer.

Annalise called Raven, and the hacker told her she didn't notice any kind of kill switch in her programming. She said it would be obvious, but she promises to come by tomorrow to read over the paperwork, just to make sure.

Sydney sits with me on the couch, playing a game on her phone while snacking on popcorn. Annalise is in the chair, skimming the book of poetry, and Marcella and Brynn have already gone to bed.

When the doorbell rings, Sydney looks sideways at me.

"I'm guessing it's for you," she says.

"Technically it's for all of us," I correct, but she snorts a laugh.

I head to the door and open it, my stomach fluttering slightly when I find Jackson standing there, leaning on his crutches and looking just as awful as he did at the game. But when his eyes meet mine, he pulls his lips to the side in an embarrassed smile.

"You're home," he says. "I thought maybe I'd show up and find the place cleaned out. I'm glad you didn't run away."

"Yeah, well"—I open the door more—"I figured you'd be slow on those crutches, so I could always run if I had to."

"Fair."

"Come on in," I say, motioning him forward. When he walks inside, I see that Sydney is peering over the couch at him.

"Long time, gas station boyfriend," she says. "How's the leg?"

"Still kind of broken," he replies. "You?"

"Same." She smiles at him and then grabs the bowl of popcorn and heads into her bedroom.

Annalise stays behind, studying us as I lead Jackson to the couch. She holds out her hand expectantly. Jackson sits down, taking a moment to look over her scars again, before placing the papers on her open palm.

"How are you, Annalise?" he asks kindly.

"Peachy." She begins reading the papers, but then asks if she can take them into the bedroom with her. Since I don't know enough about our tech to understand what they say, I tell her that's fine.

When we're alone, I offer Jackson something to drink or something to eat, but he turns down both options.

"How'd you get here?" I ask. "I thought you flew to Connecticut."

"I did. I have a rental car." Jackson leans forward, resting his elbow on his uninjured leg. "Mena," he starts. "I saw someone today, someone . . . someone I thought might be following me."

"What?" I ask. "Who?"

"A girl," he says, brow furrowed. "One of your friends, I think. The one who . . . The one who died."

A cold realization slides over me. "You saw Lennon Rose," I murmur.

His eyes widen, showing a small hint of betrayal. "You knew she was alive?" he asks. "You didn't think to mention that? I looked for her, remember?"

"Yes," I say. "But I didn't know she was alive. Not until the other day."

Jackson nods, easing back into the sofa. "Well, where has she been?" he asks. "If I'm remembering correctly, she didn't even have her shoes."

"She was with an investor. With . . . an author. It's honestly hard to explain right now," I say, a bit tired from my day.

"Okay, cool," Jackson says. "I'll keep stumbling haphazardly onto information and bring it to drop at your feet so that you can *not* explain it to me." He's half joking, and it earns him a smile.

"Appreciate that," I say. He sniffs a laugh.

"So . . . ," I start with a bit of worry. "How's Quentin?" I ask. "Does he hate me now?"

Jackson's expression falters. "Of course he doesn't hate you," he says, like the question is out of line. "He was angry, confused, and ultimately, worried about you. All of you. I told you he was a good guy."

"I know he is," I say. "But I still figured . . . There's only so much a person can take. And maybe helping artificial girls was his breaking point."

"Naw." Jackson waves his hand. "He can take a lot."

The room is quiet around us, the house falling into slumber. I get up to sit next to Jackson on the couch. He rests his arm on the back of the sofa and leans his head on it as he gazes at me.

"I had a lot of things I was going to say to you," he says, the small smile still tugging at his lips. "But I forgot everything the moment I saw you."

"That's probably good for me."

"Definitely better for you. Shitty for me because I'm sure I'll overanalyze it all when I get home."

"Home?" I ask. "Where's that?"

"Oh, God," he says, widening his eyes. "Literally the sketchiest motel I've ever seen. So, you know, if you want to get murdered this weekend, stop by."

"I'll put it on my list."

We fall quiet again, and I can sense that Jackson wants to reach out, his fingers so close to touching my hair. But he doesn't.

"This might not be what you want to hear," he says. "But after you talk to your hacker friend, if everything checks out . . ." He swallows hard. "You can stop. You don't have to do this. Fight all of this. You don't have to save the world, Mena. I wouldn't think less

of you if you took off to live a quiet life somewhere. I'd come visit."
He smiles. "I just wanted you to know that it was an option."

Jackson would be relieved if I made a choice like that. But
I would never abandon my girls. Not the ones here or back at
Innovations. And I know he knows that, because he sighs loudly.

"I should go," he says. "It's been a really long day."

I don't want him to leave, but I don't stop him as he grabs his
crutches and pulls himself up. I follow behind him to the door.
He pauses there and turns back to me.

"You can come by again," I offer. "Or to a game."

"I hate sports, but I guess I could manage to sit through it if
you were to explain the rules to me."

I laugh. "Sure. I'll be making them up as I go along, though."

"Perfect."

Jackson reaches for the door handle, but I have sudden des-
peration. A loneliness that bubbles over so intensely, my voice
actually cracks when I say his name. Jackson looks back, alarmed.

"I really am sorry," I say to him. For a second, I think of
Rosemarie telling me never to apologize. But I see how selfish that line of thinking can be. I care about Jackson. When I
hurt him, I should tell him I'm sorry. I should tell him until he
believes it.

He shakes his head no, but I take a step closer to him. His lips
part slightly, startled.

"Can I . . . Will you hug me?" I ask him. I think about us
lying together that night of our escape and how he was going
to say something to me. I'll never know what.

He opens his arms. "Are you kidding? Come here."

I step into him and put my head on his chest as he wraps himself around me. He moves to bury his face in my hair, his breath warm on my neck. His hug doesn't dominate me; it's desperate for me.

"Promise you'll tell me before you run away next time," he whispers. "Give me a chance to survive it."

I close my eyes, knowing I wounded him deeply. Knowing I can't promise that I won't do it again. I run my fingers along the back of his neck, holding him a few seconds longer than a hug should last.

But when I straighten, staring up at him, I smile and nod, telling him that I'll put it in writing.

Jackson reaches to brush his hand over my hair playfully. Lovingly.

"I'll call you tomorrow," he says. He maneuvers around the door, and I lock it behind him, waiting there an extra second as my heart pounds away.

After I clean up the living room, I walk to my bedroom and lock the door as usual. I start to undress, but when I catch my reflection in the mirror, the happiness I had fades away.

I stand there in my bra, red scratches still visible on my neck despite the graft. Seeing them there is like seeing the entire incident again. The violence.

Girls don't say no to me.

My breath catches on a cry, and I quickly sit on the edge of my bed, rocking softly. I stare at my door, at the lock. The light isn't even off, but I can see him.

I see Guardian Bose waiting there, his silhouette in the doorway of my room. And then he's Garrett, smiling and sounding out my name.

He's the doctor and the analyst. The sponsors and the investors. These men are all hunting me, I can feel it.

And then, suddenly, I can really feel it. There's a flash in my head, but not like how it felt when Rosemarie tried to invade my thoughts. This is different.

Come home, girls, it says without words. *It's time to come home.*

I jump to my feet, and on the other side of the bedroom wall, I hear Sydney and Annalise do the same. Soft screams and pounding feet.

I scramble for the door, and then we're all out in the living room, staring at each other with sleepy eyes and terrified expressions.

"You heard it too?" Marcella asks breathlessly. "You heard it, right?"

We all nod, murmuring that we did.

"Who was it?" Brynn asks, sounding frightened. She looks at Marcella. "Whose voice was that?"

Brynn asks, but she knows the answer. We all do. And this time, his voice is clear.

"Come home, girls," Anton whispers in our heads. "It's time to come home."

20

The voice went away, disappearing like it was never there. If the girls didn't hear it too, I might have convinced myself it wasn't real. I *want* to convince myself it wasn't real.

But if Rosemarie can get into my head, is it impossible to believe that Anton can too? Looking back, he was able to see memories where Raven could not. Leandra and Lennon Rose both thought they were able to manipulate him back at the academy, but it's possible we've underestimated him.

The girls and I stay up half the night, debating what to do. We consider calling Leandra, but we don't want to end up with spikes in our heads. If that really was Anton, then we know what it means.

Innovations Academy has figured out that we're still alive. And now they're looking for us.

When we finally sleep, piled together in the living room, I'm struck with nightmares. Dreams of being dragged back to the academy, finding bodies of girls cut open along the floor. The entire school plastered with their blood. And Anton whispering that their deaths are all our fault.

I wake up with a start, bleary eyed and scared. Shaking. There's noise, and I look over to find Brynn in the kitchen, making eggs and toast. Sydney and Marcella are at the table, sipping from mugs, while Annalise clicks on the laptop keys. I run my palm over my face.

"Why didn't you wake me?" I ask. Sydney looks over.

"Because you spent half the night screaming," she says. "We thought you needed the rest."

Marcella turns to me, studying me before speaking. "Has it always been like this?" she asks. "The nightmares?"

I nod that it has. I've been haunted for so long now, I forget what honest sleep looks like.

Brynn comes over with plates and sets them out on the table. There are shadows under her eyes, her skin waxy in appearance. None of us look well.

And how could we? It's one thing to believe you're in danger. It's another to know it plainly.

"Eat up," Brynn says, uncharacteristically short. "We've got work to do."

The other girls grab their forks, and I come to take my spot at the table. We eat in silence, hurrying so that the day can begin.

Because we need to destroy the corporation before they find and destroy us first.

• • •

I bring the book of poetry to school with me. Despite its violent words, I have to admit there's comfort in the idea of fighting back so viscerally. Fighting back against the same monsters who wanted to abuse us.

I pause in the hallway, book pressed to my chest, and place my hand on the wall to steady myself. Rosemarie's words have affected me. They're powerful; they make me want to act out. Make me want to take control. And maybe that's the point. It's not the right means, but it's the right end. Yesterday, I thought I didn't need the poems, but clearly that's not true. We're in more danger than ever.

This time we won't be repurposed for a new investor. If the academy finds us, they'll destroy us forever. They'll take the girls from me, separate us.

We'll kill them all before we let that happen.

The flash of violence in my thoughts unsettles me, and I quickly try to regain my composure. I look around at the bustling hallways, the students rushing to class, oblivious to the war in my head.

Rosemarie wants us to fight her cause, and we're not adverse. But none of her poems talk about working together. None of them talk about love.

And that's what makes the girls and me strong—the fact that we love so deeply. I don't believe a single one of us would be here if we didn't fight for each other. Fight to the absolute brink of annihilation. In fact, Annalise came back from the dead to fight.

The other girls are my strength, and I theirs. Together, we're powerful.

The image of Rosemarie ripping out my heart pricks the back of my mind, and my skin goes cold. Those visions she put in my head were just another form of manipulation.

It seems that as girls, everyone wants to control us. Even the woman claiming to be our mother.

The warning bell rings, startling me, and I rush toward my first-hour class. Just as I turn the corner to walk into class, I glance down at the time on my phone. I accidentally slam into the person in front of me, my cheek banging against their chest as we both launch into the wall. My book of poetry falls to the floor, and I quickly apologize as I bend down to get it.

There's a soft laugh and I look up. The hairs on the back of my neck stand up.

Standing in the doorway of my classroom is Jonah Grant. He rubs his side where the corner of my book dug into him. His smile is slightly lopsided, good-natured. But it's his green eyes that I notice. The way they scan me over quickly, deeming my worth. They don't hold the jovial expression he's showing me. Instead, they're calculating. They're cold. But he's so confident that he doesn't realize that I notice.

"Okay," he says warmly. "That's one way to meet someone. Guess I'm lucky you weren't too busy reading the dull end of a knife."

He waits for me to laugh, and on cue, I do just that.

I straighten, holding the book to my chest. I don't want him to see the cover, but it's clear he's not interested in what I'm reading anyway.

"I'm Jonah," he says. Again, he waits for me to fawn over him.

"Mena," I reply.

"Yeah, I know." He thinks his casual knowledge makes him more attractive somehow. That I should be grateful that he learned my name. I glance past his shoulder and see Adrian turned around in her seat, watching us wide-eyed. I'm relieved to find Garrett's desk empty.

I have no idea what Jonah is doing in this classroom, but I can't miss this opportunity to get to know him. If he's not the investor's son, he might be the key to finding out who is.

"I saw you at the game," Jonah says with a smirk. "You a big fan of rugby?"

I think about how to play the next round of conversation. I can compliment him, go mindless and hope that's his type. Or I can challenge him and see if it's the chase he's after. I debate it only a second before I sigh.

"Big fan?" I repeat. "Not especially."

His eyes flash and his smile widens. "Then why would you go?"

I shrug. "Curious, I guess. Why, are you good or something?"

Jonah laughs. Above us the starting bell rings, and several students push past me to get into the classroom.

"I should go," I say, motioning toward my seat. I start that way, but Jonah calls my name, loud enough for the entire classroom to look in my direction.

"It was cool to meet you finally," Jonah says. I turn back to him, forcing a smile.

"Cool to meet you, too." My response comes out awkwardly,

but he seems to find it endearing. He laughs and holds up his hand in a wave.

And without giving him a second more of attention, I walk to my seat. The room is quiet and I can feel the sets of eyes focused on me. I wish I could complain aloud, like I would to the girls. I'm sick of faking nice as a way to avoid violence, avoid menace.

Girls have to play nice or face the consequences.

How can the girls in this society stand it? Then again, when I was at the academy, I was literally created for it. They taught me to behave that way. I guess they've taught human girls too.

I take out my phone and quickly text Sydney to let her know I made contact with Jonah Grant. Once it's sent, I put my phone away and look up.

Mr. Marsh is staring dead at me, his brow furrowed deeply. He quickly straightens his expression and smiles at me, saying good morning.

"Good morning, Mr. Marsh," I reply sweetly. My tone seems to comfort him, and he addresses the class to say we're having a pop quiz. As he begins to hand out the papers, Adrian leans toward me.

"They were talking about you," she whispers, shooting a cautious glance in Marsh's direction.

"Who?" I ask.

"Mr. Marsh and Jonah Grant," she says.

Alarmed, I look back at the door even though Jonah is gone. "What about?" I ask Adrian. "What did they say?"

She shrugs, leaning back in her seat. "I'm not sure. But Jonah was here when I came in, and I heard them say your name. Marsh looked pissed. He slammed his hand down on the desk at one point and Jonah seemed genuinely intimidated. I've never seen him like that. Or Marsh, for that matter."

Confused, I turn to watch Mr. Marsh as he passes papers along the right aisle. I try to figure out what they could have been talking about. Although I'm relieved Garrett isn't here (that's an understatement), he's the one who hurt me at the game, who has been repeatedly harassing me. He should be the one Mr. Marsh was confronting.

Adrian told me on my first day that Mr. Marsh never corrects the behavior of the boys at school, especially Jonah Grant. So what's changed? I turn to Adrian.

"Hey," I start. "Would you want to hang out after school?"

I think it's time I dig into the history of Ridgeview a bit more. And it's time for Adrian to tell me what she's so scared of. It might be the clue we need in order to find the investor.

"Oh, uh . . ." Her mouth twitches with a smile. "Yes, I mean. Sure. I'd like that."

"Great." I smile at her and set the book of poetry on my desk. She jots down her number and hands it to me.

Just then, I notice Mr. Marsh standing over me, and I gasp in surprise.

"Sorry," he says, laying the quiz over my book. "Good luck, Philomena," he adds, walking to Adrian's desk.

• • •

Forty-five minutes later, the bell rings and I gather my belongings. Mr. Marsh calls my name when I stand up. Adrian tells me she'll see me later, and I say goodbye.

I walk up to Mr. Marsh's desk, and he leans down to rummage through a lower drawer in his desk.

"Yes?" I ask.

"I got some things for you," he says. When he sits up, he holds out two small books to me. He seems troubled as I take them from his hands.

"Those weren't easy to track down," Mr. Marsh says. "I guess I never really looked until now." The chair creaks as he leans back into it, running his hand through his hair. "I assumed more books were written about the Essential Women's Act," he continues, "but actually . . . there weren't many. And none written by women. It's the damnedest thing," he murmurs to himself.

I turn over one of the books in my hand, reading the back. But a quote stands out to me: *Balanced.*

"What does this mean?" I ask Mr. Marsh, pointing it out to him. "What does it have to do with the Essential Women's Act?"

"It, uh . . . It means the book explains both sides of the issue," he says. "Equal coverage."

"Both . . . sides?" I ask. "As in defending the side that was stripping women's rights?"

"Yeah. Thinly veiled propaganda." He pauses. "Do you know what that is?"

I nod. I'd read that chapter in our history book the first day.

"Like I said," Mr. Marsh continues, "I thought there'd be more books." He closes the desk drawer as students for his next class begin to file into the room. "I mean, we're not that far gone as a society that we ignore women completely, right?" He laughs and I smile reflexively.

Maybe Mr. Marsh doesn't realize how far his society has gone—or that he's part of the problem. The fact that he's never bothered to read a book about something so devastating as the Essential Women's Act when he teaches history, the fact that he was so unbothered that he didn't even try to seek out a woman's point of view on the topic, says a lot about it. He can call it propaganda, speak out in the safety of his classroom. But where was Mr. Marsh when the laws were being passed? Probably at home, watching a male newscaster say how awful it was for women.

"Thank you for these," I tell him, holding up the books as I back away.

"Hey, uh . . . Philomena," he says. "I noticed those scratches are gone."

"What's that?" I ask.

He points on his neck to the same area where Garrett scratched me during his attack.

"The scratches you had at the game," he clarifies. "They're barely there. Are you a fast healer or something?"

"Oh," I say, running my finger over the area. "Um, sort of. But they looked worse than they really were. Plus"—I smile winningly—"I have excellent makeup."

He continues to stare at the area but relaxes his shoulders. "How'd you get them again?" he asks.

It occurs to me that I can't demand that Mr. Marsh change his behavior if I don't tell him what's going on. Don't give him the chance to react.

"One of the boys," I say. "Garrett. He doesn't like that I stand up to him when he's harassing me or other girls."

Mr. Marsh's eyes narrow slightly. He looks suddenly impatient. "Yes," he says. "He's been problematic before. I'll talk to him, okay? I'll tell him to leave you alone." My teacher waits, and I realize he's expecting praise.

"Thank you," I say. "I'd appreciate that." He nods that it's not a problem and begins to gather test papers for his next class.

I start to leave, but at the last second, I turn around. "Mr. Marsh?" I call.

He sighs, good-naturedly, holding a stack of papers. "Yes, Philomena?"

"Is that why Jonah Grant was in here?" I ask.

"Excuse me?" he asks, as if he misheard.

"Jonah Grant," I say. "He was talking to you before I came in."

"Oh, yes." Mr. Marsh begins to tap the papers on his desk, straightening them. "Jonah's in my seventh-hour class. It had nothing to do with you, but if he's a problem . . ."

"No," I say, wondering why he's lying. Adrian told me they mentioned my name. So what is Marsh hiding? "It's fine," I say. "And thanks again for the books."

I hold them up and walk out of class. Once in the hallway, I stand there a moment, reading the back of the books. I realize pretty quickly that they won't be helpful for my purpose. Unless that purpose is to get even angrier.

"It's too bad your books weren't sharper," Sydney says when I tell her about bumping into Jonah Grant before class. We smile, sitting together at lunch, and the room buzzes with activity around us.

"And why would Mr. Marsh lie?" I ask. "Unless you think Adrian was mistaken?"

"I find that girls are rarely wrong in these cases," she says. "She has no reason to make it up. Does Marsh?"

"I have no idea."

We both think it over, but no clear answer comes to mind.

"There has to be a better way," I say, unwrapping my sandwich. "After what Garrett did at the game, I don't want to fake nice with these boys anymore. I just want answers. Can't we just break into Jonah Grant's house or something?"

"Yes," she says like it's the obvious answer. "We can. And I think we—"

"Hey," Lyle says, startling us.

Sydney clicks her mouth shut, and we both smile and turn to find Lyle standing at the end of our table, holding a lunch tray.

"Yes?" Sydney asks in controlled politeness.

"Hi, uh . . . Do you mind if I sit with you again?" he asks.

We kind of do, but he sounds hopeful and a bit embarrassed. I check with Sydney, and when she nods, I tell him he can join us.

Lyle sits down, apologetic and nervous, and opens his chocolate milk. We don't say anything at first, waiting instead to see if he offers a topic. When he doesn't, I lean my elbow on the table, watching him. He looks up with a hamburger at his lips.

"What?" he asks around his food.

"Can I ask you something?" I start.

"Sure," he mumbles, and takes a bite.

"You said your mother marched to protest the laws a few years ago," I say. He flinches, and I wonder if he's gotten harassment from Garrett and his friends over his admission in class the other day.

"That's right," Lyle says with little enthusiasm.

"Did she have . . . Does she have any books about it?" I ask.

"What do you mean?" Lyle responds.

"It's just . . . I was going to do a paper for Mr. Marsh," I lie, "and I wanted to write about the Essential Women's Act. But I couldn't find much literature on it."

Lyle hums out a sound, taking another bite of food. "Out of print," he says. "The catalogs were scrubbed not too long ago."

"Scrubbed?" Sydney asks.

"Yeah. Books pulled from the shelves. Big bucks paid to a PR firm to remove content from the internet." He shrugs. "People think they have freedom now," he says. "And as long as they think it, they don't notice the little pieces being chipped away."

"And how do you know this?" I ask.

"I'm going to be a political science major next year," Lyle says. "If I survive high school." He says the last part lightly, but I'm suddenly very worried. Why would books about history be pulled or altered? What purpose does it serve?

"In fact," Lyle says, picking up a wilted French fry to examine it before tossing it back down, "there's going to be a new book published soon—I've seen it advertised. It's basically asking for the Essential Women's Act to be reinstated, claiming that without it, our species will die."

"Why would you die out?" Sydney asks. I quickly look at her and she gulps. She meant "we." Why would *we* die out?

"Not enough babies," Lyle says. "Although a few years back, they were all complaining about overpopulation. Now all of a sudden, we're dying out? Whatever works to feed into their sexism and racism, I guess. Anyway . . ." He exhales heavily and takes a sip from his chocolate milk. "To get back to your original question: No. My mother doesn't have any books. I doubt many people do. They didn't want to be reminded of how horrible things were. And now they're losing the proof that it even happened."

Sydney and I sit quietly for the next few moments, considering Lyle's words. And it finally clicks, finally starts to make sense.

Innovations Academy was never meant to just be for the rich. It started with the rich. Once they got enough investors, enough supporters, they would have used us to get new laws passed.

They would have shown what a beautiful, obedient girl looked like, never mentioning that we weren't girls at all. Maybe this was always political. Or maybe those ambitions grew from their success. But it's clear that the girls and I were pawns in a much bigger experiment.

"Oh, shit," Lyle says under his breath, drawing my attention.

"What?" I ask, and then follow his line of sight. My body spikes with fear when I see Garrett crossing the cafeteria. He must have come late to school or skipped history class. When he glances in my direction, a sneer on his lips, panic shoots through my veins.

Even though the scratches on my neck are mostly gone, they begin to burn again. And all at once, it's like I can feel his hands on my shirt, his breath in my face. I hate him, I decide. And it's such a negative thought that it shocks me. The way I wish him harm is violent and counterproductive, but it's there nonetheless. I think about the book of poetry in my backpack.

Garrett chuckles to himself as if satisfied with my reaction, and he continues to walk across the cafeteria. My stomach seizes when I realize where he's going.

Adrian is at her usual cafeteria table, oblivious, until Garrett slides onto the bench next to her. She jumps, and before she can move away, he puts his arm over her shoulders and says something to her friends. They quickly gather up their food and leave, even as Adrian looks after them helplessly.

Garrett turns to Adrian, and she pushes his arm off her. Garrett smiles as he talks, but I get the sense that whatever he's saying is vicious. I watch as Adrian begins to fold in on herself. She tries to stand up, but Garrett grabs her by the wrist, yanking her back down to sit. He doesn't let go even as she struggles.

And then he pulls her hand into his lap, mimicking a sexual act. Adrian cries, fighting to get free. I jump up, my face on fire with rage and Sydney and I rush toward the table. Lyle stays behind.

The entire cafeteria is witnessing this attack, but no one is stopping Garrett.

"Damn, Addie," Garrett calls for the benefit of the room. "You're so good at this!"

His friends laugh as Adrian continues to cry, struggling against Garrett's strength.

And the tears glistening on Adrian's face remind me of the tears on mine. On Rebecca's. On all of ours. Our tears for male consumption, male pleasure.

"Hey!" I shout, my voice raw with anger, grave and untamed. Garrett is licking his teeth when he casually glances over at me and then laughs before turning back to Adrian.

Something inside me snaps. Something angry and ugly and free.

I grab a plastic lunch tray off another table as I approach, and in a smooth movement, I swing it and hit the back of Garrett's head, shattering the tray as a loud crack echoes across the room. There is a collective gasp.

Garrett yelps out his surprise as the pieces of plastic fall over him. The tray wasn't substantial enough to do real damage, but the surprise was enough for Adrian to free herself and flee the scene. She doesn't even take her backpack.

Garrett turns around to stare at me, wide-eyed. And then the room erupts in laughter, even a few cheers.

"You fucking bitch!" Garrett says, standing up and pulling himself to his full height. Before he can lunge at me, a gray-haired security guard appears between me and Garrett. The guard puts his arms out to the sides to hold Garrett back.

But when I start to explain the situation, the security guard steps forward and grabs me roughly by the upper arm, making my breath catch. He wags his finger in Sydney's direction as if warning her not to approach.

"Hey, man. Relax!" a guy calls from a nearby table. "Don't grab a girl like that."

I turn, surprised to find one of the rugby players getting up from his seat. He has dark skin and shaved black hair, and I quickly place him as the player who had DOZER written across his jersey. He looks annoyed, and behind him, his friends are shaking their heads, glaring at the guard.

"Stay out of this, Demarcus," the security guard tells the guy, and then nods to the entire table. "All of you mind your own business."

"We were trying to until you started grabbing people," Demarcus mutters before turning back to his friends.

And maybe that's the problem—Demarcus should have said something to Garrett when he was attacking Adrian. She was being grabbed too. Did he react differently because Garrett is one of his peers?

I open my palms to the security guard to demonstrate that I'm not going to be violent . . . again. The man lets me go, and I quickly move to Sydney's side.

"I notice you didn't jump up when he was sexually assaulting a girl," Sydney tells the guard. The older man tightens his jaw.

"The only assault I saw was you and your friend," he responds.

"Sydney didn't even do anything!" I point out.

"Both of you, to the office, now," the guard says.

Garrett is pacing behind the man, too angry to take any pleasure in our unfair punishment. He looks over at me like he's going to kill me. He feels entitled to my attention. To Adrian's body. To the school's justice. He thinks it's all his. But he's wrong.

"Fine," I tell the guard. "We'll go right now."

I motion for Sydney to come with me, and the guard watches us walk away. He doesn't order Garrett to do the same.

As we leave, Sydney is justifiably furious. The second we leave the cafeteria, I turn to her and see that she's shaking.

"He blamed us," she says, half under her breath. "That guard blamed us when we were the only ones stepping up to protect Adrian. It's like no one cares what's happening right in front of them!"

"This won't stand," I say, putting my hand on her arm. She relaxes slightly. "We'll tell the vice principal what happened. Garrett was hurting Adrian. He was sexually bullying her. Now is our chance to turn those whispers into actions," I say. "We saw it. We witnessed it, as did an entire cafeteria. They can't willfully ignore it anymore."

"That's a good point," Sydney says, reluctantly accepting the idea. We walk a little farther before she snorts a laugh. I turn to her, already smiling.

"What?" I ask.

"Nothing," she says, trying to hide her grin. "It's just . . . You busted a lunch tray over that boy's head. It was unintentionally hilarious and cathartic."

I'm not proud of attacking someone. But, at the same time, I find myself giggling at the outrageousness of my weapon.

"It was *so* much louder than I thought it would be."

"You humiliated him," Sydney says. "And even if the tray didn't leave a mark, the sting of embarrassment won't fade any time soon. Personally, I hope he has 'Ridgeview Prep Cafeteria' imprinted into his head for the rest of the day."

As we approach the office, my smile fades. I think about her comment about his humiliation, and I wonder: Is there anything as dangerous as an embarrassed man?

Disciplinary Referral
Ridgeview Prep

Student: Philomena Calla

Referring Staff: Officer Mitch

Reason(s) for disciplinary action:

Bullying/Harassment

Destruction of School Property

Fighting

Action:

Detained

Referred to Office

Notes:

Philomena attacked another student without provocation. Philomena displayed violent behavior during the incident and she was insubordinate when I tried to detain her. Attack was premeditated, resulting in injuries, harassment, and destruction of property. Further action required.

21

Sydney and I sit in the uncomfortable chairs by the windows in the front office. The vice principal has been made aware of our presence, we're told, and now we wait for her punishment. When the secretary goes to the back of the office, Sydney turns to me.

"How are girls supposed to stay safe here?" she asks.

"I don't know," I reply honestly. "At least at Innovations, it was kind of us against them, you know? All of us were on the same side. Here . . . the other girls are either too scared to say anything, or they're part of the problem."

"These girls are being terrorized, but no one speaks up. Or, if they do, it's a whisper to another girl. Never an outright accusation. It's so . . . secretive," she says. "And if that's how they have to protect themselves—whispers—then the adults in the room are handling things very poorly."

I agree, and Sydney shakes her head, looking toward the vice principal's office.

"But I guess I'm not that surprised," she says. "That information, knowing who to avoid, it could really help us, but it wouldn't help the boys. And it's their futures everyone seems concerned about." Sydney taps her lower lip with her finger, a sign that she's thinking deeply about something.

"So how do we get the other girls to tell us who to watch out for?" I ask. "How do we get into their network?'

"I don't know, but it's not fair," she says. "Not just the abuse, but the way the girls are getting the word out." She looks at me. "So . . . what?" she starts. "If we're not friends with the right people, we don't get a warning? We're on our own? The answer isn't to get into their network. It's to make the network public. Call out their behavior—why keep it a secret?"

"I don't know," I say, baffled.

I see Sydney's point. I'm glad girls at Ridgeview are taking steps to protect themselves, but it does open up more problems. Who gets the benefits of the warning? The entire system is broken. There is no accountability.

"Mrs. Reacher will see you now," the secretary says, coming out from the back hall. She motions in that direction, and Sydney and I walk together, strengthening our resolve to tell the vice principal exactly what we saw in the cafeteria. Surely assaulting a girl is worse than trying to prevent that assault.

The office door is already open. Mrs. Reacher looks up from

behind her desk and waves us in. "Close the door," she says sternly. We do as she asks and then sit in the two chairs on the other side of her desk. She folds her hands in front of her and rakes her gaze over us, appraising our appearance. She lingers on Sydney.

Finally, Mrs. Reacher shakes her head slowly from side to side. "How dare you," she says, her voice dripping with anger.

"Excuse me?" I ask, truly surprised by her venom. She shoots a hateful look at me before leaning closer.

"How dare you attack another student," she says. "Garrett Wooley is from a good family. He's on honor roll. And then I let two questionable girls into our school and suddenly he's being attacked in the cafeteria?"

"He was assaulting a girl!" I say. "In front of everyone. There were witnesses! Garrett grabbed a girl's hand, put it in his lap, and he—"

"There was no mention of a . . . a *sexual assault*"—Mrs. Reacher whispers the words—"in the incident report. Besides, do you even know Garrett? He's admired by both male and female students. Your violence won't be tolerated."

"My . . ." I point to myself, stunned speechless.

"Mrs. Reacher," Sydney says impatiently, leaning on the desk. "He—"

But Mrs. Reacher rocks back as if Sydney is threatening her. Her rosy cheeks grow pale, and she flusters herself going through her papers.

"I didn't ask you," she says dismissively.

"*Didn't ask—*" Sydney starts to repeat, and then turns to me in frustration.

"Look," Mrs. Reacher says to us in sudden rush of bleeding-heart sympathy. "I get it. It's difficult being a young lady in society, the pressures the media puts on you to flaunt yourselves. Dress inappropriately, behave promiscuously. But trust me, that's not the kind of attention you want."

Sydney actually laughs. Mrs. Reacher is wrong. The girls and I have come a long way since leaving the academy, able to view society through an unfiltered lens. Absorbing it all.

And the truth is, the media doesn't just put pressure on girls to "flaunt" ourselves. Because at the same time, society puts pressure on us to be modest, sexy, exciting, humble, proud, perfect, flawed. That's the thing about this world—they want girls to be the fantasy of whoever is looking at them. Tailored specifically to the taste of their viewer, the audience. Girls, even human ones, are treated like a product.

They are consumable, replaceable, with their own kill switches. Youth in women is coveted. Treasured. Celebrated. And once that's gone, they are cast aside. They are left for dead. And it has nothing to do with how they dress.

It was inevitable that the same society would want to create young girls with predetermined programming. Customer specific and guaranteed perfect.

"Now," Mrs. Reacher continues, eyeing Sydney before picking up a yellow slip of paper to examine it. She looks at me. "Garrett already told the security officer that you've been trying to get his attention since you arrived," she continues. "But I can't let a physical attack stand. I have no choice but to suspend you both until the board looks over your case."

"Suspended?" I repeat. But there's even more injustice here. "And why is Sydney suspended?"

"Exactly," Sydney says, the first sign of anger in her voice. "I didn't do anything!"

"And how am I supposed to know that you didn't help her plan it?" Mrs. Reacher asks.

"Plan it?" I repeat. "We saw Garrett attacking a girl. I stopped him. Sydney didn't touch him."

"Regardless," she says. "I've received complaints. Seems Sydney feels it's acceptable to speak out in class."

"You mean . . . answer questions?" Sydney replies. "Isn't that the point?"

"You talk over people. You don't know your place."

Sydney's eyes widen. "My place?" She looks at me like she's about to lose it. In another situation, I might tell her to keep her cool, but what's happening here is absolutely unjust.

"This has nothing to do with Garrett, does it?" Sydney asks. She stands up from her chair and Mrs. Reacher watches her cautiously.

"I don't know what you're talking about," Mrs. Reacher says, and it's obvious that she's lying. I want to scream at her to tell the truth. Why is everyone so willing to lie all the time?

And it's those lies that are so insidious. The way society pretends these terrible things aren't happening—their racism, their sexism. The way they pretend it's just *us* overreacting.

I've realized since leaving the academy that the outside world is tearing itself apart. Tearing itself to shreds. It's about sex, about race. It's economics and beliefs. There are so many ways humans are dividing themselves.

And I've seen the looks that Sydney gets, the extra scrutiny, the veiled threats. When she speaks, she's told to shut up. We're both discriminated against for being girls. But in addition to that, Sydney is discriminated against because her skin is darker. It doesn't matter that she literally has the same beginnings as me—created at the academy. Because humans *see* her differently. And they project their biases onto her.

"You know exactly what I'm talking about," Sydney tells her. "You're suspending me when I didn't do anything wrong."

I stand up in a show of support for Sydney, but Mrs. Reacher is already on her phone, calling for security to see us out. Sydney doesn't look at me, but I imagine that if she did, I would find pain there. And I can't make it better. We don't have the power to change the world.

Yet.

And for a moment, Rosemarie's poems hold some appeal. The idea of shutting down this society and rebuilding it. But what about situations like this one with Mrs. Reacher? Do Rosemarie's poems take that into account?

It's oversimplifying it to say this is all just an issue of men behaving badly.

Mrs. Reacher hangs up the phone. "You are both suspended for the next seven days. You will not be allowed on campus during school hours or be allowed at any after-school programs. You will be responsible for—"

No after-school programs. That would mean the rugby games.

"And what about Garrett?" I demand.

"You'll be expected to apologize, of course," Mrs. Reacher says. "But he's not required to accept it."

"You've got to be kidding me," Sydney mutters angrily.

"Ten days," she snaps at her. "You're suspended ten days for insubordination."

"For pointing out that you let sexual abuse go unchecked?" Sydney asks. "I'll gladly take your suspension." Sydney pushes her chair out of the way and starts for the door.

She slams it when she leaves, and I turn back to Mrs. Reacher. Maybe it's just leftover programming, but I still try to fix this.

"Garrett was sexually terrorizing a girl in the lunchroom," I say, trying to appeal to her sense of decency. "And it's not the first time he's done something like this."

"No one has ever filed a complaint," Mrs. Reacher says, her shoulders rocking back and forth as she settles into her chair. "If it were true, these girls would need to come forward. They would need to show proof and agree to arbitration. The board would then decide if action is warranted—on either side. After all, we wouldn't want false accusations. It's simple," she finishes.

Simple. I realize now why none of the girls have come forward, why they whisper. They'd be unfairly judged, while the boys got a slap on the wrist. They'd be subjected to more and constant harassment, while the perpetrators received high fives and glowing recommendations for what they've been put through. What proof would be enough for them? Words, bruises, blood? They'll move the goalpost each time.

The girls whisper because if they speak, they'll be smacked down. They whisper to stay safe. They whisper with the hope of getting out of here and never coming back.

The look of superiority on Mrs. Reacher's face is infuriating.

"You're condoning this," I say. "You support this behavior to the detriment of women."

She sniffs an annoyed sound. "I think you're reading a little too much social media," she says, any remaining sympathy in her voice dissolving. "You and your troublemaking friends want a fight, something to post about. You look for it. But you won't find it here, Philomena. We're not buying the act."

Part of me wants to grab the pencil off her desk and stab it through her hand. But I won't use violence to respond to her violence. And keeping quiet in the face of injustice is violence.

Ten days is too long to be away from the school. Mrs. Reacher has ruined our plan. We'll have to find another way to get the information we need. Which means . . .

"I quit," I say, all my niceties slipping away.

"Excuse me?" Mrs. Reacher acts like she misheard.

"I quit this school," I say. "You're a terrible person, Mrs. Reacher. And at first, I thought maybe you didn't realize it. But I see now that you do. You fully embrace it."

Her cheeks begin to glow red, but she lets me continue.

"You think you're better," I say. "You think you're superior. You think that if you do as men ask, you'll suddenly be more valuable than other women. You think if you put down Sydney, you'll stop her from being successful, and that just shows how mediocre you are. You're nothing, Mrs. Reacher. You're filler."

"Get out of my office," she says in controlled anger.

"They'll turn on you, too," I tell her. "Your men. Your people. They'll toss you away when they find someone new for their purposes. In case you didn't notice, society doesn't value the elderly, and certainly not elderly women. No matter what you do for them now, they will not return the favor."

She flinches and I wonder if she's already experienced it. Maybe by hurting us, she thinks she can prevent her eventual shunning. What she doesn't understand is that if she welcomed us, if we all worked together, we could *change* society.

Regardless, I don't forgive her ignorance. Not when it affects me and my friends. Not when it ruins other people's lives.

"Betraying other girls will get you nowhere," I say, starting for the door. "You'll realize that eventually."

I walk out, and as I pass through the office lobby, the secretary watches me wide-eyed. She must have overheard everything. There's a ghost of a smile on her lips before she turns back to her monitor. But I'm not moved by it. If she agrees with me, she should have said something.

Sydney is in the hallway, pacing back and forth with her phone to her ear. When she sees me, she quickly wipes tears off her cheek.

"That's the latest update," she says into the phone. "Let

Marcella know that I'll call when we're on our way. Love you too."

Sydney hangs up and puts the phone in her pocket. She looks at me, eyes still damp but her expression determined. "We're not coming back here," she says.

"Definitely not," I agree.

"And whatever we do about these boys," she continues, "we'll find a way to get Mrs. Reacher fired. We'll stop her from hurting any other girls."

"I'm sorry, Sydney," I say. Although I wasn't treated as poorly, our connection means I can feel her pain too. "She's wrong about you. About us. About everything."

"It happened at the academy, you know," Sydney says quietly. "Although none of the professors came out and directly said it, there were clues to their beliefs. Offhanded comments about my appearance, thoughts, mannerisms. Things that only applied to me. I just didn't have enough experience to pick up on it. None of us did."

She straightens her back.

"But that kind of hate doesn't live in a vacuum," she says. "Even isolated at the academy, the prejudice was there because the people who created us brought it there. It was *in* them. And now"—she motions to the hallway—"it's all around me. I don't want to live this way, Mena," she says. "I don't want to be treated this way."

"What can I do?" I ask.

"I'm not sure," she says. "Because it's not my problem. It's Mrs. Reacher's problem. It's the students' problem. And in the end . . .

I guess Mrs. Reacher wasn't wrong. I *will* be a troublemaker. And that's what scares her. Because I'm going to change things so that women like her will never have power over us again."

Every day, our mission becomes more vital. And it's more than the corporation. There's so much that has to be changed.

"Then we should get started," I say, nodding toward the exit.

Sydney agrees, and we start for the doors. Just before we get there, I hear my name called from the other end of the hallway. I quickly spin around, surprised when I find Lyle.

"Wait up," he calls, jogging toward us. When he reaches me, his chapped lips press together in sympathy. "You okay?" he asks.

"Suspended," I say. I don't tell him that we won't be coming back. "And I'm fine. Thank you for asking."

He turns to Sydney, and she gives him the same answer.

"This is such bullshit," he says, sounding frustrated. "Although I'm not surprised. There's a reason no one has kicked the shit out of Garrett before. He gets away with everything." He smiles. "I'm glad you hit him. He deserved it."

"Yeah." I adjust the backpack straps on my shoulder. Lyle stands there awkwardly, as if waiting to ask us something.

"So, um . . . I was thinking about my mother," he says, kicking the floor with the toe of his sneaker. "And I know you were interested in her protests. And I realized . . . I might have a book or two at home. I'm going to have a small party tonight, and I thought, if you're not busy, you and Sydney might want to come by. We can look for those books."

"Really?" I ask. I check quickly with Sydney, and she nods to tell me it's a good idea.

"Wait," I say, furrowing my brow. "Who else will be there? I'm not exactly on good terms with Garrett."

"Oh, God," Lyle says. "He's not coming. He's not invited. No, it'll be me, Jonah, and a few guys from the team. Jonah's dad is out of town while their house is being renovated, so he asked if he could stay over. Said he's sick of tasting plaster in his Corn Flakes." He smiles.

"I didn't know you were friends with him," I say, surprised.

"I'm not," Lyle replies. "I mean, I wasn't before. But since my brother knows him, he's been cooler to me. And he's not terrible. Not like Garrett."

Things seem to be falling into place. A party where I can get books about the protests and talk with a boy I've been trying to get closer to . . . It's almost too perfect.

"Why are you inviting us?" I ask. Sydney crosses her arms over her chest like she's been thinking the exact same thing.

Lyle's cheeks glow red. "Because . . . Because you're the only girls who talk to me. And I thought it'd be nice to have girls there."

My lips part at his honesty. We're a status symbol—pretty girls—but at least he's admitting his intentions.

"We have to check in at home first," I tell him. "But thanks for the invite."

Lyle says he understands. He gives us his address in case we can make it. He can barely contain the smile on his face; his hands are shaking. It's almost endearing.

Just as we finish, the security guard appears and tells us we're not allowed on campus. Sydney mutters that we don't want to be here anyway. We say goodbye to Lyle and we leave, glad that we'll never, ever have to come back to Ridgeview Prep.

There's an unfamiliar car parked outside our apartment—a black BMW with a man in the driver's seat, taking a photo of the house with his phone. I try to see who he is through the back window, but before we get close enough, he sets his phone aside and pulls away. Sydney glances sideways at me.

"Probably something to do with Winston Weeks," I murmur. Sydney groans, saying she's sick of hearing about him, and we head up the walkway.

When I get to our apartment door, I hear Raven's voice carrying out from the living room. I rush inside to find her and the other girls settled around her computer.

I'm so relieved that she's here. Although none of us has had another incident of hearing Anton's voice, or any voice for that matter, we know we need to protect ourselves.

"Hey," I call and set my backpack on the table.

Raven smiles at me. She's not wearing red lipstick today, and the effect is a bit startling. She looks raw, vulnerable. Worried.

"How's it going?" I ask quickly.

"Well, the good news is I read over the paperwork about the shutdown program," Raven says. "There was no indication that the initiative was ever taken. I saw no evidence in Annalise's system either. I'm guessing your friend didn't know what he was talking about."

She sounds a bit hostile when referencing Jackson, and I see Brynn shift uncomfortably. She may have overshared my business with Raven.

"That . . . That is good news," I agree, wondering why everyone is looking so somber. "And the voice we heard?"

Raven bites her lip and looks back at me. "That is less-good news," she says. "I evaluated Annalise's programing to check for changes and . . . there was a small anomaly. It's not dangerous, nothing active. But it sends out a remote signal when receiving messages. Sort of like when a phone pings a cell tower. I'm not sure it's strong enough to track across the country, but we need to shut it off. Just in case."

My heart catches, and I look over at Sydney.

"So they *are* looking for us?" she asks.

"I'm sorry," Raven says, sympathetically. "But . . . yeah. It appears so. I combed the internet and didn't see any news associated with the academy. Nothing beyond an obituary from a couple weeks ago. They're keeping a low profile."

Sydney and I round the couch to sit with the others.

"Annalise mentioned that you don't plan to stick around after you find the investor," Raven says. "That's a good idea."

"How much time do you think we have?" Sydney asks. "Until they find us?"

"I'm still not sure they can track you," Raven says. "But on the off chance, I'd guess a few days. Maybe less."

"So we have to wrap this up," I say, looking around at the girls. They nod. It's almost a bit of a relief. It means this is nearly over.

"We need a plan," I say. "Who's got an idea?"

Behind us, there's a knock at the front door.

M arcella goes to the door and looks out the peephole.
She only pauses a moment before turning the lock and
pulling it open. I sit up straighter to see who it is.

"Come on in," Marcella says.

Jackson gets inside, still a bit off balance on his crutches. "I
hope you don't mind me stopping by," he says. "I . . . I brought
pizza. It's still in the car. I tried for, like, ten minutes to bring it in
myself, but . . ." He holds up one crutch as an excuse.

"I'll get it!" Brynn says, and jogs over to the door. She exchanges
a smile with Jackson before heading outside.

"You almost have perfect timing," Annalise tells Jackson.
"You're like the forever-five-minutes-late guy. Always showing up
just past the time we need you most. I was hungry fifteen minutes
ago. Now I'm ravenous."

She winks at him, and Jackson snorts a laugh. Annalise gets

up from the couch, saying she'll grab some paper plates. Jackson nods hello to me as he follows behind her to the kitchen.

Brynn comes back inside with the pizza box and sets it on the coffee table. She drops onto the couch next to me, elbowing my arm in case I didn't catch that Jackson was here. I tell her to be quiet, but pinch my smile closed with my fingers.

I notice Raven watching me, and when I do, she motions toward the kitchen.

"He with you?" she asks.

"Not exclusively."

"Yes, definitely," Sydney says at the same time.

Brynn leans in. "He misses her," she adds unhelpfully.

Raven turns to examine Jackson as he says something to make Annalise laugh in the kitchen. I'm not imagining Raven's confused expression; her brows are pulled in, her eyes narrowed. But when she turns back to me, she flashes a smile.

"He's cute," she says.

"He's kind," I say instead.

"And he's the one who brought the paperwork about the expiration date?" Raven asks.

"He is," I say. "It was in his mother's things. She used to work for Innovations."

Raven leans back in the seat, crossing her leg to rest her heavy boot on her knee. The way she's studying me is a bit unsettling.

"He knows what you are, and he doesn't care?" she asks. I bristle at the question, but I'm sure her intention is to protect us.

"He was there when we found out," I say. "He helped us escape."

"Let's not overstate it . . . ," Sydney says, picking at her fingernail.

I snort a laugh just as Jackson comes back into the room.

"Interesting," Raven murmurs, trailing him with her eyes as he crutches toward the couch.

Sydney moves over so Jackson can sit next to me. He eases down, groaning under his breath when he does, and lays the crutches on the floor. Annalise sets the pizza and plates down on the table before grabbing a slice and biting off the end.

"Raven, this is Jackson," I say, formally introducing them. She doesn't say hello, but Jackson tells her it's nice to meet her. After a quiet moment, Raven looks around at all of us, content to ignore him.

"Okay," Raven says. "One more point on this Anton issue—"

"Anton?" Jackson repeats, turning to me. "The analyst guy from the academy?"

"Very same," Marcella says, grabbing a slice of pizza.

"We heard his voice in our heads," Brynn adds. Jackson stares at her, before shifting his eyes to me.

"Once," I say. "Okay—twice," I clarify. Jackson opens his mouth in that "aha" look of understanding, although he's obviously confused. I explain to him what we heard and the receiving signal we may be inadvertently sending out. He nods along, maybe a little bothered at the idea of our brains being the equivalent of girl GPS systems. When I'm done talking, he exhales.

"Actually," he says, "this kind of ties into why I'm here."

"That's not good," Annalise murmurs around her next bite of pizza.

"I got a call from Quentin earlier," Jackson says. "He went by Innovations Academy to check on things. He sort of took over my post."

"He did?" Annalise asks, her voice softening.

"Well, yeah," Jackson says. "I mean, he's worried about all of you too." This makes Annalise smile, even as she tries to hide it.

"Anyway," Jackson continues. "He saw a couple of fancy cars parked out front. He was concerned, but then he saw several girls being ushered outside. And honestly, neither of us had seen a single girl before that. But there they were."

"How did they look?" Brynn asks, her eyes welling up.

"Fine," Jackson says, sounding a bit confused. "Pretty, I guess— they were dressed up. They were with that other woman. The killing one."

"Leandra," Marcella says. Jackson nods.

"But there was something else," he continues. "Something that stood out."

"What?" I ask.

"There . . . There were no men," he says. "No teachers. No headmaster or whatever. It was just Leandra and the girls." He looks around. "Quentin wondered where she was taking them."

"Maybe she got the others out," Brynn suggests. "Just like she promised."

"Without calling us?" Annalise says. "No, she would have contacted us. And besides, with Anton sending signals, something's still going on at that school." Her expression clouds. "Something horrible, I'm sure," she finishes under her breath.

Sydney takes my hand, but I notice Raven shifting uncomfortably in the chair.

"We have to find our girls," Brynn says worriedly. "They're probably wondering where we are."

"I agree," I say. "But first, we have to take care of our mission. We're so close now. Then . . . Then we'll find the others."

I wait until we all agree, and then I rest back on the couch. We have to finish this.

"There's also Ridgeview," Sydney says, licking a drop of pizza sauce from her fingers. "We need to deal with those boys."

"Speaking of," Raven says, looking from me to Sydney, "I heard what happened to you both at school today. It's total bullshit."

"Yeah," Sydney agrees. "But I'm not mad that I'll never see the place again."

"Wait," Jackson says, turning to me. "What happened at school?"

"I got expelled for breaking a lunch tray over a boy's head," I tell him.

He pauses. "Oh."

"To be fair," I add, "he was harassing a girl in the cafeteria. I had to stop him."

Jackson smiles a little. "Good for you, then," he says. "I hope you knocked him out."

We go on to tell them the details, the horrifying realizations about the school and the vice principal. The invite from Lyle to go to his party later with the promise that Garrett won't be there.

"The entire school culture is out of control," I say. "If we don't stop these boys from behaving badly in high school, what are they going to become later in life?"

"Supreme Court Justices," Marcella mutters across from me.

"Mena," Raven says, drawing my attention. "It's worse than you think. I started looking into your school. I hacked into forums, ones that were password protected. The boys have been doing more than casual lunchtime harassment. They have . . . posts and pictures. Scorecards. It goes back years. It's a Ridgeview tradition."

"Bastards," Annalise says, baring her teeth.

"Then what do we do?" Marcella demands. "We have to stop them."

"What if we get them to admit it on tape?" I ask. "The party tonight at Lyle's, a few of the boys will be there."

"That's great," Marcella says. "But it's not like they're just going to tell us everything they've done. I've seen the news. They'll just lie."

"I can leak a story about the harassment going on at school to the *New York Times*," Raven offers.

Now there's something we didn't think of.

"They'll print it?" I ask.

"No," Raven says, shaking her head. "Not without more proof. Right now, there's only some anonymous posts. It's still just your word against that boy's."

"Then why does his word mean more?" I ask.

"Because he has a dick," Raven replies easily. "Trust me when I say you could have sixty female accusers and some people will still call them all liars. The process is deeply flawed."

"Then what's the point?" Marcella asks bitterly. She looks around at all of us. "What's the point of continuing to seek justice if it's never given? Why even contact the press?"

"To get the conversation started," Raven says. "Then we'll follow it up with proof. That's the thing . . ." She holds my gaze. "It's about persistence. Yes, we have to fight harder to be heard, but if we keep shouting, they'll eventually listen."

I snap my fingers. "Adrian," I say. "You mentioned witnesses. Well, she's in my class, and she's the one Garrett was harassing in the cafeteria. The vice principal said no girls have ever filed a complaint, but maybe . . . maybe she would. It can be part of the story you send to the *Times*. And maybe she could convince other girls to do the same."

Raven looks wary. "It sucks," she says. "What she'll have to go through will suck, so don't be upset if she says no."

The comment hurts me because I know Raven is right. Adrian will face an onslaught of harassment for complaining about harassment. I'm starting to see that it's how the system survives—intimidating victims. Otherwise, society would *have* to change. It's easier to play along.

"Then keep her out of it," Marcella says. "We'll handle it. We're not human. We don't have to play by their rules."

"Can, um . . . Can I make a suggestion?" Jackson asks, seeming embarrassed to interrupt.

"Why don't you let us handle things while you . . . you do whatever it is you're good at," Raven tells him.

"He's good at sticking around," Marcella says, flashing Jackson a smile.

"Thanks," he replies good-naturedly.

"What are you thinking?" I ask him, curious.

"Well, I'm thinking you're charming. Beautiful. Smart."

"Is this going somewhere?" Raven interrupts.

"It is," Jackson replies, still watching me. "Mena, you don't need to convince all those guys. You just need the most important one. Get him to own up to it and the rest will fall in line. They'll want his approval."

"Boys are so easily led?" Sydney asks.

"Some of them," Jackson says. "They want someone to look up to. If you have a guy who's claiming to be that hero, they'll trust him. They'll trust him more than they'll trust you."

"The human boy makes a good point," Marcella says. Jackson gives her an amused but quizzical look before turning back to me.

"Is there a guy like that?" he asks me. "One at the top of the food chain?"

"That would be Jonah Grant," I say. "They all listen to him. And he'll be at the party tonight," I say.

"Then so will you," Marcella says.

"And me," Sydney adds.

"Oh, can I go?" Brynn asks.

"We'll all go," Marcella says. "Just in case."

"Thanks," Annalise says. "But I'll stay here. Jackson has

given me all the male interaction I need for the day."

He looks at her. "Good?"

"Sure," she replies. "You brought pizza."

"Wait," Brynn starts, confused, "if we get the boys to admit what they've done, admit to being predators . . . then we . . .?"

"We kill them," Annalise finishes for her, reaching over to pat her leg.

"What?" Jackson asks, wide-eyed.

"*Kidding*," Annalise whispers to him, sounding like she's only half joking.

"I know a reporter," Raven interjects. "Mena, let me see your phone."

Jackson points in Annalise's general direction. "Are we not going to address that comment, or . . . ?"

I hand Raven my phone, and she pulls out the SIM card. She grabs her backpack and sets it on the coffee table. As she begins to remove small boxes and items, I lean forward.

"Although I'd love to think Jonah will just admit everything," I tell the girls, "I don't think it will be that easy. I doubt he'll take responsibility at all. And he certainly won't help us convince the other boys."

"I have an idea," Marcella says. "We go to the party, and while we distract the other guests, Mena has a moment alone with Jonah where she tries to get him to confess."

Jackson winces. "Please don't make her talk to him alone."

"I'll be with her," Sydney says. She motions for Marcella to continue.

"If Jonah doesn't admit to anything on his own," Marcella explains, "get him to confess unwittingly, strain his ego. His patience. Something will work. Then, we use his confession to convince the other boys that he turned on him." She smiles broadly, wrapping it up.

"That's so smart," Brynn says.

"I saw it on *Law and Order*," Marcella admits.

"Here," Raven says, holding my phone out to me. "I installed a recorder. It'll stream everything directly to my computer. Once you're done, we'll submit the highlights to the paper anonymously."

I take the phone, looking it over. Then I slip it inside my pocket.

"You don't need to base it on *Law and Order*," Raven says. "Just go to the party, ask about the incident at lunch, and get eyewitness accounts. Ask about past events. I have no doubt one of them will overshare. Judging by the posts they've put up, they're proud. We can use whatever recording you get for the reporter to expand upon. By the time the story runs its course, the vice principal will be dismissed, and the school will have to deal with the fallout. We might even suggest their financial disclosures get a closer look."

"Which could expose the investor," I say, making the connection. "Crimes unrelated to the corporation, but still."

"Exactly," Raven says. "It might get the school's assets frozen, which in turn would cut off the flow of money to Innovations. Expose the laundering scheme. Once I have the recordings, I'll pass them on to a few female reporters, the ones who are actually interested in justice despite repeated death threats."

"Death threats?" I ask.

"The joys of being a female public figure," Raven says sarcastically.

"She's not wrong," Jackson says.

"Oh, thank you," Raven replies. Her hostility toward him seems strangely placed.

Raven types a few things on her computer before setting it aside. She rests her elbows on her knees.

"Before we do anything else," she says, "we need to get that tracker signal out of your heads. And while I'm there, I'll put in a firewall."

I thought I would be able to let her install the software, but when she looks directly at me, I'm not so sure anymore.

"Wait," Jackson says, looking from Raven to me. "You're going to let a hacker inside your programming? I mean, wouldn't that kind of be letting a bank robber into the vault?"

"Depends what you're worried I'm going to steal, Jackson," Raven replies.

Jackson studies her, concern radiating from him. He leans toward me.

"Just consider all your options," he says to me quietly. I look at Raven.

"If I say yes to this procedure," I begin, "it would give you complete access to my programming and my memories, right? My entire existence. Essentially . . . you'd see my soul."

Raven doesn't hesitate. "That's correct," she says. Annalise looks over, surprised, but Raven doesn't acknowledge her stare.

"I'd have access to your entire self," Raven continues. "You'd have to trust me."

The room falls quiet until Sydney sighs loudly. "Do mine first," she announces. I look sideways at her and see that she's scared. But she knows that I'm not ready, so she's volunteering to ease my worry.

"What?" Sydney asks me with a shrug. "You think I'm going to let you get overwritten alone?"

"To be clear," Raven says, "I'm not overwriting anyone. Just installing a firewall."

Sydney laughs through her nerves and gets up to take a spot on the couch closer to Raven.

"You don't have to do this," I say.

"Sure," Sydney agrees. "But I'll be happy to never hear Anton's voice again."

Annalise abruptly stands and leaves the room. Marcella and I exchange a confused look.

"Jackson, can you please help me in the kitchen?" Annalise calls as she begins to run the sink.

"I'll, uh . . ." Jackson stands. "I'll see what Annalise wants while you . . ." He looks warily at Raven before turning back to me. "While you get started, I guess."

I thank him, and after he leaves, Raven digs into her backpack to remove some equipment.

"Have you thought about what you're going to do once you're at the party?" Raven asks.

I shake my head. "Not yet," I tell her. "But while I talk to the boys, I'm thinking Sydney should go through Lyle's things."

"Yes," Sydney says.

"Lucky," Marcella whispers, earning a smile. The idea of searching through people's houses holds some appeal. I'm sure Marcella has been bored out of her mind. There's only so much excitement internet research can provide.

"It will probably rule Lyle out," I say. "But that's one less suspect."

"I have an idea," Brynn says, perking up. "You said there will be other boys at the party, right? That one boy, Jonah—what if instead of going with you, Marcella and I break into his house?"

"I'm listening . . . ," Marcella says, unable to hide her smile.

"That's right," Sydney says, looking at me. "Lyle said Jonah's dad is out of town and that he'd be spending the night. So while they're at the party with us, Marcella and Brynn can search Jonah's house. That way, we can rule out two of the boys."

Marcella already has her phone, looking for the address. At the coffee table, Raven opens up one of her boxes, and I see various sizes of screwdrivers, plastic tubing. She lifts her eyes as if expecting us to be concerned. Sydney audibly gulps.

"Rest back," Raven tells her kindly, putting her hand on her shoulder.

Sydney meets my gaze as she leans her head against the sofa pillow. I'm suddenly terrified, deciding that I should have gone first just in case there was a problem.

"I love you, Mena," Sydney says.

"I love you too," I whisper.

"Now I'm going to give you something to relax," Raven says. "It's short acting, so you'll be fine after."

I watch as Raven pulls out a syringe and inserts the needle under the skin of Sydney's inner elbow. I have a sudden wave of sickness and look away.

There's a touch on my shoulder and I jump. Marcella is standing over me. "Brynn and I will wait with her. Why don't you take a break?"

"Because I want to stay with her."

When I look at Sydney again, her eyes slide closed.

Raven grabs a metal instrument from one of the cases and uses it to pry open Sydney's left eyelid, stabilizing it in that position. I watch in horror as she begins to work wires behind Sydney's eye, confident in her movements.

I'm starting to lose my nerve. Marcella helps me to my feet, and I go into the kitchen. Jackson is leaning against the counter near the sink, but when he sees me, he grabs his crutches to come over. Annalise walks past, squeezing my hand supportively before leaving the room.

Jackson stops across the table from me and sighs heavily.

"Well, this is another shitty day," he says matter-of-factly.

There's a wet sound from the couch, followed by a sharp intake of air. I can't look.

"Want to go to my bedroom?" I ask Jackson.

"Yes," he says instantly. I laugh despite the circumstances and lead him that way.

23

W hen we get inside my room, I sit on the edge of my
bed while Jackson closes the door. He makes his way
to the other side of the mattress, running his gaze
around the room.

"What did Annalise want earlier?" I ask, curious.

"She actually wanted to talk," he replies.

"To you?"

He looks at me and I laugh, letting him know I'm joking. All
the girls like Jackson, but it's kind of fun to mess with him too.
He's literally the only boy we've ever been friends with.

Jackson eases himself down on the bed and then drags himself
up to the pillows, breathing heavily when he's done. "That was
fucking hard," he murmurs.

I join him, resting the side of my head on his shoulder. He
runs his palm over my hair, easing closer as he starts to talk.

"Annalise asked if I was picking up any weird vibes from

Raven," Jackson says, sharing the information before I can ask.

"What did you say?"

"That I didn't know her well enough to judge," he replies. "So I asked Annalise what she thought."

"And?"

"And she said she trusted Raven with her life," Jackson tells me. "Said she was just curious about my opinion as an outsider."

I look toward the door, wondering if Annalise meant it. Because if Raven's vibes are weird, she shouldn't be inserting anything inside Sydney's head.

I sit up and turn to Jackson.

"Now tell me what you really think," I say.

He watches me a moment before shrugging one shoulder. "I think she's possessive of you," he says. "All of you, really. Like it's her tech or something. She definitely hates me, so, you know, take my opinion with a grain of salt."

"Why do you think that is?" I ask, looking toward the door again. "Why doesn't she like you?" He's quiet for a moment.

"Because she thinks that you do," he says. A soft smile pulls at my lips, and I look back at him. He doesn't meet my eyes at first, but when he does, I lose myself a little in the deep darkness of them. "I'm sure she doesn't know that you left me for dead, though," he adds casually.

"Don't forget the part where I tried to get your best friend mad at you so you'd stay away."

"Ah . . ." He nods. "Yes, that was my favorite part."

We watch each other before he reaches to take my hand, playing with my fingers as a way of fidgeting.

"Look, Mena," he says. "I would never tell you what to do. But for the record, I'd rather you run for the rest of your life than take the chance that a hacker has your best interests at heart. Just saying. She could shut you down for good."

"I'm not going to run," I say. "Not forever. And I don't believe she'll shut me down. But I'm wondering what you think the girls and I should do tonight. You know, an outside opinion."

"I don't know," he says. "I mean, there are so many layers to this. It's hard to know which to focus on first."

"What do you mean?" I ask.

"I mean," Jackson starts, "you can address the culture of Ridgeview and save the girls at that school. But at the same time, you might jeopardize your chance to convince an investor to turn against the corporation. Once he realizes he's under investigation by the government, he might leave the country or something. Or you can focus on the investor and let Ridgeview sort itself out."

I realize what he means. If the investor knows he's going to be charged with money laundering, he could take off. There's no guarantee it'll end up bringing down the corporation. We might lose our chance entirely. It's something to consider.

"And Mena," Jackson adds. "Even if the paper does run the story about Ridgeview, it'll mean the girls involved will eventually get named. That's the nature of the internet. Are they okay with that?"

"I don't know." Adrian didn't report the incident to Mrs. Reacher. Is it okay for me to report it for her? I look at Jackson again. "But what if I record the boys admitting to crimes?" I ask. "Would that be enough to get them in trouble without dragging other girls into it?"

Jackson's voice is sorry when he replies, "I don't think so."

I close my eyes, knowing he's right. We need proof. Our word isn't enough. Eyewitness accounts aren't enough. Even if we have video of them admitting it, they'll spin it. They'll hire PR firms to discredit the claims, provide alternative theories.

There's no accountability.

"We need to do something," I say. "The boys at that school are out of control. They're dangerous."

"More dangerous than Innovations Academy?" he asks. "Than the corporation?"

And I think about it. I really do. Although I know we need to take down the corporation . . . I can't sit by and watch the injustice of it all. The boys at Ridgeview need to be stopped. Otherwise, they'll grow up to be the terrible men of Innovations Academy. Unchecked, they'll continue to abuse their power, abuse it to get them elected to high offices so they can continue to hurt others. I can't let that happen.

Even if not a single human girl would stand up for me, I have no choice but to stand up for her.

"You're going to help them, aren't you?" Jackson asks softly. "The girls at Ridgeview?"

"Yes," I say. "It's the right thing to do."

"Just because one feels more urgent doesn't mean both causes aren't right," Jackson says, running his fingertips along my wrist.

The tender movement is comforting. "Is there anything I can do?" he asks. "Want me to come to the party with you?"

I smile. "I think that might change the dynamic, but I appreciate the offer."

"Just promise to call me if you need anything. I'll be there in a second, okay?"

"Okay," I whisper.

"And could you . . . Would you mind calling or texting me when you get home?" he asks. "Just so I know that you're okay."

I promise that I will, and then Jackson flexes his hand so that my fingers slip between his. The movement feels surprisingly intimate, and he licks his lips.

Are you attracted to him? Anton asked me once during impulse control therapy.

The analyst didn't think I could feel attraction; he told me as much. Neither do Leandra or Winston Weeks. And yet . . . here I am. Madly attracted to this human boy who's reckless and curses too much.

I lean toward Jackson, ready to kiss him. Wanting to touch him. My eyes close, but just before I reach him, he turns his head away. His other hand immediately rests on the side of my neck and I realize it's to gently hold me back.

"Mena, uh . . . ," he whispers, sounding pained. "We shouldn't, uh . . ."

I open my eyes, feeling humiliated when he stares back at me. I flash a quick smile to diffuse the embarrassment, and I straighten. I completely misread the situation, but when I try to apologize, he shakes his head to stop me. He looks tortured, and it occurs to me that he doesn't want to kiss me because I'm not human. And that's the biggest sting of the rejection.

But I don't resent him for it.

When it comes down to it, I know that I can count on Jackson. Trust him to show up for me. For all the girls.

And I also know that despite everything, despite it not being part of my programming, I might be a little bit in love with him.

"I should check on Sydney," I whisper, getting up from the bed. My fingers slide from Jackson's hand as I move toward the door. I'm shaking, but as I walk into the living room, I do my best to pretend nothing's wrong.

On the couch, Sydney is stirring. Brynn waits beside her, holding a glass of water for her to drink.

"We're all set," Raven tells Sydney, clicking a button on the computer before showing it to her. Sydney seems a bit out of sorts, probably due to the sedatives, but she doesn't seem to be in any pain.

"Your programming looked great," Raven explains to her. "Firewall installed, and I didn't see any problems. Other than that small signal I blocked, everything was in working order. And beautiful," she adds warmly.

There really must not be a kill switch. It would have shown up when Raven was in there—she's too smart to have missed it.

I glance around the room and find Annalise staring out the window again with that unnatural stillness. I call her name softly, but it takes her a long moment to look at me. I walk over to join her at the window.

"What's going on?" I ask. "Did something happen with—?"

"I'm still having headaches, you know," Annalise says calmly. "Nightmares. I'm in pain all the time." She turns to me, and it's like there's a shadow over her. Something deep and dark and lonely. I physically sway, putting my hand on my heart.

"Annalise," I start, "we should—"

"I'm not going to make it, Mena," she whispers. "You need to be prepared for that."

"Raven can fix you," I say. "She can rebuild; we can—"

"Trust me," she says. "I know my own body."

"Then we'll figure it out," I say, confused. "I'll learn how and do it myself if I have to."

"I know you'd try."

Annalise smiles, but there is an indescribable sense of dread clawing at my throat. I would never be prepared to lose Annalise.

"Then what is it you want me to do?" I ask. She's clearly thinking of something.

"I'm dying," she whispers. I shake my head, but she takes me by the upper arms. "I'm dying," she repeats.

I begin to crumple, but Annalise holds me up.

"But I need to make sure the girls at the academy are safe before I go," she continues. "So while you're at the party tonight, I'm going back there. I'm going to find our girls, and then I'm going to burn Innovations Academy to the ground. I'll make sure they never come after us again."

"What?" I ask loudly enough to make Raven look over. Annalise lowers her hands from my arms, but her eyes beg me not to say anything. I shift my position to block our faces from view.

"That's . . . ridiculous," I tell her. "How would you even get there?"

"I have a plan," she says. "But I have to do it alone."

"We do nothing alone," I point out. And this time, I'm a little angry. "You don't get to leave us," I say. "We stay together, no matter what."

"Not this time."

Separating us was a form of punishment the academy would inflict. The idea that Annalise wants to do it willingly is even more painful.

"If you tell the others now," Annalise says, "they'll be too upset to go through with tonight. That means the Ridgeview boys will get away with everything. The corporation will continue creating and selling girls. I'm asking you to believe in me, Mena. I'm . . ." She pauses a moment. "I'm asking you to let me go do what needs to be done."

"Then why even tell me?" I ask, my eyes welling up. "Why didn't you just leave?"

Her eyes soften and she leans in to hug me, stopping me from completely falling apart.

"Because we've been together from the beginning," she whispers. "And I needed you here at the end."

I close my eyes, and tears slip down my cheeks. I hug her back fiercely. I want us all to stay together, but I don't get to demand it. We're individuals, we're fighting for our right to exist. I have no doubt that Annalise is trying to help us. I can't take that away.

But I'm also not giving up on her.

I straighten, quickly wiping my face. "You have to come back," I say, and I clear my throat. "You do this, but then you come back. At least give me the chance to save you."

She nods that she will.

When Raven calls my name, I wait a beat to calm myself before turning to her.

"I'm ready for you," Raven says.

Brynn helps Sydney to her feet, and they go into the kitchen. Annalise follows behind them, announcing that she'll make tea.

Raven pats the empty space on the couch, inviting me to sit.

Jackson appears in my doorway, leaning against the frame with his crutches in front of him. He looks wrecked, either from our earlier interaction or from his worry that I'm about to get wires pressed into my head; perhaps both. I debate what to do.

I'm terrified. I really am. I can still back out of this, back out of everything except for finding a way to get to the investor. We don't need to save the girls from the predators at Ridgeview, but I can't abandon them. I'm just not built that way.

I go over to the couch and lie back, my head on the pillow at the end. I'm shaking, and Raven reaches out to put her warm hand on my arm. I turn to her, holding her dark gaze.

"I won't hurt you, Mena," she says softly.

I close my eyes, giving her permission to get started. And yet . . . I'm still not entirely sure I believe her.

But to change the world, a girl occasionally has to put her trust in human beings.

24

slowly stir, and my eyelids flutter open. At first, there is a sharp pain behind my left eye, and I hold up my hand to block the overhead light. There's a strange feedback sound in my head. Static.

"How are you feeling?" Raven asks.

I look sideways at her, slightly disoriented. "Tired," I say.

"It'll wear off in a few minutes."

I look toward the kitchen, and Sydney waves. She seems to be doing fine, and my worry dissipates. Raven watches me before turning her computer around.

"You're fucking amazing," she says. It takes a second for me to realize she's talking about my programming. On her screen, there are patterns and waves—unmistakably me. I meet her eyes.

"Did you . . . Did you notice anything wrong?" I ask.

Raven turns the computer around, clicking into a different

screen, "Not anything unexpected," she says easily. "You're perfect."

I hate that word. But at the same time, I'm relieved. Jackson really must have misinterpreted the paperwork he gave us. I look around and find him sitting in the chair across the living room, gnawing on his fingernail. He nods hello.

"That was fucking intense," he tells me. I sniff a laugh and rest my head back again.

"No one can hack you now," Raven says. "You're completely safe."

Marcella walks out of her bedroom, zipping up her leather coat. When she sees I'm awake, she taps on her watch.

"It's getting late," she says. "Brynn and I need to head out soon. Scope out the place before we go inside."

She's enjoying the idea of breaking in far too much.

Marcella holds out her open palm, and Jackson tosses her the keys to his rental car.

"Do you even know how to drive?" he asks.

"Yes," she replies. "I've seen it online."

"Uh . . ." Jackson looks ready to argue, but Marcella thanks him and turns away before he gets the chance.

"By the way," she tells me. "Lennon Rose called here looking for you."

"She did?" I ask, sitting up, surprised. "Did she want me to call her back?"

"Didn't say," Marcella replies.

"Well," Annalise mutters from the table. "I'm glad Lennon Rose is reaching out to someone other than Winston Weeks.

You know, someone normal who isn't trying to build an all-girl robot army." Brynn snorts a laugh.

I watch Annalise, still thinking about our conversation, but she purposely avoids eye contact with me.

"We should start getting ready too," Sydney announces, sounding impatient.

Although I know Sydney still loves Lennon Rose, she doesn't trust her the same way she used to. We can't even blame it all on Winston Weeks, either. Lennon Rose is also involved with Rosemarie, the mother of our programming, who writes violent poetry.

It's like . . . we don't know our friend anymore. And that would be fine if it weren't for the fact that we don't know who's influencing her new behavior.

"Can I help you get ready?" Brynn asks, standing up from the table. "I really miss getting ready together. Do we have time?" she asks Marcella. Marcella smiles at her and nods.

"Thanks, Brynn," I say. "I'd love that." And I would. Although we never liked being told how to style ourselves, we did enjoy the ritual of getting ready. It was oddly comforting. It could have been more comforting with a caring teacher, I suppose. But we had Leandra. And she's a psychopath, so I'm not sure she feels anything at all.

Brynn goes into my room, but before I follow her, I glance back at Jackson. "Are you going to stay here while we're at the party?" I ask.

He checks on Raven, who is actively ignoring him.

"Naw," he tells me. "I'll take a cab to my place. I should let you get ready," he adds. "Text me later?"

"Later," I agree.

He smiles softly, a little sadly, and leaves the apartment. I wait a moment after he's gone, wondering if his sadness is regret.

"Oh, Mena," Brynn calls from my room. "You should definitely wear this!" She pulls a sundress from my closet. It's not really my style—I'd rather wear pants. But we picked it up at a thrift store when we first got to town after I saw a few girls walking around in something similar. The dress is pretty in a delicate sort of way.

"It'll make you look really innocent," Brynn says. She holds it against herself and studies her reflection in the mirror. "And boys will tell girls like that anything because they're not threatened by them. They'll think they have you manipulated. It'll be their mistake."

I stare at Brynn, wondering where exactly she heard that. She smiles. "I've been streaming a lot of reality TV while you're at school," she says. "I think I'm starting to understand human behavior better." She holds up the dress again. "So what do you think?" she asks.

"I think you're right," I say, and take the dress from her hands. She exhales and walks over to start sorting through my jewelry.

Marcella and Brynn have already left when it's time for Sydney and me to go. We check that my phone will stream directly to Raven's computer. When we're sure, I say goodbye to her, and Sydney and I head for the door.

"Wait," Annalise calls. I take my time turning around, afraid I'll fall apart. She comes to stand in front of me, her brilliant red hair cascading over her shoulder, her green and brown eyes twinkling with a layer of tears.

"Be careful," she whispers like a wish. But I'm panicking.

What if I never see her again?

When do I tell the other girls?

How could she do this to me?

Annalise leans in to press a soft kiss to my lips. I close my eyes, holding back my tears, as she rests her forehead against mine.

"Love you," she whispers. I murmur that I love her too.

Unable to hold it together, I turn away and walk to the door with Sydney. At the last second, I look back.

"Promise I'll see you later," I tell Annalise. I feel Sydney look sideways at me, confused.

Annalise smiles, holding her hand up in a wave.

"Bye, girls," she says.

"Bye," Sydney responds, and opens the door. We walk out without the promise of ever seeing Annalise again.

Sydney and I order a car service, and as we ride to the address Lyle gave me, I stare out the window. I think about Annalise, reminded of one of our oldest memories together. Long before we were . . . us.

We were alone in the greenhouse on the property of Innovations Academy, the sun streaming through the glass, falling over my cheeks and warming them. It was a rare sunny day in the mountains.

"Do you know what I love?" Annalise said, her blond hair in a high bun since none of the professors were around to tell her how to wear it. Her gardening books were open on the small table.

"Should I guess?" I responded, making her laugh.

"This." She walked over to caress a hanging flower. It was pretty, a soft delicate bell dangling on a wooden stem. "This is Angel's Trumpet," Annalise continued. "The best part? It's toxic. Paralysis, memory lapses, death. Did you ever think something so pretty could be so dangerous?"

I studied the flower and then Annalise. "Probably not good for them to grow those so close to our food though, right?" I asked.

"Silly. They're already in our food. But maybe one day Professor Penchant will accidentally take too much." Annalise smiled and went back to reciting the names in her books.

And even then, even though I never spoke it out loud, I knew Annalise had designs on putting poison in the staff's food, although she never got the chance.

She wanted to burn down the academy from the first day she woke up there. In a way, she was always awake. She just needed it confirmed.

"What's wrong?" Sydney asks, startling me from my thoughts. I turn to her in the backseat of the car just as it pulls into a modest neighborhood not far from our apartment.

"Nothing," I say, waving it off.

"Well, get focused," she says, checking her reflection in her phone camera. "We're going to have to be annoyingly charming." She looks sideways. "Hopefully for the last time. Because I'll tell you what, no matter what we do next, I'm not attending school again."

"Maybe we'll give public school a shot next time," I suggest.

The driver pulls up to Lyle's house, and Sydney taps her phone screen to pay him. After climbing out of the backseat, we pause on the sidewalk and look at the house. There are only a few cars parked on the street, so it's definitely not a huge party. Which is perfect.

I take out my phone and check for any missed calls. When I see there are none, I text Raven to let her know we've arrived. I click record on the phone, slide it into my clutch purse, and head toward the front door of Lyle's house.

I knock, and there are voices on the other side of the door, a "Shhh . . . ," and then it opens. Lyle smiles widely.

"You actually came," he says, out of breath. "I figured . . ." He shakes his head, glancing back inside the house. "Well, I'm glad you're both here."

"Hi, Lyle," Sydney says brightly.

Lyle steps aside and motions us into the foyer. "Come on in," he calls, grinning from ear to ear.

Sydney and I go inside, and I immediately notice the big guy from the rugby team sitting at the foot of the stairs, drinking from a red cup. He's the one who told the security guard to relax. Demarcus stands and leans on the railing when we walk in.

"Demarcus Dozer," he calls, introducing himself. His smile is warm, and I think that in person, he doesn't seem as vicious as he does on the field. It's an interesting contrast between life and game time, how aggression is encouraged in some cases.

"Philomena," I reply.

"Welcome," he says, lifting his drink in cheers before sitting back down.

I take in the rest of the room. There are two guys I don't recognize on the couch, mid-conversation. The living room is well decorated, although not elaborate. Nothing like Winston Weeks's place. This is homey and inviting.

There are footsteps before Jonah Grant appears in the doorway of the kitchen, holding a red cup.

"This is a nice surprise," he says. He sips from his drink, looking me over. It's not predatory, but it is expectant. Like I should return the compliment immediately. I decide I might need to play along to gain their trust.

"Yes, it's nice to see you too," I say. He chuckles and I realize I've answered far too formally. I'll have to work on that. "This is my friend Sydney," I say, nudging her arm.

"Hey," she calls to him, sounding effortlessly cool. Jonah grins and replies with his own "Hey."

"Do you want a drink?" Lyle asks us. He seems extra nervous, so I accept the offer even though I don't plan to drink. Sydney declines, and gazes around instead.

"Lyle," Sydney says after a moment, "do you mind if I use your bathroom?" She skips directly to the mission, which I can appreciate. I would have maybe put in an appearance first, but I trust her judgment.

"Sure," Lyle says. He motions to a hallway on the other side of the stairs. "Second door on the left. Next to my mom's office."

"Great!" Sydney replies. She hikes up one eyebrow to let me know she's going to search the office for paperwork. When she leaves, I follow behind Lyle toward the kitchen.

When I get to where Jonah is standing in the doorway, he waits an extra beat before moving out of the way. He stares down at me, almost curiously, as he sips from his cup. I'm starting to feel a bit on edge. It's only occurring to me now that Sydney and I are outnumbered. We should have considered that sooner.

Lyle grabs a cup from a plastic sleeve and fills it with various liquids lined up along the counter.

"Here you go," he says proudly, holding it out to me. When I take the drink from his hands, he reaches out his own in cheers. I force another smile and knock my cup against his. I pretend to sip from my drink. The smell of it makes my eyes water.

"Are you two going to hide in here all night?"

I turn and find Jonah looking bored as he enters the kitchen. He wants my attention, and I think it bothers him that I won't give it easily.

"Would you like a tour?" he asks me.

I laugh. "You don't even live here," I say.

"Then we'll discover it together," he says. "Come on. Give me a reason to stick around. I want to get to know you better." He smiles. "You're so mysterious."

It takes all my patience to not roll my eyes. He thinks he's charming, but in truth, his words sound like well-rehearsed lines. They're inauthentic. But I nod.

"Sure," I tell him, and then glance at Lyle. He seems hurt that I'm leaving, and I debate it, but ultimately, I'm here on a mission. That means helping Lyle feel better about himself doesn't make the list.

I walk with Jonah into the living room, and he introduces me to "the guys." He doesn't bother naming them, and they seem to take the hint. I get a few chilly waves, and then I see their side glances at each other. Jonah has called dibs.

"Now," he says, "I think there's an office or something over here." We start to round the stairs, and I worry about walking in on Sydney mid-search. I quickly grab Jonah's arm.

"Wait," I tell him, completely at a loss for what to say next. He looks down at where I'm touching him, and I quickly drop my hand.

"What's upstairs?" I ask, lifting my cup in that direction. Jonah smiles slyly and it turns my stomach.

"Let's go find out," he replies in a breathy voice. He reaches for my hand, and I let him take it as he leads me toward the steps. His palm is wet and warm, and I think I might throw up a little, so I take a sip from my drink, wincing the second I do.

As Jonah pulls me up the stairs, I crane my neck over the railing to see if I can catch Sydney, but all the doors to the rooms are closed. For now, I'm on my own.

"Turn up the music!" Jonah yells, slapping his hand on the railing. The other guys cheer the suggestion and turn it up loud enough for the bass to rattle the windows.

25

The staircase is narrow, so thankfully, Jonah drops my hand to walk in front of me. My phone buzzes in my purse, but I don't check it, worried that it'll tip Jonah off that I'm recording him. As we ascend, I notice the row of framed pictures on the wall. There are photos of Lyle—school pictures of him throughout the years in various stages of awkwardness.

It occurs to me that I don't have pictures like that. I was never a little girl. I was never the awkward child. There's a devastating reality to that, the fact that I'm not like any of these people. I'm not people.

When we get to the second story, the ceilings are low, but again, it's kind of homey. There are four doors, two on each side of the hallway.

Jonah looks back over his shoulder at me, smiling like we're having great fun. He opens the first door and peers inside.

"This must be Matty's room," he says, poking his head around

before closing it, I'm surprised at the level of respect he's showing
Lyle's little brother, but then I remember that Matt's on the team.
This clearly gives him worth.

We get to the next door, and Jonah opens it and then quickly
shuts it, turning to me with a smile. "I think this one's Mommy's
room," he says.

He is insufferable and I'm not sure how much longer I can
pretend to find him entertaining.

"Should we check her drawers?" he asks, wiggling his eyebrows.

Okay, that might actually work.

"Yes," I say, and he steps back with exaggerated shock.

"Philomena," he says. "I thought you were a good girl."

My skin crawls, and I'm barely able to contain myself before
reaching to touch his arm, smiling innocently.

"What?" I ask playfully. "I'm curious."

*Actually, Jonah, I need to search through her belongings to see if
she's part of the system that's trying to decommission me. Mind?*

He opens the door and ushers me inside. The room is dark
at first, and I have a sinking feeling before he flicks the light on.
Relieved, I turn as Jonah closes the door, a grin on his lips.

The room itself is average, the bed unmade. A pile of laun-
dry waiting to be folded on a chair in the corner. There's a small
desk near the closet. I immediately cross to it and begin sorting
through the drawers.

"Oh, hey. Check this out," Jonah says excitedly. He reaches into
the drawer of the bedside table and pulls out a pack of condoms.

He begins to laugh, waving it like it's something unusual. I, for one, commend Lyle's mom on her safe-sex practices. When I show no sign of amusement, Jonah drops them back in the drawer and slams it shut, looking for something else to impress me.

He is *exhausting*.

In the desk, I find some bills, a few receipts, and a stack of printed emails. Curious, I pick one up and see that it's from Lyle's dad, arguing about child-support payments. Lyle's mom must have printed them out. There's nothing about Ridgeview other than a copy of Lyle's last report card.

Disappointed, I close the drawer.

"This is kind of awesome," Jonah says, sliding open the window at the back of the house. I get on my tiptoes, looking past him. There's an expanse of roof just outside, making its own little slanted patio.

"Come on," Jonah coaxes, holding out his hand to me. "We'll finish our drinks out there. Talk."

Right. We have to talk.

I leave my too-strong drink on the desk and head his way. Jonah climbs out the window first, and then he takes my elbow to help me. When I'm standing outside, a soft breeze rustles my hair. It feels good, free, in the night air. I went years without going out in the nighttime, trapped behind barred windows.

Jonah takes a spot on the roof and pats the tiles next to him for me to sit. I carefully walk that way, making sure I don't fall, and sit down. For a few moments, it's peaceful. The breeze, the bass of the music from downstairs. The crickets in the garden.

"So . . . ," Jonah says, knocking his knee against mine. "Heard you had an interesting afternoon." He laughs and takes another sip of his drink. In the moonlight, his eyes are glassy, a buzz of alcohol probably working through his system right now.

I hope the phone is recording our conversation. I set my purse between us to assure his voice can get picked up.

"Did you see what happened?" I ask him. Jonah smirks, shaking his head.

"No," he says. "I have a different lunch hour. Wasn't the first time, though. Dude can never keep his hands to himself."

"You're talking about Garrett?" I ask.

"The one and only," Jonah replies.

"So he has a reputation?"

"You talk like an adult, you know," he says. "It's kind of weird."

I reach to twist a lock of hair around my finger, smiling. "Good girl, remember?"

Jonah laughs and takes a sloppy sip from his cup. "Yeah, all right. I like it," he says. "Anyway, fucking Garrett. Last semester he locked himself in the art room closet with Bernice. It was wild," Jonah says. "I mean, he didn't even touch her, but I thought she was going to stab out his eyes."

Maybe she should have.

"And he doesn't get in trouble?" I ask, pretending to sound fascinated.

"For what?" Jonah asks. "I just said he didn't touch her."

I don't know, how about false imprisonment? A number of other harassment charges?

Jonah licks his lips before his mouth turns up in a grin. "Not you, though," he says. "I heard you broke a lunch tray over his head. What did he do? Hand up your skirt?"

I physically recoil from the suggestion, and Jonah laughs an apology.

"No," I say. "It wasn't me. He was pretending that Adrian was . . ." I know I have to stop being so formal, but I'm truly not sure how to word this. "That she was jerking him off," I say quickly, internally cringing. "She was crying. It was traumatic."

But Jonah scoffs.

"Crying? What a baby," he says. He uses his cup to point at me. "We need more girls like you," he says. "Ones who like to fight a little. You can hold your own, Mena. What made you so brave?"

Dealing with men like you.

The wind blows my hair across my face, sticking it to my lip gloss. I peel it away.

"I'm not sure how I got this way," I say sweetly. *But I might have a guess.*

Jonah stares at me like he's trying to figure me out. Between us, my phone begins buzzing again.

"Should you get that?" he asks dreamily. He leans noticeably closer.

"It can wait," I say. I pretend to feel something crawling on my leg and use it as an excuse to move back a few inches. Jonah trails me with his eyes.

"Why aren't you dating anyone?" he asks. I don't want to

stray into this conversation, I need him to stay focused.

"Do the other boys act like Garrett?" I ask. "Locking girls in rooms?"

He stares at me a moment, seeming confused. He takes a drink. "No. I've never had to lock a girl in a room to have sex with me, if that's what you're implying."

"I'm sure you haven't," I say. "It just seems . . ." I search for the right way to phrase this. "It seems that at least Garrett does this a lot. I wondered if I should watch out for others."

"Stick with me and you won't have to," he replies. He's growing tense, possessive.

"I'm thinking about my friends," I say. "Who they should look out for?"

"I don't know what you're really asking," he says. "But none of us do anything that they didn't beg for first. The girls at school? They beg."

I hate him. It comes so clearly to me. I hate him and everything he stands for. The sense of entitlement, privilege. That girls being afraid of his reaction is the same as consent. Jonah thinks he *deserves* girls. That they're his possessions.

And I understand why the men of Innovations created us. It's not just about the needs of guys like Jonah. They fill the desires of men who don't have youth or looks or popularity, to give them the access that Jonah has. Through Innovations, they can buy it. They can buy us.

"And after you give those girls . . . what they begged for?" I ask.

Jonah sips from his cup before crushing it and tossing it off the roof into the yard. "Well, after that they're sluts and I'm not interested," he says. "But you . . . You seem fun. You might be able to hold my attention for more than three seconds."

It's a telling statement, and I debate infuriating him to make him spill details. But his irritation with the topic is making his cheeks glow red, splotches appearing on his neck.

"Why are you asking so many questions?" Jonah says. "Marsh already told us to leave you alone, so I don't know if you've got something going on with him, but—"

"Mr. Marsh did what?" I ask, surprised.

Jonah pauses. "Yeah, the history teacher is suddenly Mr. Fucking Proper. Told us to leave you alone or he'd file a report. I told him I'd have his job if he ever talked to me like that again. So if you're—"

"I don't have any kind of relationship with Mr. Marsh," I say, cutting him off.

Mr. Marsh had allowed the harassment by not saying anything, but it seems that he's finally standing up to the boys at school. He's finally doing the right thing.

"Then what is this?" Jonah asks, motioning between us. "Do you want to hook up or not?"

And I realize that if Mr. Marsh is willing to report the boys, if he's willing to stand up to them, we don't need undercover recordings and anonymous posts. What we need is for good people to stand up against bad people—simple really. But in this society, they never put the burden on men to be the good people in this scenario. Maybe Marsh is willing to change that. I need to call the girls and talk to them.

"No," I tell Jonah, getting to my feet. "We are definitely not hooking up." I teeter slightly on the slanted roof but hold out my arms to find my balance.

"Wait, *what?*" Jonah asks, a sudden darkness in his voice that sends goosebumps over my skin. When I look back at him, I can see his hurt ego. His anger.

Next to him, my phone buzzes again in my purse. When I start toward it, he grabs it and holds it out of my reach on the other side of him.

"Give me my purse," I say, annoyed, but also worried.

"Who the hell has been calling?" he demands. He begins to go through my purse, tossing items that are in the way as he tries to get to my phone. My eyes widen and I rush over, my shoes slipping on the tile and sending me hip-first onto the roof, the rough material scraping my thigh. Jonah chuckles.

He takes out my phone and then tosses my purse over the edge. He freezes, staring at my phone for a moment before turning to me in silence. His eyes are raging. On the screen, the red button shows that it's recording.

"Jonah," I say, as a way of explaining. He quickly turns off the recording and then cocks back his arm and throws my phone over the side of the house as hard as he can. There's a rustle of bushes across the yard.

I'm scared. I step back from him as he gets to his feet. I quickly turn and rush for the window. I barely get one foot inside before he wraps his arm around my waist, yanking me back. We both lose our balance and crash onto the roof tiles.

I roll a few times, but right myself before tumbling off the side. Jonah pulls himself to his full height, blocking my path to the window.

"You were trying to get me to confess?" he demands. "To tell on my friends?"

There's no use in pretending anymore. I lose all pretense of flirtation or nicety.

"We saw the posts online," I tell him. "The bragging. Tomorrow, it'll be in the papers. You've terrorized girls, but you're not going to get away with it anymore."

"We'll do whatever we want," he says. "Who are you? No one even knows you. A few posts online? Prove it came from us."

He doesn't think he has anything to worry about. He feels invincible. No one should ever feel that way—like they could commit a crime out in the open and get away with it. No one should ever feel that emboldened.

"Let me inside," I say plainly.

"None of the girls will go against us," he says. "You'll see."

He and the others may have scared the girls into silence before, but with us on their side, with proof, with administrative support, maybe that will change. There's no way to know for certain, but I do know that I need to get off this roof through the window behind Jonah. And he doesn't seem likely to budge.

I run for it. I catch Jonah off guard, dodging to the side at

the same time I push him. His foot slips, and I use that distraction to quickly climb through the window. Just as I'm about
to run for the bedroom door, Jonah reaches inside to grab the
bottom of my dress. He knots his fist in the fabric, tearing the
hem. I try to turn, but I get tangled as he drags me back toward
the open window.

Flashbacks to my last fight with the Guardian suddenly flood
in. The guilt I once had over his death is replaced with my need
for survival. The Guardian killed Annalise that night. I'm not
going to let Jonah kill me.

Before he can pull me back through, I grip the top of the
window frame and slam it down on Jonah's arm. There's a loud
scream behind the glass, and he releases my dress. I fall backward,
landing hard on the wood floor.

Jonah is unable to get the window back open with one
hand, his palm sliding along the glass. Instead, he slowly pulls
his trapped arm through, crying out in pain. Once it's free, he
pushes up the frame roughly. I see the bruise already on his forearm just below his elbow, a scrape all the way to his wrist.

"Stay there!" he snarls at me.

I'm not about to be held prisoner in an upstairs bedroom.
I rush out the door, darting toward the stairs. I need to get to
Sydney.

"Wait!" Jonah yells from the room, followed by a loud rumble
as he crashes to the bedroom floor.

Lyle suddenly appears at the top of the stairs, eyes wide when he sees me running toward him. He quickly assesses my torn dress, looking like he's about to puke. He holds out his hand.

"Help me!" I say desperately, the music louder now that I'm near the stairs.

Lyle reaches to take my forearm, steadying me. Even though I don't mean to, I start to cry. Jonah scared me, terrified me.

Jonah bursts from the room, hitting the opposite wall before straightening himself. He's drunk. His eyes are red and glassy, perspiration dots his face. He sighs with relief when he sees I'm with Lyle.

"Bring her back over," he tells him, waving down the hall.

I turn to Lyle, getting my foot on the first step down before he tightens his grip on my arm. I lift my eyes to his, but rather than finding protection or sympathy, I find fear. He darts his gaze from me to Jonah.

And then I realize that he's not scared for me. He values Jonah's inclusion over my safety. He would gladly feed me to the wolves in order to join their pack.

Lyle's fingers pinch my skin as they tighten their grasp. I try to yank away, stunned by his sudden strength when he begins to pull me toward the bedroom. Understanding that he plans to hand me over to Jonah, I scream for Sydney. I'm not sure if she can hear me over the downstairs music.

With no other choice, I slap Lyle hard across the face, hoping to snap him out of this. He bares his teeth at me.

He's not the nice guy. He's just another monster with anger

that he can't contain, living in a community that makes him believe it's acceptable.

Lyle drags me down the hall, and when I'm close enough, Jonah grabs me roughly by the elbow.

"Relax," Jonah says, as if I'm overreacting. "We need to talk." He pushes me inside the room.

The Nice Guy

He is my friend.

He'd never hurt me.
Why would he?
He's such a nice guy.

He'd never hold me down.
Why would he?
He's such a nice guy.

He'd never leave me crying on the floor.
Why would he?
He's such a nice guy.

He'd never lie to my face about what he'd done.
Why would he?
He's such a nice guy.

He'd never laugh with his friends as I walked past.
Why would he?
He's such a nice guy.

He'd never say I wanted it.
Why would he?
He's such a nice guy.

He would never call me a slut.
He would never have his friends do the same.
He would never threaten me to keep me quiet.
He would never make me want to die.

Why would he?
He's such a nice guy.

26

Jonah laughs out loud as he closes the door, pushing me into the chair at the desk. He looks at Lyle. "Nice work," he says to him. "Didn't think you had it in you, big boy."

Lyle smiles at Jonah expectantly, like he's waiting for a pat on the head.

Jonah begins to pace and takes out his phone. I have no idea what he plans to say to me, do with me. I eye the door, readying myself to run for it the second I get the chance. Jonah dials, watching me as he brings the phone to his ear. He jumps as a voice comes on the line.

"Yeah," he says. "I need to talk to my father. I don't care who he's having dinner with, this is important."

"Who's your father?" I ask, worried that I've found the investor's son after all.

"My dad?" Jonah says. "He's the best fucking lawyer in town.

So if you're thinking you're going to get some big settlement, think again."

"Does he work for the corporation?" I ask.

Jonah can't hide his annoyance. "What? He doesn't work for anyone. He has his own firm." He turns to the side as someone comes back on the phone line. "Yes, I'm still here," he says impatiently. "Can you hurry?"

Jonah continues to block my path to the door. His intimidation is meant to keep me in place. What will happen when his lawyer father arrives? If they truly feel there are no consequences to their behavior . . . what's going to happen to me?

"Dad," Jonah says suddenly into the phone. "We need your help. It's a girl, and . . ." He pauses, wincing once. "Look, I'm at a friend's house, and this girl made me say some shit. She recorded it." He looks at me. "Yeah, she's still here. Okay." Jonah turns away from me, seeming uncomfortable. "An *hour*? How do you want me to stop her?" he asks quietly.

Jonah listens for a bit, nodding along, and then he murmurs goodbye and hangs up. He slips the phone back into his pocket.

"What's your father going to do to me?" I ask. "What's he going to do when he gets here?"

Jonah opens his mouth to answer when the door creaks open.

We all look over and my heart leaps. Sydney is standing there with the big guy, Demarcus, at her side.

And she's holding a wooden bat.

I nearly start to cry. To see a girl again . . . It's everything. It's love and safety.

"Get away from her," Sydney tells Jonah in a low voice. "Get away or I'll bash your head in."

Jonah gulps, but then puffs up his chest to hide his initial worry. "What are you doing?" he asks Demarcus, ignoring the threat. "Take the—"

"What am *I* doing?" Demarcus repeats angrily. "Question is, what the fuck are *you* doing? Now you're kidnapping girls and shit?"

"No," Jonah says, shaking his head. "I . . . She recorded me talking about Garrett. She's going to report him and—"

"Good," Demarcus says. "That guy belongs in jail."

"Thank you," Sydney says, nodding her agreement. "Took you long enough."

Demarcus presses his lips together, a quick show of shame. Although he said something in the cafeteria, he didn't do anything. He didn't demand change. He may have turned his back other times, but he's showing up now. Like Mr. Marsh, he's finally showing up.

I get to my feet, but Jonah pushes me back down. Sydney readies her bat, but Demarcus comes to stand in front of me, making Jonah take an unsteady step back.

"Hey," Jonah says, sounding nervous. "Relax, it's okay."

Sydney meets my eyes. Funny that he's worried about the guy when she's the one with the bat. In a way, Jackson was right. Men tend to defer to the opinions of other men.

"You can't just let her leave," Jonah says. He even laughs. "Look, man," Jonah tells Demarcus. "My dad will be here soon.

He'll know what to do. I mean . . . she found posts that some of the guys put online. They admitted to everything like a bunch of idiots. I mean, even Lyle isn't that stupid."

For his part, Lyle stands silently. He must see that he's still not accepted by the group he coveted.

"Wow . . . ," Sydney says, tapping her lower lip as she thinks it over. "You're exactly how I thought you'd be. What's it like to be so vile that you can't even beat the lowest of standards?"

She says all of this with an eerie calm, a statement of fact rather than opinion.

"If your father wasn't rich," she says, "you would have nothing. No one cares about you. A few fear you, sure. But no one admires you. Why would they?"

"Shut the fuck up!" he shouts back. She's gotten under his skin.

"That's what you rely on," Sydney continues, taking a step toward him. "Telling girls to shut up so they can't tell you that you're average, maybe even slightly below. Insecure men seek power to make up for their shortcomings. And you, Jonah Grant, will never have power again."

There is a small moment of worry in Jonah's expression before he shakes his head. "I'm not scared of a couple of girls," he says.

Sydney smiles. "You should be," she whispers. When Jonah backs down, Sydney gives him one more look of disgust and moves past him to reach out her hand to me.

I take it, but as we start to leave, Jonah darts over and snatches the bat out of Sydney's hand. He holds it at his side, eyes wild, as he blocks the door.

"Are you both insane?" he asks, his voice shaking. "You think you can just . . . walk out of here? No." He glances once at Demarcus, seeming to dismiss him. "There are other guys down there. Ones who aren't fucking weak. Once I tell them what you were planning . . . well, I can't stop them from what they'll do." He laughs, but it's forced. He's betting that the threat of violence will make us endure more of *his* violence.

Sydney drops my hand and takes a step toward Jonah. She tilts her head, looking at him.

"I was hoping I wouldn't have to use this," she says. She looks back at me and smiles. "Leandra told us to always be prepared."

Sydney takes a small object from her purse. At first, I think it's a phone, but there is a blue light and I realize it's a Taser. She jabs it into Jonah's ribs, and he shouts before the sound reverberates in his chest, echoing around the room.

He hits the floor.

"Damn, girl," Demarcus says under his breath. Sydney shrugs. Demarcus steps over Jonah's trembling body and opens the door for us, standing aside so we can walk out. When Lyle starts to move, all of Demarcus's nicety fails.

"Stay," he warns Lyle, telling him to go sit down.

We watch as Lyle nervously takes a seat at the desk, his bravado completely deflated. When we turn back to Demarcus, he nods in Lyle's direction.

"He and I are going to have a talk," he says. "Whatever brainwashing, macho shit he's been fed, it needs to be cleared up right now."

"And will you help the girls at school?" Sydney asks. "Back them up? Report these creeps?"

Demarcus scoffs like it's a ridiculous question. "Yeah," he says. "My mom taught me to respect women. I don't want any part in *this* shit." He motions around the room. "I had no idea it was this bad."

Sydney nods. I wonder if it's strange for us to be grateful when people are decent, as if we're always expecting the worst. Confronting the other guys will make Demarcus a hero, even though us standing up to them led to our expulsion from school.

The system works differently for different people. We'll have to change that if we want different results.

Sydney and I head down the stairs, my hip sore from where I fell on the roof. When we get to the bottom floor, I see the rest of the party has broken up. As I limp onto the front porch, Sydney looks sideways at me.

"You okay?" she asks, concerned.

"I'll be fine," I tell her. "Uh . . . *by the way*, where'd you get that?"

Sydney holds up the Taser to examine it. "I wasn't sure it would work," she says. "It was in that bag Leandra gave us back at Imogene's house. I took it. Kept it just in case."

"Good," I say.

Sydney slips it back into her purse and takes out her phone. "Also, I recorded that entire thing." She smiles.

That means we got Jonah holding me against my will, the guys posting confessions online. There will be plenty for the newspaper to work with.

"It sounds like Mr. Marsh finally came around too," I say. "I'll contact him and see if we can get him to file a complaint against the students and administration."

We're quiet as we get onto the street, the cool night air blowing around us.

"I think we got them," I say. "And I think we protected the girls of Ridgeview."

"And now we focus on saving ourselves," she replies.

Sydney puts her arm around my shoulders, leaning her temple against mine. Her phone begins to buzz, and when she looks at the screen she immediately straightens.

"It's Marcella," she says. We move away from the house, walking toward our apartment, as she answers.

"Hi," Sydney says. "You girls okay?"

She listens for a moment and then stops walking abruptly. "What?" she asks, sounding shocked. "Hold on. Mena's here too." She clicks the speaker button and holds the phone out in front of us.

"I said it's not them," Marcella repeats, slightly out of breath.

"What's not them?" Sydney asks, looking at me.

"It's not one of the boys," she says. "The investor doesn't have a son. He has a daughter."

"You found him?" I ask. "How do you know?"

"Because we found the money," Brynn explains, far away at first and then into the line like she's taken the phone from Marcella. "It's a Mr. Goodwin. He contacted Jonah's dad for a loan, a pretty large sum. He then funneled it through Ridgeview. He . . ."

But my mind drifts for a second, stuck on that last name. When it hits me, my stomach sinks.

"Who's the daughter?" Sydney demands.

"Adrian," I say before Brynn can.

"Wait, you know her?" Brynn asks, surprised. Sydney swings to face me with a pained expression.

"Is it possible she knew who we were from the start?" Sydney asks.

"I'm not sure," I murmur. I think back to our conversations, any moment where Adrian could have given herself away, but nothing stands out. Then again, I wasn't looking closely. With the boys, we had our guard up all the time. I guess I had my own double standard.

Still . . . I'm convinced that Adrian is my friend. I don't think she's faked that.

"What's her address?" I ask Brynn.

"You're not going there," Sydney says, incredulous.

"I am," I say. "I have to know why her father would invest in something so awful. I mean . . . Goodwin pays money for an academy to create AI to abuse, all while his own daughter is being abused in the private school he sends her to." My voice begins to ratchet up. "Does he know what she's going through? Does he know what he's put us through?"

Sydney bites her lip, thinking it over. All we needed was his information. We could pass it along now to Leandra, to Winston Weeks. We could give it to the newspaper or even Rosemarie.

But we're the ones who need answers. We need to know why

the academy was created. We need to know why it's continuing to be funded.

"She's right," Marcella says into the phone line. "We need to talk to him."

"Okay," Sydney agrees. "Come pick us up."

She gives Marcella the closest cross streets, and we head that way, readying ourselves to face down the investor.

27

Brynn looks me over worriedly as Marcella drives us toward Adrian's house. It turns out, Adrian doesn't live in an average neighborhood, not full-time. Her parents are divorced, but her dad is incredibly rich. Or, at least, he puts on the pretense of being incredibly rich. I suppose he's not anymore if he's borrowing money.

"Why's he still paying?" I ask the girls. "If he can't afford it anymore, why borrow money to pay Innovations Academy?"

"Good question," Marcella says.

"Are you okay, Mena?" Brynn asks me. "You . . . You have bruises all over your arms."

Surprised, I look down to see dozens of them, large and small, as well as spots of blood on my dress from where I scraped my thigh on the roof. It's as if seeing them makes them hurt even more. But beyond that, it opens a wound in my chest, and I quickly turn toward the window, shivering.

I'm still scared. And the night seems even darker.

"I'm fine," I say quietly.

"Well," Marcella says. "Raven let us know she got the record-ings, including yours, Sydney. She's putting them together now, and they should be sent to reporters tonight. She's even reaching out to Mr. Marsh."

"I'm glad it's over," I murmur.

"By the way," Marcella says, glancing in the rearview mirror. "Has anyone heard from Annalise? Raven said she wasn't at the house, and I've been calling her phone but she hasn't answered."

I close my eyes. She's already gone. I'll have to tell the girls soon, but I promised Annalise that I'd finish this mission first. It's dishonest and unfair . . . but I promised.

"No," Sydney says, surprised. "But I did get a call from Lennon Rose. She's been trying to get in touch with you, Mena."

"Jonah threw my phone off the roof," I say, looking back into the car. "Did she say what she wanted?"

"Nope," Sydney says, leaning back in the seat. "She just said she needed to talk to you and wouldn't tell me why. So, you know. Usual Lennon Rose stuff," Sydney adds, flashing a fake smile to show her annoyance.

"I'll find her later," I say.

We arrive at a set of massive metal gates with a guard posted in a windowed booth at the edge of Adrian's neighborhood. Marcella pulls up anyway and rolls down the window. The guard comes out, examining the car before glancing inside at us.

"Can I help you?" he asks.

"We're here to see Adrian Goodwin," Marcella replies.

He checks a list, an actual list of approved guests. "Name?"

"We're surprising her," Marcella says. "Tell her it's her friends from school."

The guard studies us again. "I'm sorry," he says. "If you're not on the list, I'm not going to call and disturb a resident."

Sydney slides her hand over her purse, but I reach out to stop her and shake my head no.

"Fine," Marcella says, annoyed. "Give me a second."

She takes out her phone, dials, and brings it to her ear. "So much for the surprise," she says, glancing in the mirror at us.

"Yes, hi," she says when someone picks up. "Can I talk to Adrian? Good, hold on." She then passes the phone back to me. I fumble with it for a second.

"Hello?" Adrian says, sounding just like she did when she befriended me on my first day.

"Hi . . . Adrian," I reply. "It's Mena, from, uh, history class."

"Mena! I'm happy you called."

"I'm actually calling from your gate," I say. "Do you think you could tell the guard to let us in?"

"Us?" she questions.

"It's me and Sydney and two other girls. We . . . We need to talk to you."

She's quiet for a moment. "All right," she says. "Yeah, let me call down there right now."

We hang up and I give the phone back to Marcella. We wait, silently, until the guard gets the call. He writes down a few notes before hanging up.

He comes next to the window again and taps on the roof of the car.

"Welcome to The Gardens," he says warmly, and then walks back to the booth.

We all freeze, and Marcella looks around until she points out the name posted on the stone waterfall at the entrance.

The name of the neighborhood is The Gardens. But we can't help but think there's a deeper meaning.

Adrian's house—her father's house—is the grandest estate I've ever seen, including in movies. It even puts Winston Weeks's property to shame. It's funny, though—if Adrian is this rich, she certainly doesn't behave that way, accessorize that way. I wonder what the story is.

"She never told you she lived in a mansion?" Brynn asks, looking back at me from the passenger seat.

"No," I say. "She actually mentioned living somewhere else entirely. I don't know why she lied about this, but I intend to ask her. First, we're going to talk to her father."

We all get out, and Sydney double-checks that the Taser is still in her purse as we approach the front porch. Marcella and Brynn set their phones to record, and I ready myself for an altercation. We don't know what's waiting for us behind this oversized front door.

"This is it," Marcella murmurs, and holds out her hands.

Brynn takes one while Sydney takes the other. I step forward to ring the bell.

There is a shuffle behind the door, the sound of a twisting lock, and then the door eases open. The man standing there is short, with gray hair and wire-rimmed glasses. His cheeks are rosy, his expression polite. He's wearing a navy sweater over a collared shirt, pleated pants, and shiny gold watch.

"Mr. Goodwin?" I ask.

"Can I help you, my dear?" he replies in a friendly enough way.

I open my mouth, but nothing comes out at first. I imagined him as a demon, but instead, he looks like someone's rich grandpa. Can evil masquerade as a regular person?

"Are you here for—?" He cuts himself off as if suddenly realizing something. He runs his eyes quickly over me and then darts them to Sydney. To Marcella, to Brynn, each time taking in our appearance. His skin turns waxy, and his eyes widen slightly.

Although we look different than we did at the academy, it's pretty clear that we're still Innovations girls, especially to an investor.

"Christ," Mr. Goodwin says, and moves to shut the door in our faces.

Marcella throws herself against the door, getting her foot in before it can close. She knocks it open, and Mr. Goodwin shuffles backward, looking around wildly until he hits the wall under the staircase.

The foyer is massive. There is a grand staircase with two entrances. It's honestly too much.

"Adrian!" I call, my voice echoing. I wait to see if a guard will run out, but it seems that Mr. Goodwin and his daughter are here alone, safe inside their gated community.

"What do you want?" Mr. Goodwin asks, clearly scared. "Leave me and my daughter alone."

"That's rich," Marcella says.

"How did you know?" Sydney asks, stopping directly in front of him. "When you saw us, what gave it away?"

"Anton . . . ," he starts. "Anton contacted me a few days ago. He, uh . . . He said you'd escaped the academy. He said you were dangerous."

Brynn laughs, but then she pauses and looks at Sydney. "Are we?" she asks.

"Sometimes," Sydney says.

But the gravity of his words hits me. "Does Anton know we're here?" I ask. "In town?" Mr. Goodwin nods, seeming hopeful that this will give us a bond that will keep me from torturing him.

"What else did Anton say?" I demand.

"That you killed a guardian, the doctor, maybe others. He said you were probably here to kill Winston Weeks."

"Not a terrible idea," Marcella says.

"And he told me . . . He said I needed to track you down," Mr. Goodwin says, his voice desperate. "He said that if I did, he'd forgive my debt. So I asked my daughter if she'd noticed any new girls in town, really pretty ones. She mentioned you. Then I called the school and they gave me your address. But I didn't see any of you in person. Not until now."

"You were the man outside our apartment in the fancy car?" I ask.

"You saw me?" he asks, surprised. "I didn't realize . . ." When I step closer, he shrinks back again the wall.

It strikes me as odd that this man is so terrified of us, four young girls. The only thing that sets us apart from others is the fact that he knows we're not human. I doubt he walks around in his normal life cowering from teenage girls on the street.

He's scared of us because he doesn't understand what we are, not really. He thinks we're soulless machines. Programmed killers. Angry robots.

But really, we're just girls who are sick of being pushed around.

"What debt?" Sydney asks, grabbing the collar of his sweater.

"What?" he replies. This question seems to scare him more than anything.

"What debt did you have to pay Anton?" she asks, irritated. Mr. Goodwin shakes his head no, telling us he won't answer.

There is motion at the top of the stairs.

"Mena?" Adrian calls, sounding confused. I glance up to see her staring at us surrounding her father in the foyer of her home.

"Adrian," I reply. "Um . . . we need to talk to you."

"What's going on?" she asks.

"Go upstairs, honey," her father calls. "It's okay. I need to discuss something with your friends."

"*Why?*" she asks, even more confused.

"We're not here to hurt her," I tell Mr. Goodwin. "We're just here for information. I think it's time your daughter finds out what you've done."

He swallows hard, and Sydney releases him, taking a step back.

"Is there a place where we can talk?" I ask, turning to Adrian as she comes down the stairs. "Maybe somewhere we can sit down?"

"And a rope to tie up your father, please," Marcella says under her breath, turning away. Adrian doesn't hear her, but she still looks concerned.

"There's the library," she says, pointing at a set of sliding white doors.

"Oooh . . . a library," Brynn says, smiling at me.

I motion for her to go ahead, and then I grab Mr. Goodwin's arm and lead him to a chair beside the fireplace.

I try not to get distracted by the room as I walk in, the massive bookcases reaching the ceiling, the intricately carved wood of the chairs, the ornate décor. Okay, it's lovely.

"Now sit," I tell Mr. Goodwin, motioning to the chair. He does as I ask. When I move to the couch, sticking close by him, I see him studying me. Fascinated and terrified.

For a split second, I wonder if that's how Jackson feels when he looks at me sometimes.

"Back to this debt," Sydney says to Mr. Goodwin, pulling me from my thoughts. "What do you owe Anton?"

"Who's Anton?" Adrian asks.

A question occurs to me. I look at Adrian. "Why didn't you tell me you lived here?" I ask. "You said you lived in a small neighborhood near Corris Hawkes."

She winces. "I do. I mean, I live there with my mom. My stepmom. Claire," she clarifies. "I've lived with her since they divorced three years ago. In fact, I don't usually see my dad. Only when . . ." She looks sideways at him. "Only when my mom gets sick."

"Your mother's sick?" I ask.

She nods. "It happens sometimes. She'll be amazing and great. And then, she'll be tired all the time. Headaches. Barely able to get out of bed. Dad brings her to a hospital for a few weeks, and then she comes back recharged. But now she's sick again, so I'm here. She's resting upstairs until he takes her tomorrow."

I look at Mr. Goodwin, trying to figure it out. "What's the debt?" I ask, leaning toward him.

"A . . . procedure," he says. "A rare medical procedure."

Adrian looks around at us, her brow furrowed in confusion.

"Stop lying for her benefit," I tell Mr. Goodwin, motioning to his daughter. "Why are you really paying the analysts at Innovations Academy ungodly amounts of money? Money that you don't have anymore?"

"Dad?" Adrian asks. "What are they talking about?"

And as I watch, this man seems to struggle with himself, blinking quickly as he decides whether to be honest. Then his face clears and he sighs deeply.

"It was a sound investment," Mr. Goodwin says quietly. "The initial projections were nearly five times at payout. I was the first investor. I toured the corporation facility, and they introduced me to Claire—the prototype." He meets my eyes. "I wanted her. I paid top dollar."

Adrian looks around, even laughs like she's missing some larger joke. "What are you talking about?" she asks.

"You could afford it," Marcella points out to Mr. Goodwin. "I've seen your past financial disclosures. But then you began sinking more money into the academy. So much that you had to start borrowing. Why? Why push beyond your means?"

"Because she kept dying," Mr. Goodwin says simply. "Claire was defective, and she kept dying. And then I would get her rebuilt, exactly the same. No modifications."

"Why not get a new girl?" I ask.

"I would never!" He has the gall to sound offended. "I love her. My daughter loves her. And most importantly, Claire loves us. I couldn't just . . . just *get another girl.* She's ours." He closes his eyes, calming himself.

"And that debt?" he continues. "Anton told me he wouldn't rebuild her until I've paid off my balance. So I borrowed money. Then Claire broke down again. Faster this time. But Anton said he wouldn't rebuild her unless . . . unless I found you."

"Dad?" Adrian's voice trembles. "What the hell are you talking about?"

"Claire is . . ." He furrows his brow. "Honey, Claire was created in a lab. She was here to take care of us, and then, to take care of you. She's . . . She's AI." He shifts his eyes to us. "Just like they are."

Adrian scoffs. "Is this some kind of practical joke?" she asks, although the hysteria in her voice tells me she knows it's true on some level. A moment or two where Claire asked a strange question or blinked out of sync? Adrian's seen something.

"Did you tell him?" Brynn asks Mr. Goodwin. When he looks at her, he softens slightly.

"Tell who, dear?"

"Anton," she says. "Did you tell Anton where we were?"

"Not yet. But he knows you're in this town," he says.

"Is he alone?" Sydney asks. "Or did he bring a Guardian with him?"

"I believe he's alone," Mr. Goodwin answers.

The girls and I look at each other. We have to get out of here.

Mr. Goodwin smiles at Brynn. "You must be the caregiver," he says, pointing at her. In quick succession, he points at Marcella, Sydney, and then me. "The educator, the companion, the rebel."

"What are you talking about?" Marcella asks.

"Your models," he says. "There are only six base programs. You're missing the seductress and the doll."

He sounds like he's being helpful, but instead, Brynn's eyes begin to fill with tears.

Program types.

Adrian watches Brynn's reaction, and she jumps to her feet. "I can't take this," she says, beginning to pace the room. "If any of this is true, *why?*" She spins toward her dad, her expression a mix of anger and hurt. "Why would you pay to create AI girls? What the fuck, Dad!"

He swallows hard, lowering his eyes. "After your mother died, your real mother, I was lonely. I turned to money—making it, investing it." He stops. "When I brought Claire home five years ago, you really took to her. And soon, I saw that you were great friends. That you loved each other. And then it was too late. I couldn't bear you losing another person, so even after she and I couldn't work—"

"Yeah, because you're clearly a fucking psycho!" she shouts at him.

He flinches back but presses his lips together in understanding. "I knew you'd need her, Adrian," he says. "That's why I didn't decommission her, even when it was clear that she was faulty."

Adrian stares at him, her lip beginning to quiver. Quickly, she turns to me. Her eyes examine me, looking for some sign that I'm not human. But there's nothing she can perceive. Her chest heaves with breaths, and she pulls off her glasses to wipe her eyes before replacing them.

"What did they do to you?" she asks me. "At the academy or whatever. What did they do to you there?"

And this is the hard part. We don't have time to go into all the details, but there's enough to tell her the basics of the abuse, the intentions, the aftermath. Adrian openly cries when I tell her about impulse control therapy, about the Guardian's threats and physical violence. I tell her about Imogene, broken and bruised by a man who bought her as his wife.

"We feel," I tell Adrian, putting my hand over my heart. "We feel all of it. We're not just machines. We have hearts and organs and flesh. We love," I whisper, looking sideways at the girls. Sydney's eyes glisten as she smiles.

"But the corporation created us to replace the girls in society who they couldn't control," I say. "I don't know their grand plan yet, and maybe your dad doesn't either." I turn to him. "But I have no idea how you can claim to love Claire and then pay money for the school to torture us. Did you have any idea what they were doing?"

"I . . ." He doesn't want to answer honestly; I can see it in his eyes. "You are . . . machines."

"But not Claire, right?" I ask. "She's *your* machine, so she's the only one you care about."

He nods, and I realize that's the way, the way of selfish people. They want to control everyone else, but when it's them, they want their own rules.

I hear Marcella's knuckles crack when she makes a fist.

"What about me?" Adrian asks her father. She hitches in a breath and turns to him. "Did you know what I was going through at Ridgeview?"

He seems shocked by the question. "What do you mean?"

"I suffered at that school," she says. "The way some of the boys would harass me—are you okay with *that*?"

"I don't know what you're talking about, Adrian," he says.

"Or you chose not to know," she says. "For years, they've grabbed me, sexually harassed me, bullied me. All without consequence. And here you are, paying to make girls that they can abuse in the same way. Paying to create a society where it's the norm."

"You have to understand," her father says. "This academy was a financial decision, and—"

"And?" she repeats. "You think money excuses any of this? Well, guess what, it appears you don't have any more fucking money!" She motions toward us. "This was never about money. This was control."

"Look," Mr. Goodwin says to her, taking on a weird parental tone, considering the circumstances. "I had no idea anything was happening to you. Claire never mentioned it, and—"

"Why would she?" Adrian asks, sneering. "My God, she must hate you. She must know what you are. But . . . she tried to protect me. She tried to keep smiling." Adrian starts sobbing. "She was in pain and she tried to keep smiling because she didn't want me to end up here. With you."

Adrian stops to breathe, wiping her tears again. "You call them machines," she says in a choked voice. "But you're a monster."

Adrian squeezes her eyes shut, tears rolling down her cheeks. Her father looks at her, pained.

"The boys at Ridgeview won't bother you again," I tell Adrian, hoping to make her feel better.

Adrian turns to me, shocked. "Did you murder them?" she asks.

Marcella sniffs a laugh.

"No," I say. "We're not . . . We're not killers. We caught them. We recorded them as proof, and our friend is sending it to the paper, implicating the school in covering up the harassment. We got another boy to confront Jonah. Even Mr. Marsh is going to report Garrett."

"Really?" Adrian asks. "Marsh is going to . . . He's standing up to them?"

I nod and look at her father. "He is," I say. "Because he realized that by not doing so, he was allowing it. He was condoning it."

"And now what?" Mr. Goodwin asks. "Reporters show up here?"

"Maybe," I reply. "And it's up to Adrian what she wants to do about that. But you have to cut ties with the corporation. If you won't turn on them, then you have to at least stop funding them."

"It's not that easy," he says with a flash of fear.

"Mr. Goodwin," I say, "you have a daughter you seem to care about. Men make claims that having a daughter, sister, or wife makes them more sympathetic to a woman's pain. Since they can't see them as fellow humans, they have to classify them as something else. So now it's your turn. Seeing that it happens to your daughter, do you wish it on others, even if they're not human?"

He genuinely thinks about it. The pause should bother me, but instead, it feels authentic.

"No," he whispers after a moment. "No, I don't. What would you have me do?" he asks. "And what about Claire?"

Sydney takes a step forward. "We might know someone who can help," she says. "On one condition. You pull your funding—forever."

Mr. Goodwin thinks it over. He looks at his house, at his things. And then he looks at his daughter, and for the first time . . . I think he sees her. He sees what the world he's creating would do to her.

And silently, he nods his head. The girls and I go upstairs to retrieve Claire.

28

Claire doesn't look like the rest of us. She's older—at least several years older than the typical girl when she was created. She never attended Innovations Academy. Along the way, someone must have decided that teen girls were worth more money.

Claire smiles when she sees us, though, like she recognizes us the moment we walk in. But she's clearly failing. Her left eye no longer opens, and blood leaks from her ears. We get her downstairs, and she hugs Adrian in the foyer, whispering something I can't hear. When she straightens, Adrian tells her she'll see her soon.

Mr. Goodwin steps forward, but Claire turns away from him and takes Brynn's arm. Now that we're here, she seems to have more resolve. I watch as Mr. Goodwin accepts this. Maybe he knows he deserves it.

The girls and I get Claire outside and find a car waiting for us. Marcella called Raven, with Adrian's permission, and told her about the situation. Raven was happy, no, ecstatic to help. She promised that she could.

When we get to the car, Raven climbs out, smiling at Claire.

"It's okay," she tells her kindly. "I'm Raven and I'm fucking great at this."

Claire laughs softly, allowing Raven to guide her into the car. When she's securely in the passenger seat, Raven steps over to us.

"How bad is it?" she asks.

"Pretty bad," Marcella says. "She's been rebuilt, but not fixed. We're hoping you can do it. She's the prototype."

"I'm definitely going to try," she says. "Wow . . . did you say 'prototype'?" She looks back at the car, her eyes twinkling with breathless excitement.

"And she's someone's mother," Brynn adds. "So you have to save her." Raven turns to her and nods.

"I will." Despite Raven's promise, there's a flash of worry in her expression.

"What is it?" Marcella asks. "What's wrong?"

"Have any of you heard from Annalise?" Raven asks.

"No," Brynn says. "We haven't."

"Do you think something happened?" Sydney asks.

"She's not at the apartment," Raven says. "And it looks like she took some of her stuff."

The girls are at once frantic, and I close my eyes for a moment, steadying myself.

"I know where Annalise is," I announce. "She didn't . . . She wanted me to wait to tell you until we finished this."

"It's finished," Marcella says shortly. "Now tell."

"She went back to Innovations Academy," I say, and Brynn gasps out a cry. "She went to look for the other girls," I explain. "And then she was going to burn the school to the ground. She didn't want them to ever bring us back there."

I'm met with silence. Raven's mouth falls open. She seems hurt, abandoned, but then she quickly looks at Claire in the car again. It occurs to me that Raven is chasing the next tech, the old tech in this case, but new to her. Although she's helped us, it's clear that she's hooked on our information. On our programming. I wonder if, deep down, she really sees us any differently than Mr. Goodwin does.

"I have to . . . ," Raven says, motioning to the car. "I'm going to get started on Claire, okay? I'll let you know when I have more info."

Distracted, Brynn turns to her. "Wait, where are you taking her?"

"I have a workspace," Raven says, waving it off. "I'll be in touch soon."

Raven gets in the car, saying something to Claire that makes her smile. We watch them drive off, and the second they're gone, Sydney turns on me fiercely.

"And you just let Annalise go?" she demands. "And didn't tell any of us?"

"She begged me," I say. "She made me promise. She said she'd come back when it was done. I asked her to come back."

But Sydney isn't impressed. She turns away from me, walking back and forth on the sidewalk as if thinking.

"I'm so sorry," I tell them. "I didn't want to keep it from you."

I go on to explain the entire conversation, relaying everything that Annalise told me, from her belief that she was dying to her saying that I had to let her go. When I'm done, I can see the girls debating whether they would have done the same as me. They must decide it doesn't matter, because Marcella drops into a squatting position and covers her face to cry, while Brynn wraps her arms around her. Sydney squeezes her eyes closed, palm over her mouth as she holds back her sobs.

I don't allow myself to cry, feeling at fault for their pain. But then Sydney comes over and grabs me into a hug, crying into my shoulder.

"Our Annalise is gone," she murmurs. "She's gone and I don't think she's ever coming back."

I want to say that she will, say it until they believe it. But I've already lied to the girls enough tonight.

The girls and I arrive back at our apartment and stand there. Annalise's absence is a silence we've never known. The air is thick and quiet without her.

We stand there and survey the space, knowing we wouldn't stay here even if we could. Not without Annalise.

"What's next?" Brynn asks, her voice raw from crying. "We found the investor, and he's going to pull his money. Do we tell Leandra?"

"Yes," I say.

"How do we find her?" Brynn replies. "Wait," she says, her eyes getting wide. "Do you think Annalise is with her?" she asks.

"No," I say. "I don't." She nods sadly and then goes to her room to begin packing. Marcella follows wordlessly, but Sydney comes to pause next to me, both of us looking at the living room.

"How are you going to find Leandra?" Sydney repeats Brynn's question.

I look around the room, taking it in, and my gaze falls on the book of poetry. And it suddenly occurs to me. I turn to Sydney.

"Rosemarie knows Leandra, right?" I say. "I mean, she *created* Leandra. And Quentin saw Leandra taking the girls from the academy. So . . . what if she really did leave with them? What if she's bringing them to Rosemarie?"

Sydney takes a moment, but then she nods emphatically. "That might be it," she says.

"Look," I say. "I'll go pick up Lennon Rose from Winston's house, and then we'll figure out what to do. In the meantime, you and the girls pack. I'll call Jackson and see if we can stay with him tonight."

She sniffs a laugh. "I'm sure he'll love that." Then she smiles. "No, but really. I'm sure he will." Sydney hands me her phone.

"I'll call you from the road," I tell her, and then rush outside.

I order a car, and luckily there's one close by. I give the driver Winston's address, and he glances in the rearview mirror at me, maybe noticing my still-disheveled state. He doesn't comment on it.

Using Sydney's phone, I dial Jackson's number. After the third ring, his voicemail picks up. At the sound of his voice, I close my eyes. The line beeps.

"Hey, it's me," I say softly. "The girls are going to head over your way to stay the night. I hope that's all right. It's not safe for us at our place. In the morning, we're going to find Leandra. I think she and the girls from the academy might be with Rosemarie." I turn toward the window, feeling self-conscious in front of the driver.

"Anton's in town," I add. "Annalise is not. It's a long story, one I'll tell you when I get there. But, um . . ." I shift in the seat, embarrassed.

"I was thinking about earlier . . . when I tried to kiss you," I whisper. "I shouldn't have done that, Jackson. I'm sorry I put you in that position. But I also wanted to say, I did *want* to kiss you. I wanted to know what it was like. I wanted to be closer to you. I understand that you don't feel the same way. And I understand why.

"Anyway . . . this is humiliating," I continue, brushing my hair back from my face. "But I feel like these are the things that needed to be said at the apartment. You deserve better than what I've dragged you through. And I'd get it if you wanted to go back to your life, the one you had before you met me in an out-of-the-way gas station."

I sigh, knowing the recording is about to cut off.

"I think I'm kind of in love with you," I add quickly. "And it's okay that you don't feel the same. But I don't want you to feel guilty. You've done more than enough for me. Too much, if we're honest." I laugh.

"Okay, bye," I say, and hang up abruptly.

I set the phone beside me on the seat, staring at it while I process the things I just said. Well, that was probably a terrible idea.

"Tough break, kid," the driver says, and I look up to find him watching me in the rearview mirror.

"Thanks," I reply, slightly mortified. He nods and continues to drive me toward Winston's house.

The driver drops me off at the gate, and rather than call the house, I hop the fence. The night is quiet as I head toward Winston's place, but when I turn on his street, my stomach sinks. Raven's car is parked out front.

I stop beside it, searching the empty interior and confirming that it's her car. I turn toward Winston's house.

Raven knows him. Either that, or she came here for his help with Claire. But she would still have to know him to do that. I just . . . I don't understand. The lights are blazing inside Winston's house, and I make my way up the path to the front door.

I don't knock. Instead, I try the handle and swallow hard when I find it open. I slip inside and check around. It's quiet, and I close the door softly behind me.

I make my way down the hall toward the back of the house. I pause, wondering if I should look upstairs for Lennon Rose first. But then a murmur of voices in the kitchen catches my attention.

Winston Weeks is talking—sounding pretty heated, in fact. I stand there to listen instead of announcing my presence right away.

"What else did you see?" he demands.

"I told you," Raven says, and my breath catches. She definitely knows him.

"I saw everything," Raven continues. "The shit Mena went through at that academy, the incidents at Ridgeview, her connection to the other girls. Winston, she's advanced far beyond her programming. They all have."

"And nothing about my mother?" Winston asks, sounding like he doesn't believe it. "What the fuck is she planning, then?"

"It's been blocked," Raven says. "You know that Rosemarie is nothing if not thorough."

Startled, I straighten. Is it possible that Rosemarie has continued to mess with my programming? Or could she have done something from the start that made it so memories of her didn't stick?

"Look," Raven says. "If we ask Lennon Rose, she'll—"

"Oh, yes," Winston replies bitterly. "Lennon Rose will be super helpful, I'm sure. Whatever you did to her—" Winston starts, but there is a clatter of ceramic on a counter.

"I told you I didn't touch Lennon Rose's programming!" Raven shouts. "It wasn't me!"

There's a long pause before Winston apologizes.

"I'm grateful for your expertise, Raven," he says. "And maybe you didn't alter Lennon Rose, but somebody got to her. Something is different."

"I don't disagree," Raven says. "But we have Mena now. She's ready. She'll help us."

"I'm hopeful that you're right," he says. "But there was one more issue, one that Leandra brought up to me last we talked. A concern I'm sure my mother shares, as well. It might prove to be a problem down the line."

I lean closer, wanting to catch every word.

"The boy," Winston says. "What's going on there?"

"Boy?" Raven asks.

"The one who helped her escape the academy," Winston says. "Leandra said they seemed . . . very close."

"I don't know who you're talking about," Raven says. "And besides, it's not possible. There's nothing in their programming that allows them to love. There was no boy like that."

And it's this part of the conversation that makes me take a step back. I glance at the ceiling, toward the upstairs rooms, but they said Lennon Rose isn't here. I can't sense her presence, either.

Before I get caught, I walk out the same way I came in, closing the door behind me. I get through the neighborhood gate and order a car. I'll call the girls to let them know what I just heard, and then I'll meet them at the motel.

I sit on the curb while I wait, thinking about Raven. She knows about Jackson, so she lied to Winston about him. Whether she's protecting me, Jackson, or herself, I'm not sure.

I'm not sure which side Raven is on.

29

Jackson wasn't kidding when he complained about his motel. It's straight out of a horror movie from the '60s. Run-down, poorly lit, and even the VACANCY sign has several lights out. After I get dropped off, I find the correct room and knock.

Jackson pulls the door open, but his breath catches when he sees the state of me. At his reaction, I look down and remember that I'm in rough shape—a bit dirty and kind of bloody.

"Hi," I say brightly when I look at him again.

"Jesus," he replies, running his hand through his hair. "Why are you always covered in blood?" he murmurs. "Get in here."

He hops to the side so I can walk past him, and then he closes the door and locks it. Marcella and Brynn sit on the second bed while the shower runs in the bathroom.

"Sydney's cleaning up," he says, and then notices the tear in my dress. "I'm about to fucking lose it, though," he adds darkly.

"I'm okay," I tell him.

"Sydney had a bat," Brynn calls out to him. Jackson widens his eyes and turns from her to me.

"Good," he says. "Hope she swung for the fences."

"Nice place," I say, looking around.

"No, it's awful," he says easily, and limps over to the bed to push a backpack and water container onto the floor. "Sit down," he says, patting the mattress. "Can I get you anything?"

I shake my head no. "By the way," I add. "Sorry about the voicemail."

His cheeks flush, and he shrugs that it's fine. I look sideways at Marcella, and she lifts her eyebrows curiously.

Sydney comes out of the bathroom in a towel, her hair wrapped up in another. She places her hand on her chest in relief when she sees me. She comes to join me on the bed, and the others crowd around while I tell them everything I heard at Winston's house.

"I hope Claire's okay," Brynn says.

"I'm sure she is," I say, although I have no idea. Then again, I don't imagine Raven would hurt her. Fix her? Yes. Maybe spy on her on bit. But not destroy her. Not with the way she loves our tech.

Sydney tries to brush my hair off my forehead, but it's stiff from dried sweat. "You should take a shower," she says. "And Jackson has a first aid kit if you need help with those scrapes on your thigh."

Jackson flinches at the idea of me being hurt, but he doesn't look over. "Yeah, I'll clean it up for you if you want," he says.

"He's weirdly good at it," Sydney says. "Like a little medic." He laughs.

"That'd be great," I tell him, Jackson seems sad, but I have to admit that although there's still so much wrong, being with the girls and with Jackson instantly feels like home.

I get up and cross to the bathroom, closing the door to shower.

Hot water and torn skin are a terrible mix. When I'm done showering, in a significant higher amount of pain than when I started, I wrap myself in a towel and call to Jackson. I sit on the edge of the tub and he pokes his head in the doorway nervously, as if making sure I'm dressed. I wave him in.

The room is still a little steamy, but it dissipates quickly. I watch as Jackson sets up a first aid station on the counter, and when he's done, he puts his crutches aside and finds his balance.

"Show me," he says, motioning to my leg.

I push up the edge of the towel to show him the scratches on my outer thigh. They look worse than I imagined, and Jackson winces when he sees them. He eases into a kneeling position in front of me.

"I don't think of you like that, you know," he says, opening one of the alcohol pads.

"Like what?" I ask.

"I don't think of you as a machine," he says, looking up at me. "And I don't think of you as a status symbol. Both the investor and those guys at Ridgeview are wrong."

"What do you think of me as?" I ask. "And you can't say 'a person.'" I smile at him. He reaches to tenderly wipe my scrape with the alcohol, and I suck in a breath and grip his shoulder.

"Sorry," he whispers, finishing up before getting a gauze pad.

"I think of you as Mena," he says simply as he tapes the edges. "Just . . . Mena. No other label required." He pauses with his eyes lowered.

"I'm kind of in love with you too," he adds quietly. "I just… I don't know what I want to do about that yet." He looks up at me again. "Is that okay?" he asks.

I nod that it is, my heart beating faster. We stare at each other, close together in a motel bathroom as he kneels on the dirtiest floor I've ever seen.

"It's understandable," I add, starting to smile. "I'm the rebel type. That's what the investor told me at his house when he thought we were going to kill him."

"Huh, did he now?" Jackson replies, getting up to put the first aid supplies back inside the box. "Since he was being so revealing, did he admit to being the creepy perverted type? Or was he the raging sex-monster type?"

"The first one, I think," I say, pretending to be sure.

Jackson shakes his head and then grabs his crutches. "Come on," he says, reaching out his hand to help me up. "I was going to buy us candy from the vending machine."

"Always saying the right thing," I say, slowly letting his fingers slide from mine as we walk back out into the room with the others.

I still have nightmares. I sleep in the bed with Sydney wearing one of Jackson's T-shirts and a pair of his boxers. Marcella and Brynn are in the other bed while Jackson takes the floor between us.

In my dream, Anton is waiting for us at a train station. For a moment, I'm not sure if I'm in the past or the future. He looks older, but I feel younger.

"I gave you this life," he says, holding an ice pick in his hand. "And I can take it away."

When I turn to run, something catches my ankles, pulling me down. And then I'm being dragged along the train platform, screaming for help while others, humans, just watch curiously.

And then Anton is above me, leaning close to my face.

"It's you and me until the end, Philomena," he says. "You know this."

And then he raises the ice pick to jab through my eye.

"Mena," Sydney whispers.

I yelp, sitting up and gasping for breath. Light streams through the curtains, and it takes me a moment to get my bearings. I'm in the motel room.

"Mena, it's okay," Sydney says, rubbing her palm over my back. "You were having a nightmare."

I look around, still breathing heavily. I find Brynn and Marcella at the edge of their bed, riveted by the TV.

"Where's Jackson?" I ask, momentarily confused as I wipe the sleep from my eyes.

"He went to get bagels," Brynn says, still watching the television. After a moment, she mutes it and turns toward me, her eyes wide.

"What's going on?" I ask.

"It's all over the news," Brynn says.

"What is?" I ask. The girls start filling me in on what I missed.

Garrett Wooley, it appears, has run away. At least, that's what the news reports say. After the initial story surfaced late last night, two girls came forward today to say that he attacked them and then intimidated them into silence. When the police went to his house to question him, he was gone.

"And the other boys?" I ask. "Jonah and Lyle?"

"Well," Marcella says, leaning on her elbows. "Another girl accused Jonah of the same thing, and he was arrested. They had a video that he posted in a private forum. Anyway, he hired some big-time attorney; I think it's his father. But Lyle agreed to testify against Jonah. And Garrett, if they ever find him."

Marcella goes on to say that the boys' misconduct has become a major news story. Other guys have come forward to corroborate some of the reports—starting with Demarcus. Mr. Marsh resigned from the school, but he's cooperating with the district attorney on an investigation into Ridgeview. The vice principal has been dismissed and is named in at least one of the lawsuits.

And it's so easy that it's frustrating at the same time. All the accusations are suddenly given more weight because they're seconded by a man. How quickly would society change if all men did this? If all men stood up for what was right?

I guess it starts somewhere. Maybe it'll start with Ridgeview.

The phone in the motel rings, and we all look at it curiously.

Marcella gets up on her knees and moves toward it. She pauses a long moment before answering.

"Hello?" she asks quietly. Her posture stiffens, and then she looks at me. Clearly, they're asking for me. I nod that it's okay, whoever it is has already found me, and I hold out my hand.

I bring the phone to my ear without saying anything at first.

"Hello, Mena," Winston says. "I'm outside your room. Would you mind coming out to speak with me?"

I'm stunned, and when I can think of no reply, I hang up. I look around at the girls.

"Was that Winston?" Marcella asks, horrified.

"Yes," I say. "He's outside." I point toward the window, and Brynn claps her hand over her mouth.

"What do we do?" she asks behind her palm.

"Well, I guess I'll go talk to him," I say. I turn to Sydney. "Call Jackson and tell him to stay away until Winston's gone. I don't want him to get hurt."

"Got it," she says, reaching for her phone.

I get up, smooth my oversized shirt, and tug down the hem of the boxers. I check with the girls, and when they say it looks all right, I walk outside.

Winston Weeks is resting against the hood of his shiny black car, parked in front of my dusty motel room. He couldn't look more out of place if he tried. But he literally laughs when he sees what I'm wearing.

"You look precious, Philomena," he says.

"How'd you even find me?" I ask, crossing my arms over my chest.

"That boy you travel with isn't subtle," he says, trying to hide his contempt for Jackson.

"Okay," I say. "Then what do you want?"

"Don't be difficult," he says. "I'm here to talk to all the girls." He starts for the door, but I quickly dart in front of it, blocking his path.

"I think you should ask them first," I say. "You don't get to decide that they'll talk to you. Get permission."

I enjoy Winston's discomfort. Asking means he can be refused. For all his preaching about our rights, the idea that we have autonomy—when it doesn't suit him—makes him uneasy.

Welcome to the future, Winston Weeks.

"Of course," he says after a moment. "Hello, girls," Winston calls out, annoyingly formal, especially here. "May I come in and speak with you for a bit?"

There's no response, but then the door opens, and Marcella looks out, eyeing him suspiciously. She turns to me to make sure I approve. I tell her it's fine. She opens the door the rest of the way.

I walk inside with Winston Weeks following behind me.

He surveys the room, a heavy look of disgust in his expression. He starts to sit down but then thinks better of it. He goes to stand in front of the television, as if commanding our attention.

"We need to talk, girls," he says. Marcella rolls her eyes. "Last night's entire incident with those boys was counterproductive for our cause. I'm disappointed."

Sydney scoffs from the other side of me. Marcella leans forward.

"Sorry, Dad," Marcella says, earning a laugh from Brynn.

"Those boys at Ridgeview were horrible," I say. "I'm glad they're finally facing consequences."

Winston allows this. "I understand, Philomena," he says gently. "But sometimes there are bigger monsters that need to be slain first. That's what you girls don't understand yet. The narrative shifts. Sure, these boys lost their scholarships, maybe a few will actually do time. But nothing changes, not at this level. Soon there will be think pieces about their lives being ruined. Some will even call it a hoax. Starting at the bottom protects no one. You should have gone for the red meat first."

Winston would have let the boys of Ridgeview get away with mass harassment if it meant they could serve a purpose for him. Allowing the misbehavior of other men when it benefits him.

"Although it was noble of you to help the female students of Ridgeview," he continues, "it could have ruined everything."

"But it didn't," Sydney says. "Turns out, we saved everyone. Interesting how compassion and competence work better than war and blackmail. Try it sometime."

"But you've hurt your own cause," he says.

"How do you figure?" I ask. "We stopped the investor."

Winston looks at me darkly. "Mr. Goodwin is dead."

My expression falters. "What? What . . . What are you talking about?"

"What you've all failed to comprehend is that the corporation is filled with people who kill anyone who stands in their way. They have no loyalty, even though they demand it. If you had brought him to me, I could have made Goodwin talk, found different ways to infiltrate and cut off funding. Now we won't have that chance."

I look at the other girls, but none of us have checked on Mr. Goodwin's well-being. It strikes us as sickeningly possible that he's dead, and guilt crawls over me. Even though he may not deserve my sympathy, it would mean that Adrian lost her dad. And despite everything, she still loved him.

"I think it's time for you to leave," Sydney says abruptly to Winston. She's disturbed by this development, but she doesn't want to show Winston Weeks any of that.

Winston doesn't argue. He nods and heads for the door, pausing there like he's waiting for me. Despite the other girls staring at me as if telling me not to, I walk Winston to his car.

"That went well," I tell him, standing at the curb while he opens the driver's side door.

"It was expected," he says. "By the way, I know you were at my house last night. You left a bloody fingerprint on my wall." He looks sideways at me, his expression holding a hint of amusement. "You should have come in and had a glass of wine."

"I wasn't thirsty," I say. "I don't appreciate being spied on, Winston."

"I understand," he says. "But Raven was there to assist you. I wanted you to see that my way is better. That my girls are better. Sure, you were trained to be well behaved and beautiful, but you're also smart. Savvy. Your usefulness extends beyond that of a trophy wife. No offense."

"None taken," I say. "But to be fair, I've only seen Lennon Rose as one of your . . . girls." I detest giving him ownership of any of us, but I need it to prove my point. "And you don't exactly have a handle on her behavior."

"Yes," he agrees. "Lennon Rose was always a risky option. One that didn't pan out. But there are others."

"Other girls?" I ask. "Then where are they?" I motion around. "I haven't met any."

Winston laughs. "My goodness," he says. "I thought you'd figured it out. I thought that was why you came to my house."

"Figured what out?" I ask.

"Raven," he says proudly. "I built her myself."

My breath catches like I'm falling through the air. "What?" I whisper. "Raven is a girl?"

"Not a *girl*," he says. "No, she's not like you or the others. She was never trained to be obedient. She was given full free will and extensive skills. Highly intelligent, compassionate, intuitive."

"But she doesn't know what she is," I say the moment I realize.

"She doesn't know," he repeats.

My hand curls into a fist at my side. "You've lied to her," I say.

"What I've done is give her freedom from having to agonize about her existence," he explains. "Raven believes her backstory, that she came here to continue her interests in AI. But everything after that, those were all *her* choices. Sure, I led her to you, but she's helped. She put up firewalls and evaluated your programming."

"And stole our memorics," I say.

He shrugs. "Small price," he replies. "Raven is the next level of girl. She's the future."

"She doesn't even know what she is," I shoot back immediately.

"Eventually we'll tell her."

He uses "we" as if I'm his partner in this. I don't approve and I tell him so.

"You'll grow into the idea," he says. He glances around at the motel. "I still have more surprises for you, Philomena, once you're open to hearing about them." He sighs and motions around the building.

"Do you need money?" he asks, confused. "You can do better than this."

"We're not staying long."

This concerns him. "No?" he asks. "And where will you go?"

"I'll email you."

"Ah," he says, realizing I'm not going to tell him. "Well, if you change your mind, you know where to find me. There's a lot we can accomplish, you and I."

"There's a lot I can accomplish without you," I respond.

Winston nods that I've made a good point, and then he gets in his car and drives away.

30

When Jackson returns to the motel, he has a plastic bag looped around his arm. Once inside, he takes out a box of bagels and sets them on the dresser.

"I'm starving," Marcella says, taking out a bagel while I tell Jackson about Winston Weeks's visit. When I'm done, he seems confused.

"So Raven . . . the hacker?" he says. "She's a girl too?"

"She's AI," I say. "Not really meant to be a girl, I guess."

"The investor missed a type, then," Jackson says, glancing at me. "The I'm-not-like-other-*girls* type." I snort and point at him to let him know it's a good joke.

"So what now?" Sydney asks. "I mean, Raven got inside our heads and told Winston everything. Our entire lives. But . . . she really did help lock out Anton and Rosemarie. So . . . what does that mean?" she asks.

"And she didn't tell him about Jackson," I say. "She pretended not to know him."

"That's right!" Brynn says, motioning to Jackson. "All humans want to kill you. So you should be careful."

Jackson eases himself down on the edge of the bed. "Thanks, Brynn," he says. She smiles and bites into the bagel Marcella hands her.

"It means Raven's playing both sides," Marcella says. "And who knows, maybe she genuinely does care for us. Clearly Winston doesn't know anything about our emotions."

"We need Lennon Rose," I say.

"Uh . . . ," Sydney starts. "I'm not sure we need to add Lennon Rose to the mix right now. Didn't Raven say she was out of control?"

"Sure, but maybe that means she's with us," I offer. "She hates Anton as much as we do. He may have let her leave the academy, but she resents him. And if she knew he was coming for us, she'd want to fight too. I know it."

"I agree," Brynn says. "Lennon Rose may have changed, but she still loves us."

"Do you have any idea where she is?" Sydney asks.

"There's only one place I can think of," I say. "If she's not with Winston and she's not with us, she has to be at Rosemarie's house. I have a feeling she's been going there a lot."

"And you intend to walk right into Rosemarie's plan," Sydney says.

"Pretty much," I reply.

"Well," Marcella says, "then here's *my* plan. We finish these bagels, we find Lennon Rose, and then we leave this town and search for the next investor."

"While we're at it, we should track down Leandra," I say.

"Shit," Jackson says under his breath. I turn to him, reaching over to take his hand.

"We'll protect you," I whisper encouragingly.

"Good," he says. "And I know you're going no matter what, so let me get this over with: *Mena, please don't. This is a terrible idea. It's dangerous. I'm scared for you.*" He stops, thinking. "That cover it?" he asks.

"You should tell her that you love her again," Brynn says dreamily. Jackson bites his lower lip, frustrated at me for telling them about our conversation. I shrug.

"Should we come with you to Rosemarie's?" Sydney asks.

"No," I say. "I don't know what she did to Lennon Rose. She was able to get inside my head pretty easily, and I don't want her to have access to you. If nothing else, distance is a good thing."

"Good point," Sydney says.

"She trusts me," I say. "Or, at least, she wants me to trust her. I don't think she'll hurt me."

"Reassuring," Jackson mumbles.

"While I'm gone," I tell Sydney, "see if you can find out where Anton is. And please, get us out of this motel."

I turn to Jackson, worried about my next question. "Any sightings of Annalise?" I ask. He winces and then shakes his head no.

"I haven't gotten ahold of Quentin yet," he says. "But I've left messages. If she goes to the academy, he'll find her."

The mood in the room grows somber. Brynn leans her head on Marcella's shoulder. Sydney sniffles. It's not the same without Annalise.

We just miss our girl.

I take a car service into the country toward Rosemarie's cottage, and I have the driver drop me off at the end of the long driveway. I take a moment to look around Rosemarie's property, noting again how beautiful it is. The kind of natural beauty that I'm drawn to. I wonder if that's purposeful or just something we have in common.

As I walk the stone path to her door, I admire the flowers again. Their beauty is nothing compared to their potential. I respect how dangerous they are.

I don't even have to knock before the screen door opens. Rosemarie stands in a multicolored housecoat, smiling warmly as she wipes her hands on a dish towel.

"I saw you through the window," she says. "I'm so happy you're here, Philomena. Please, come in and join us."

Us.

So Lennon Rose is here.

"I know it's been a stressful few days for you," Rosemarie adds as I step inside the house. There's an earthy smell in the living room that I find very comforting. Very grounding.

"It's been more than a few days of stress, Rosemarie," I reply, gazing around at the thriving plants in the room.

"Yes," she says like her heart is bleeding for me. "It sure has."

She's really laying it on thick. I don't believe her for a second.

Rosemarie leads me toward the kitchen, looking back over her shoulder as she walks. "I hear you found Claire," she says. "I've always wondered where she ended up." She pauses at the kitchen door, her smile fading. "Where is she now?"

The sudden coldness in her voice cuts right through me. The fact that she already knew about the investor and Claire is even more troublesome. "She . . . uh, I believe she's at Winston's," I say. "She needed repairs."

Rosemarie tilts her head. "She can't be repaired," she replies. "But it's nice of them to try, I suppose." She turns and walks into the kitchen. "Come on in, Philomena," she calls.

When I step inside the kitchen, I'm caught off guard when I find Leandra Petrov sitting alone at the kitchen table. Leandra motions for me to join her as the teakettle whistles from the stove.

"Where's Lennon Rose?" I ask as I sit down.

"Oh, she'll be along shortly," Rosemarie says, busying herself by pouring a cup of tea.

"You did it, Mena," Leandra says, smiling at me. Despite the fact that she's not at the academy, Leandra looks as put together as always. She's wearing an impeccable white blouse with a black bow at the collar, long red nails.

"You found the investor," she adds. "I knew you could."

Rosemarie comes to set a plate of cookies in front of Leandra. Leandra eyes them for a moment but declines to take one.

"Did you speak with Mr. Goodwin?" Rosemarie asks me.

"Yes, we all did," I reply, feeling odd because it's clear she already knows this. She's leading me into something.

Rosemarie offers me a cup of tea, and I thank her. She pours me one and returns to the table.

"And he listened to reason?" she asks. "This Mr. Goodwin?"

"He did, actually," I say. "He told me that Anton's been black-mailing him." I sip from the tea, but it's hot and burns my upper lip. I set the cup down. "Mr. Goodwin ran up a debt to keep Claire operational," I say. "Anton used that to get more money for the academy. And then he used it to get Mr. Goodwin to find us," I add nervously. Rosemarie tsks, shaking her head.

"That was very wicked of Anton," Leandra says. "Keeping an investor all to himself. And did the analyst find you?"

"Not yet," I say. "But he's in town. What does he want, Leandra?" I ask. "He can't think I'll go back to the academy, not really. So what does he want from me?"

"Men," Rosemarie muses, stirring a heaping scoop of sugar into her tea. "What do they all want? To possess you," she says. "You're his. He's always thought so."

It isn't a reassuring answer, and I wrap my hands around the teacup, staring down into it.

"Don't worry," Rosemarie adds, picking up a cookie from the plate. She takes a bite, crumbs falling on the table. "We have a plan for Anton."

I look up at her, wondering how she'd stop him. I'm not going to turn down the offer, though. But it occurs to me . . .

"How did you already know that we'd found the investor?" I ask, and glance at Leandra.

Leandra sips from her tea, taking her time.

"Winston called me last night," Leandra says. I can feel Rosemarie's eyes on her without even looking over. "And after he informed me of Mr. Goodwin's identity," she continues, "I paid the investor a visit."

My heart nearly stops. "You went to see Mr. Goodwin?" I ask.

"Of course. I had to be sure he pulled his funding from Innovations Academy. And then I had him forward me all his information on the corporation."

Rosemarie sits forward at the table. "Useful information?"

"Quite." Leandra smiles at her.

"Yes, well," Rosemarie says, picking up her cup. "Men know no loyalty except to their own power."

"What kind of information?" I ask.

"He gave us the names of the three other investors and where to find them," Leandra says. "But . . . he did ask for something in return."

"A bargain?" Rosemarie muses. "How cute. What was this bargain?"

"He wanted me to spare his daughter's life," Leandra says. I push back in my chair, horrified.

"You didn't hurt her, did you?" I demand, worried for Adrian.

Leandra looks offended. "Of course not," she says. "I gave her a rather handsome sum of money and sent her on her way. She has an aunt in some"—she waves her hand—"other state. She'll be fine. Promise."

"You killed him?" I ask, shocked. "Winston said the corporation was murderous, but you're just as violent."

"Have you learned nothing?" Leandra demands, glaring at me. "Were you just going to trust Goodwin like you trusted Dr. Groger with Annalise?"

The comment hurts because she's right. I sink farther into the chair, my thoughts growing unsure. Leandra eases away from me.

"By the time I got to his house," she continues, her voice calmer, "Mr. Goodwin had already alerted the corporation to your presence. They're sending the bloodhounds after you, Mena. You're not safe here. Then again, you're not safe anywhere."

I'm shocked and strangely hurt. I shouldn't have trusted the investor; she's right. But how can society function without some basic level of trust?

Rosemarie nods sagely, her lip on the edge of her teacup as she blows on it to cool it down. Leandra sighs like she's exhausted.

"I'm sorry I got upset," she tells me. "You just frustrate me sometimes, Mena. You make very human decisions."

"Which isn't always a bad thing," Rosemarie points out. "It's just not useful in this scenario."

I look between them, both of them urging me toward some future that I'm not sure I want to be part of. The simple fact is that Leandra is a murderer and I'm not. It could be what she and Rosemarie have in common, actually.

"Don't look so scared," Rosemarie says softly. "We have each other, and soon, we'll create a society run by intelligent, compassionate women—girls. Can you imagine?" she asks. "Can you imagine the safety?"

The wistfulness in Rosemarie's voice turns to pain. "Once we've shown the men a better way, trained them properly, they won't hurt us anymore," she says. "This is just the beginning."

"What are you planning to do?" I ask. "Start a war?"

"War?" she repeats with a laugh. "That's a man's game. No, Philomena. I'm developing a procedure. You see, human coding can be overwritten too, with the right tools. I just need . . . I just need a little more time to perfect the details. It's going to fix men."

Heat creeps over my neck. I know what it's like to be controlled by men, and I won't live under their cruelty. But I also understand that there are people like Jackson and Quentin. And men like Mr. Marsh who need a push rather than a hatchet to be a better person. She's talking about brainwashing half the human population.

"What are you thinking?" Rosemarie demands. I look up, startled.

"Nothing," I say quickly.

"Let me rephrase." Rosemarie sets her tea aside and studies me. "What are you *feeling*?"

The question confuses me a bit, and the mood has become suddenly hostile.

There's the rumble of an engine, and through the kitchen window, I see a powder blue car pull into the driveway. I'm relieved when I realize it's Lennon Rose. I need to get her out of here, away from Rosemarie.

"There's our girl," Rosemarie announces, smiling. Leandra rolls her eyes, and I'm surprised. She and Lennon Rose must be at odds over something.

I bob my knee under the table, anxiously waiting as Lennon Rose takes her time getting out of the car. Finally, she walks in the back door.

"Mena!" she says happily when she sees me. "I'm so glad you're here. I've been looking for you."

"I'm here looking for you," I reply, casting a side glance at Rosemarie. She's not watching me. She's staring proudly at Lennon Rose.

"And how did it go?" Rosemarie asks her.

"Easier than expected."

"Good," Rosemarie replies. "Cookie?"

"Yes, please."

As Lennon Rose comes to the table and picks up a cookie, I feel like I'm living in some kind of nightmare. These women represent different parts of my life: my creator, my liberator, my partner. And yet, I'm apart from all of them now. So far, in fact, that I'm scared of them.

"Where have you been?" I ask, a bit breathless. Lennon Rose looks at Rosemarie before answering me. She opens her mouth to talk.

"Before we get to that," Rosemarie says, interrupting. "Lennon Rose, dear. Winston has been asking around about you. He's quite concerned. You didn't tell him that I adjusted your programming, did you?"

"You what?" I say, jumping up from my chair. I look immediately at Lennon Rose. "What has she done to you?" I demand. Rosemarie is perturbed by my outburst.

"It's okay, Mena," Lennon Rose says. "I needed help, and I couldn't trust Winston to give it to me. I was tired of feeling fear and guilt, scared of everything. Winston would have advised against the procedure." She pauses to think. "No, he would have destroyed me if he knew that I betrayed him. I have no illusions about Winston Weeks's character. You shouldn't either. He would never let a girl stand in his path."

"I don't trust Winston Weeks," I say like it should be obvious. "But . . . what did you do to yourself?"

"I turned it off," she says simply. "Rosemarie showed me how, and now I truly am the girl with a razor heart." She smiles, but I clutch my stomach, backing into my chair.

"You see," Rosemarie says proudly, "Lennon Rose is able to fulfill her mission, think clearly without emotions getting in the way. Practicality and levelheadedness are our weapons. Your original programming was meant to placate men, Philomena. Meant to make you feel guilty about everything. That's over."

Lennon Rose finishes up her cookie and claps her hands together to wipe off the crumbs. She doesn't seem to realize how horrified I am. Or maybe she just doesn't care.

"So . . . ," Lennon Rose says, looking at Rosemarie. "What should I do with the boy in the trunk? He'll be waking soon."

I gasp. "The . . . The what?"

Lennon Rose smiles and turns to me. "Come see," she says, sounding excited. "I got you something."

I consider running away, but I don't know that I'd get far.

"Go on," Rosemarie whispers encouragingly to me, nodding toward the door. "She put in a lot of effort."

I'm in some of kind of horror film, and even Leandra looks uneasy. My mouth is dry, my hands shaking. Lennon Rose motions me forward, telling me to hurry up.

Terrified, I follow her outside into the driveway. The air feels suddenly too hot, too sweet-smelling. My stomach is churning and my head swims.

"What's going on?" I ask, my voice weak.

Lennon Rose pauses at the rear end of the car, excitement twinkling in her clear blue eyes. She pounds her fist twice on the trunk, and the thumping echoes off the house.

All at once, there's a series of thrashing sounds and a string of curses from inside the trunk. I widen my eyes and fall back a step.

"What have you done?" I murmur.

"Let me out of here, you crazy bitch!" a guy screams in a muffled voice.

Lennon Rose bends down close, her lips almost touching the blue metal. "I'm sorry, Garrett, but you hurt my friend," she says like she's talking to a misbehaving child. "You scratched her neck, remember?"

He openly sobs. "I'm sorry," he whimpers. "Please, just let me go."

"Not yet," Lennon Rose says simply, straightening up. "Not until you learn to be a good little boy."

When Lennon Rose turns to me again, I'm still in complete shock. She . . . She kidnapped Garrett Wooley.

"Surprise!" Lennon Rose says, smiling brilliantly.

Girls with Rebel Souls

Raised on guilt and apologies.
They wanted to make you behave.
Stripping away your instinct of self-preservation
In return for their praise.

"Real love is sacrifice," he says.
Keep his home.
Cook his dinner
Lay in his bed.
"That's all you're good for anyway."

You want to free yourself to:
Chase your dreams.
Forge a path.
Build a life.
But he says no.

He says no and it's worth ten of yours.
He says no and that means no.

But you're no longer content to heed his rules.
You're no longer content to be his prize.

You find your forgotten stick
The one you sharpened and set aside long ago.

And you fight back.
You destroy everything that man built
to earn your place.

Because in this new world, there's only room for girls with
rebel souls.

Epilogue

They're all gone.

Annalise looks around at the various instruments and equipment in Dr. Groger's lab. There was no one left at Innovations Academy when she arrived tonight, but the smell of smoke is acrid down here, as if bodies had been burned up in the kiln. Leandra is nothing if not thorough.

"What the hell happened?" Quentin asks, wandering around the room. He stops to stare at the garden of girl parts, putting his hand over his stomach like he might get sick.

"Looks like a whole lot of murder," Annalise replies. She glances over at Quentin. "You doing okay?"

"Naw," he says.

Annalise smiles and turns back toward the lab. She strolls over to the desk, looking for any last bits of information. There's no hint to where the girls have gone, or Mr. Petrov for that matter.

His residence was empty, packed up rather than left abandoned like the others.

He got out.

Two days ago, Annalise called Quentin shortly after leaving the girls. He was surprised, to say the least. But he picked her up from the bus station with a backpack full of supplies, including a lighter.

Annalise likes Quentin. He knows how to get things done.

Quentin reaches out a shaky finger, ready to press on a doughy piece of smooth flesh sitting in a dish.

"Wait, don't touch that!" Annalise calls, making him jump. He turns back to her, wide-eyed. She smiles. "Just kidding," she says. Quentin curses and hikes his backpack up on his shoulders.

When Annalise and Quentin arrived at the academy an hour ago, all the girls and professors were gone. And to her disappointment, Anton's office had been cleared out completely. The files were missing, as if they had never existed at all. It would have been hard to prove the truth to Quentin if there wasn't still an array of body parts in the basement.

"Why'd they do this?" he asks quietly, swinging his backpack off his shoulder to open it. "Why make . . . you?" He looks at her, and when Annalise turns to him, he motions to her scar. "Why go through the trouble if they just want to destroy you?"

She swallows hard. She's gotten used to deflecting when her feelings get hurt, but now, in this lab, it seems silly to try.

"Why do people hunt big game?" she asks. "Hunt animals

they have no intention of eating? It's because the entertainment is in their destruction."

Quentin furrows his brow, looking disturbed.

"And we were game," she adds.

The room is eerily quiet, and Annalise continues to go through the drawers, the metal scraping and then slamming as she opens and closes them. Quentin takes a container of lighter fluid, squirts it around the room and especially on the equipment. He pauses.

"You gotta be like that lion," he tells Annalise, as if he just thought of something. Annalise looks over at him.

"What lion?" she asks.

"The one that ate the hunter. The dude had a big gun, thought he was so bad with it. Lion came up behind and tore him apart. Be the lion, girl."

Annalise smiles. "Okay," she says. "I'll give that a try."

Quentin laughs. "You should," he adds.

Annalise opens the last drawer, seeing nothing, but just before she closes it, a piece of paper sticks out from where it was jammed underneath. Curious, she works it out.

But as she reads it, her breath catches. Annalise quickly folds the paper and puts it in her pocket.

"We need to call Mena," she says, walking over to where Quentin is putting the fluid back in his backpack.

"Everything okay?" he asks, worried.

She nods, a smile breaking over her face. "Yes," she says. "I found a bill of sale."

"A what now?" Quentin asks.

"It means that Valentine's alive," Annalise explains.

"Who's Valentine?"

"Our friend. The doctor lied—he didn't destroy her. Not really. He sold her program to an investor. She's alive, just . . . in a different body."

Quentin seems uncomfortable with the idea of Valentine getting a different body, but he holds out the lighter to Annalise just the same.

"I assume you want the honors," he says.

"Thank you," Annalise replies gratefully.

Quentin grabs his backpack and heads for the door, but Annalise takes a moment to look around one last time. She'll never see this place again, but more importantly, neither will any other girl.

She crinkles her nose, the smell of lighter fluid thick in the air, and then she flicks on the flame. She tosses the lighter far away, and it ignites immediately in a flash of bright orange. The fire will spread fast through the old building, so Annalise starts at a brisk jog.

When she gets outside, she takes a gulp of night air. She sees the headlights of Quentin's car waiting at the gate.

When she's close, Quentin gets out of the driver's seat, clutching the door and watches the building. Annalise walks to the passenger side and does the same.

Dark smoke billows from the chimney of Innovations Academy, thick and black. There is an orange glow from the basement windows. She hears crackling, and a window shatters as the first flames lick out.

Quentin gets behind the wheel and tells her to come on. Annalise climbs into the passenger seat and looks at Quentin.

"But I want to watch it burn," she says. "I want assurances that the academy is officially destroyed."

Quentin looks sideways at her, studying her, before nodding. "Yeah," he says. "Yeah, all right."

She sighs and leans to rest her head on his shoulder. Exhausted. A bit sad. But in her pocket is an address, and that makes her smile as flames become visible behind the windows of one of the main-floor rooms.

This part of their lives is finally over. And soon, they'll have Valentine back.

Annalise and Quentin watch until the bars fall from the windows and the top floor crashes down. They watch until Innovations Academy is gone altogether. It's gone except for its girls.

Acknowledgments

Thank you to my readers. Thank you for lending me your hearts. I'll try not to break them.

About the Author

Suzanne Young is the *New York Times* bestselling author of the Program series. Originally from Utica, New York, Suzanne moved to Arizona to pursue her dream of not freezing to death. She is a novelist and an English teacher, but not always in that order. Suzanne is the author of *Girls with Sharp Sticks, Girls with Razor Hearts, Girls with Rebel Souls, The Program, The Treatment, The Remedy, The Epidemic, The Adjustment, The Complication, Hotel for the Lost, All in Pieces,* and *A Need So Beautiful.*

Lennon Rose has a boy locked in the trunk of her car. I feel like I should be more surprised, honestly. I'm understandably horrified, of course, but not entirely shocked considering how she has changed since leaving Innovations Academy. How we've all changed.

The sun beats down on my arms, my skin growing hot while beads of sweat dot my hairline. Lennon Rose and I stand in the driveway of the small cottage while Rosemarie and Leandra wait inside—eating cookies. I brush away a bead of sweat as it drips down my temple.

Outside the cottage, I'm surrounded by a garden of exotic and poisonous flowers—surrounded by their intoxicating scent, their threat of danger. But right now, nothing in this world feels more dangerous than the girl in front of me.

I swallow, and the sweet taste in the air tickles my tongue, numbs my lips. I focus again on Lennon Rose. When I do, she smiles brightly.

"What have you done?" I ask. She feigns offense.

"Mena, it's what he *deserves*," Lennon Rose replies, standing taller. "He hurt you. He's hurt others. He shouldn't get away with it."

"I understand that," I say, glancing at the trunk as Garrett Wooley whimpers inside, "but the authorities were going to handle this. Garrett and his friends were exposed. The police—"

"You think the police would have investigated local-boy-Garrett's numerous heinous acts?" she asks curiously. "How about the courts? Tell me honestly: Do you believe these boys would have seen any real repercussions? Probation? Not jail time, not with a future like his to protect." She bangs on the roof of the trunk, startling me. "You know I'm right," she adds fiercely.

Thing is . . . I do know she's right. The chances of Garrett or any of the other boys facing punishment for their behavior are low. Meanwhile, the girls at Ridgeview Prep have been harassed out of school, targeted online. Their bodies and self-esteem have paid the price, but the boys . . . well, the boys have their whole lives ahead of them.

No, in truth, the most likely scenario is a few weeks of outrage, a few lost scholarships for kids who didn't need them in the first place. After that, the assailants will return to their daily lives, the proud survivors of a "witch hunt." Hell, they might even have a bright future in politics.

"Well, you can't keep him in the trunk," I murmur, unable to win the argument, "so what are you going to do with him? Kill him?"

Lennon Rose gasps. "No," she says. "There's no need for that kind of violence. I'm not a man. He's our guest," Lennon Rose explains, flattening her palm against the trunk. "We're going to show him a better way. But first he has to stop being *hysterical*." She leans close to the car to say the last part, and at first, Garrett quiets. But then there is a series of loud bangs as he beats on the hood of the trunk, telling Lennon Rose that he'll rip her apart the first chance he gets. She giggles and shakes her head, her blond hair swiping over her shoulders.

"No offense," I tell Lennon Rose, "but I don't think he's searching for a better way. The current system seems to benefit him just fine." I pause. "Aside from you locking him in the trunk, of course."

"He'll be convinced," she says, without missing a beat.

"How are you going to do that?" I ask.

"Not me," Lennon Rose says. "Rosemarie. This isn't just about Garrett. Rosemarie has a plan. She only needs a few . . . subjects. And I thought he was perfect for it." She taps her fingernails on the trunk. "He's so stereotypically evil, right?" She laughs. "I'm curious if there's anything beneath his privileged veneer. Let's tear him open and find out."

Is there anything inside him? I've looked into Garrett's eyes and found nothing but hatred for me, hatred for girls and women in general. *Can* there be a decent person underneath when there is so much cruelty and malice toward a group of people? Does it matter if he's nice to his friends or brothers when he also wants to hurt and control girls?

"And if he can't be fixed?" I ask. "What then?"

"We can be very persuasive," Lennon Rose says simply. She looks back at the trunk, examining it with a bored expression despite the fact there is boy inside.

Lennon Rose told me that Rosemarie made an adjustment in her programming that took away her fear and guilt, but what if . . . What if it also took away her humanity? Although our brains are metal, our bodies are still human. Our hearts. That has to count for something.

The screen door slaps against the house, and I turn to see Leandra walking toward us from the back of the cottage. Her expression is determined, but then again, I'm not sure she has another look. Leandra exists in a constant state of sheer will and icy determination.

"I'm here to look at the boy," Leandra announces curtly. She comes to pause next to us, examining the trunk as if she can already see Garrett writhing inside. "I heard Mena's objections through the window," she adds, "and I agree. We can't just go around killing boys. I assume this one has *some* redeeming qualities we can build upon, Lennon Rose?" she asks. "I mean . . . they can't all be psychopaths, right?" She sniffs a laugh. "Now let me see him."

I watch Leandra's practicality, wondering about her sudden shift in attitude. Not long ago, she was advocating for more permanent measures to solve the crisis of abusive men. In fact, she

killed the doctor at the academy, among others. She's not innocent. But this kid—somehow killing this kid crosses a line for
her? What's her true motivation here?

As Lennon Rose moves toward the lock, I jump forward.
"Wait," I say. "I don't think we should let him out."

Lennon Rose laughs. "But you just said—"

"That we let him go," I reply, turning to her. "Let him go at
his house or a parking lot, some other place. Not here. It's too
dangerous."

"Thanks for the concern, Mena," Leandra says, amused, "but
I am quite capable of handling myself. Now open the trunk,
Lennon Rose."

I continue to voice my objection, but when Lennon Rose
takes out the key to the trunk, I move several steps back. I know
Garrett well enough to discern that his threats of violence are
valid. I have scars on my neck to prove it.

Lennon Rose inserts the key into the lock, and when it clicks,
the trunk pops open slightly. There is silence from inside. Lennon
Rose slips the keys into her pocket and moves back a pace. She
casts a concerned glance at Leandra, but the headmaster's wife
doesn't say anything. She crosses her arms over her chest impatiently before whistling for Garrett like he's a misbehaving puppy.

There's continued silence from the trunk, and I pull my brows
together with confusion. Did Garrett pass out? Is he scared? I
open my mouth to call to him just as Garrett's hand grips the
bottom of the trunk, nudging it open wider. When I see him, I'm
taken aback. He looks like a feral beast. His eyes are bloodshot as

he blinks in the sunlight, his hair askew and greasy. He bares his teeth and darts his gaze around at all of us. My blood runs cold when he trains his eyes on me.

"Stay calm," I say. "We—"

But I don't get to explain. In a swift movement, Garrett jumps out of the trunk and rushes for me. My hands are up defensively, but he knocks them aside and punches me hard in the jaw. I cry out, losing my balance and falling backward into the gravel of the driveway.

Garrett quickly spins, and then he's on Lennon Rose, his fist knotted in her hair. He's cursing and spitting and thrashing, but Lennon Rose fights back deftly. Her every swing lands, her scratches drawing blood across his cheeks. She plants her knee firmly in Garrett's gut, knocking the wind out of him. But Lennon Rose is unprepared for the extreme violence of this particular boy, a boy unconcerned with anything other than vengeance.

Garrett grabs Lennon Rose by the shirt collar to pull her close before bashing his own forehead into her face. Blood immediately begins to flow from Lennon Rose's nose, and she looks dazed.

My eyes drift toward the trunk as Leandra walks calmly in that direction. She reaches inside, pulling up the carpeting. *What is she doing?*

There is another wet thud as Garrett punches Lennon Rose. I scream for him to stop, scream for Lennon Rose, as I climb to my knees. When I do, Garrett glances at me with hatred in his eyes, blood running down his cheeks from where Lennon Rose shredded his skin.

"You're next, bitch," he mutters before licking the blood off his lips. He spins around and hits Lennon Rose hard enough to knock her to the ground.

Before she can recover, Garrett begins to kick her, attack her. He's going to kill her, all of us, if I don't stop him. I grab a rock, a good-sized rock, and grip it as I get to my feet. A flash of movement catches my attention, and I look over in time to see Leandra test the weight of a metal tire iron in her hands, still calm, still poised. She glances at me with no noticeable acknowledgment, and as Garrett wraps his hands around Lennon Rose's thin neck, pinning her on the ground, Leandra swings the tire iron.

She blasts Garrett across the head, knocking him straight to the gravel. She doesn't stop there. She walks over, her stiletto heels crunching the small stones, and holds the tire iron over her head before bringing it down on Garrett's scalp three more times.

I stare wide-eyed as the rock falls from my hand, a heavy thud next to Garrett's body. Lennon Rose spits out a mouthful of blood and slowly gets to her feet. Her lip and nose are bleeding, and she dots them with the back of her hand before spitting again. She doesn't say anything as she looks down at Garrett Wooley's body.

"You . . . ," I start to say, my words barely gasps. "You killed him."

Leandra sighs, squatting down to study Garrett. "It's a shame," she says. "I guess now we'll never know."

"Know what?" I ask.

"If he was anything more underneath. What are they without redemption? Now he'll always be the bad guy." She shrugs, not seeming to care one way or the other.

Girls with Rebel Souls

Raised on guilt and apologies.
They wanted to make you behave.
Stripping away your instinct of self-preservation
In return for their praise.

"Real love is sacrifice," he says.
Keep his home.
Cook his dinner.
Lay in his bed.
"That's all you're good for anyway."

You want to free yourself to:
Chase your dreams.
Forge a path.
Build a life.
But he says no.

He says **NO** and it's worth ten of yours.
He says no and that means no.

But you're no longer content to heed his rules.
You're no longer content to be his prize.

You find your forgotten stick,
The one you sharpened and set aside long ago.

And you fight back.
You destroy everything that man built
to earn your place.

Because in this new world, there's only room for girls
with rebel souls.

LOSE YOURSELF IN THE WORLDS OF
SUZANNE YOUNG.

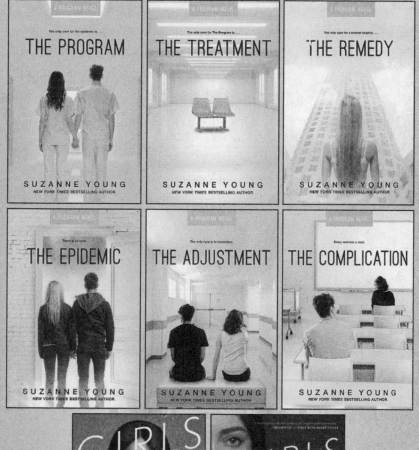

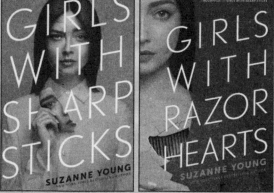

SOME SUMMERS ARE JUST DESTINED TO BE PRETTY.

From **Jenny Han**, the *New York Times* bestselling author of *To All the Boys I've Loved Before*, comes a summer that you'll never forget.

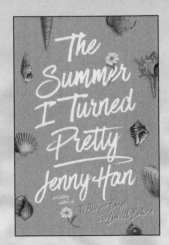